A Fine and Private Place

A FINE AND PRIVATE PLACE

Freda Davies

CARROLL & GRAF PUBLISHERS
New York

Carroll & Graf Publishers
An imprint of Avalon Publishing Group, Inc.
161 William Street
16th Floor
NY10038-2607
www.carrollandgraf.com

First published in the UK by Constable,
an imprint of Constable & Robinson Ltd 2001

First Carroll & Graf edition 2001

ISBN 0-7867-0909-X

Printed and bound in the EU

'The grave's a fine and private place,
but none, I think, do there embrace.'

Andrew Marvel

Chapter One

Moonlight washed over the graves as the dead of five centuries slept in the red earth. Mendelssohn's Wedding March hiccuped to an end in the church, relieving unseen listeners who had been gritting their teeth and praying for silence.

The heavy door opened then slammed shut, a key grating as it was turned in the lock. The organist trudged away along the narrow path to the vicarage and bodies rose from behind the churchyard wall.

Three stood, the fourth was supported, snores punctuating his movements as his friends dragged him to the church door. Cider-fuelled laughter helped them with their load along the nave. They laid it reverently on the floor between the choir stalls, roses from the altar put between crossed hands.

'If he dies of fright, he'll be ready for his burying,' echoed with giggles as the conspirators crept away.

The night was still once more and the dead slumbered on. A figure behind a tombstone stirred, checked wreaths were back in place on the mounded earth and went home.

'By damn, he's in a hurry!'

The dark BMW had been travelling fast towards the main road, almost forcing the van into the ditch. Steve Perry restarted the stalled engine as his companion swore steadily.

'Sure as hell he's not off to see some woman,' Steve muttered as, with 'Bryce and Son, Plant Hire' emblazoned on each side, the van continued its journey.

'You know summat I don'?' Terry Butcher asked. His dark eyes were bright with malice.

'Who'd go chasing women this time of the morning?' Steve reasoned. It befitted his foreman status and his years of wedlock.

'Get away from 'em more like – or their 'usbands.'

'You should know.'

They were driving towards Tolland, dreaming on a long loop of road which kept it far from the mad skelter of the A48. It was a quiet village in a curve of the River Severn, old grey houses clustering around the church of St Barnabas.

Facing the church was the George Inn, a long, low building, small windows puncturing its walls. On a rise behind the church the red sandstone of Tolland Manor was almost hidden by trees, a vast Cedar of Lebanon dominating them all.

Steve drove past the church and Terry saw the door was open, a woman busy sweeping the porch as confetti played hide-and-seek in the verge outside the gate.

'Oo got married Sat'day?'

'Pam Mitton,' Steve said. 'Noel Abbott she married, from Cheltenham. It's far enough away for him not to know all Pam's got up to in the past. Still, if the size of her belly's anything to go by, he's no monk.'

Steve drove on out of Tolland, passing a row of council houses, most of them with immaculate gardens. Half a mile along the road was a large, double-fronted house, paintwork glistening in the early light.

'Boss not up yet,' Terry said as he noted upstairs curtains still drawn and secret. ''E's usual out inspectin' by now.'

'You just be thankful he's in bed and not seeing what time you get on the job.'

In a depot behind the house and separated from it by

8

a curtain of trees were lorries and earth-movers, all carrying the Bryce logo.

'If 'e'd let I 'ave a van to take 'ome there'd be no need of you fetchin' I o' a mornin'.'

Steve grinned. 'I remember what happened when old Noah did try that. Right little knocking-shop you made of it – and you never got to work in time. Cost the boss money, you did. He won't forget that in a hurry.'

'If 'e's so keen on cash, 'ow come these bloody mobiles?'

Terry flipped open the phone he had taken from his pocket and angrily punched numbers.

'You've got to switch it on if you want it to work.'

The advice was ignored and Terry went on punching. 'Bet t'was David's idea.'

'If it meant spending money on staff safety, of course it was.'

'Safety? It's on'y so's owd Noah can check up on us mornin', noon and nigh'.'

'No problem is there? As long as you're where you're supposed to be.'

'All the owd bastard wants is to move us on quick as 'e can and make sure we don' lose un 'alf a day's profit.'

'You'd be the same in his shoes.'

Terry was silent, pocketing his phone as Steve slowed the van and parked in a gateway which led to a field.

'I'll give you a hand with the cans,' Steve offered.

Terry removed himself slowly from the van and stretched lazy muscles. Jerry-cans of fuel oil were carried to the long-armed machine Terry was to drive. On one side of the field was the new gash of a drainage ditch. A stack of pipes waited for the soil to be opened.

Refuelling complete, Steve was ready to leave. 'Got your lunch?'

Terry hefted his haversack and there was the clink of cans.

9

'If the old man catches you drinking on the job he'll sack you.'

'I 'ont be drivin' on the 'ighway,' Terry protested. 'An' wha' 'e can' see, can' 'urt.'

Steve surveyed the length of the field untouched by the digger. 'You've got a full day's work here. When you get to the hedge make sure you don't break through. Sir Edward was most insistent on that. Under but not through.'

Terry muttered a comforting stream of obscenities to himself as he swung up into the driving cab.

'Collect you at four thirty,' Steve shouted.

There was a nod from Terry and the roar of a huge diesel split the morning.

The drainage ditch progressed in length as Terry methodically cut out turf and soil, laying them neatly aside. He thought of Noah Bryce breakfasting in his warm house, a wife to see to his every need, a son as dogsbody in yard and office. Then there was the field's owner, Sir Edward Driffield. Stinking rich and with an energetic blonde in his bed every night. Clear Gloucestershire air became filled with exhaust fumes speckled with Terry's curses on the heads of everyone who had an easy life.

The morning passed slowly. Terry was good at his job and the ditch was ruler-straight, the ridged soil tidy. Once more he poised the long arm of the earth-mover ready to dig but this time he hesitated. Something was different. Terry switched off the engine and lifted his haversack before climbing out of the cab.

'Time for a break any'ow,' he told the grass as he landed.

With a can open and half-drunk, Terry ambled over to the ditch to see what had caused him to sense change. Something had slid from the heaped soil, dropping back into the trench from whence it had come. Terry leaned over to look and his blood chilled. A huddle of bones lay exposed.

There was no sign of hide or fleece so it could not be a diseased animal hidden from the authorities, he decided and peered more closely. Foot bones had been pulled free of what looked like the remains of a shoe. For a while Terry stood and thought, then he grinned.

'Can' work while you be lyin' there,' he told the bones. 'Not legal, diggin' up a grave.' He pulled the mobile phone from his pocket. 'This'll get owd Noah runnin'.'

It did.

Noah Bryce was angry. 'Why didn't you ring me first?'

Terry lounged with the graceful ease of a fit young animal. He was still handsome, his features not yet coarsened by age and hard living. Under heavy brows which almost met above his nose, Terry tried to look innocent.

''Ad to dial 999 fust, boss. P'lice'd 'ave my balls I didn'.'

Noah Bryce was a tall stick of a man, his white hair still plentiful and his seventy years carried with restless energy.

'Get in the car. David'll find you work in the yard. There's nothing more you can do here today.'

'I gotta stay 'ere.'

Terry swept aside overlong dark curls with a muscular hand and an earring glinted. An unhealthy purple mottled Noah Bryce's skin as his temper flared.

'Who says so?'

'I do, sir.' The policeman was respectful but the voice with its local accent was firm.

'PC Draper.' Noah Bryce was not impressed by the rank. 'Butcher works for me. You can talk to him at the yard.'

'It would be wise, Mr Bryce, if you left Terry here until Detective Inspector Tyrell arrives.'

'Tyrell? Who's he?'

'The officer taking charge of the investigation, sir. He's on his way from Lydney so he won't be long.'

'And while we wait around I'm losing money!'

'Can't be helped, I'm afraid, Mr Bryce. Not in a murder case.'

'Murder! That's all you people can think of these days. This Inspector . . .'

'Tyrell.'

'He won't be any better. Where there's a corpse, there's a camera. I suppose he fancies himself on TV – like the rest of them?'

Martin Draper was the community policeman responsible for Tolland. He knew Noah Bryce of old and had the scars to prove it.

'As you say, Mr Bryce.'

The elderly man nodded towards the bones in the ditch. 'Is that one of the Gloucester lot?'

The media had been busy for weeks with news of body after body discovered in the city.

'I doubt it, sir.'

'Why?'

'First glance, it's not a girl – that leg bone's too long. He'd have been a very tall chap, I should think.'

Noah Bryce pressed thin fingers to his lips. 'How long has – it – been buried?'

'I couldn't say, sir. Forensics are very good these days. It'll take time but they'll pin it down pretty well.'

There was the sound of a car being driven fast and stopping quickly. Doors banged and PC Draper went to meet two newcomers. The three policemen talked briefly before going to the ditch and peering in.

Noah Bryce was impatient, restless. 'God's sake! How long's all this going to take?'

There was only Terry's lazy grin as an answer and his employer stormed off.

'Can't you talk to Butcher now so I can get him back to some kind of work?'

The tallest of the trio turned to face him and he was assessed by shrewd hazel eyes.

'And you are . . .?'

Martin Draper hurried to explain. 'Bryce, sir. It's his driver, Terry Butcher, who reported the skeleton.'

'I'm Detective Inspector Tyrell, Mr Bryce, and this is Detective Sergeant Clarke.'

The inspector was young for his rank, with thick, light brown hair and a pleasant smile on regular features. Clarke was older, wide and dark, with a cap of black curly hair and ears showing signs of many a hard rugby tackle. Both men wore grey suits, the inspector's fine worsted fitting him perfectly while the sergeant's bulged, strained by heavy muscles.

Tyrell was courteous. 'If you would like to return home, Mr Bryce, we'll get Butcher back to you as soon as possible.'

Noah Bryce lost some of his bluster and the high colour faded from his cheeks. Without another word he stalked off to his car and drove away. He was almost home before he had time to wonder at his dismissal from the scene and his unthinking obedience.

Terry fared no better. Expecting to spend a pleasant day lounging in the field as he watched experts at work, he was relieved of every scrap of his knowledge in a matter of minutes. DI Tyrell thanked him for his help, DS Clarke promised to arrange for an official statement to be made and PC Draper drove Terry the short distance to the Bryce depot and the rest of his day's work.

'We'll have to let Gloucester know about this,' Tyrell said as he looked down at the jumbled bones.

'They'll expect it to be their pigeon – in case there's any connection.'

'It's too old.'

'How d'you know?'

13

'I don't – not for certain. One thing's for sure, we can't do anything until the police surgeon declares it dead.'

The scene-of-crime team had been waiting with its usual mix of patience before Chris Collier, the police surgeon, arrived in his well-worn Volvo. Tall, thin, his fine blond hair sparse, he managed a tired smile for Keith Tyrell.

'A messy one?'

'Not really. We just need you to certify he's dead.'

They walked to where the drainage ditch was marked with police tape.

'If anyone's been under soil that deep they'd have found it hard to breathe,' Dr Collier remarked.

The two men looked down at the bones.

Collier sighed. 'I'd better go down and have a shufti.'

'I doubt you'll find a pulse,' Tyrell said.

Humour might help with the work but however long the body had been buried, someone would be grieving after today's find.

'Have you been down?' the doctor asked.

'No. I had a quick look and checked the soil up here. There were a few buttons visible but I've left everything to the forensic team.'

'They've had plenty of experience these past few months – poor bastards.'

Tyrell was handed the medical bag to hold while Dr Collier leaped nimbly into the ditch, walking forward carefully until he was close to the pathetic heap he had come to examine.

Squatting, he peered this way and that, concentrating on what was left of the shoe and seeing scattered buttons, some still attached to tiny scraps of fabric.

'Found somewhere to put your thermometer, Doc?' DS Clarke called out cheerfully.

Chris Collier squinted up at the two police officers, backed by the overalled SOCO team.

'One day, Sergeant Clarke,' he promised.

'Is it one for Gloucester, Dr Collier?'

DI Tyrell's deep voice brought instant quiet. Too many of the men and women present had taken their turn digging by hand for the bodies of young girls.

'I very much doubt it.'

'Reasons?'

'The femur is that of someone taller than I am, so it's most likely a man. Then I'd guess from the way the clothing has virtually disappeared he's been here for a very long time, certainly more than twenty years.'

The doctor continued his inspection.

'Anything else?' the DI asked.

'The skull's missing – probably still to be dug out. Except for the axis the neck vertebrae are all present and tangled up with them are dog tags.'

'Dog tags?'

'Yes, Sergeant Clarke, dog tags,' Inspector Tyrell said. 'Worn to make sure any corpse on a battlefield could be named.'

'Give us a hand up,' the doctor asked and DS Clarke obligingly hauled him out of the ditch.

DI Tyrell beckoned to the waiting specialists.

'You know what to do. The skull's still under so go carefully. Make sure every single artefact, as well as the human remains, are collected and logged.' He waited for Dr Collier to finish writing his notes. 'Anything in particular Forensic should look for, Chris?'

'Get them to pay special attention to the sternum and ribs.'

'Why?'

'I don't want to commit myself at this stage but they've a different appearance from the other bones.'

'Estimated time of death?' Keith Tyrell asked with a wry grin.

'Long before his rightful time. That was true of so many poor devils in the war if that's when he died.'

'Could he have been caught in an air raid?'

15

'No bomb killed him, I'll go bail for that,' Chris Collier insisted. 'The bones were still in normal arrangement, quite neat and tidy really until the digger disturbed them.'

'Deliberately buried?'

'That would be my guess.'

'Thank you for confirming mine,' Keith Tyrell said as the two men shook hands. 'Oh, by the way, you said dog tags. More than one?'

'They looked like duplicated discs.'

'Not an official death then. There'd have been one tag left on the body and one to mark the grave.'

'A secret burial?'

'Undoubtedly, but he'll have been reported missing. Then there are the buttons.'

'Why? What's so important about them?'

'If I'm right, I'll have a helluva lot of extra paperwork and be expected to be diplomatic.'

Dr Collier's eyebrows rose in an unspoken question. 'Our body just might be American.'

The bell tinged twice as the shop door opened and closed. Mrs Fell looked up.

'Morning, Mrs Seymour. How's your Alan now?'

The words were kind but Mrs Fell's eyes glinted in a pudgy, thin-lipped face under tightly permed grey hair.

'He's very well, thank you.'

'He was lucky.' Mrs Fell spoke loudly, knowing others in the shop listened. 'Sleeping it off in church, he could've caught a chill. And poor Mrs Mitton, she was so upset all her lovely flowers ruined.'

'That wasn't Alan!'

'Course not. It's just a pity his friends were so irre- sponsible. That's the trouble with young people today, no thought for others.'

It was a long way to the nearest supermarket. Mrs Fell

knew she could speak her mind and still not lose too much custom.

The village shop was the end cottage in a row behind the George. A massive extension at the back had resulted in a spacious modern flat above a large store with a wide range of goods. Tolland's seclusion had attracted highly paid commuters as well as senior citizens with the money to find a genteel existence. There were tins of consommé beside the baked beans, smoked salmon in the chilled cabinet and firelighters alongside candles to grace a dinner table.

'You all right, Mrs Roberts? Anything I can get you? Something your wholesaler doesn't carry, perhaps.'

Myra Roberts, landlady of the George, shook her head. 'I've just come in for some biscuits. Sam likes one with his coffee.'

Mrs Seymour's purchases were ready for checking. 'I suppose you've had the police round?' Mrs Fell asked her.

'Me? Why?'

'The dead man in the field – soldier I heard. Probably there since the war. You're born and bred here and the Seymours, they go back a long way in Tolland. I expect you've got relatives know what went on.'

'My mother was from Blakeney and my father was a prisoner in Germany. He didn't get home until the war was over.'

Mrs Fell shook her head and tutted. 'Pity you couldn't help the police get it cleared up. Someone round here must've buried the poor lad and plenty could tell a thing or two, if they've a mind. I'm sure it's very upsetting, no one knowing whose family's involved. I mean, you've got enough to worry about with your Alan. It's all right for Mrs Roberts – she'll be getting extra trade from reporters.'

Myra Roberts fielded the malice and laid a packet of biscuits on the counter.

'If there's media interest we'll both benefit,' she told

Mrs Fell, 'but I can assure you the prices in the George won't change.'

Mrs Fell flushed with anger and banged the till hard as her customers paid their bills and left. When they were walking away Mrs Seymour stopped and turned to Myra Roberts.

'It's true, isn't it? Everyone's on edge, the police coming and going.'

'It's still early days but they won't give up till they've finished ferreting. Trouble is, who knows what they'll turn up.'

'He should have backed Pete Simons!'

'Daddy's little boy couldn't have done that.'

'No? Instead, he gets promoted and Simons is docked to sergeant.'

'Pete was lucky to get that. I heard the brass were ready to bust him, a beat job at the very least. It was his DCI went bail for him.'

'Whittaker?'

'He understood about Pete being on edge – his wife divorcing him.'

'It's still no excuse for belting a prisoner – like he did.'

Reason was drowned out by a phone buzzing in the next room. Keith Tyrell answered it, the voice in his ear ending the comments he had been enduring.

Leaving his critics to slash at him in peace he walked the short distance to the office of Detective Superintendent Mortimer and its open door.

'Come in, Keith. Sit down.'

Mortimer's body was tired and it showed in his face. 'Update?'

'The remains are those of an American soldier, a PFC Benjamin Gordheimer reported AWOL just before D-Day.'

'That was quick!'

The Pentagon had creaked a little but spat out a fax with military efficiency.

'Dog tags proving their worth, sir, even after fifty years.'

'Could it have been an accident?'

'Unlikely. The body looked as though it had been laid out for burial before being covered.'

'In a ditch?'

'No, sir. Probably a bomb crater.'

'In Tolland? You're joking!'

'Draper, the community man for the village, he's done his homework. Very early in the war German bombers navigated by rivers on moonlit nights. Tolland's on the larger of the two bends of the Severn – '

'And the silly buggers thought it was Gloucester.' Mortimer shook his head to clear disbelief. 'I suppose it was the aircraft factory at Brockworth they were after.'

'A stick of bombs fell across the fields near the river. No one was killed, no property hit, just holes in the ground. Some of the craters weren't filled in until after the war.'

'A very handy grave. Evidence of murder?'

'We're waiting for Pathology, sir. Chris – Dr Collier – noticed something odd about the ribs and sternum. Possible damage by shotgun pellets.'

Mortimer swore softly, impressively. 'Not an army rifle. That means a local job.'

'There's every likelihood the murderer's dead, sir.'

'Of course there is, dammit, but the American Army's involved. That means we'll have to lean over backwards making amends for us killing one of their boys instead of the bloody enemy.'

'Can I pass on any questions from reporters to the press office?'

'Good idea. They're all experts after taking their turn in Cromwell Street.' Mortimer was silent for a moment, his features heavy. 'Since you're not chasing someone likely to kill again, I can only give you Sergeant Clarke and the community chap . . .?'

'Draper, sir.'

'Warn them there'll be no overtime – resources are a minus quantity. First call must go to the Gloucester case and God knows when that mess will be cleared up, or what it'll cost. I don't suppose the digging's finished.'

Like every policeman in the county force Tyrell had been appalled by the horror unfolding daily.

'Any family with a daughter missing must be afraid she's buried there.'

The super shook his head. 'Poor devils. Every day they contact Gloucester, full of hope, and what for? To know for sure their child's dead? When they find out how . . .'

Both men had read pathology reports on recovered bodies.

'That's one problem I don't face. The Gordheimer parents must be long gone.'

'There'll be someone alive who remembers him and still grieves,' Mortimer warned.

'And at an age to be very vulnerable – as is anyone involved in the killing and cover-up. They've all got to be at least seventy. Maybe we'd better put the grave-digger on red alert.'

'I've heard of this theory of yours, Keith. Mind you, I've friends in Belfast who've said much the same as you.'

'That when someone murders they trigger off a chain of death?'

'It was so in Ulster, I'm told. Witnesses having heart attacks or strokes, grieving relatives developing terminal illnesses.'

'It all adds up to extra funerals, yet the murderer can't be charged with those deaths even if he killed as surely as with a bullet.'   •

'What if your American died accidentally?'

'Manslaughter? It's possible, I suppose. What I do

know is that murder or not, the chain's been suspended for fifty years. The question is, will it go on claiming casualties now the body's surfaced?'

'That's up to you, lad. Isn't the second part of your theory that the number in this chain of death, as you call it, depends on the way the investigation is carried out? If you're right, it's you who has to proceed with caution.'

'With all the witnesses officially geriatric, I'll be walking on eggshells,' Tyrell promised.

The CID office went quiet as soon as Tyrell walked in. Resentment was a silent tide flowing his way and he assumed it was because of his recent promotion and the Simons' enquiry. He could not know the greatest part of the antipathy was envy of his looks and athletic build, the easy way he wore good clothes. Nor was the DI aware he had an aura of authority, enhanced when he spoke, his words always quiet, deep and free of the local accent.

Almost everyone in the room studiously avoided Tyrell's glance. Only Sergeant Clarke looked up.

'Are we to go on working from here or do we get one of the nice, new, shiny vans?'

'No such luck,' Tyrell said. 'A facility in the village is to be put at our disposal.'

'What happens if you don't find the guy who did it?'

The voice was the one which had referred to him as Daddy's boy and Tyrell studied the owner. Very short black hair on a bullet-shaped head, prominent eyes and a thick neck with a strangling collar.

'I get to carry the can all on my own. If I've cocked up or made an error of judgement, that would be fair, wouldn't it?'

Tolland's village hall smelled of dust and sweaty

21

trainers, sheets of children's work with crayons and paint adding the only touches of cheerfulness. Boxes around the room held the supplies sent from headquarters. They contained one well-used computer and printer, an old fax machine and large quantities of forms. There was also a civilian to man the newly installed phone. Maria Gilbert was the middle-aged widow of a police sergeant.

'A Mrs Poynter's already been in, wanting to know where she's supposed to run her playgroup.'

'Mrs Poynter?' Tyrell looked to Martin Draper for help.

'She's Lady Driffield's little shadow.'

'Good, then Lady Driffield will be able to find her a space somewhere.'

PC Draper was uneasy. 'Her ladyship may make a fuss.'

'Tough. We wouldn't even have this place if Washington wasn't looking over HQ's shoulder. Let's got on. Do you need any help, Mrs Gilbert?'

She was unpacking a kettle from a box and was surprised by the question. 'That's very kind, thank you.'

Jackets were stripped off and, in a very short time, tables and chairs had been moved, trestles stacked, equipment arranged.

'I'm ready for coffee,' Mrs Gilbert said. 'How about you?'

'Great!' Tyrell said with a grin and looked even younger.

The three policemen went over the information they had obtained from the villagers. It did not take long, Ben Gordheimer's name dropping into Tolland memories so deep no ripples appeared.

'I've got a list of sorts,' PC Draper reported. 'There were a couple of local girls who went mad about Yanks and nylons in the war. One of them married and went to live on a Kentucky hill farm but it wasn't what she expected. She stuck it out and was still there when she died ten years ago. The other one liked the way she could earn well. When things were quiet after D-Day she drifted off to London and disappeared without trace.'

Tyrell was sceptical. 'The whole of the Forest was saturated with Americans in '44. I can't believe those girls were Tolland's only contacts.'

'No, sir, they weren't. Tolland Manor was requisitioned in 1940 and used as a Land Army hostel.' PC Draper smiled. 'Regular visits by truck-loads of American soldiers for dances and so on.'

'Especially the so-on.' DS Clarke imagined the events.

The DI was interested. 'Are any of the land girls still in the area? They might remember Gordheimer.'

'I've made enquiries, sir. There're three – all married to local men.'

'The family at the manor during the war. Driffield?'

'Old Sir Montague was alive then. He had two sons away in the army and a daughter in the Wrens. The youngest daughter was in boarding school and not allowed to mix with the land girls in the holidays.'

'Where is she now?'

'Here, sir, in Tolland. Miss Caroline, the locals call her. Before the war ended her father had a massive stroke and she left school to look after him. He lingered twenty years or so, then after his death she stayed on as a kind of housekeeper for her eldest brother and his wife. When they died and their son, Sir Edward, took over, she had a cottage on the estate done up for herself.'

'In time we'd better have a word with them all,' the DI decided, 'and any staff the Driffields had who are still alive.'

'There's only old Mrs Slade. She's the one who's been giving me all the gossip,' PC Draper admitted. 'Kitchen maid at the manor, she was. The rest of the staff died or moved away years ago.'

'Well done, Draper. You carry on listening to gossip,' Tyrell said with a smile. He turned to his sergeant. 'We'd better start interviewing the land girls. It's not a long list.'

'And they're all pensioners,' DS Clarke added morosely. 'Won't remember a damned thing they don't want to.'

'Maybe not – but someone knows what happened. It'll take patience, and plenty of it. Facts we need will have become hidden, some buried I've no doubt. Still, in a village like Tolland, there'll be talk.'

DS Clarke had a healthy cynicism. 'Even after fifty years?'

'Yes, Sergeant, and we have to listen more carefully than usual, even if the CPS will ignore us completely when it's all over.'

'Mrs Slade, sir,' Martin Draper said apologetically. 'She knows all there is to know about past, present and future life in Tolland but she keeps on about flowers on a grave being too high. She's demanding police action. I thought you should be warned.'

'That's all we need,' DC Clarke groaned. 'A witness ready for the funny farm.'

'It's hardly a new experience for us. Now, let's get at the land girls.'

The DI began to lead the way out.

'Girls?' Brian Clarke exploded as he followed. 'They're all older than my mum!'

'What about Mrs Slade?' PC Draper called after them.

Tyrell turned. 'We'll get to her in time. I mean, flowers on a grave? It hardly needs our mini-murder squad rushing into action.'

Chapter Two

Peggy Arkwright had married Len Phelps soon after the war ended. From a piece of waste land on the outskirts of Gloucester they had carved a small market garden which, in more recent years, had evolved into a garden centre.

'I've heard talk of this place,' DS Clarke said as he searched for space in the car park. 'Plants do well from here.'

'Martin Draper said the food was good. I gather the son-in-law trained as a chef.'

There was an air of leisure, of prosperity. Sheds and greenhouses were well kept, the paths in good condition and recently swept. Wheeling barrows and directing hoses were men and women in jeans and uniform green T-shirts.

The Phelps' house was set back from the busyness of the gardens. Once two derelict cottages, it glowed like a jewel.

'Come in, come in,' the woman who answered their knock insisted.

The smell which bellied out at them was the first thing they noticed. It reminded the DI of hopeless slums he had had to visit, yet there was no sign of poverty. Mrs Phelps clapped her hands excitedly and led the way from the front door. Tyrell had time to see good furniture with the dullness of dirt, thick carpets that had long ago given up the struggle against grime.

In a sitting-room cluttered with chairs and tables, Mrs

Phelps turned to beam at her visitors. Keith Tyrell needed only a glance to imprint the woman in his memory. The faded reds and blues of her long, limp dress of Indian cotton, the strings of amber beads, might have suited a young girl but Peggy Phelps had white hair. It was fairly clean, flowing around the lined features of an old woman before wisping thinly near her waist.

The smile she gave them was that of a happy child. Her eyes were large and vague, the irises an indeterminate colour and edged with the opalescence of age.

'Sit down, sit down.'

The two men tried to do as she asked but the couch and chairs overflowed with gardening magazines and discarded clothes. Mrs Phelps smiled encouragement as they pushed aside enough debris to allow them to sit.

'When she knew about the skeleton, my daughter said you'd come.'

'Tolland Manor in 1944 – you were one of the land girls,' Tyrell said.

Mrs Phelps clapped her hands together yet again, making the beads on her thin chest bounce.

'1944! I was only eighteen and it was such fun coming to the country.'

Tyrell guessed she had been born in Birmingham.

'I hated the uniform,' she confided to DS Clarke. 'The dungarees weren't as bad as the breeches and shirts for best – but we did have wellingtons! Not everybody was allowed them in the war – we needed them on the farms. I loved it. Standing in the fields and just hearing the food grow.'

Her expression was blissful, faded eyes looking through the window and seeing only the sunshine of fifty years ago. DS Clarke looked at Tyrell and nodded towards the woman lost in her memories. A forefinger went to his temple in a screwing gesture.

Tyrell shook his head.

'The Americans, Mrs Phelps. Can you remember them?'

The strange eyes swung to him and focused for a moment.

'Dear boys, so cheerful and full of life as they faced the horror that was to come – the invasion, you know.' She frowned, her happiness clouded. 'So many were killed.' With reality her youth had gone, she was old and frail, then her lips curved in a smile. 'Everyone said they were such fun at the dances – and there was ice-cream. Peach ice-cream.'

'Ben Gordheimer,' Tyrell said. 'Do you remember him?'

'Who?'

'Ben. Ben Gordheimer.'

'I never bothered with names, there was no point. They were all going away to die.'

The simplicity of her answer was chilling but Tyrell knew he must pursue the wayward thoughts.

'Have you names, addresses, of any other land girls? Those who left the area after the hostel closed down?'

Mrs Phelps blinked and was back with her guests. 'I'll ask my daughter. Anthea knows about such things.'

The door opened and a knobbly man of middle height stormed in, his shirt the same green as those of the garden workers.

'What the hell you doin' here?' he wanted to know.

The man wrenched off his cap and the whiteness of his bald head was stark against the weather-beaten red of his face. Tyrell stood and explained the reason for their visit and Mrs Phelps' co-operation.

'Co-operation? You'll be lucky! Peggy can't even remember to blow her own bloody nose. You want to know about 1944? She was assin' about playin' farmers while I was in North Africa. Yanks?' He turned and spat, adding to the mess in the grate. 'They're like the bloody Germans. Best dead.'

Tyrell's eyes flashed. 'One did die in Tolland, Mr Phelps.'

27

'One less to worry about then.'

DS Clarke intervened. He had heard of the DI that if he was icily polite, watch out.

'If you say so, sir, but we have to ask questions, just the same.'

'Your daughter may have the addresses of land girls who lived at the manor,' Tyrell continued, a steel edge to his deep voice.

Len Phelps quietened, no longer tossing his head like an angry ram. 'I'll ask her. Anthea's got the business brains round here. She keeps things like addresses on her computer. Got a number I can have?'

DS Clarke obliged.

'Anthea's got everything pin-neat in her office,' her father declared proudly, seeing the men out as his wife daydreamed.

'Christ! No wonder the gardens are so tidy. The old boy must spend all his time there – and who could blame him. Even the muck heaps must smell better than that house.'

'Not the best housekeeper, our Mrs Phelps,' the DI agreed, 'but all she needs is a good pair of glasses.'

'No way! She's as nutty as a fruit cake.'

'You were too busy holding your nose to watch her properly. OK, she's got used to the smell but by not wearing glasses she can stay as young as she chooses to be. You must admit it's a marvellous system for living the life she wants.'

'Anyone who enjoys even one day in that midden must be batty.'

'She's not. If she can't see things clearly, there's no housework to bother with. The son-in-law cooks, the husband stays out in the garden and the daughter sees to the rest.'

DS Clarke mulled over the idea as he unlocked the car doors.

28

'I'm glad she didn't make us a cup of tea.'

'The interim pathology report confirms the possible date of death and interment coinciding with the victim going AWOL.'

Superintendent Mortimer had sent for Keith Tyrell. The older man had a briskness of manner born of a good night's sleep. He took a sheet of paper from a file.

'There's this photo from his brother – it's better than the army one from Washington.'

Smiling for the camera, PFC Gordheimer had been a dark, handsome youth with a cap of curly black hair. Tyrell guessed him to have been intelligent and maybe a little shy.

'When you've seen them as they are now, it's hard to accept the changes.'

Tyrell nodded. 'After all these years and with no flesh left, the shock of a violent death is muted.'

'But it was there at the time,' Mortimer reminded him, 'and we need to know which bastard was responsible.'

Tyrell carried the thought back with him to the over-large incident room. He had taken only a few steps into the hall before he stopped. Chairs were in a welcoming group and there was the smell of polish mingling with the perfume of flowers.

'Mrs Gilbert?'

Her smile was merry. 'I was bored and started a bit of cleaning. Then, half an hour ago, two women came in with flowers for the American. There was no grave so they brought them here.'

'Had they known him?'

'I got them talking. In 1944 one had been living near Broadway, a nurse in a hospital. The other's the daughter of a man who died in Changi jail. The mother's bedridden but she wanted flowers brought. "Something she's never been able to do for my dad." Funny how it can still bring tears – even after all these years.'

'Any messages?'

'None, I'm afraid.'

'Good, then we can get back to the land girls.'

Beyond a garden of sparse colour, the Bryces' house looked like a place in which even a mote of dust dare not linger. The bell was answered by Noah Bryce, anger flushing his skin as he recognised his visitors.

'If you haven't come to tell me I can get the drainage job finished, you're wasting your time.' The thin wattles of his neck shook. 'I'm losing money every day you hang about.'

'Then perhaps you'll let us talk to Mrs Bryce as soon as possible?'

DS Clarke nearly smiled. The DI was being polite again. He might be the youngest inspector in the county CID but he could sound like an old-fashioned head-master with a cane in one hand.

'My wife?' Noah Bryce was momentarily shaken. 'Why do you want to talk to her?'

'She's the Sheila Knight who was a land girl living in Tolland Manor in 1944?'

Colour began to drain from the old man and eyelids hooded his thoughts. 'What of it?'

'We're talking to all the people who might be able to give us background information. Mrs Bryce is one of them. May we see her, please?'

They were led to a sitting-room with solid furniture and neutral colours. Every possible surface gleamed and the only sign of life was a petal which had fallen from a silver vase of roses.

When Mrs Bryce came she was slim and neat in a plain blue dress and cardigan. Not even the awkward-ness of arthritis could hide the beauty which had once been hers, although she did nothing to enhance it. Thin blonde hair was streaked with white and drawn back from her face, ruthlessly exposing the calm mask of age behind which she hid.

Mrs Bryce invited the policemen to sit and her husband fussed them to a sofa.

'What is it you want to know, Inspector?' The woman's voice was soft, controlled, yet there was curiosity in her pale blue eyes.

'We're having difficulty finding anyone who knew the American soldier buried in the field your husband was contracted to drain.'

'I resent your implication!' Noah Bryce barked.

'Nothing was implied, Mr Bryce. All I want to do is talk to your wife. I'm sure you're a very busy man, sir. There's no reason to detain you when you must be needed elsewhere.'

Noah Bryce refused to be dismissed from the room. He stood behind his wife, glaring at the two policemen as Tyrell handed Mrs Bryce the photo of Ben Gordheimer.

'Did you know him?'

She examined the likeness carefully. Her husband peered over her shoulder and redness stained his throat, surging upwards.

'Of course my wife didn't know him. She's not the sort to run around after Americans when she was engaged to me.'

'Mrs Bryce?'

'I've told you, she didn't know him.'

'I'd like your wife to answer for herself, sir.' The DI was stern.

The old man rocked furiously. 'You're harassing her! Leave her alone!'

His eyes bulged and his cheeks were purpling as they watched.

'Noah, remember what Dr O'Brien told you,' his wife said gently. 'These gentlemen are only doing their job. When they've finished, David can see to the drainage in Sir Edward's field and you'll get paid.'

Bryce looked pleadingly at his wife, his body arcing towards her.

'Perhaps you'd better leave,' she said to Tyrell. 'I'll show you out.'

At the front door Tyrell stopped and faced her. 'Ben Gordheimer?'

'I never met him,' Mrs Bryce said and closed the door behind them.

'God! What a possessive old bastard!' Brian Clarke was annoyed. 'And mean? It was only her suggestion about him getting paid that shut him up.'

'You're right. I also saw a man desperately near another stroke – and she knows it.'

'Another stroke?'

'Didn't you notice he dragged his right foot a little the day we met him? It's worse now and he was busy keeping his right hand out of sight.'

'She'd be better off if he blew a fuse for good. He can't be much fun to live with.'

'He's her job – and she's not a woman to neglect her duty.'

'Is that all marriage is when you get old?'

'Old? It's nothing to do with age but yes, for a lot of older couples, maybe duty is a part of it. Perhaps it's just love.'

'Not in that house.'

'There,' Tyrell said, 'I think you're right.'

'Mrs Mitchell?'

They had been directed to an extension built at the side of a large and prosperous farmhouse. The elegant woman in tweed and cashmere who answered the door looked tired, wary. She inspected their warrant cards thoroughly before allowing them in the house.

PC Draper had warned them what to expect. By the well-guarded fire and dressed in the expensive wool of a country landowner, sat the withered hulk of a man who raised the eyes of a child to them.

'Mr Mitchell?'

Tyrell walked forward and shook the man's hand. For a second there was strength in the grip, then the huge body relaxed back in its chair. The once-handsome head moved restlessly until he found the familiarity of his wife.

'Cake.'

She went to him and stood with her hand on his shoulder. She was defensive, protective of her husband. Tyrell recognised they must have been a very good-looking couple until the creeping tendrils of Alzheimer's switched off the sharpness of a brain.

Mrs Mitchell sat beside her husband, holding his hand. The innocent old eyes closed and he dozed.

'You want to talk to me about the body you found?'

'Did you know Ben Gordheimer?'

'Since I first heard the name I've been trying to remember. There were so many boys who came to the manor at that time. They all arrived at once, there was a lot of noise, then they were gone.'

'Perhaps this will help?'

Tyrell gave her Ben Gordheimer's photo. She studied it carefully, then shook her head.

'No. I don't think so. I'm sorry. It was all so long ago – and I wasn't much interested in Americans. After they'd gone we heard more than half were killed in the first week of the landings.'

There was mourning in the peaceful room.

'Did you ever go to the army base with the other girls? We were told the Americans used to send a truck.'

Mrs Mitchell smiled wickedly and, for a moment, the two men saw the beauty and the fire that had been in her.

She chuckled. 'The passion wagon.'

'Not your style?'

'No. Anyway, I'd already met Roland when he was home on leave and I worked on this farm for his father. His mother would soon have split on me if I'd "gone off with the Yanks" as she would have called it.' She looked at the man she had married so long ago. Weariness eased and her face was luminous. 'He was worth waiting for.'

'Are you still in touch with any of the land girls who were here in 1944?'

'I thought I might be asked that.'

Mrs Mitchell gently released her hand from her husband's grasp and went to an antique desk, unlocking it and taking out a sheet of paper.

'I've made a list for you. We haven't met in years – just exchange Christmas cards and let each other know we're still alive.'

'If you recall anything . . .?'

'I'll let you know.'

The two men returned to the car and DS Clarke shook his head.

'Bloody pathetic!'

'The Mitchells? You think so?'

'Don't you?'

The DI sat quietly as his sergeant started the engine and drove along the lane to the main road.

'Of the three houses we've visited today, in which one did you feel at home – have a sense of happiness and contentment?' Tyrell asked.

'But he's a vegetable!'

'So? He's the man she loved and married and she's clearly got a lifetime of good memories to think about as they sit there together. It's not how many women would cope, I grant you that. Mrs Mitchell can – and does.'

'If we're lucky, when she's sitting doing all that remembering, something useful might crop up.'

DS Clarke changed gear and turned on to the main road, revving the engine hard.

'I think we've stirred up a few pools this morning,'

Tyrell said, half to himself. 'I wonder if she'll make contact?'

'Who?

'One of the women was holding something back, I'm sure of it.'

'Which one?'

'We'll just have to wait and see.'

The incident room smelt of fresh coffee and Mrs Gilbert was waiting with a fax.

'From a garden centre. A list of addresses.'

Brian Clarke was surprised. 'That was quick!'

Tyrell grinned. 'Our Anthea's supposed to be the business brain.' He handed over the data given him by Mrs Mitchell. 'Names and addresses. Possible leads. Add them to the ones on the fax and ask home stations for assistance. You'd better send them Gordheimer's picture.'

'A fax of a fax? It won't be very clear. There's no scanner so this computer's no help.'

'It's all we've got.'

'Maybe not. You've a visitor.'

Keith Tyrell looked round the hall, empty but for the two of them and Brian Clarke heading for the toilets.

'From the American Embassy,' she said. 'Major Gifford, Military Attaché's office. He said he'd wait for you in the George.'

'Damn! Gloucester was supposed to see to all that.'

'They did. This chap came along to view the scene of the crime and meet the officer in charge.'

There was a disturbance at the door.

'Mother, you shouldn't be here.'

'It's a police station, isn't it? I've every right.'

Keith Tyrell saw an elderly lady, small and determined. She was pushing away the restraining hand of her daughter, a woman in her forties with the air of someone near the end of her tether.

35

Maria Gilbert intercepted the pair.

'If it's a local matter, you really need to see PC Draper.'

'Young Martin's no good to anyone. He keeps on being very polite and doing bugger all,' the old woman snapped, her little button nose twitching with anger.

'Mother!'

'It's true. Never been the same here since they sold off the old police house. You always knew where to find the bobby – and he couldn't crawl in a car and sneak off to Lydney or Gloucester out the way. New people moved in there now. Bloody foreigners!'

'The Jenkinses are very nice, Mother, and they're not foreigners. Mrs Jenkins' mother lived in Tolland when she was a girl.'

The private row seemed set to continue indefinitely, the old woman used to pulling rank on her daughter to get her own way. She was dressed in the full black of the recently widowed, her felt hat skewered in place with an aggressive hand. Keith Tyrell fought back a smile.

'There seems to be a problem. Can I help?'

Little eyes of polished granite stared up at him. 'Who are you?'

Tyrell explained, offered his warrant card and introduced Mrs Gilbert and then DS Clarke as he returned to the arena.

'You're a proper policeman?'

As the daughter exclaimed, 'Mother!' a stifled sound came from Brian Clarke and Maria Gilbert bent to the papers on her desk.

'Very proper,' the DI assured his visitor. 'And you are . . .?'

'Elsie Slade. Mrs. I buried my Fred a week back and that's why I'm here.'

'There was something wrong with his death?'

'No. I kept telling the old fool to go easy in the garden, he was too old for it. Would he listen? Out hoeing his onions when he dropped. Still, peaceful he looked when we found him. He could have had years more if he'd listened but he shut his ears to me a long time ago, he did, didn't he, Agnes?'

The daughter looked at Tyrell, pleading for his patience with her mother. He smiled at her and turned to the little termagant.

'If you're the Elsie Slade who used to work up at the manor in the war, then you're just the person I want to see.'

She was suspicious. 'What about?'

'American soldiers used to visit Tolland Manor. You were there at the time.'

'What if I was? We weren't allowed in the Land Army quarters – and they had to stay away from us, too.'

'Come on, Mrs Slade. A lady of your intelligence? Are you trying to tell me you never saw or heard anything that went on amongst the land girls?'

'Maybe – and maybe I've forgotten it all.'

The DI recognised a formidable adversary. 'What would it take to help you remember?'

Calculations went on behind eyes as unblinking and clear as a child's. 'Get something done about the flowers on my Fred's grave.'

'I'd like to help but it's really a matter for the vicar – unless, of course, a crime's been committed. Has it?'

Elsie Slade's mouth closed in a mutinous line and her patient daughter shook her head.

'They're different,' Mrs Slade insisted. 'The flowers are different.' Suddenly, she was a tired old woman. 'Why won't anyone believe me?' she asked, her voice trembling.

'Mother, we've been to Dad's grave again and again. The wreaths are all where Reg Warren put them when he filled Dad in.'

'I don't care. When I went to the grave the day after we buried him, the wreath from me wasn't as high as my knees. I noticed because the fern at the side tickled and I bent down and scratched. Sunday, after church,

37

that bit of fern had moved. It was sideways and higher up.'

'That's all you have to go on?' Keith Tyrell asked gently.

'It's enough – or it should be.'

There was frustration, helplessness in the look she gave him.

'If I know Mrs Gilbert, she's got the makings of a good pot of tea somewhere handy. Come and sit down and I'll arrange for her to get the vicar to come and talk to you. After that, if we all put our heads together, we may be able to clear up the mystery.'

Tension eased in the little figure and Mrs Slade allowed herself to be led to a chair. Her spirits returned as she rejected seat after seat until she found one which would not snag her new coat.

'Can you cope?' Tyrell asked Maria Gilbert. 'I should get over to the George and see this embassy man. All Mrs Slade needs is tea and sympathy – and a date with the vicar.'

Maria Gilbert smiled. 'You go ahead. I'll phone the vicarage while the kettle boils. Brian and I might even get her chatting about Tolland in wartime.'

'I'll be back as soon as I can.'

Tyrell left the ugly rectangle of a room that reminded him of stewed tea from urns, curling sandwiches, Cubs and Brownies. It was only a matter of yards to the back door of the pub but he stepped into a different world.

The George was the haunt of countrymen. Its small rooms were dark caverns, their walls lined with settles of wood as solid as that of the tables. There were no fakes in this place, the Forest oak dark with age.

In the bar was a fair sprinkling of customers. Most were middle-aged or elderly and they all stopped talking, watching Tyrell's every move. It was like the station canteen but without the aggression.

'Mornin',' said a man in his fifties and too young to be of use in the investigation.

Keith Tyrell acknowledged the greeting with a nod. 'Good morning.'

No one moved, yet the DI found himself silently directed to a corner where a stranger was sitting. There was amusement in the half-smile on a square face, its strong features topped by military-cropped blond hair.

'Major Gifford?'

The major stood and was almost as tall as Tyrell. The handshake they exchanged was watched by every pair of eyes in the George.

'Beer?' the American offered. 'It's very good for English brew but your secretary won her bet.'

'Bet? Mrs Gilbert?'

'I hoped it would be cold. She said, "No way".'

'They're a bit traditional here. I believe much of the ale's brewed on the premises and no self-respecting Englishman would dull his taste buds drinking such liquid iced.'

The two men used easy conversation on a neutral topic to take stock of each other. Keith Tyrell saw a man a few years older than himself who had the stance of someone superbly fit. The major's slacks and tweed jacket were well cut, casual, allowing him to blend in with the background. As for Gifford, he approved of the firm set of Tyrell's mouth, the quick intelligence in his eyes.

'Can we talk here?'

Keith Tyrell grinned. 'Not unless you want all we discuss spread on the village grapevine.'

'Bugs?'

'Not the electronic sort. I should imagine every word is picked up and remembered by someone you thought half-asleep.'

'Jeez! It seems such a harmless place.'

'It probably is but they have their own ways. There'll be great suspicion of anyone who hasn't lived among them for the last thirty years.'

39

'Will it take that long for you to get the answers you want?'

'I hope not. Someone in Tolland knows what happened to Gordheimer. It's been kept a secret for fifty years and it'll take more than a little patience to get the village to release the details.'

'How much patience has your boss got?'

'He wants a result but we're not a highly expensive unit. An inspector and a sergeant. We may be CID but there's no overtime.'

'There is Mrs Gilbert,' Gifford said. 'She tells me the best crisps are the ones with a little bag of salt.'

Tyrell was puzzled.

'Her winnings,' the major explained with a grin.

Amicably, the two men went back to the makeshift incident room in time to hear a cultured voice protesting.

'. . . but Mrs Slade, who on earth would want to disturb your husband's grave, even slightly?'

Reverend Nicholas Hatton, a small man in a worn grey suit and shining white dog-collar, was too gentle to be a match for Elsie Slade.

'There's been goings-on, Vicar, and well you do know it,' she scolded. 'Only two days after Fred's funeral young Alan Seymour nearly died of fright, didn't he, Agnes?'

Agnes Morse nodded in silence.

'Waking up in church and thinking he was dead! I ask you? Young people today – nothing's sacred.'

Reverend Hatton tried to pour verbal oil on troubled waters. 'That was just a prank.'

The oil fuelled a firestorm.

'Prank? That's what you call it? Betty Seymour still can't sleep nights, not with her boy's nightmares. Screaming his head off he is – until he wakes himself up.' Elsie Slade scarcely paused for breath. 'And what about Maggie Mitton? All that effort to get her Pam married decent before she dropped the baby and what happens? Whoever left Alan in the church and let him think himself dead, they'd pinched flowers off the altar. No crime, Vicar? You got time I'll soon put you straight!'

'Mrs Slade.'

The headmaster was back in the DI's voice and the black-clad little virago was silenced. Her noisy breathing gradually slowed and the bright red spot in each cheek quietened to a peony flush. Sharp eyes flicked to the American and she lifted her chin to take in his height.

'Who's he?'

Mrs Slade was given a courteous bow. 'Clayton Gifford, ma'am. Major, US Army.'

'A Yank. Better sit down – you're giving me a crick in the neck.'

'Thank you, ma'am.'

He did as he was bid, entertained by the feisty little lady.

'I suppose you're here because of the bones?' she said.

'He was a soldier, ma'am. There're a couple of people still alive back home who knew him as their brother. They want to make sure he has a proper burial.'

'So what's stopping you?'

'An English coroner's court. Then there's the need Ben Gordheimer's folks have to know why he had to lie in a field for fifty years.'

Elsie Slade nodded sagely. 'It's best to know.'

'So you'll talk to us?' Tyrell asked.

She looked up at him and saw a man she could respect. 'If I do, what about my Fred's grave?'

Agnes Morse was almost in tears as she began to argue with her mother. The vicar joined in, waving his hands helplessly.

'Who was the undertaker?' Tyrell's words were quiet but they cut through the din.

41

'Frank Cobbett,' Reverend Hatton said with relief. 'A very good man.'

'Should be for what he charges,' grumbled Mrs Slade.

'Mother!'

'Well, it's true. I could manage it for my Fred but Agnes'll have to dig deep to bury me.'

'Your daughter has plenty of time to save up, Mrs Slade,' the DI said firmly. 'In the meantime, I suggest Reverend Hatton contacts Mr Cobbett – '

'Agnes can do that,' her mother insisted, determined not to lose control of the situation.

'No,' the inspector decreed and Elsie Slade subsided. 'The churchyard is the vicar's responsibility. He can invite Mr Cobbett, along with the sexton and yourselves, to meet at the grave. Once there, you can decide if there's been any change. Reverend Hatton will let us know if there's need for police involvement. Now, will you talk to me here?'

Elsie Slade pursed her lips as she wondered if she had extracted all she could from her visit.

'You can come to the house when we've sorted out Fred's grave.'

'Very well,' Keith Tyrell agreed. 'I've plenty to see to in the meantime.'

'Will he come too?' she asked, twitching her head towards the major.

Tyrell and Gifford exchanged brief glances.

'If the major is still in Tolland when you agree to see me, I'd be glad of his assistance.'

'If you're going to find out what happened in the war, you'll need all the help you can get.'

The inspector leaned towards her. 'Believe me, Mrs Slade, I'll find the answers I'm looking for,' he assured her, his words deceptively soft, 'and no one will stop me.'

With Elsie Slade's departure there was peace, time for the DI to outline a schedule for his small team.

The American was curious. 'Mrs Slade is a witness?'

'She probably never saw a thing,' Tyrell said cheer-fully, 'but she can be very useful.'

The major was sceptical and looked it.

'Put it this way,' Tyrell began, 'if you want to crack a nut and use a hammer, the chances are you smash it to smithereens and get nothing edible.'

'But with the proper tool?'

'Exactly. A village like Tolland has a very hard shell. Our Mrs Slade could be just the right nutcracker.'

Chapter Three

The car turned off into a narrow lane and gently bumped its occupants towards a house they could glimpse through gaps in the hedge.

'This lady's important locally?' Gifford asked.

'One of the Driffields of Tolland Manor,' Keith Tyrell explained. 'She was there in '44.'

As Brian Clarke stopped the car outside an open gate, Tyrell turned in his seat to face the American.

'I'd be grateful if you could wait here, Major Gifford. Should there be a chance for you to come in, DS Clarke will fetch you.'

'OK, Inspector.'

Tyrell and Clarke made their way to the door, noting the care that had been lavished on the garden. The bell ringing brought unseen dogs barking. With the door open, two labradors ran round legs and on into the garden, released by an attractive woman, her grey-blonde hair loose and curling on her shoulders. In jeans and a man's yellow shirt, its collar up against the lean lines of her neck, she studied them calmly.

'Can I help you?'

The expensively accented voice was low and husky, her amber eyes bright with interest. Tyrell knew her to be in her late sixties but she defied the clock. He explained their mission and the two men were invited in.

'Come through. I've just made some tea.'

The kitchen had been added to the original house.

Beyond it a conservatory stretched into a garden which surrounded the glass enclosure with flowers and shrubs. At a circular table spread with newspapers and magazines sat a man with the same lines of breeding as their hostess. He rose awkwardly, age and stiffness hampering him.

'My brother, Bobby. May he stay?'

'If you wish.'

The woman busied herself pouring tea into mugs. Bone china, Tyrell noticed as he accepted his and drank.

'Have you had any luck, Inspector?' Bobby Driffield asked.

'Not yet, sir, although there is a little movement.'

'How on earth are you managing it? Fifty years ago Tolland was in a state of flux, people coming and going all the time.'

'The chances are Ben Gordheimer was interested in one of the land girls. Although we've only been able to talk to three of them, we've been given names and addresses of others who may have been here at the relevant time. In turn, they could lead us to a solution.'

Bobby Driffield frowned, adding to lines pain had engraved in his features. 'Sounds feasible, I suppose. And when you find the girl?'

'It's unlikely she's the one who killed and buried Gordheimer but she may have an idea who did. A jealous local man, perhaps. Another soldier.'

'Peace or war, Inspector, human emotions remain the same.'

'But in wartime,' Keith Tyrell said softly, 'weapons, and the skill to use them, are more easily available.'

'I understood it was a shotgun blast that killed him.'

'Did you, sir?'

The extent of Bobby Driffield's knowledge made Tyrell stiffen. The press had quickly lost interest in the dead American and forensic details had not been released.

'How did you come to know that, may I ask?'

'Someone mentioned it, I believe.' The smile was friendly. 'You know how people talk.'

Tyrell wondered if a fairly senior officer had been indiscreet. He must have gossiped in a club of some kind, or over a dinner table.

'And you, Miss Driffield,' Tyrell said as he turned to her, 'have you any memories which could help?'

'Me, Inspector?' Her smile was pleasant. 'I was a schoolgirl. When I was home in the holidays I was banned from fraternising with land girls. They used the old servants' quarters and so were completely cut off from us – beyond the green baize,' she said with a smile. 'My father considered their part of the manor had become Sodom, Gomorrah and a Parisian brothel all rolled into one. When they left he insisted every room they'd used was completely scoured and repainted.' She laughed gently, although bitterness echoed. 'I almost expected him to demand an exorcism.'

'That is interesting,' Tyrell said. 'I've been told your father suffered a massive stroke in 1944. He must have improved considerably to have been able to make plans for renovating the manor.'

The silence lasted a fraction too long.

'You never knew my father, Inspector,' Bobby Driffield said wryly. 'Even handicapped as he was he could make his orders clear. Very clear.'

Brother and sister looked at each other and gained strength as Tyrell took the faxed photo from his pocket.

'Perhaps you may have seen this man at some time?'

Caroline Driffield accepted the paper and glanced at it briefly. 'Oh dear, my glasses. Can't see a damned thing without them.'

She went swiftly from the room, walking with the

grace of a much younger woman. In her absence Bobby Driffield talked of Tolland in the years since the war. When his sister returned her eyes were hidden by spectacles.

'Sorry, Inspector, I can't help you.' The photograph was handed back. 'As I told you, it would have been more than my life was worth to be caught amongst the land girls.' Her smile was infectious.

'And the Americans?'

She shook her head. 'My father disapproved of them. Every time a truck-load arrived at the manor he became incandescent.'

'She's right, Inspector. He was a fine man in many ways but an archetypal WASP. White Anglo-Saxon Protestant,' he said, smiling at Brian Clarke's puzzlement, 'especially the Protestant part. He still hadn't come to terms with Bloody Mary burning some way-off relative.'

'Do you remember the vicar we got in the war?' Caroline Driffield asked her brother. 'Genuflections and crossing himself all the time?'

'Was that the chap Papa tried to get the bishop to move on for being too high church?'

She nodded. 'Quite unsuccessfully, of course. The bish was like everyone else at the time – glad of any help he could get. Anyway, Father John was too old to go elsewhere. "He was a nice, unparticular man",' she quoted.

Her expression was soft, her eyes blank as she lingered in a happier existence. Tyrell moved to put his mug on the table and the sound brought her back to the present.

'I'm sorry. Old memories carrying one away.'

'Perhaps they'll stir up some we could use?'

She shook her head. 'Nothing.'

Tyrell was silent, holding her eyes with his until she lowered her gaze.

'There is one way you could be of assistance, Miss Driffield.'

'Of course. If I can.'

'You have influence locally. If you were able to encourage the villagers who were here in 1944 to talk freely to us, we could complete our task and move on.'

'Seems fair, Caro. I could have a word, too,' Bobby Driffield offered.

'You overestimate my powers, Inspector.' Her laugh was light, unforced. 'I'm really retired from involvement in Tolland affairs since I moved here – out to grass, that sort of thing. You should apply to our nephew Edward's wife. Lady Driffield is the *force majeure* now.'

Tyrell savoured the atmosphere her words created and noted Bobby Driffield's careful examination of fingernails.

'Miss Driffield, waiting in the car is Major Gifford from the American Embassy in London. He's here to help with our enquiries, on behalf of Ben Gordheimer's relatives. May I ask you to see him?'

She hesitated for a moment, unsure.

'Poor devils! It must be hard for them,' her brother said. 'Wheel him in, Inspector.'

Bobby Driffield stood, forcing himself to smooth movement. He marshalled the strewn papers and spectacle cases, depositing them on a convenient window seat as Sergeant Clarke left to fetch the major.

By the time the two men arrived in the kitchen, Caroline Driffield had washed mugs and made more tea from the massive kettle steaming gently on the Aga. Introductions were swift and courteous, and Clayton Gifford beamed at the Englishness of the scene.

'It's good of you to see me, ma'am.'

'Not at all, Major Gifford.'

'You've had contact with the dead soldier's family?' Bobby Driffield asked.

'Yes, sir. A sister and brother are still alive, although

48

Mrs Mandel's in poor health. The brother's a retired professor of law living in New York. I've talked to him and he's very anxious to know what happened here.'

'He must be.' Bobby Driffield's voice held the measure of his concern.

'If you can understand, sir, all the family have known for fifty years is that PFC Gordheimer was a deserter who had disappeared off the face of the earth. No body to mourn over and bury, just the disgrace of a man who supposedly ran away from the D-day fighting.'

Caroline Driffield sipped tea and then cradled her mug. 'What is it you need to know?'

Clayton Gifford hardened, somehow looking much older. 'I'm army, ma'am. I have to try and discover if Gordheimer did go AWOL before he was killed. If not, his record must be altered.'

'After fifty years does it matter?'

'Yes, ma'am, it matters. Very much. Then, for his family, there's the shame they've carried on his behalf. It may be a burden they can shed.'

'We'd be the same, Caro.' Bobby Driffield turned to the major. 'If we can help, we will. I occasionally pop into the George for a pint, so I can go this evening and start getting the message round.'

'I'd be grateful, sir.'

'So would I', Tyrell echoed. 'I'd guess Tolland is a place where no one helps the police in case it's seen as informing on a neighbour.'

'Of course it is,' Caroline Driffield agreed cheerfully. 'Centuries of smuggling on the river – old habits die hard, Inspector, even if you're not revenuers.'

Gifford was fascinated. 'Smugglers here?'

'You have to remember the great rivers were the ancient highways. Before good roads and railways, the fastest transport was by boat,' Bobby Driffield explained. 'Tolland was important then, a sizeable port for the hinterland. There was much trade coming in – especially from France.'

'It sure looks the sleepiest of places now.'

Caroline Driffield chuckled. 'Nothing much is missed. A dozen people could describe you right now, Major. Half of them you'd never have seen but they'd have had a good look at you and the details would be accurate.'

'And, if nothing's changed,' Tyrell added quietly, 'there's more than one could help us with the death of that GI.'

'You're right, Inspector,' Bobby Driffield agreed. 'I'll go down to the George early tonight.'

The drive back to Tolland was short and silent. Only as Brian Clarke hurried into the village hall did Clayton Gifford stop and turn to the inspector.

'Something was going on back there. What was it?'

'I don't know. I sensed resistance for some reason.'

'Was that why you got me in?'

'I thought your plea for help might open up a crack in the defences.'

'Why should they be defensive? Have they got something to hide?'

'It's their village – and I don't just mean they live here. For generations the Driffield family decided what happened in Tolland, protected it, if they felt it necessary. They still do to some extent and a proportion of the villagers will go on expecting it of them.'

'Surely that sort of thing's as dead as a dodo – even in England?'

'Is it? Oh, I know new people have moved in and most owe no allegiance, or a tied cottage, to the manor. Many things have been modernised but not the community structure. The village still exists in layers not visible to the naked eye. Sandwiched somewhere are the facts I need.'

Major Gifford saw the hard line of Tyrell's jaw, the firmness of his mouth.

'It's as you said. No good using a hammer.'

'I have to think back to Tolland as it was fifty years ago. Many of the houses had no running water. There were earth closets in the garden and a Driffield at the manor controlling homes and jobs – such as they were.'

'Are you saying the Driffields don't want the police upsetting the village – like parents not wanting their children questioned?'

'Especially if they know one of the children might be guilty? It was against that kind of background Gordheimer was killed and the secrecy began. All I can do is insert questions here and there and wait for the ripples.' Tyrell smiled, a hint of devilment appearing. 'I think I've started something. Now I just have to let it run.'

In the hall Maria Gilbert and PC Draper were deep in conversation.

'. . . may have just been attention-seeking,' the policeman said.

'She's always been one for that, I should imagine.'

'The talk in the George was that her Fred dropped dead to get away from her tongue.'

'Mrs Slade and the flowers,' Tyrell said, his words earning instant attention. 'Any joy?'

Martin Draper nodded. 'The vicar's rung the undertaker who'll be over as soon as he can. There'll be those two, Reg Warren the gravedigger, Mrs Slade and her daughter. I've had a look at the grave. It's neat and tidy so I can't see a charge of desecration sticking.'

'Until the vicar tells us he's not happy and a crime may have been committed, we keep out of it.'

'Yes, sir. Willingly.'

At PC Draper's heartfelt tone Major Gifford raised a quizzical eyebrow. 'Problems, Inspector?'

Keith Tyrell was reading the latest data printed out by Mrs Gilbert.

'Problems? No, not really – at least, not ours.' He tidied the paper away in a folder. 'If I'm wanted I'll be up at the manor. Coming, Major?'

'What about Mrs Slade?' Maria Gilbert asked. 'Now she knows the flower situation's in hand she's expecting you for tea.'

The inspector marched towards the door.

'If she has to wait for us to see her, she may get mad enough to let out more than she's decided to so far.'

It was a short drive to the three-storeyed manor house on its knoll above the village. Tyrell could see fresh paintwork and no signs of decay. Windows gleamed and smooth lawns rose to the weathered sandstone. Gravel on the drive crunched impressively as Brian Clarke drove up to the front door.

'They're not short a bob or two,' he said as he braked and switched off the engine.

'How does a family like the Driffields keep going?' the major asked Tyrell, in counterpoint to the sound of their footsteps.

'Old money and good investments. Draper heard a whisper there was an enormous boost from slavery in the eighteenth century.'

DS Clarke rang the bell and stepped back and it was the inspector the woman who opened the door saw first. She might have been good-looking but for the scowl which greeted them.

DI Tyrell offered his warrant card as he introduced the trio. He sensed the woman's thoughts shuttered from him as she took stock of her visitors.

'I don't understand why you're here.' The words were carefully modulated, a fraction too loud for courtesy.

'We would like to talk to your husband, Lady Driffield.'

'Why?'

'It was in his field the skeleton was found,' Tyrell reminded her.

'Sir Edward's already made a statement. He assured me that was the end of the matter.'

'It is – but we would like to talk to him.'

She waited, unconvinced. Her perfume reached them and Tyrell savoured it. Guerlain?

'I believe Sir Edward could help us hurry things along,' he said.

'In what way?'

'That's something I could discuss with him?'

Tyrell stood four-square. He smiled pleasantly and Brian Clarke could have warned her not to mess with the DI.

Lady Driffield shrugged her shoulders. 'You'd better come in.'

She watched like a hawk to make sure they traipsed no dirt in on their shoes and it gave Tyrell time to study her. Of medium height she was slim, with an impression of strength. Her clothes were expensive, the almost-uniform of navy skirt, sweater and frilled shirt-collar. Thick, blonde hair was held back by a wide velvet band and drew attention away from a heavy jaw line. Skilful make-up increased lip fullness and the width of her eyes. Not strictly pretty, Tyrell decided, this was a woman who had worked hard to improve on nature.

'Wait there.'

Tyrell and his companions obeyed, looking at each other with raised eyebrows. From inside the room they could hear low voices. Papers rustled, then Sir Edward appeared, a welcoming smile on his pleasant face.

'Come in, gentlemen.'

After Lady Driffield had stalked out, Tyrell went into an oak-panelled room which was a combined office and study. Orderly files and a computer terminal, its screen in use, were on a large partners' desk in front of the window. Solid chairs of buttoned red leather curved around the fireplace and Sir Edward invited the three men to sit.

'Something come up about the skelly, as my sons will insist on calling it?'

He bore a resemblance to his aunt and uncle, with the same lean lines. His hair was thinning, reddish, and a moustache barely hid the mark of a repaired cleft lip.

'How can I help you?'

Sir Edward looked at each man in turn. His gaze lingered on the American, completely at home in the old-fashioned setting.

'Major Gifford is attached to the American Embassy,' the DI explained. 'He's in Tolland in a dual capacity.'

'Of course! The man was presumably a serving soldier when he died. Red tape in the Pentagon?'

'There is indeed, Sir Edward, but PFC Gordheimer has not been forgotten by his family. I'm also here on their behalf.'

Sir Edward shook his head. 'It makes the bones a real person – having family to mourn him. When young Butcher caused such a stir with his digger it all seemed rather a lark. Max and Oliver, my sons, rang up from school quite excited by the whole thing. They were also furious that by the time they got home the dust would have settled.'

'That's just it,' Tyrell said. 'We have to keep the dust circulating until we can show what Ben Gordheimer was doing in Tolland, why he died and who buried him.'

'Mm. A tall order for you after so many years.'

'But not impossible – with your help.'

'Mine?'

'Yes, Sir Edward. If you could give the lead, be seen assisting us, it might swing a few of the older villagers our way. With luck, they might tell us what they can remember.'

'Naturally, Inspector. Since the remains were found on my land I have a personal interest in the matter.'

54

'But as you were born in 1953, no personal involvement.'

Sir Edward looked more carefully at Tyrell and a hint of wariness appeared.

'You've done your homework.'

'We've all been well trained.'

The distant faint burr of a ringing telephone stopped and Sir Edward smiled disarmingly at Tyrell.

'I'd better do all I can to help – otherwise you might have me up on a charge of some kind.'

The atmosphere in the small room lightened. While DS Clarke relaxed his massive thigh muscles and stretched first one leg, then the other, Major Gifford cast an appreciative glance at a couple of dark little pictures at the side of the fireplace.

The door was thrust aside by Lady Driffield who carried tension in with her. There was high colour in her cheeks and her eyes were flashing, dark.

'I understand you called at Bowden Cottage before you came here,' she accused Tyrell.

Like the other men, Sir Edward had risen at her entrance. He was quickly at his wife's side, not touching her, using his proximity to calm her.

'Lady Driffield. You have a problem?'

She glared at the DI. 'You're dealing with Tolland matters. It would have been more civil to have called on my husband before you went to see his aunt.'

'Our visits are not social affairs, far from it.'

Blonde hair was tossed and swung imperiously. 'There are proper ways of doing things and you should be aware of them.'

'Oh, I am, Lady Driffield.'

Tyrell's eyes held hers. He saw anger mixed with an emotion he could not immediately recognise. In his nostrils was the smell of dusty blazers, battered textbooks. A dim voice eulogised a dead writer. Jane Austen. Consequence, that was what was so important

55

to Lady Driffield. He had ignored her and that had been his crime.

'I assume Miss Driffield phoned you?'

'Yes.'

Keith Tyrell could see the pattern, the older woman pushed to the sidelines, needling the young upstart so intent on status. Jane Austen would have been proud of him, the inspector decided as he thanked his host and prepared to leave.

'There's nothing else I can do?'

'No, thank you.'

Ever courteous, Sir Edward escorted them to the door. 'Was my aunt able to help?'

'Not really. Maybe in time something may occur to her. With your assistance someone in the village might come forward with useful information and we can be on our way.'

Sir Edward grinned, the scar on his upper lip suddenly white. 'As my sons would say, Inspector, don't hold your breath.'

Gravel spurted as DS Clarke spurted away.

'You sure touched a nerve back there,' Clayton Gifford chuckled. 'The lady of the manor! Now I've seen everything.'

'Very huffy you saw the aunt first,' DS Clarke said. 'She didn't like it one bit.'

Content, Tyrell lay back in his seat. 'Tough.'

'Mrs Slade sent her daughter to find out when you were going to see her,' Maria Gilbert greeted the inspector as he returned to the village hall. 'Apparently, she needs to know because of the sandwiches. If you don't hurry they'll start to curl – and she said not to forget the Yank.'

'Have we time for a wash?' Tyrell asked as Major Gifford laughed and DS Clarke headed for the toilets.

'Brian will have to hurry. He's expected in Gloucester for a briefing.'

The sergeant stopped, turned and was suspicious.

'What's come up?'

'The trial – you were due to give evidence. Greenwell? You helped arrest him.'

'I wasn't supposed to be called yet.'

Maria Gilbert checked her notes. 'Mr Hinton's had a whisper the defence are gunning for you. Undue force.'

'There wasn't! I only tackled Greenwell and brought him down. It's not my fault the stupid bastard didn't know how to fall and his leg broke.'

'Obviously no rugby player, our Mr Greenwell,' Tyrell said. 'It's a classic move,' he explained to the American. 'Make the arresting officer look bad to the jury – to take the sting out of the fact the leg fractured after Greenwell had held up a shopkeeper, robbed the poor devil and then beaten her senseless.'

'It makes me feel right at home.'

'DCS Hinton's waiting,' she reminded them.

'You'd better get there on the double,' the inspector advised Clarke. 'Any news of a replacement?' he asked Maria Gilbert.

'Not yet – but I did remember to ask.'

'Can I help?' Clayton Gifford offered.

'Any good at taking notes?'

The major reached into an inside pocket and produced an electronic notebook. 'This do?'

'As long as you don't wipe it clean or the battery dies on you.'

'Fresh one this morning. Anything else?'

'I hope you can eat extra sandwiches. I've a feeling we'll be expected to clear the plates.'

They walked to Elsie Slade's home and were on first-name terms by the time they reached it. Well beyond the

George, it was the end house in a terrace of four stone-built cottages behind low walls. Keith Tyrell opened the gate and caught the full beauty of the early roses Fred Slade had tended with such care. He guessed the fatal bed of onions lay at the back of the house.

Tyrell lifted his hand to knock. Before he could do so the door was opened by Agnes Morse, smiling with relief. Followed by the American, the inspector bent his head to make sure he missed the lintel. They were in a tiny hall almost filled by a narrow table smothered in ornaments. Full-blown roses on the wallpaper were hidden by heavily framed pictures so dark with age it was impossible to see their images.

'I'm so glad you've come,' Agnes Morse said. 'We've been to the grave. Mr Cobbett says all the wreaths are there and Reg Warren is sure they're just where he left them. Mother was upset so I brought her home quick as I could. She's in the parlour. You go on in and I'll go and make the tea.'

It was warm in the small room, a coal fire in the grate glowing red and throwing out enough heat for hell. At the far side of the hearth sat Mrs Slade, a resplendent widow in her black dress, its collar held by a gold brooch winking in the firelight.

Keith Tyrell smiled at the bright little eyes following every movement. He could see that without her hat white hair was limp and sparse on the crown, the pink of her scalp exposed in all its vulnerability.

'You'd better sit down. I can't be looking up at the two of you all the time. Where's the other one?'

Tyrell explained his sergeant's hasty departure and Mrs Slade savoured the upset in her plans caused by an unthinking chief superintendent.

'You'll just have to eat his tea, then – can't have waste. Anyway, you're both big enough to manage.'

Agnes Morse brought in the teapot, its china belly festooned with red roses. The motif was repeated on the cups filled for them as well as on the plates for the sandwiches. Crustless and moist, they were filled with succulent ham or smoothly beaten egg, each one enough for a meal.

'These are delicious, ma'am,' the major said when he was allowed a moment's respite from eating.

Elsie Slade sat up proudly and settled her cup in its saucer. 'I learned well from Mrs Turner. She was cook up at the manor. Big woman she was, tall and skinny, all bones – but her pastry was so light you had to hold it down to eat it.'

Clay Gifford reached for a tartlet crammed with fruit and cream. When he bit into it pastry crumbs floated away from him.

'See what I mean? Hers were better. Mrs Turner's. Agnes made those. Got the touch, Agnes has – and a proper training in college. She was cook up at the manor for Miss Caroline when she kept house for her brother.'

Tyrell nodded. 'We met him. Bobby?'

'No, he's the younger one – and his name's Peverel. Bobby's what the family call him.'

Agnes returned with a refreshed teapot.

'I mean young Eddie's father,' Elsie Slade insisted.

'Sir Edward, Mother,' Agnes protested.

'Eddie he was when he came in here as a boy. Nice lad. His father was Sir Hilary. Had a bad war, Sir Hilary, in one of they Jap camps. It took him a long while to get fit again. Then he met Lady Lavinia and they had Eddie. Lovely family. Mrs Turner was still there, so was Mr Everett, the butler. He'd been old Sir Monty's batman in the first war and he kept going for a while after the old man died. It was his legs took bad – ulcers big as dinner plates. Retired to the Maples, he did.'

Tyrell had seen the large house near the centre of the village, its Victorian style back in fashion and hideous with boudoir curtains.

'Nice house.'

59

'Ah – and he left a good bit too, to his nephew over Painswick way. Very careful man, Mr Everett.'

Mrs Slade was in full flood. Gifford silently ate and drank, leaving the inspector to steer the dusty memories.

'Was Mr Everett still at the manor when you worked there?' Tyrell asked Agnes Morse.

It was her mother who answered. 'His legs were terrible by then. Anyway, after Lady Lavinia got thrown and broke her neck, Sir Hilary shut himself up for a while. Miss Caroline took over and she sort of stayed on. Proper gentry, Miss Caroline.'

Elsie Slade's thin lips clamped together as though to prevent the escape of the words 'unlike some' which hung, unspoken, in the air.

'So, Mrs Morse, when did you leave the manor?'

'When Eddie and his wife come to live there,' her mother snapped. 'Agnes wasn't good enough for them, a village girl and local trained. Chef they had to have – not that Lady Driffield would know good food. She's not used to places where they keep a decent table.'

'That's true of most big houses these days. Very different before the war, I expect.'

Agnes began clearing the table and her mother's eyes gleamed.

'That's very true,' she said. 'Plenty of staff before the war. For a start, in the gardens there was Mr Stanley, then my Fred and two others – even if one of them was Billy Warren. Simple, he was, but he could dig like a tractor. Mr Josephs, he was the gamekeeper. Lived in Bowden Cottage Miss Caroline's had done up.'

Tyrell interrupted the flow. 'In the house?'

'Mr Everett. He had a footman and a bootboy, then there was a parlourmaid, two housemaids, a tweeny who cleaned backstairs. Mrs Turner and me in the kitchen – and Iris Hughes, poor girl, was scullery maid. She got killed at Brockworth in a bus when the airplane factory got bombed.' Elsie Slade looked into the movement of the fire and mourned. 'Change of shift at dinner time, it was. Buses coming and going. The Gerries got the lot.'

It was time for the inspector to bring the old woman back in line. 'There wouldn't be many left in the manor after the call up.'

'You're right, that Ernest Bevin had the lot. Only ones left were too old or feeble – and me, of course. I had to look after my old mother. Bedridden, she was. Sir Monty went to Gloucester and saw people so I could stay here and look after her. Eight years she lay upstairs in this very house. Happiest time of her life she used to say.'

Mrs Slade dreamed in the firelight. Agnes had put more coal on the fire and the flames licking round the chunks were yellow and bright. Tyrell made a sign to Gifford and the American unobtrusively drew out his tiny computer.

'Not many to keep a place the size of the manor going in wartime. How many was it?' Tyrell asked.

'Well, there was Mr Everett, he was too old for the war but he was in the Specials. Mrs Turner – I wouldn't have liked to be the one who asked her how old she was.'

'And you, did you live in?'

'No, I couldn't because of Mother.' She leaned towards Tyrell and whispered. 'Mother's commode.'

He smiled at her. 'The other staff all lived in?'

'Course. Nice rooms they had. Dolly Buckle used to clean them Wednesdays.'

'Was that her only day?'

'No. Mondays washing, Tuesdays ironing, then Thursdays Sir Monty's rooms and Fridays downstairs in case there were visitors for the weekend.'

'Did she help out if there were dinner parties?'

Elsie Slade gazed at the inspector. 'You know summat about big houses.'

'A little. Did she? Dolly.'

'Needed all the work she could get, her Walter only good for starting babies and falling in a ditch dead

61

drunk and drowning. Eight, he left her with. Silly woman. I'd have knocked the bugger off his perch long before that.'

'Tell me about the land girls. Who looked after them?'

The major recorded information as Tyrell guided Mrs Slade. In a very short time there was a list of all the residents of the manor in 1944.

'Knowing the village as you do, you'd have been wise to any of the local boys keen on land girls.'

'None better. Most land girls didn't stay long. Some did if they were on particular farms, like Enid Carpenter-as-was. She got hold of Roland Mitchell that way – now there was a catch. The Mitchells were county people and Roland real handsome. Enid did all right for herself. Then there was Len Phelps. He chased Peggy Arkwright till he caught her – silly bugger. Everyone told him he was a fool but he had to have her, even if she was off with the fairies half the time.'

'Was that all?'

'No. Jimmy Mitton was in the navy. He married Beryl Sykes and they went off to South Africa. Sheila Knight-as-was married Noah Bryce. He was in the REME and based at Ashchurch.'

'He was lucky.'

'That's Noah. He got home quite a bit and got extra long leaves when he bust his arm – a starting handle kicked back, or so he said.'

'When was that?'

Her eyes dimmed and her lips pursed in a tight little ring as she thought hard. 'It was well on in the war. Before D-Day – he missed the landings because of it. Cleaned up afterwards, did Noah. His dad had a scruffy smallholding and barely made enough to feed a cow let alone a family. After the war Noah got hold of army surplus cheap and did it up. Look where it's got him today!'

'I've met his wife.'

'Nice girl, Sheila. Not stuck-up like some. Good with lambs, they said. Noah was always more keen than her but she did wed him. Their David's a real gentleman – not a bit like his father.'

The fire had reached the stage of bursting with heat again and Elsie was obviously tired with the strain of the day and her memories. Tyrell, ready to leave, began to thank her.

'You'll come again?' She was anxious. 'No one wants to hear about the old days any more.'

'I need to, Mrs Slade, but it'll take Major Gifford and me some time to recover from all that marvellous food.'

Elsie Slade was startled. The American had been forgotten as she roamed her youth.

'That poor skeleton!' She looked up at Keith Tyrell. 'It's all graves, isn't it? When you're old they matter. You stay in them so long once you're there it's got to be done right because you're on your own.'

It was a tired old woman who sat bowed in her chair.

'When Fred was here I could go on at him. They all think I'm a stupid old woman but seeing his grave's all right – that's all I can do for him now.'

'He's earned the right to lie in peace.'

She smiled at Tyrell, a twinkle appearing in the little eyes.

'Aye. I gave him what for when he was alive – he knew it was just my way.'

The two men escaped at last into the cool of an early evening, marching in step towards the village hall.

'God! I feel I've been stuffed and roasted!'

'You have been,' the inspector said, 'but I think, at last, I've begun to get the real flavour of Tolland in 1944.'

'Not many men and a helluva lot of strange girls?'

'Until the Yanks arrived,' Tyrell grinned at his companion.

63

'They sure stirred up something – but what?'
'Or who?'

Only PC Draper was to be found in the hall. Maria Gilbert had gone home, leaving a message for the inspector that DS Clarke's replacement would arrive next morning.

'Anything new?' Tyrell asked.

PC Draper looked worried. 'Yes, sir. Reverend Hatton is taking advice on what to do next. I think it means he's praying.'

'After the meeting in the churchyard?'

'Yes, sir. I wasn't there, of course. I only know what the vicar told me. The undertaker and the family confirmed the wreaths were all there. The gravedigger assured them the wreaths were where he'd left them, even if the one from Mrs Slade might have been turned round a bit. Someone tidying, perhaps.'

'But?' Tyrell asked.

'Warren, the gravedigger, waited until Mrs Slade had gone. Then he told the vicar the soil under the wreaths wasn't as he left it.'

'How much soil?'

'All of it.'

'You're joking!'

'No, sir. Reg Warren insists someone's tampered with the grave.'

Chapter Four

'Martin?'

A slight stammer betrayed tension in Reverend Hatton as he stood in the doorway of the village hall.

'Has anything happened?'

'Before I talk to the bishop I wanted to make sure there was something to tell him. If there is, it means calling in the police.'

The cleric looked hopefully at the group of solid-looking men.

'You'd like us to check? Unofficially?' Tyrell asked. The vicar's curiosity extended to the tall American.

'This is Major Gifford, US Army,' Tyrell said, adding, 'seconded from his embassy.'

'Of course! The skeleton found was American. Everything has been so impersonal and official, Major, but if you would like me to hold a service for the poor man, I'd be more than willing.'

'That's most kind of you, sir. Private Gordheimer was Jewish but any prayers said on his behalf must help.'

'Oh dear. If his family members are strictly orthodox they may resent my intrusion.'

'Late tonight, when it's morning in New York, I'll be talking to his brother, Professor Gordheimer. With your permission I'll put your suggestion to him.

'Would you? How awfully kind of you.'

'Fred Slade's grave,' the DI reminded them.

With his hands waving in an unspoken apology,

Reverend Hatton angled his body in the inspector's direction.

'Oh, yes, Inspector Tyrell. Fred was an old rogue but he died speedily and peacefully – as we should all like to be taken to our long rest.'

The vicar nodded rhythmically and succeeded in resembling a lop-eared rabbit.

'Unfortunately, there's a possibility Fred's rest was quickly disturbed,' Tyrell said. 'Perhaps we could go to the churchyard now, sir? If you're ready?'

'I would be so grateful.' Hands flapped. 'With all the problems in Gloucester . . .' he began, then hurried away.

Waiting for them at the church gate was Reg Warren, a small barrel of a man with his hands in his pockets. Work-stained clothes were moulded to his body. Above them, on a short neck, a round head with a crust of earth-brown hair made him look like a freshly dug swede. The DI listened to Warren's account of the changes he had noticed.

'What we really need is a long, thin steel rod. Is there anything like that handy?'

The vicar tutted and frowned anxiously at each of them in turn. Warren was deep in thought, his gaze on the wreath of roses and ferns that had triggered the present crisis.

'Lightnin' conductor. Don't know if they's steel.'

It was hard for the man's words to be understood as they escaped through uneven, stained teeth. The vicar stared up at the tower.

'Not that one,' Reg Warren said. 'The old un. In the shed.'

He lumbered off followed, at a nod from Tyrell, by PC Draper.

'We'd better move the wreaths,' the inspector decided.

He lifted the one from Elsie Slade first, depositing it carefully on a nearby tomb. The vicar and Major Gifford

66

helped so that when Reg Warren and PC Draper returned carrying sections of the old conductor, the grave was stripped, expectant.

'I'd better do this – in case there are objections later.'

Tyrell selected a length of the metal that suited him. He began in one corner of the grave, inserting the rod as far as it would go without undue pressure. The soil was soft, easily penetrated. He repeated the manoeuvre at regular intervals along the diameter. On the third thrust the metal travelled only a few inches. Tyrell tried again further on. The rod was stopped short.

'Something?' Gifford asked.

The DI nodded. 'I'd better be systematic. Take notes, Draper. I'd like the rest of you to watch so you can be witnesses to what I do.'

Carefully, and in an orderly pattern, Tyrell probed the loose soil. Whatever it concealed was almost as long as the grave, in some places almost as wide. No one spoke. All eyes were intent on the metal rod, shining now where it had been scoured by the earth.

'Make sure your notes are dated and timed, Draper,' the inspector ordered. 'Reverend Hatton, I think you'd better phone your bishop while I go and give my boss a headache.'

'What about they rods?' Reg Warren asked as the vicar hurried away. 'I likes things tidy.'

'Leave them where they are,' Tyrell said. 'It would be best if you came back to the hall with us, Mr Warren, and I can get your statement completed before the experts arrive. Draper, you stay here. I'll try and get the nearest SOCO team to do the preliminaries. Gloucester will have to organise the forensics. They have all the possible teams but I'll do what I can to hurry one up.'

'Thank you, sir.'

'There's no need to tell you the biggest problem will be sightseers.'

Already there was a row of heads peering over the

churchyard wall. The DI could hear the clink of glasses and guessed regulars from the George were the first to gawp at the scene.

'You think it's a body?' Gifford asked Tyrell.

'Don't you?'

The two men marched the short distance to the village hall, Reg Warren lumbering behind them.

'If you want to hide a body, where better than in a graveyard full of them,' Tyrell said, 'and in a grave freshly dug.' At the hall he unlocked the door. 'It could be someone's old carpet,' he added, convincing no one.

'Whatever it is, it must have been put there after Fred Slade's funeral.'

Reg Warren was settled in a chair next to a desk.

'Can you see to the kettle?' Tyrell asked the American. 'I think we're in for a long, hard night.'

As the DI began to take down the gravedigger's statement, Clay Gifford assembled mugs and made sure they were clean. It was not long before Reg Warren was laboriously reading and signing sheets of paper. That done he was off to the George where his experiences would be worth a few beers from someone else's pocket.

'Poor Elsie,' Tyrell said. 'She'll have to be questioned thoroughly to find out exactly when those blasted flowers changed height. She was the only one who noticed.'

'I guess she'll love it,' Clay Gifford said, grinning. 'Anything more I can do to help?'

'Thanks, but no. While I'm waiting for the invasion I'll file Warren's statement. Yours and mine will have to be done independently, then you could go back to your hotel.'

'And miss all the fun?'

Reg Warren pushed open the door of the George's bar.

'Didn' you plant owd Fred deep enough, then?' came

from a little man who resembled a moulting ferret and was seated a comfortable distance between the beer pumps and the toilet.

'Course I did, Cyril. Deep enough for somethin' else to go in on top.'

Reg watched a pint of beer cream to a head.

'On the house, Reg,' said the landlord.

Sam Roberts was a burly, balding man in his forties and not unhappy with the thought of all the thirsty journalists who must soon invade the village and his pub. Reg's thanks were drowned in his first, long gulp of home-brew.

'Well?' Cyril Mitton was impatient. 'What's in there wi' owd Fred?'

'Dunno. Didn' get to dig un up. Vicar's in a right takin', goin' on about the bishop – and that Inspector Tyrell 'ad I out the way afore anythin' 'appened.'

'So what you all doin' there? I saw you go off an' fetch summat along o' the bobby,' Cyril said, his false teeth clicking.

'Lightnin' conductor. 'E wanted a rod for pokin'.'

'Who did?'

Reg drained his glass before replying. 'Inspector.' He looked at his listeners and waited.

'Put a 'alf in for un,' Cyril grudgingly told the landlord.

Sam Roberts did so but Reg only saw the emptiness at the top of the glass.

'Better fill it up, Sam, or he'll never tell us,' Steve Perry said with a laugh. 'Come on, Cyril. Get your money out.'

Only when there was a full glass within his reach did Reg recount for his audience the inspector's antics with the metal rod. Questions were hurled at him but he shook his head.

'I 'ad to make a statement,' he said importantly. 'Inspector Tyrell did write it down 'isself.'

'If it's a body, we'll all be making statements.'

Steve Perry's voice was quiet but it cut a silence as Sam Roberts cleared glasses and wiped the bar.

'At least it'd be a fresher corpse than the last one dug up,' he said.

'And if it's fresh, who put it there?' Steve asked. 'It must have been someone in the village.'

'Who killed it, that's what I want to know?' Cyril Mitton muttered aloud.

'We'll 'ave police everywhere,' an old man creaked from his corner.

Steve Perry chuckled. 'What you got to hide, Tossy?'

'I've nothin' to be afraid of,' he snapped at the younger man, 'but you just wait – all of you. If there's a murdered body in with Fred, there'll be nothing any of you can keep to yourselves. They'll have it out of you and in they Sunday papers.'

'I got nothin' to 'ide,' Cyril protested.

Malevolence gleamed from faded eyes. ''An't you, Cyril? I could tell 'em a thing or two about you.'

Cyril Mitton was annoyed and his teeth rattled. 'Tossy Reynolds, I never murdered no one – and well you do know it.'

'Dudn' matter. They'll keep on at us till there's no secret left in Tolland, you wait and see. What I knows about you, what you knows about young Steve. They'll 'ave it – mark my words.'

The bar was quiet, each man with his own thoughts and sudden fears.

'Give us another, Sam,' Steve Perry said and cleared his throat.

Tossy Reynolds rocked in his corner. 'You mark my words.'

'Keith! What the hell are you playing at? You're as bad as one of those bloody dogs the French train to sniff out truffles!'

Six foot two of brawn in an expensive suit and topped by dark curly hair only lightly paled with grey, Detective Chief Superintendent Hinton marched through the rapidly crowding village hall like a bull elephant in must.

'Sorry, sir. SOCO's just confirmed it is a body. They're taking it slowly, so we won't know much more for a while.'

'I'm assuming first stage procedures are in operation and second stage in hand?'

'Yes, sir.'

'Keith, you know I can't leave you in charge of this one.'

'Expected, sir. Who will it be?'

'DCI Whittaker.'

Tyrell stiffened. 'Yes, sir.'

'You keep on with the skeleton enquiry, of course – unless Whittaker needs an extra pair of hands. Who else was working with you?'

'DS Clarke, Mrs Gilbert and Draper, the community officer. DS Clarke's in Gloucester for Greenwell's trial. Major Gifford took notes for me earlier today.'

'Gifford. That's the embassy man?'

Tyrell beckoned the major over and made the introductions. The two men took stock of each other and liked what they saw.

'Clarke's replacement?' Hinton asked the DI.

'I was just told someone was coming – not who.'

'They can be used by Whittaker too,' Hinton warned.

'This new body could mean a murderer on the loose – it must take priority. Still, if it was only buried after a very recent funeral, at least it can't have been put there by that bastard in Gloucester.'

'No, sir.'

'Any hope of finding your elderly murderer?'

Gifford's interest was triggered by the senior man's question and Tyrell faced two pairs of expectant eyes.

71

'I think I can guess who shot him but there's no evidence as yet.'

Hinton's gaze was shrewd, assessing. 'That obvious?'

'Not really, sir, but there is a pattern emerging.'

'Can't you push and get it resolved quickly?'

Tyrell shook his head. 'Tolland's a secretive place. Ask too many questions and the inhabitants seize up.'

Hinton nodded. 'Protecting one of their own. If that's so, you'd better warn Whittaker.'

'I doubt he'd welcome my advice.'

'Perhaps not. We'll see how it goes. Let me have the report on your case as soon as possible. Direct to me. It's my office the American Ambassador's aide keeps phoning for a result.'

'It's a long way from being ready, sir. Hunches and guesses wouldn't rate too highly at the CPS.'

'Will it concern them?' Hinton queried. 'We've got to keep costs down as much as we can and I can't see the CPS approving court time for a crime committed in 1944.'

'No, sir, but I'm using their guidelines.'

'Of course, Keith, you're right to do so. If someone's going to be labelled a murderer, even if they're pushing up the daisies themselves, it must be done by the book.'

There was the sound of new arrivals.

'Looks like duty calls,' Hinton said, his face grim. He shook the American's hand in farewell. For Tyrell it was, 'Your father will be proud of you.'

'Sir!'

'Sorry, I forgot.' The chief superintendent was as rueful as his rank permitted. 'Give him my best. Last time I talked to him he said he didn't see nearly enough of you and that pretty wife of yours. Seemed to think it was all my fault.'

As the senior man strode into the mass of people coming through the door, Gifford turned to Tyrell.

'What was all that about?'

'Family. Best kept out of the murder business.'

'Is your father a cop?'

'No,' Keith Tyrell said with a laugh.

Amusement drove away his usually serious expression and Gifford saw something of the man behind the professional mask. Tyrell sobered and was once again the efficient policeman.

'I'd better see about our statements.'

The start-up routine of a new enquiry swung into motion, oiled by too much practice in recent months. As officers and equipment flooded in, the noise level in the village hall rose.

'Tyrell!' The call cut through the hubbub.

'Sir?'

The inspector regarded his immediate superior with equanimity. Detective Chief Inspector Richard Whittaker was older than Tyrell, not as tall and less well built. He was very carefully groomed, the silk tie he wore perfectly in keeping with a man determined to succeed. It emphasised the hard line of his jaw as well as ice in the blue eyes above a narrow nose and thin lips.

'Who's this?'

Tyrell gave Gifford's name and rank, adding his status at the embassy in Grosvenor Square.

'You're welcome to work with Tyrell, Major. Just make sure you don't get in the way of my investigation. It takes precedence.'

'OK, Chief Inspector. Your Mr Hinton's already made that clear.'

'The report on your case, Tyrell. Immediately.'

'Sorry, sir. The chief super said it was to go direct to him.'

'I don't believe you.'

Keith Tyrell's jaw tilted ominously. 'That's your privilege. Sir. Would you like me to put the call through to Mr Hinton so you can check?'

There was a stillness between the two men, then Whittaker smoothed his tie.

'That won't be necessary. I've no doubt the case and your investigation methods are completely irrelevant.'

The DCI swung away and headed towards more important matters.

Clay Gifford was amazed by the exchanges. 'Who the hell's yanking his chain?'

'Whittaker's ambitious. He won't rest until he's a chief constable.'

'There're two kinds of ambitious people,' Gifford said. 'One works all the hours God sends and the other kicks in the teeth of anyone they see as competition.'

Keith Tyrell grinned. 'You've decided the category you put him in? Take my word for it, Whittaker works hard and he's damned good at his job.'

'He sure is touchy where you're concerned. Any reason?'

'Does he need one? I'm young for my rank – and I'm a graduate entry.' At Gifford's look of enquiry he added, 'Oxford. Law.'

'And you settled for being a cop? Hell's teeth! You could have made a packet as an attorney!'

Tyrell looked around the room with its peeling paint-work and the smell of decay mixed with stale urine and bleach.

'This is what I wanted.'

Gifford shook his head in disbelief. 'You must be mad.'

With the DI he watched the village hall become a major incident room. Telephone cables snaked to hand-sets and the latest computers which had appeared as if by magic. Mrs Gilbert's desk with its ancient terminal was shunted into a corner. Men and women in uniforms or practical suits moved with a purpose and, in a remarkably short space of time, DCI Whittaker had an arena in which to brief his team.

'You'd better stay for this, Tyrell.' His words carried across an expectant hush. 'Afterwards you can carry on with your enquiries – unless I need you for something else.'

'Yes, sir.'

The reply came with a calm cheerfulness but Gifford noticed several officers speculating, like himself, as to the reason for the tension crackling in the air.

Whittaker's briefing was efficient. In a hushed room the team heard that the body found was that of a dark-haired male, approximately five feet ten and a hundred and sixty pounds. Not young. There had been severe damage to the head and face. Until the post-mortem had been completed little else could be decided. It was thought the man was not an IC1, nor an IC3.

'What does that mean?' Gifford whispered.

'Possibly Asian or Mediterranean.'

'In Tolland?'

Heads turned and eyes glared at the whisperers. The DCI almost smiled at his team's loyalty.

'It's house-to-house. Any strangers seen, when and where – you know the ropes.'

'Clothes, sir?' a woman detective asked.

'No help at all, I'm afraid. There were none.'

The import of his words hit home and a buzz of sound exploded. Whittaker held up his hand.

'The man was naked – and if that fact leaks to the press I'll have the guts of someone in this room no matter who they are. Or how senior,' he added, staring at Tyrell and Gifford. 'If anyone you question asks about clothes, just tell them they're not important at this stage because Forensic's dealing with them. Rumours will already have been circulating in the village and I want you to push on as quickly as possible. Don't come back until you've got some answers.' The DCI glanced towards a tall, angular woman behind a stack of clip-boards. 'DS Rogers has the allocations. See her for your maps and sheets and get going.'

'It'll make a change for her from pouring his bloody tea for him.'

75

The speaker was a thin man with the yellowed fingers of a heavy smoker and he earned a ripple of laughter among the assembled detectives and uniformed officers as they moved into action. In a short space of time the hall was almost empty.

'Inspector Tyrell?' A PC hardly out of his probation looked anxiously at him. 'I have to take your statement, sir.'

'Of course. Major Gifford and the vicar?'

'Detective Sergeant Rogers is to do those.' Keith Tyrell was surprised. DCI Whittaker must have some hang-up to take time out for pettiness. He smiled at the very young man.

'You are?'

'Cole, sir.'

'Come on then, Constable Cole. Let's get it done.'

With Tyrell's quiet steering through the procedure the statement was soon signed and filed along with Reg Warren's.

'Thank you, sir.' PC Cole was pleased to have completed his task so painlessly. 'I have to fetch the vicar.'

'The vicarage is beyond the church. There's a gate into the garden from the churchyard.'

'Thank you, sir.'

'Try the church first, Reverend Hatton might be there. If he's praying, just get near him and cough.'

With the departure of PC Cole there was time for the inspector to take stock. In a far corner DS Rogers was questioning Clay Gifford. They were too far away for Tyrell to hear what was being said until the major raised his voice in anger and 'No, ma'am, he did not!' reverberated.

Keith Tyrell went outside into the cool of the early evening and waited for Gifford.

'Whittaker will land you in the shit if you don't watch out,' Gifford warned as soon as he stood beside Tyrell. 'Any problem with the autopsy and you get the blame.'

76

'Specifically?'

'Marks on the body. Because of the absence of clothes the end of that rod you used has punctured the skin.'

'I assume DS Rogers wanted to know if I'd used more force than was needed?'

'How did you know?'

'It's what I'd have asked. There's no problem. Our pathologist is spot on. She'll have the rod I used and be able to separate my damage from anything the murderer inflicted.'

'You'd better hope the vicar doesn't allow himself to be bullied.'

'And suggest I was Neptune hurling his trident? I can't see it. He's not the most positive of characters, I grant you, but I'd guess he's a stickler for the truth – even if he were to be stoned to death for it. He's got the elements of a martyr, our Reverend Hatton.'

The quiet of the evening was soothing. In the distance a car engine was being revved hard and, in their imaginations, they could see a mechanic attentive to the sound.

'It's a strange place, Tolland. Just how did Ben Gordheimer end up here?' Gifford said.

Tyrell's smile was enigmatic.

'I suppose you know?'

'Not for sure. How're you fixed for dinner? You're very welcome to come back with me. If Jenny's not home you can even help me cook it.'

The lane was narrow, hedges high on either side. A wide gate stood open and Keith Tyrell drove into the garden of what had been a farm worker's cottage. The simplicity was still there, starkness softened with new windows, a porch, the glass of a modern conservatory peeping out from a corner. Keith unlocked the front door and attended to a sophisticated alarm.

'It's linked to the nearest police station,' he explained,

'and I'd rather we sat in peace than had a couple of the local boys here at the double.'

Clay was surprised. 'Do all police have this set-up?'

'No. Jenny's a psychologist and she works in a local hospital – psychiatric cases. I like to know she's safe when I'm out at night.'

They walked through the little house and Clay had time to see fresh colours, simple furniture, an absence of clutter. In a corner of the main living-room was a computer and, beside it, a chessboard. The carved ebony and ivory figures faced each other in the middle of a conflict.

'Who's your opponent?'

'A friend in London, Stephen Childs. He's CID too and usually beats me hollow.'

'He must be good.'

'A grand master.'

Clay whistled softly as Keith walked on to the back of the house. The kitchen had been extended from the original. It was well equipped and immaculate. Keith reached for tumblers and there was scotch on ice for Clay, orange juice for himself.

The American sipped and his eyes opened wide in appreciation. 'This is a good one.'

'My father would be down on me like a ton of bricks if I kept anything else. His mother was a Scot from Islay.' He lifted a salad from the fridge. 'Pasta OK with your steak?'

'Fine by me.'

Keith worked swiftly, chatting as he cooked. Plates were set out and cutlery for three arranged. The pasta was drained and cream was being added to garlic and mushrooms when wheels scrunched in the driveway. 'Jenny,' he said.

The front door opened and was closed firmly. There were quick steps then, 'That smells good.'

Jenny was tall, slightly built, attractive, her dark hair short and shining. Keith dropped a kiss on the top of his wife's head and she leaned against him, closing tired eyes.

The American looked away, giving total attention to the amber drops at the bottom of his glass. The sense of union between the two was more intense than a passionate embrace would have been and he felt an intruder.

'I'm Jenny.'

He shook the offered hand. Her face had come alive from its weariness. The eyes were large and bright, assessing him with a candid gaze. Jenny's scrutiny did not last long and she smiled her acceptance of him.

The meal was a lively one, Clay Gifford surprised at the transformation of his colleague. Keith was no longer an imposing, astute professional. He had become a younger man, with a lively wit and rich humour, pouring good wine for his guest as he made sure his wife ate well.

Jenny was banished to the sitting-room as Keith cleared away the supper things, Clay helping.

'I don't know how I had the gall to eat all that after the food we were stuffed with earlier but it was great. Thanks.'

'Jenny was called out very early this morning and would have been too tired to eat properly. It was cooked and you were here. It did her good.'

'Glad to have been of use.' Clay leaned against the counter as the dishwasher hummed busily. 'Tell me honestly, am I in the way of your investigation?'

'Not at all,' Keith said with a laugh, the sound gentle and deep. 'Besides, investigation in a village where normal methods don't apply?'

The kitchen tidy once more, Keith led the way to the living-room. Gentle light from a lamp showed them Jenny asleep on the couch and Keith covered her with a blanket.

'I'll be on my way,' Clay whispered. 'Can I get a cab out here?'

'You'll do no such thing. I'll drive you back to your hotel – why do you think I've been on orange juice all evening?'

Clay liked the integrity of his new friend. 'You sure do take your work seriously, right down the line.'

'Most of us do. It's the only way,' Keith said as he reached for his car keys.

Ushering his guest from the house he stopped to unplug the phone and set the alarm.

'Will she be OK?'

'Jenny'll sleep like a baby – she needs that to break her tiredness. Tomorrow she'll be as bright as a button and run rings round both of us.'

By the time Clay Gifford reached Tolland next morning the hunt for the new killer was well under way. There was a buzz, an air of purpose in the village hall, terminal screens constantly rolling with bank after bank of information.

The smell of fresh cigarette smoke mixed in with the stale and the tang of coffee fought strong aftershave. Some of the desks had ordered surfaces, others were cluttered with papers and files laid down haphazardly.

A wall was festooned with photographs of Fred Slade's open grave, as well as of the curiously pale body it had contained. One showed it on its side, the face obscured. Other photographs were more revealing, the horrific mess of bone and flesh where once had been a face, the lines of puncture marks from the lightning rod's delving.

PC Draper hurried towards the American. 'Thank God you've come, sir!'

'What's up?'

'It's Mrs Slade. Last night DCI Whittaker sent DS Simons to question her. He's good but she'd have nothing to do with him, nor the DC with him. Then, this morning, Mr Whittaker went himself with DS Simons but she still won't talk. The DCI was livid when he got back just now. He wanted DI Tyrell and you.'

'What've we done?'

PC Draper grinned. 'I heard a whisper old Elsie will only talk to that nice Inspector Tyrell and the Yank.'

'She'll feed us!' Clay Gifford protested. 'And I've only just had breakfast.'

'There's no hurry, sir. DI Tyrell had already gone to the hospital in Gloucester by the time Mr Whittaker came back here. Noah Bryce has had a stroke.'

'Noah Bryce. Should I know him?'

'Mrs Bryce is one of the land girls Inspector Tyrell interviewed. The man who dug up the skeleton worked for Mr Bryce.'

'For Pete's sake! It's like everything in this place is tied with invisible strings!'

'It feels like that at first, it did to me. I think that's why Elsie Slade wants Inspector Tyrell. He seems to sense where the strings are and doesn't go barging through them, causing unnecessary trouble.'

'As did her other visitors from the police – is that what you're saying?'

'Could be, sir.'

'But why ask for me?'

PC Draper tried to look innocent. 'Perhaps she fancies you, sir?'

A flurry of activity at the door heralded the arrival of Whittaker. He was handed a printed sheet and a file, glancing at their contents.

'Briefing. Two minutes.' He caught sight of Gifford. 'There's no need to detain you, Major.'

The American sensed the undercurrent of spite which tainted all of Whittaker's dealings with Keith Tyrell. No Tyrell, someone had to suffer. He smiled and gave a cheery wave as he left the incident room and its claustrophobic atmosphere.

Someone was hurrying after him. 'Major Gifford!'

He turned. 'Mrs Gilbert. Can I help you?'

'For the inspector – when you see him.' She handed him an envelope. 'Some follow-ups from other forces. Land girls. He'll understand. Excuse me, I must get back before I'm missed.'

At a loose end Gifford walked towards the churchyard where a tent covered the grave of the late Mr Slade. His companion in death had long gone and the American hoped that somewhere Fred Slade was enjoying all the activity.

Even at that hour there was a small crowd and it was easy to spot journalists, each seeking an edge to their story. The villagers were saying nothing. Keith was right, Gifford thought. Tolland is an entity, separate from all that's going on.

He looked again, seeing the village from Tyrell's perspective. A few spectators had a closed look to them, the sealed eyes, ears and mouths of the three monkeys rolled into one. Old-style villagers, Gifford decided, presuming newer residents were safely shut away behind the fashionable curtains and blinds of their modernised cottages, barns, farmhouses. Only their children whizzed about on expensive mountain bikes, the designer clothes and loud voices completely ignored by those for whom living in Tolland had not been a new experience for several generations.

'It's a terrible thing to have happened.'

The voice came from behind and Clay Gifford swung to look at the speaker. Reverend Hatton was wringing his hands as though to squeeze out his anguish, his thin, wispy hair lifted into a halo by the light wind.

'Yes, sir. It is.'

'Have the police really no idea who the man was?'

'Not yet.'

'To think two strangers to Tolland have been buried here, shovelled secretly into the earth with no blessing to comfort their souls.'

'It's their families who go through hell.'

'You're quite right, Major Gifford. Your poor soldier's loved ones have had to wait so long for knowledge. When will they be able to lay him to rest properly?'

'Soon, I hope.'

'You still don't know if he was a deserter?'

'I'm told it's unlikely but we have to be sure – for the record.'

'At least you know who he is. I wonder how long it will be before the man found last night can be named? All over the country families are missing a father, a brother. They'll be waiting in dread for a knock at the door.'

'It was very hard for the Gordheimers. I talked to his brother last night and he told me it's only now they can start grieving properly.'

'After fifty years it seems incredible but I can understand how it must be for them.'

White-garbed SOCO men and women moved in and out of the little tent, evidence bags tucked out of sight in cardboard boxes.

'Inspector Tyrell is busy?'

Gifford explained about the Gloucester hospital.

'A stroke, you say. Do you know who?'

'A Noah Bryce.'

Reverend Hatton sighed. 'Poor Noah. He's had one or two slight strokes in the past but his dear wife has nursed him back to health. He really should have retired and let David run the business. I suppose when you've worked as hard as Noah to build up a firm it's hard to let go of the reins – even to someone as capable as your own son.'

There was another sigh. This time the sound caused Clay Gifford to look sharply at his companion. He sensed a personal misery and wished Keith Tyrell was there with his uncanny understanding of all things Tolland.

Reverend Hatton invited the American to the vicarage for coffee. As they walked through an increasing drizzle the cleric gave out the historical data on the church of St Barnabas much as a small child repeats its eight-times table. Gifford was still wondering what the other man had on his mind that was causing such turmoil when they went into the ivy-covered porch of what could have been a very attractive house.

'Major Gifford, my dear,' the vicar called to a dim figure carrying a tray.

'How nice.'

Mrs Hatton was a squarely built woman in dull clothes, her hair scraped back from a face sagging with the weight of her burdens. She smiled formally at Gifford.

'Come into the study, there's a fire there. I know it's nearly summer but on a day like today . . .'

Her husband opened a door for her and she went into the study, laying down the tray on his desk.

'I'll go and get another cup.'

A pleasant half-hour passed but Gifford could not lose the idea gnawing at him. The vicar and his wife were very worried people, especially Mrs Hatton.

'It must be strange to be flooded with police again so soon,' Clay Gifford said.

While Reverend Hatton squeezed distress from his fingers Mrs Hatton sighed heavily.

'It's so upsetting,' she said, adding, 'for the villagers,' a little too hastily.

The vicar jammed a damp log in the centre of the fire as his wife rocked in her chair. Gifford remembered Keith Tyrell's warning and was silent.

'Does Inspector Tyrell have any idea who killed the soldier?' Mrs Hatton asked after an uneasy pause.

'He hasn't told me.' Gifford spoke gently, careful not to break the tension. 'It's likely Ben Gordheimer was buried in that particular field because of loose soil from the bombing.'

The vicar's wife was surprised. 'Bombs?'

Gifford nodded. 'In the early days of the war the field

was one which took part of a stick of bombs during a raid aimed at Gloucester – so I was told.'

'Those bombs,' Reverend Hatton said. 'Warren, the gravedigger you've already met, it was his Uncle Billy who had the task of filling in all the craters – when he had the time. Years it took him, I gather. Tractor fuel and manpower couldn't be spared for anything as trivial as filling-in odd holes in those days.'

'So, in early '44 there was still work for him to do?'

The vicar frowned, then blinked rapidly. 'I see what you mean. A ready-made grave. Then . . .'

'Someone who knew about the crater also knew about Ben Gordheimer's body.'

Mrs Hatton had been staring into the twisting smoke of the fire for some time. It was the vicar's turn to sigh.

'A parishioner?'

'Perhaps.'

'Another American?' Reverend Hatton hoped.

'The truck they all came in went straight to the manor. They couldn't have known about the craters.'

'I suppose not.'

'And now history's been repeated.' Gifford spoke quietly. 'Somewhere, a body, and here, in your church-yard, a newly filled grave. Loose soil quickly dug out.'

They were all picturing the scene.

'After the Slade funeral, when did it rain?' Gifford's questioning was easy, unforced.

'Rain. Let me see.' Deep furrows were carved in the vicar's brow. 'The funeral was on the Thursday. Did it rain before that weekend or after it, my dear?'

Mrs Hatton was slow to answer. 'Not until after the wedding on Saturday. I thought it was threatening when I went to the church to practise on the Friday evening but it had cleared by the time I left.' She looked at her husband, distress twisting her homely features. 'I did lock the door. I'm sure I did.'

85

'Of course, my dear. You're so very reliable.'

'I remember thinking about Will as I turned the key.'

'Will is our younger son, Major Gifford. He'd been staying at home for a few days. After he left, my wife went to the church to practise her organ-playing for the wedding next day.'

'I'm not very good,' she confessed, 'but there's no one else who'll do it.'

'And next day the door was unlocked?' Gifford asked.

'Yes – and flowers from the altar strewn along the aisle.' Mrs Hatton was annoyed at the desecration. 'Mrs Mitton had worked so hard to do everything nicely for that daughter of hers – '

'My dear!'

'I don't know how they got in – the vandals. I'm sure I locked the door behind me.' Her lips were a thin line of stubbornness.

'Was it an old key?' Gifford asked her.

'Yes, very.'

'Then there's probably someone in the village who has one,' he suggested.

'Oh, no! I'm very careful about that sort of thing,' the vicar insisted. 'Warren has one – and Ken Downing. He's the vicar's warden.'

'Perhaps a previous minister was not so careful?' Gifford said.

Reverend Hatton brightened at the idea. 'I see what you mean. One of the Tolland families may have had a key for years and a youngster got hold of it.'

'So, that Friday night there was some sort of horsing around in the church but no rain. Saturday?' Gifford asked.

'Saturday was very busy. Mrs Mitton and her family were seeing to the flowers and leaflets, that kind of thing.'

'And still no rain?'

'No.' Mrs Hatton was sure. 'Not until late Saturday evening, then it poured. It was still raining when Nicholas went across for early communion on the Sunday. It had stopped by matins. Eleven o'clock.'

In the distance a bell jangled and Mrs Hatton rose to answer it. She was stiff and tired, lumbering a little in her sensible shoes. The bell rang again, impatience in the renewed sound.

The vicar was seeing in his mind's eye the churchyard on that wet Sunday. 'The rain would have washed away any traces?'

'I guess so.'

There was a man's voice in the hall, not loud but peremptory. Mrs Hatton returned, closely followed by two men.

'Detective Chief Inspector Whittaker.' He was barely controlling his anger as he offered his warrant card, then waved at his companion, a thickset man with white skin and wearing dark clothes. 'Detective Sergeant Simons.'

Whittaker stared at Gifford.

'The major was good enough to join us for coffee,' the vicar explained.

'And now I'm here to interview Reverend Hatton,' Whittaker said, clipping out the words.

'Then I'll thank you kindly, ma'am, and you, sir, for your hospitality.'

'Come again, Major Gifford. Any time,' Mrs Hatton said as she saw him to the front door and watched him go.

Gifford was accosted by a journalist but the American's size and good humour got him free of harassment and he strode on. When he reached the village hall a car pulled up and Keith Tyrell emerged from it, waiting for Gifford to reach him. The major delivered the papers from Mrs Gilbert.

'Sorry I missed you. I had to get to the hospital.'

'How is the old man?'

'Not good. He just lies there staring up at the ceiling. Not long ago he was charging across a field to give me hell.'

'Prognosis?'

Keith Tyrell shrugged his shoulders. 'If he can get through the next forty-eight hours he may survive but his movements and speech will be severely limited.' A phone rang in the hall.

'That reminds me. Something I want to check with Jenny.'

The two men were barely noticed as they made their way to Maria Gilbert, tucked away in a corner behind her computer. She greeted them with a smile.

'There're a couple more faxes from other forces. Only two of the women they were asked about are still alive. One is on holiday in Majorca and won't be back for six weeks. The other can't remember anything useful. She says she always shut herself away with a book whenever the Yanks turned up.'

Clay Gifford laughed, the sound merry, hearty, in the echoing room with its grim photographs.

'It's the effect we have on people.'

Keith Tyrell was talking to his wife, Mrs Gilbert and the major trying hard not to listen. Odd words were hard to resist. 'Recessive' was one, 'dominant' another. 'Chance of brown?' was clearly a question that mattered. The final check complete, the DI ended the call.

'The file on Gordheimer?' he asked Mrs Gilbert.

It was produced instantly and Tyrell flipped over sheets, his finger tracing down the data on a selected page.

'Got it. Ben Gordheimer had brown eyes.' He frowned, puzzled. 'It makes a tidy pattern yet, somehow, it doesn't feel right.'

'Give,' Gifford said.

'Noah Bryce has grey eyes, his wife's are blue.'

'And?'

'I met their son, David, this morning. His dark hair

88

has a little grey in it and his eyes are brown. From an old biology lesson I remembered something I just checked with Jenny.'

'Two blue-eyed parents can't have a brown-eyed child. And grey counts as blue,' Gifford said slowly. 'I had that lesson too.'

'How old is David Bryce?' Maria Gilbert wanted to know.'

'Late forties – early fifties,' Tyrell said. 'Just the right age to be Ben Gordheimer's son. He's certainly not Noah Bryce's.'

Chapter Five

The shop was quiet.

'That's Miss Caroline's order. She says she'll pick it up on her way back.'

'Back from where?' Mrs Fell asked.

Chrissie Warren blinked, then frowned at the question. Mrs Fell waited, rolling her eyes in despair.

'It's so I know how long I've got to get it made up. I mean, if she's gone to Newnham, I've got half an hour. If it's Gloucester, I can take all afternoon.'

The face of the stolid woman cleared. 'Gloucester. With Mr Bobby – about his hip.'

'Poor man. Isn't he supposed to have a new hip soon?'

Chrissie concentrated on the question, the effort pulling lines around her mouth. 'His blood. Makes it risky,' she said at last.

Mrs Fell tutted sympathy. 'Anything you want for yourself, Chrissie?'

'Suet – and a tin of plums.'

'Plums are on the top shelf by the door.'

Chrissie Warren walked slowly along the aisle, searching carefully.

'That cottage of Miss Driffield's must be easier to keep clean than the manor. How long is it since you stopped working for Lady Driffield? I know it was before I bought this place from the Simpsons.'

Dark eyes regarded Mrs Fell unblinkingly until she felt an uncomfortable heat.

'Three years last February.'

'That was soon after Sir Edward and his wife moved in, wasn't it?'

'Two weeks.'

'My, and you'd worked at the manor how long?'

'Since I left school.'

'You finished at the manor the same time as your Barry, didn't you? Sir Edward wanted new ways, I expect.'

'It weren't Sir Edward.' Chrissie flushed a dull red. She bent over her purse then put the exact coins on the counter. 'It weren't Sir Edward.'

'Not an easy person to work for, I should imagine – Lady Driffield. Your husband's still at the manor. I suppose the cottage goes with the job?'

Once more Mrs Fell was subjected to a calm stare and she encountered an intelligence which surprised her. Chrissie Warren shuttered her thoughts and silently took herself and her shopping away from Mrs Fell's questions.

In her corner of the incident room Maria Gilbert sat at a computer. Near her Keith Tyrell concentrated on a list. Clay Gifford straddled a chair, his arms resting on its back.

'Do you think it was Bryce killed Gordheimer?'

Tyrell shook his head. 'No. I don't believe he did the shooting or the burying, though I could see he was in a hell of a state for some reason.'

'Could he have been involved somehow?'

'He's got a good head on his shoulders – at least he had until this last stroke. Don't forget Noah Bryce was still in charge of his own business. Can you see him sending a digger to work in the very field where he'd buried a man he killed?'

'Nope.'

'Mind you,' Maria Gilbert said slowly, 'if he'd married

a girl carrying an American baby, then the skeleton coming out of the field – '

' – would have been like a skeleton coming out of the closet,' Gifford said.

'It still doesn't explain . . .' Tyrell was silent as he organised his ideas.

'What?' Gifford wanted to know.

'Just a feeling I had when I was talking to someone.'

A constable brought a file to Mrs Gilbert and she went to enter its contents in one of the new terminals dotted around the room.

'Talking about feeling,' Gifford said. 'The vicarage this morning. The Hattons were worried about their son, Will – especially Mrs Hatton. She was on another planet at times.'

'You've locked into the system that works in Tolland,' Tyrell said with a grin. He seated himself at Mrs Gilbert's computer and tapped in a request. After waiting, he read the screen's contents. 'No William Hatton in our records. I'll try Wilson.'

Another blank, as there was for Wilbert Hatton.

'Maybe it's nothing criminal. A girl pregnant?'

'Possibly.' Tyrell pursued an elusive memory. 'A boy I was at school with was called Will but his full name was Willoughby.'

This time the entry produced results.

'Got it. A student at Aston University, Birmingham,' Tyrell read from the screen. 'Two minor drugs offences. Possession. Not a registered addict.'

Gifford was curious. 'What kind of drugs?'

'Cannabis. Quantities too small for much dealing.'

'No hard stuff?'

The inspector shook his head.

'They were too concerned. It was more than just being scared of him caught with the odd joint,' Gifford insisted.

'If anything else comes out that might have a bearing

on the new murder it had better be filed or Whittaker'll have you shipped back to Washington in chains.'

'Definitely a new experience! As for the Hattons, the coffee was vile and we talked about the weather – very British,' Gifford grinned. 'Specifically, when it rained after Fred Slade's funeral.'

'You were after a likely time for the extra burial?'

Gifford nodded and Tyrell cleared the screen, ready for a new document. Details of organ practice, keys, vandalism were filed into the computer and a printed copy placed on Whittaker's desk.

'Did you get hold of Professor Gordheimer last night?' Tyrell asked.

'Sure, I did. He sounded what you'd call a "nice chap".'

'Is he coming over?'

'His sister's not so good. When the medics have got her fit to travel they'll both come over.'

They were interrupted by the return of the DCI. He did not wait to become updated with his paperwork.

'Major Gifford!' Barely controlled anger made Whittaker's voice shake. 'You've been questioning my witnesses!'

'If you mean the Hattons, I was invited in for coffee. I guess what we talked about was the same topic of conversation in every house in the village.'

'You interrogated them without proper procedure,' Whittaker stormed. 'As a result, any evidence they could give will be useless in court.'

'Excuse me, sir,' the inspector said. 'Major Gifford is not a serving police officer. He's someone the Hattons liked and wanted to talk to as a friend.'

'And, as a friend, he has them nicely confused about the facts.'

Disdain curled the lips of the DCI. Behind him was the dark mass of DS Simons, his bright eyes flicking from one to another, missing nothing.

'There's a print-out on your desk of all the relevant information given to Major Gifford.'

Whittaker stalked off to his desk like a disgruntled rooster and picked up the sheet, reading and rereading it before he looked up.

'It'll do for now. Tyrell, get yourself to that damned widow's and find out what you can.'

'Mrs Slade? Yes, sir. Who do I take with me?'

'She wants the American major for some strange reason,' Whittaker snapped.

The American major stood to attention and sketched a salute, West Point style.

'Mother's waiting for you.' Agnes Morse smiled a welcome. 'Thank you for coming. I know Mum can be a real devil when she sets her tongue to it but the others who came . . .' She shook her head and opened the parlour door for them. 'I'll go and make some coffee. I expect you could do with some.'

Clay Gifford looked doubtful as the inspector smiled his thanks.

'Go on in,' she said.

Today, Elsie Slade wore a white blouse under a black cardigan. Strain had dragged fresh lines in her face but at the sight of the two men she straightened and a smile brightened her eyes.

'We'll have some proper coffee now you've come.'

'Mrs Morse is just making it,' Tyrell assured her as he and Gifford obediently sat where the imperious little finger pointed.

The American looked at the fire. A small heap of coals and gentle flames. No roasting was imminent. If they were not expected to eat too much it could be quite an interesting session.

Agnes Morse pushed open the door and Gifford got to his feet to help her settle a tray heavy with thickly

94

buttered scones, shortbread, fruit cake. The coffee was fetched and poured, rich and aromatic.

Clay Gifford sipped. 'This is great!' he told the women. 'I don't usually get coffee like this in the UK.'

Agnes beamed. 'Miss Caroline gets the beans for me in Cheltenham. She's very good that way.'

'No side, Miss Caroline,' her mother agreed. 'Not like some.'

The sniff was an audible condemnation while Agnes waved cheese scones enticingly.

'It's been a hard time for you.'

Tyrell's voice held sympathy, an invitation. Elsie Slade looked at him suspiciously but met only understanding. She sagged in her chair.

'You were kind,' she said at last, her Gloucestershire burr more noticeable. 'I'm no fool, I know you only did something about my Fred's grave because you wanted to get me to talk. The manor and the land girls, that's what you were interested in but very good you were, you and the major. People can say what they like about the police, I speak as I find. Young Martin Draper made sure Agnes and me got home before . . .' Tears rose.

'I'm sorry the grave had to be opened.'

'You won't have to get Fred up again, will you? He was laid there so peaceful.'

'No, I don't think he'll be disturbed. Besides,' Tyrell's smile was gentle, 'have you any idea how much paperwork it would take?'

The atmosphere in the stuffy little room lightened and the full-blown roses on the wallpaper reminded Tyrell. 'Were the flowers in your wreath from the garden?'

Elsie Slade nodded, then smiled wistfully. 'Fred loved roses. When they were ready for cutting he'd bring them in and put them down by me. Go off without saying a word.'

There were tears in Agnes Morse's eyes. Tyrell had an image of the quiet man expressing, in the only way he knew how, his love for the woman who talked for the two of them.

'They're still lovely – the roses,' the inspector said. 'I've not seen them last so well in a wreath.'

'Betty James did it for me. She used that green spongy stuff.'

'Oasis,' Agnes said.

'That's it. Like putting flowers in water it was. The day of the funeral, after everyone had gone, Agnes and me, we went back to the grave.' Elsie Slade was quiet, remembering.

'It'd been terrible leaving Dad there on his own – so cold,' Agnes told them. 'We wanted to go and say good-night to him and make sure he was all right. Reg Warren had done a good job. Everything was neat and tidy and he'd arranged the wreaths so they were like a blanket, the flowers keeping Dad warm. He did love flowers so.'

'I knew the roses would need watering,' her mother said. 'You got to keep topping up that green stuff. Friday night I took water with me so I could see to the roses and talk to Fred. Reg Warren put my wreath where Fred's head would be.'

'Saturday?' Tyrell asked.

Elsie Slade shook her head.

'We started out but there was so much noise from the George we turned back,' Agnes said.

'Pam Mitton's reception,' her mother explained. 'Half the men there wanted to bed her and the other half probably had already. They were the ones celebrating their escape. All over the place they were.'

'In the roadway?' the inspector wanted to know.

'Aye – and hanging on the churchyard wall, dead drunk.'

Elsie Slade's lips were disapproving. 'Still, Mittons. What d'you expect?'

'When did you go again?'

'Next morning – Sunday. I thought it was just as well

it had rained so hard and washed away some of the muck.'

'You went to the grave after church in the morning?'

She nodded.

'What time would that have been?'

Mother and daughter consulted each other silently.

'Half-past twelve?' Elsie Slade suggested. Agnes shook her head. 'More like quarter-past.'

Clay Gifford amended his electronic notepad. 'Was everything the same?' Tyrell asked. 'No. I bent over to feel how damp the green stuff was and I didn't have to bend so far. At my age you're a bit stiff so you know about things like that.'

'Was that all?'

'No, it wasn't. A piece of the fern had been broken off. Nice fern it was Betty used. When I bent down on Friday it tickled just below my knee, under my coat. It wasn't broken then. Sunday, that piece was facing away from me – and broken. A shorter piece was nearest to me and it brushed against my coat above my knee.'

'You're sure?'

'Positive!'

Tyrell turned to Agnes Morse. 'Did you notice anything unusual?'

She frowned, trying to remember. 'The card on the wreath from Jack and me, it was a bit skewiff. I straightened it but I thought it might have been rain that moved it.'

'Was it straight on Friday?'

Agnes searched her memory for the scene, then nodded slowly. 'Yes, I'm sure of it. The other wreaths, I wouldn't know.'

Tyrell turned to her mother. 'Chief Inspector Whittaker does need you to make a statement.'

Her eyes flashed. 'He stopped me going to Fred's grave.

'That was his job.'

'Not the way he spoke to me – as if it was none o' my

business. I told him, that's my part of the grave you're digging up. Double grave me and Fred bought and paid for. Fred went in first so it's my place they've been pulling to bits. It didn't make no difference.' She lay back in her chair and was a tired, unhappy old woman. 'I only wanted to make sure they'd let Fred alone. There was a girl there in one o' they funny overalls. She was nice. She said she see to the roses. Will you look for me? Make sure she's done it?'

Tyrell promised. 'A statement? Only the facts. The dates and times you noticed things.'

'Can't you do it here?'

'Not really. I could ask PC Cole to do it for you at the hall.'

'Is he any good?'

'He took mine.'

Her eyes widened and Tyrell saw irises that had paled with age.

'You had to make a statement?'

'Of course. All major witnesses do.'

'What about Agnes?'

'We'd be very grateful if she could come with you and have her statement taken at the same time.'

Elsie Slade looked into the fire, thinking hard. A decision made, she looked up at the inspector.

'If you'll come with me.'

Flanked by Agnes and wearing the new hat bought for the funeral, Mrs Slade made her entrance into the busy din of the hall. Whittaker saw her and approached with a welcoming smile.

'I'm here because of Inspector Tyrell,' she informed the DCI before he could say a word and then swept onwards, a reincarnation of Queen Victoria wearing her 'We are not amused' expression.

PC Cole was brought out of hiding, his shyness Elsie

Slade's undoing. Between them the required statement was soon prepared.

'Kid gloves for her, Mrs Gilbert. Pull out all the stops,' Tyrell begged.

'She's that important?'

'If we want Tolland people on our side in this new investigation, yes. It was her Fred's grave that was desecrated and the village will take its lead from her. That's why I got her to walk in today.'

'So, I keep her sweet?'

'As only you know how,' Tyrell said with a grin.

'By the way, a message from Ipswich CID. One of the land girls living there recognised Gordheimer though she'd only seen him once or twice. All she could tell them was that he was waiting for a girl who cycled to meet him. She never had any idea who the girl was. Still doesn't.'

'Cycle?' Gifford asked.

Tyrell frowned. 'It suggests distance but how did they know when and where to meet?'

'I guess the phones worked, even in wartime Tolland.'

'I expect they did – what there was of them. There'd have been one in the centre of the village – but used by a girl who was secretive? Apart from that one, the manor would have had a phone, the vicar, doctor, a few farmers, that would have been all. Thank you, Mrs Gilbert. Every detail helps.'

As Gifford and Mrs Gilbert talked of changes since the war, Tyrell opened the Gordheimer file. He was not left in peace for long as Whittaker leaned on the desk.

'You've had your tea and biscuit break, now let's see some real work. The body arrived in Tolland somehow. Alive or dead, we don't yet know.'

'Can the pathologist help? It should be possible to tell from post-mortem changes if the corpse was carried over someone's shoulder or lay in the boot of a car for some time.'

'Been reading your textbooks again?'

Tyrell ignored the sneer. 'No one's going to carry someone that size very far,' he argued reasonably, 'in which case the man came to the village either alive or in some form of transport. If he was already dead he could have been dumped here from anywhere in the country.'

'Procedure, Tyrell. We assume he was breathing when he got here, so get out and start asking questions. DS Rogers has a list for you.' Whittaker smiled, the pleasantry failing to reach his eyes. 'You've been assigned WDC Paige but I need both of you house-to-house. She can help with your historical research when I've finished with you.'

The DCI went off, a man on his way to importance. Gifford saw him go and ambled over to Tyrell.

'Me being put in my place.' Tyrell explained the routine questioning.

'What can I do?' Gifford asked.

'When Cole and Mrs Gilbert have finished with Elsie and her daughter, can you escort them back home?'

'That fruit cake hasn't gone down yet, dammit!'

Tyrell grinned. 'You'll just have to suffer for your country or get them to put some in a doggy bag for me.'

'Why the concentration on keeping her on your side?'

'Because she's been a tremendous help with the Gordheimer murder. She doesn't know it – and I want to keep it that way. I'm sure there's still more to come. Then, if she's willing to help with the latest murder enquiries, it might tip the scales with the other villagers.'

'DI Tyrell?'

He turned to see a halo of auburn curls, angry green eyes under winged brows, freckles on a clear skin and a mutinous expression. Behind him Clay Gifford went off reluctantly to talk to Agnes Morse.

'WDC Paige.'

Tyrell nodded courteously. 'You've got the list of houses we're to check?'

There was no softening in the girl. 'They're all out in the country.'

'Map?'

She showed him the paperwork and Tyrell picked up a wedge of statement forms.

'Let's get on with it, then. I'll drive.'

Her lips tightened in temper. 'Don't you trust my driving? Sir?'

'I've not experienced it, so it would be unfair to comment. However, I'd rather not be driven by anyone as mad at someone as you are.'

The inspector led the way to his car. Only when they were whisking between tall hedges to their first destination did he risk a glance at the girl. She was studying the map.

'Berryhill Farm – next lane on the left.'

The DI parked the car on the verge just short of the turning and switched off the engine.

'I'm not going to any interviews with you spitting nails. Let's have it. What's wrong?'

There was a determined silence.

'WDC Paige, we have a job to do. Both of us. You're not in any fit state to do yours and that's my responsibility.'

The girl looked down at her hands. They were small, neat-fingered. He guessed she must have had difficulty making the minimum height for the force.

'You've been transferred. Where from?'

'Haven't you been told? All boys together?'

'No.'

'I was at Cheltenham. A DI groped me and I slapped him hard, so everyone knew. The super threatened me with a charge of assaulting a senior officer. I warned him that if he did that I'd have the bastard on a harassment charge. I got transferred here.'

'You've a right to be angry. If it's the DI I have in mind

it's only a matter of time before he's facing a charge of some kind. It still doesn't explain why you're so mad today.'

'You were supposed to have DS Simons. I was sent here to replace him in Whittaker's team. Instead, I get Whittaker being po-faced, telling me it'd be better to leave Simons where he is because he's a damned good copper. There's a few think it wasn't Simons' fault he lost seniority – the DCI must be one of them. He said I was to help you – and he made it very clear I was being demoted.'

'By working with me?' Tyrell smiled wryly. 'I've had better compliments.'

'No, not because of you.' The girl was anxious not to be misunderstood. 'I mean, a fifty-year-old murder? It's hardly urgent.'

'Isn't it? You have to keep in mind the victim came to this country as a fit twenty-year-old, ready to fight Nazism. He's shot, here in Tolland, and hidden away. The US Army lists him as a deserter. Back home his parents die, wondering what happened to their son. His brother and sister are elderly and frail – time's not on their side. When they do get to bury him properly after all this time, they need to know why he was killed – and who did it. We owe them that much.'

'I suppose so. How can you ever hope to find out?'

'Tolland knows. Get under the skin of the village. Be accepted as a not-too-harmful parasite and wait.'

'What for?'

'After a while, what Tolland knows, you will too.'

'Won't the usual procedures help you get the facts more quickly?'

He shook his head. 'All they'll get you is closed doors and an even tighter lid on memories.'

Freckles moved as her forehead wrinkled. 'Would that apply to the new murder?'

'I don't see why not.' The inspector switched on the engine. 'Let's try it. Who lives at Berryhill Farm?'

'The Seymours.'

'Seymour. That rings a bell. Who was here before us?'

She checked the notes. 'DS Moore and DC Richards.'

'They obviously didn't get anything or Berryhill Farm wouldn't be on our list.'

'Well, what do you expect of a couple of men?'

With the fury back in her voice, Tyrell switched off the engine.

'That's enough! In every job there are men who see women as either dykes or bimbos and they do it for two reasons. Either they're arrogant and stupid or they're afraid and stupid.'

The green eyes were shadowed, hidden from him.

'If you categorise all men as mindless idiots are you any better?'

Tyrell waited.

'No. I'm sorry, sir.'

They drove up the track to the farmyard in silence and a black and white collie dog tethered to a kennel barked a warning to the household. Before there was time to knock on the nearest door it was opened.

'You look like police. What's up now?'

A broad, comely woman stared at them. Her arms were bare and folded across an apron dusted with flour. Warrant cards were produced for inspection.

'Mrs Seymour. I'm Detective Inspector Tyrell and this is WDC Paige.'

The woman's face cleared to a welcoming smile. 'Inspector Tyrell! Come in – and you, miss.'

They were ushered into a large, airy kitchen. It was warmed by an Aga and smelled of fresh bread, bubbling soup. A corner of the massive pine table was cleared of flour crock and scales.

'Sit yourselves down. Would you like tea or coffee? You could have cider, if you'd rather. Make it ourselves, we do.'

'Thank you, Mrs Seymour. We'd better not.'

'No, of course. You'd be on duty.'

'Apart from that I can't risk going to sleep in the middle of the day.'

'Come on,' she scolded with a smile. 'It'd take more'n our cider to knock out a big chap like you.'

'Another time, perhaps,' he promised. 'You had two of our colleagues here asking questions.'

Disgust coloured the broad face. 'Town boys. Thought we weren't too bright.'

'More fool them. Now you've had time to think a bit – talk things over with the family – has anything come to mind?'

Mrs Seymour shook her head. 'No. The other two asked about seeing strangers but none of us had. My husband, he's cousin to Agnes Morse's Jack, he's been trying to remember. Wendy, our daughter, she's training at Gloucester Royal, she wasn't here the weekend of Pam Mitton's wedding – not that she'd have been invited. Not Pam's sort, our Wendy,' she added proudly.

'Your son. Alan?' Tyrell asked.

'The silly fool! Just turned eighteen and knows it all! He wasn't up to seeing anything. The night before the wedding he was out with some of his friends and got so drunk he had to sleep it off and walk home in the morning. The nightmares he's had! Serve him right. He'd taken some of his father's cider.'

'Is he about?'

'Alan's with his dad in Tuppenny Field. They'll be home for their dinners in half an hour or so.'

'I'd like to talk to Alan before I go.'

'Then have a drop of broth while you wait. It's ready for the men – and there's plenty.'

'That's very kind of you, Mrs Seymour,' Tyrell said as his WDC tapped the list and the map.

'Sir?'

He ignored her and smiled at Mrs Seymour. 'There's

104

no point in going off and having to come back – and that broth of yours smells good.'

'I'll put the two of you in the dairy. It hasn't been used for that for years, not since Bill and me took over from his dad. I'll send Alan in to you when he comes home and you can be private.'

The room was pleasant, the bowls of soup huge, the bread soft inside a crust which crackled.

'They're certainly good cooks in Tolland,' Tyrell said as he finished his meal and sat back from the table.

Paige was still struggling. 'There's too much for me.'

They heard a heavy vehicle driving up to the farm-house. Doors slammed and there was the sound of voices. In a matter of minutes Alan Seymour appeared, his face still damp from a hurried wash.

'Come in, Alan. We don't want to keep you from your meal longer than we have to.'

'You're the inspector that goes to see Auntie Elsie?'

Tyrell nodded. 'And this is WDC Paige.'

On another occasion Alan might have shown a greater interest in the policewoman. He shifted from one foot to another as he tightened the roll of his shirt-sleeves above nut-brown arms scratched from branches.

'What'd you want?'

'Sit down, Alan. You don't mind if WDC Paige takes notes?'

Alan shook his head, his eyes wary.

'Now, the night before Pam Mitton's wedding.'

Alan groaned. 'Who told you? I bet it was Auntie Elsie. Why can't she keep her mouth shut?'

'It wasn't her and it doesn't matter who told us. Anything to hide, Alan? I thought it was just a case of too much cider and fat-headed friends.'

'My friends are OK.'

'Are they? You passed out and they carried you to the church, stretched you out in the aisle and covered you with roses from the altar. Who had the key?'

'I don't know. I was out of it.'

105

'Let's take it step by step. You left here – what time?'

'About seven.'

'Armed with supplies of your father's cider. I've had farm-brewed cider. If it's really good it could fuel rockets. How many bottles did you fill from the barrel?'

'Two. Old pop bottles. Dad would've noticed if I'd taken more.'

'You met up with your friends. How many?'

Alan was prepared to stay silent until he met Tyrell's stern gaze.

'Three.'

'So, there'd be at least a couple of large glasses apiece. What then?'

'We went to the George. The others had lager but I stuck to cider.'

'The strong stuff?'

'I was all right till I went outside,' the boy protested. 'It was the fresh air.'

'That's cider for you,' Tyrell agreed cheerfully. 'Your friends decided to put you in the church for a lark. Who got the key?'

Alan refused to speak.

'It's natural to defend your friends but think about it, Alan. When you woke up you were lying on your back covered with roses. I've no doubt it was only done to give them a laugh and you a scare.' Tyrell leaned forward, his expression grave. 'Suppose you'd vomited while you were unconscious. It's something drunks do – a natural reaction. What then, Alan? You're no fool, far from it. Would you have been able to walk home in the morning?'

The boy's resistance drained from him and he slumped in his chair. The DI gazed at him, Alan shifting uneasily.

'Well?'

'I'd have been dead.'

106

'Agreed. Now, the names of the boys with you that night.'

The two officers watched Alan's struggle with his conscience then, 'Ben Keyte, Peter King, Mark Ryan,' were listed slowly.

'Are they all eighteen?'

'Mark's twenty.'

'And they all live in Tolland?'

Alan nodded.

'I'd like to talk to them.'

Alan started to get up. 'I'll fetch them.'

'Sit down! I want to interview them one at a time, without there being a chance of you making contact with each other. Do they all live on farms?'

'Ben's at Keyte's Farm, Peter lives with his grandfather at Mayhill.'

'Mark Ryan?'

'Thorn Farm.'

'I suppose you're all leading lights of the YFC?' Tyrell asked as Paige checked lists.

Alan looked away.

'We're due to visit all those farms, sir,' Paige said.

'Good. Alan, while I talk to your mother, I want you to make a statement – and don't leave this room.'

The inspector made for the kitchen.

'Everything all right?' Mrs Seymour asked anxiously.

Her husband pushed aside his plate as Tyrell explained the situation to the bewildered parents.

'We can take all the boys off to the hall, maybe the nearest police station, where they'd be interrogated. Or we can try something else.'

The Seymours consulted each other silently, then both nodded.

'We'll see he's learned his lesson,' Bill Seymour promised before turning to his wife. 'I told you they'd find out.'

*   *   *

107

Three phone calls later two more Land-Rovers arrived at the farm, then a battered Volvo estate car. In each was a very scared young man accompanied by a furious parent or guardian. One by one the boys went to the dairy and were questioned thoroughly. Only when they had made and signed a statement were they allowed to go back to their vehicles and wait until Inspector Tyrell was ready to talk.

'The real reason for our investigation is the death of an unknown man buried in Fred Slade's grave,' he told the men and women assembled in the dairy. 'Today, we've had to deal with a minor incident.'

DI Tyrell stared at each culprit in turn.

'What you did was stupid, thoughtless. You could easily have cost Alan his life. That's something you – and he – will have to live with. It's not an experience I'd enjoy having on my conscience.'

He let them suffer his wrath in a long silence.

'You all know Mrs Slade. Try to imagine what it's like to bury someone you've lived with for nearly fifty years and then, almost immediately, have the grave desecrated.'

'Do you know who the man in the grave was?' Peter King's grandfather asked.

'No. We'll find out, make no mistake. In Tolland there'll be people who might have noticed something trivial and dismissed it from their minds. If you hear of anything, however small, please get the information to us. As soon as we get a solution, Fred Slade – and his wife – can be left in peace.'

DCI Whittaker was furious.

'You did what? Those boys should have been brought in for questioning.'

'They're witnesses, sir, not murder suspects,' Tyrell argued.

'By their own admission they're guilty of breaking and entering – and vandalism.'

'Actually, sir, only entering. They had old Mr King's key, left over from when he was vicar's warden twenty years ago. The vandalism was removing flowers from the vases on the altar. The CPS, as well as the magistrates, would laugh us out of court. Instead, the families are embarrassed and hopping mad with the boys. They're all the more willing to help us. It's not a bad exchange.'

'The influence of your new American friend? I'm surprised you didn't give the tearaways badges and swear them in as deputies.'

Tyrell steadied his breathing. 'It does no harm to get Tolland people ready to talk to us.'

'You should have gone for a career in public relations,' the DCI advised, spite colouring his words. 'With your connections you'd have done well.'

'Perhaps so, sir,' Tyrell said. 'The pathologist's report, is it finished?'

'It arrived while you were out.'

'May I see it?'

'I'll save you the bother. Death was caused by a blow to the back of the skull. The ever-handy blunt instrument. One that left splinters.'

'Has the wood been identified?'

'Oak.'

'That's odd. Oak in furniture is usually well seasoned. It must have been rough wood. The damage to the face?'

'It was inflicted after death. There were more splinters and the features were obliterated. Nose smashed, jaw bones fractured, cheek bones as well.'

'Dental records?'

'Not much use. It looks as though the victim wasn't too keen on dentists. There had been the odd extraction – no fillings. Actually, he had quite good teeth.'

Whittaker's animosity was suspended as he worked through facts and ideas.

'Prints?' Tyrell asked.

'The tips of all the fingers were damaged. The pathologist suggested that after he died he might have been grating cheese – without the cheese.'

Tyrell shuddered at the thought.

'To do all that, someone must have had a cool head and a strong stomach,' Whittaker decided.

'Yet the first blow, the fatal one, suggests a loss of control,' Tyrell reasoned.

'Two of them?'

'It's possible. One kills in anger, the other disposes. They're both here in Tolland,' Tyrell said softly. 'I'm sure of it.'

'First priority is still the identity of the victim. The pathology data's gone to the whizz-kids in Gloucester. They may be able to produce a computer-enhanced picture we can give to the press.'

'The clothes the victim came in have almost certainly been burned by now but there is the car he came in.'

'You're sure that's how he got here?'

'Aren't you?' Tyrell asked Whittaker. 'No taxi driver's come forward.'

'A local's car? With the corpse in the boot?'

'It is possible,' Tyrell said as Whittaker shook his head.

'Excuse me, sir.' WDC Paige was looking at Tyrell. 'A Mr Ryan on the phone for you. He said he was Mark's father.'

The DI moved quickly, Whittaker following, although he had difficulty hearing much of the conversation and paced impatiently until Tyrell stopped talking.

'Well?'

'The Ryans' cowman. He was parked in a lane with a girl. A car passed them, driven very fast, heading for the Forest. He thinks it might have been after midnight.'

'You're certain it was that night?'

110

'The girl was due to be at Pam Mitton's wedding next day.'

'The car?'

'He thinks a Mercedes, dark colour, quite old.'

'Too much to hope for a number.'

'No headlights on the parked car – and the cowman did have his mind on other things.'

'Get him in – and the girl.'

'He wouldn't tell Mr Ryan who she was. My guess is the girl's either under age or her father would castrate him. Maybe both.'

'Simons!' Whittaker shouted. 'Start a hunt for a dark-coloured Mercedes, old registration. Gravel pits, quarries, lakes – '

Tyrell intervened. 'Excuse me, sir.'

Whittaker's frown was not encouraging. 'What is it?'

'The train of thought of the cool-headed one. He buried a body where there were other dead bodies.'

'You think he'll have done the same thing with the car? A car park?'

Tyrell shook his head. 'If he chose a regular park it would be empty at night and the first arrivals next morning would see it and remember. Much more likely it's been left with other old cars.'

'A scrapyard?'

'No. The owner, workers, they might spot an extra one. My bet would be a site where cars are dumped and left to rust until the council carts them off. By now the Mercedes might be missing a few items and will look the part.'

'Makes sense,' Whittaker begrudged. 'Simons, any old car tips this side of Cinderford – to begin with.'

DS Simons groaned audibly. 'Yes, Guv.'

Whittaker turned his attention back to Tyrell. 'Since you're so good at getting information from the locals, you'd better get back to it. We haven't got all day.'

The inspector collected WDC Paige and they were

walking to his car when Maria Gilbert came running after him.

'A message from Major Gifford. He's been called back to London for a couple of days and asks you to persuade the vicar to delay the service for Private Gordheimer. His brother, Professor Gordheimer, is flying over from the States and wants to be present.'

'Great!'

Tyrell grinned at the bewildered policewoman.

'A living, breathing brother. That should stir up some old ghosts and get them walking again. Someone's bound to talk now.'

Chapter Six

The smell of fresh coffee woke Keith and he drank it as Jenny was getting ready for the day. Lying back in the warm bed he watched her rub her hair dry.

'Do you want to talk about it?' she asked.

Keith was aware only of her sparkle, the smell of soap and talc. She was everything that was clean. He reached out a long arm and pulled her to him, burying his face in the fragrance of her.

'What is it?' she whispered and waited.

At last he began to talk. Of the people he had interviewed, good people living worthwhile lives.

'What's wrong with that?'

'With the Gordheimer murder I thought I could ask my questions, write my report and leave Tolland intact. Everything had happened so long ago.'

'And now?' Jenny's eyes were wide, candid, the mind behind them accepting no prevarication.

'Noah Bryce is in hospital. Then this new murder. Everything, everybody, will have to be checked and rechecked.'

'Surely that's only to be expected?'

'In a village like Tolland, any community come to that, there're things that happened in the past which've been forgotten. They're harmless now – they hurt no one. After this investigation Tolland will have nothing it's allowed to hide.'

'Is that such a bad thing?'

'Perhaps not. Lesser crimes may come to light and be dealt with.'

'Like the boys in the church that night?'

'That's typical. A petty thing Martin Draper would have seen to very effectively and few the wiser. Now it's all on record.'

'If they've learned to leave a drunk in the recovery position it's a plus!'

'OK, I agree, it's a crime of sorts and murder's a drastic disease. It has to be rooted out.'

'Are you afraid too much that's healthy might have to be sacrificed?'

'No, it's more than that.'

Keith stared at the ceiling, trying to organise his thoughts. It was important for him to express himself clearly.

'I sense whoever killed and buried Ben Gordheimer deliberately hid behind the fabric of the village. In wartime maybe it wasn't so hard to do. The trouble is the same thing's happening again, I know it. The entire population, the innocent as well as the guilty, will have to go through the mincer for us to get at the ones we want. No one will be left unsacrificed as the murderers try to save their skins. I can't help thinking of Elsie Slade, her daughter, the Hattons – '

'They'll survive.'

'Not all of them. Noah Bryce's stroke – was that triggered by the skeleton surfacing? If he dies that's one down to me.'

'No,' Jenny argued, 'it's down to his reaction to your questions.'

'That's the point. He might have something on his conscience that's nothing at all to do with the killing but I go barging in and he ends up in hospital.'

'Given what you've told me of his medical history and his temper, the stroke was inevitable – even if he'd never met you.'

'I wish it was as simple as that.'

'Tolland villagers have been coping with worse than you for centuries.' Jenny rolled on to her elbows to see his face. 'Are you telling me you're on a par with the plague?'

Keith smiled at her teasing. 'By the time Whittaker's finished with them, they'll probably feel they've had that as well.'

Jenny cocked her head to one side. 'Come to think of it, that's how Cromwell must have seemed. Very good for the soul but a right pain in the backside.'

For Keith the day began to look more hopeful. 'You've described Whittaker perfectly.'

'When's the nice American coming back?' Jenny wanted to know. 'He'll keep you cheerful.'

'Haven't a clue. He's probably waiting for the Gordheimer brother to arrive. Mind you, it's just as well Clay's not here, I wouldn't have time to look after him. Whittaker's got us all at full stretch.'

'Making his presence felt?'

'Not really. The body has to be identified quickly if we're to pick up any leads with breath in them. And, if Simons doesn't find that damned Mercedes where I suggested, my neck's on the block.'

'Listen, Buster! If there's any chopping to be done I get first crack at it. Coming home tired out last night?'

'Still, I slept well.' Keith grinned at his wife. 'There's no real hurry yet, is there?'

The landlady of the George was keeping an eye on the barrels being unloaded. Myra Roberts was little and neat, the red which kept grey at bay in her hair matching a fiery spirit.

'How's your mother?' she called to Agnes Morse.

'Bearing up, although the reporters are getting her down. D'you know one woman just opened the back door and walked in? Said she'd heard people in the country expected neighbours to pop in that way, then wanted to know how Mother felt when she'd heard there was a body in with Dad. I ask you!'

'I bet your mum sent her off with a flea in her ear.'

'Getting angry helped Mother – and that's no bad thing. You know, I'm worried about her,' Agnes confided.

'She's not ill?'

'No, just listless. It's the idea someone she knows dug into Dad's grave. She says it's like being burgled by a friend and not knowing which one.'

'The police haven't been too bad, have they?'

'Well . . . some of them have riled her but she'll talk to Inspector Tyrell any time. I have to stop her coming down to the hall whenever she's a mind to see him.'

'I've heard he's very polite. Did he ever discover who killed the Yank in the war?'

'I think he knows – but how can he prove it after all this time? Anyway, with this new murderer on the loose he'll be busy with that.'

Myra Roberts shivered. 'Maybe it's someone we know – the new killer.'

'I'm sure it's what Inspector Tyrell thinks. He's sharp, mind you, for all he's so young.'

'My Sam says you're answering questions before you've even realised he's asked them. I wouldn't want to be around him if I'd a guilty conscience.'

Agnes laughed. 'I'd better get on.'

'Another of your dinners?'

'Yes, at Benham Abbey. The new people there want to get into charity work. They're quite nice, not pushy at all.'

'Pushy? We've got more than we want of that right here in Tolland,' Myra said bitterly, 'as you know to your cost.'

'Oh, I'm better off as I am now, even if Jack says between Mother and the dinner parties Miss Caroline gets for me, he and the boys see less of me than ever.'

'I never thought when you started going round cooking meals in people's homes you'd be so busy. You haven't time to do me some pot meals and pasties, have you? I don't want to buy in frozen stuff but there's no way I can keep up with the numbers.'

'I suppose I could. I'd need good mince and stewing steak. You won't get many vegetarians amongst the journalists.'

'It's the police. Hungry as hunters when they come into the bar.'

'Well, that's what they are,' Agnes reminded her. 'Hunters.'

'Have you any idea how many dark-haired, middle-aged men there are on the missing persons list? Of course we've checked it!'

WDS Roger's fury was evident to all in the fall-out zone of the incident room.

'Who's Penny talking to?' Tyrell asked a weary CID man whose tie was awry and collar open beneath a stubble of tiredness.

'Press office.'

'Anything new since last night?'

'Simons found the car – what was left of it. There must be a good market for Merc spares near Soudley.'

'Was that where it was?'

'A dump in behind some trees and not far from the A48. Not easy to spot.'

'Fingerprints won't be much use,' Tyrell said.

'Forensic got there sharpish but it was still too late. There's an impressive collection, I understand. Some of them real tiny.'

A new voice joined in. 'Everything starts young in the Forest of Dean, didn't they warn you?' It was DS Clarke looking fresh and rested.

The DI greeted him warmly. 'I heard Greenwell's waiting for sentencing. A good verdict.'

Clarke beamed. 'There were a couple of old rugby players on the jury. What's the situation with the skeleton?'

'More or less on hold because of this.' Tyrell waved his hand at the busy incident room.

Clarke nodded towards the collage of photographs showing the naked victim in all his last vulnerability. 'Still no idea who he is?'

'No. Hair type suggests an Arab, maybe Greek, Italian, Pakistani. No one's sure. Forensic's trying to patch up what remains of his fingerprints using computer enhancement – they're not hopeful. It's really a practice exercise for them. Even if they got a match it would be no use as evidence.'

Tyrell explained about the cheese grater and Brian Clarke began to feel queasy.

'Morning, sir.'

Emma Paige was alert, ready for work. Tyrell introduced her to Brian Clarke and the two eyed each other warily.

'Does this mean I'm moved again?' the girl demanded to know.

'I've no idea,' Tyrell said. 'For the moment, we all go where we're sent.'

Brian Clarke nodded in the direction of the trestle table set out below the photographs.

'Looks like they're getting ready for a briefing.'

DCI Whittaker might have had a busy night, an early start, but his shirt was crisp, his hair bright.

'Right. Listen up!'

The call for silence brought instant quiet, except for DS Rogers organising the hand-out of paper.

'The dark blue Mercedes has been located and it belongs to a Halam Kemal with an address in Birmingham. Kemal was hauled out of bed late last night and questioned. He insists he lent the car to a friend of his. It's possible the man buried in Tolland churchyard is Mehmet Orhan, also from Birmingham. Mrs Orhan is

118

accompanying Kemal to the mortuary and they will try to identify the remains. We should know yes or no by eleven.'

'Orhan. What kind of name's that, Guv?' a CID man asked.

'Turkish. That ties in with the hair type but we'll just have to wait for confirmation. In the meantime I want a list of any, I repeat, any reference made to Birmingham in your interviews in the village. Check through statements, notes, your memories – if they're still working. Then check again. We've at last got a smell of a lead and I want us to be ready to follow it through.'

'No matter what,' Tyrell murmured to himself.

It was enough to attract Whittaker's attention. 'That includes you, Inspector Tyrell. I want anything that might link the skeleton with Birmingham. Old sins and their shadows, that sort of thing. It's a long shot but I want every aspect covered.'

'Yes, sir. I'll go through the paperwork.'

There was no need for Tyrell to check his files. Peggy Phelps was from Birmingham, the ex-land girl who lived in a world of her own. How would she cope with the vigorous questioning by a murder squad under pressure?

Clay Gifford's voice was there in his mind. 'Too worried' kept echoing silently and Tyrell could picture the Hattons' distress, their son at a Birmingham university. The boy had a police record for drug abuse, however minor the offences might be.

The DI was certain of one thing. Tolland had better brace itself to be torn asunder.

The police presence in the village might be like that of an occupying army but the inhabitants insisted on living their everyday lives as normally as possible.

Cubs and Brownies regrouped in the vicarage and Cyril Mitton complained loudly about his regular bingo being banished from the hall. He was only silenced when Sam Roberts offered the use of a room in the George. This was no help to the mothers of very young children. They became extremely vocal, protesting to anyone who would listen, a need for the playgroup to continue.

In the church Mrs Hatton struggled to master hymn music while Lady Driffield, aided by her anxious acolyte, Elaine Poynter, arranged flowers. In the nave two village women polished pews and ledges as they grumbled about stuck-up flower arrangers, the crush in the George at lunchtime and Mrs Fell's high prices.

It was half an hour short of midday when the phone call came from the mortuary. The body now had a name. Mehmet Orhan, aged forty-two, had been married with three daughters when killed and interred with Fred Slade.

Data streamed from computers, faxes and phones. The Orhans lived in a Birmingham suburb that was home to a high percentage of Turks. He owned his semi-detached house, making a steady living as a factory worker.

Whittaker was annoyed. 'It doesn't make sense! There must be another angle. No quiet, law-abiding shop-floor slave borrows a car to come secretly to a village like Tolland.'

'Did he tell his friend, Kemal, why he wanted the car?' Tyrell asked.

He and Whittaker were the senior officers in the room, waiting while all the other ranks collected copies of an accurate photo of the dead man.

'Kemal was of the opinion Orhan seemed excited. He thought he had a way of getting his hands on some cash,' the DCI said.

'Was he badly in need of some?'

Whittaker thought of his own children. 'No more than most men with three daughters.'

'A factory worker earning well in Birmingham would probably have a car of his own. Why didn't he?' Tyrell asked.

'He did. A year-old Audi. His wife wanted it to take two of the girls to a party in Solihull. The Mercedes in Soudley was Kemal's second car. He drove down in a brand new model.'

Tyrell pursed his lips as ideas meshed and formed a pattern. 'They're living it up for immigrant labour. What else did Orhan do?'

'That's what we're waiting to hear from his local nick.'

'And Kemal? The friend with two Mercedes. What's his source of income?'

'Mr Kemal is in electronics – so he told us when he arrived. He's being checked out as well. While we wait, any Birmingham links in your skeleton case?'

Tyrell outlined the involvement of Peggy Phelps, then added Clay Gifford's comments on Will Hatton.

'You mean their son was here at the time Orhan was buried?'

'I don't think so. He'd gone by the time his mother left the house to go and practise in the church. The local boys I talked to hid until she'd stopped playing. They even waited until she'd got back to the vicarage. Their high jinks would have taken a little time and I'd bet they were pretty noisy in the process. The grave-opener must have had to lie low while they were there.'

'Before?'

'I doubt it. Elsie Slade and her daughter were at the grave for some time. We could talk to her again. She might have heard Mrs Hatton start up.'

'It's got to be Friday night. Convince me why.'

'Elsie and Agnes. They're sure the grave hadn't been touched when they left it Friday night. Saturday was busy, people coming and going round the church all the time. The George was at full flood for the reception and the party afterwards. Quite a few of the drinkers used the churchyard, for one reason or another, until it started to rain.'

'No evidence in the mud of interference with the grave and any earlier signs washed away.' Whittaker's lips thinned in anger. 'He's a lucky bastard.'

'What puzzles me is the connection Orhan had with Tolland.'

'It'll surface.'

Whittaker looked round the room. Apart from himself and Tyrell there was no other ranking CID officer.

'You can go and interview the Hattons. A statement this time on their son's movements while he was at home. We'll leave it to Birmingham CID to pull in Hatton junior.'

DI Tyrell and WDC Paige waited for the door to be opened. They had time to see the vicarage was badly in need of refurbishment. What was once glossy white paint curled grimy and dull away from windows. Moss spread across the path to the front door, its lush green at odds with scrawny flowers standing listless in weed-choked beds.

'It's you, Inspector. Do come in.' Reverend Hatton had a distracted air. 'You're here officially?'

'Yes. This is WDC Paige. If I could talk to you first, then Mrs Hatton? Separately.'

Shrewdness quirked in the vague grey eyes. 'Is it a parish matter?'

'In a way. It does involve a member of your family.'

The vicar closed his eyes and Tyrell guessed the prayer was heartfelt.

'You wish to question us about Will's visit. Please, come into the study.'

The room was dank. Papers were in tidy piles on the

desk but all other surfaces had the dimness of dust and apathy.

'Your son's a student at Aston University,' Tyrell began as Emma Paige opened her notebook.

'In his second year.'

'I understand he was staying with you about the time Fred Slade's grave was opened. I'd be grateful if you could tell us the exact times of his arrival and departure – as well as any movements he may have made away from this house.'

'Will is suspected of something?' Reverend Hatton was bewildered by the idea.

'No, I'm not aware he is.'

The vicar's tension eased a little. 'Will arrived on the Thursday, the day of the Slade funeral.'

'Time?'

The vicar looked for advice at an elderly etching of Jerusalem. 'He was here in time for lunch. Perhaps twelve fifteen.'

'How did he travel?'

'By car. It's an old one Julian, our elder son, passed on when he went to live in France.'

'Did he leave the house? Visit anyone?'

Reverend Hatton shook his head. 'No. Will had come to see us. He did not go out until he returned to the university.'

'And that was?'

'Friday. Five o'clock.'

'You're sure?'

'Yes. My wife and I prayed together, then we had a cup of tea.'

'What time did she go to the church to practise?'

'How did you – ? You're very efficient, Inspector. It was late, about eight o'clock. She came home and made cocoa at, say, nine thirty. We were in bed by ten.'

Emma Paige checked and double-checked times and movements with the vicar, making sure she had an accurate record. When she was satisfied, Reverend

Hatton called his wife into the room. She was nervous and Tyrell was reassuring her when the phone rang and the vicar excused himself to answer it in the hall.

Tyrell was discussing with Mrs Hatton the difficulties of heating a large house in winter when the door opened.

'Inspector Tyrell.' Reverend Hatton was white with anger. 'I've just had a call from a friend of Will's in Birmingham. My son is in a police station being questioned as a murder suspect.'

'Nicholas, no!' Mrs Hatton was trembling. 'He can't be. The shock might trigger – '

She covered her mouth with shaking fingers, the eyes above them huge with fear. Clay Gifford was right, Tyrell decided. It was likely the boy had been well on his way back to Birmingham when Fred Slade's rest had been disturbed yet the parents were too frightened for him to be innocent. Of what? Something involved their son and it scared the wits out of them.

'Would you please both sit down,' the inspector urged. 'Your son is not a suspect – not more than anyone else. In a murder enquiry every detail, however small, must be followed up. That includes your son's visit home at a time when a man was killed, possibly here, in the village.'

'But Will was with us all the time,' his father insisted.

Mrs Hatton, her shoulders bowed, wept quietly.

'It might help if you could tell me the reason for his visit.'

'No! No, we couldn't. It was a private matter – a family matter,' the vicar said.

'We're in the middle of a major investigation and I'm afraid all normal courtesies must go by the board, sir. We know your son has had two convictions for drug use. I'd hazard a guess he's being questioned about his source, or sources, of supply in case there's a link with the murdered man.'

'Will stopped all that,' his mother protested.

Her husband was weary, defeated. 'It happened in his first term. Others on his course persuaded him to experiment with the dreadful stuff. Will was not convinced as to its supposedly beneficial effects and he ceased to use it of his own accord.'

After Reverend Hatton stopped speaking Tyrell let the silence linger. He thought it more likely two court appearances for possession took away much of the dubious pleasure of cannabis. Leaning forward, he spoke gently.

'Why did he come home that Thursday?'

The parents refused to answer.

'We will find out,' Tyrell promised. 'Wouldn't it be better if you could tell me now and get it cleared up quickly?'

'Is this what they mean by police harassment?' the vicar wanted to know in a gesture of defiance.

'No, sir. This is a very small part of what may be necessary for us to arrest a murderer and enable Mrs Orhan to bury her husband.'

The woman was angry. 'But Will didn't kill him!'

'I'm prepared to accept that, Mrs Hatton, but I do need to know why he was here.'

She sighed, the sound a long agony. Her husband went to her and patted her shoulder awkwardly. There was an elusive dignity about him as he faced Tyrell.

'Will came to tell us he had had to have a blood test some weeks ago. He had been trying to restrain a friend of his who was having a fit. Will was bitten – his hand.'

'Hepatitis or HIV?'

'The friend is HIV positive. As a precaution Will had to be tested. He wanted to prepare us in case the result . . .' The father's voice faltered.

'How long ago did this happen?'

'Some weeks. I'm not sure.'

'Test results take a long time to come through but

there's a very good chance your son will be clear, especially if the wound bled and was cleaned quickly.'

'It's better we're ready for the worst,' the vicar said.

'"Blessed is he that expecteth nothing, for then he cannot be disappointed",' Tyrell quoted.

There was the faintest glimmer of humour in Reverend Hatton. 'It's a useful maxim, Inspector.'

'I'm sorry I had to be so intrusive but we do have to know everything that occurred in Tolland that week – and why.'

The boy's mother was haggard. 'Does it have to be common knowledge about Will?'

'We would rather the village did not know.' The vicar's request was made with a quaint formality.

'No one will hear it from WDC Paige or myself,' the inspector assured the anxious pair. 'What you have told us will have to be verified and filed, of course. We hear a lot in our investigations. If information is irrelevant to our enquiries, it doesn't reach the public.'

The vicar made a supreme effort to return to normal conversation. 'Orhan, you said, Inspector? Not an English name.'

'No, sir. Mr Orhan was originally from Turkey, although he has lived in Birmingham for some years.'

'Ah, Birmingham. That's the connection.'

'So it would seem, sir.'

The vicar let his thoughts wander for a moment. 'How strange . . .'

'Strange, sir?'

'This Mr Orhan was, I take it, a Muslim?'

'It's probable.'

There was a hint of a smile in Reverend Hatton's eyes. 'That will upset Elsie Slade.'

There was no time for the inspector to consider anyone's feelings, especially those of journalists flooding the village. In spite of constant lenses monitoring police activity, house-to-house questioning had to be completed as quickly as possible.

The blue Mercedes must have been driven to the village and parked somewhere before being moved to Soudley late on the Friday night. Tolland was not the place where a strange car could appear and not be noticed but the first reports back from the police teams were not promising.

Whittaker thumped his desk early next morning. 'I don't believe it! There's no suggestion Orhan had ever been here before, yet he gets himself, and a flashy car, into the village as though they were invisible. He must have had to ask directions from somebody.'

'Perhaps he did.'

Tyrell's voice was quiet, reflective, causing a silence in the restless, smoke-laden air.

'Oh yes, Inspector Tyrell? And who do you suggest?'

Whittaker's curled lip made it clear how much help he expected.

'If Orhan was attempting blackmail and expecting money, his quarry would have been contacted earlier – maybe several times. Supposing he came here for the pay-out? It could have been arranged in a way that made sure no one saw him arrive.'

'And the car?'

'There must be plenty of places where it could have been hidden from view.'

'No way.' DS Simons shook his head at Tyrell's suggestion, delighted at the chance to contradict him so publicly. 'There's nowhere around the village that can't be seen by someone. The odd driveway behind a barn, that sort of thing. Gateways usually lead into fields and farmers are like bloody old women about their land and trespassers.'

'That's it, then,' Whittaker decided. 'I want the village covered again.'

His order was greeted with groans, masculine and feminine. The DCI ignored them all.

'Flash the photo of Orhan around. Some bastard's holding out on us. Get out there and, for God's sake, get some answers this time. Push hard and make it clear we're not going to be messed around.'

The teams began to disperse.

'Tyrell!' Whittaker called. 'You and your little band of warriors are joining me on this one, so no sneaking off for tea and cakes.'

'Sir.'

Tyrell kept a pleasant expression fixed in place as he went to collect his list of houses to be visited.

Emma Paige's eyes were huge. 'Is the DCI always this down on Inspector Tyrell?' she whispered to Brian Clarke.

'This is one of the good days – mind you, Whittaker blows hot and cold. If he thinks the DI's useful, he treats him just like anyone else helping him up the ladder.'

'What's bugging him? Is it because the DI gave evidence against Simons in that enquiry?'

Brian Clarke shook his head. 'The aggro was there way before that. It didn't help when the inspector was made up from sergeant very young. Whittaker believes it was influence.'

'Was it?'

'I thought so at first – until I worked with him. Tyrell got the rank because he's bloody good. He'll be overtaking Whittaker soon because the DI's going far and he's going fast. So will you if you remember he doesn't mind if you forget to say "sir" but he can't stand being called "Guv".'

'Go on then, tell me. The influence. Whose? The chief super?'

'No way. Hinton's as straight as they come, so's Super Mortimer. Tyrell's father is a judge. Sir John Tyrell?'

Emma shook her head.

'Court of Appeal, mostly. He's based in London and there's some old country house on the Wiltshire border that's been in the family for a few hundred years. The

128

DI gets that – and the title – when his old man coughs.'

'Our Mr Whittaker not happy about the idea?'

'He'd give his eye teeth for it. It's just the sort of lifestyle he fancies.' DS Clarke leaned confidentially. 'Mind you, I bet Whittaker fancies Mrs Tyrell too. So would anyone married to his hard-faced bitch of a wife.'

Teams went, worked hard and returned frustrated. The inhabitants of Tolland were polite but had apparently been oblivious to anything leading to the murder of a stranger in their midst.

When every house had been covered, every motorist, cyclist, pedestrian stopped and asked for help, DCI Whittaker was tight-lipped with fury.

'Simons! Have you got an overnight bag?'

County policing might appear less hectic than the town variety but DS Simons, like the rest of the CID, took the precaution of keeping an emergency kit in his car.

'Get it,' Whittaker said. 'We'll have to go to Birmingham. Now!'

Simons headed for the door.

'Tyrell! Repeat the background checks on anyone who's moved into Tolland. Chase up that old woman and get her gossiping. By the time I get back I want an angle. Understand?'

'Yes, sir.'

Tyrell watched with relief as Whittaker swept out. As the sound of a car being driven away fast lessened with distance he turned to face a hushed expectancy.

'You heard the DCI. Trace back everyone in Tolland who hasn't lived here since the day they were born. As soon as you find out where they've come from, get on to the appropriate force and see if anything's known. All requests for help must be classified "Urgent". We've got to get – '

The door opened and Superintendent Mortimer stalked in. Deep lines were engraved from his nose to the edges of a mouth held in tight control and Tyrell sensed the other man's pain.

'Where's DCI Whittaker?'

'On his way to Birmingham, sir.'

'Leaving you in charge?'

'Presumably until you got here, sir.'

Now Tyrell understood the DCI's dash to the Midlands. Mortimer was due to retire soon and, as the date approached, he was becoming increasingly abrasive. Whittaker had left his favourite enemy to catch the flak.

'What've you done?'

Tyrell detailed the work being carried out at each of the computer terminals. As he spoke, phones rang and were answered. Diligent officers were making notes, collating data. No one was idle.

Mortimer surveyed the room, the paperwork on Whittaker's desk. He was about to speak to Tyrell when he turned away, hiding his face. Picking up a file he opened it and appeared to study it intently but the DI could see the older man's grasp crumpling the stiff cover. When his fingers relaxed, the sound of Mortimer's breathing was quieter. He straightened up and faced Tyrell.

'Keep me informed if you turn up anything.'

'Of course, sir.'

'My office will find me.'

Mortimer's skin was pallid, beaded with sweat which was beginning to trickle down the lines in his face. He swung away from Tyrell and walked stiffly back to his car.

'Is he OK?' Brian Clarke asked.

'Far from it. He obviously wants to carry on as normal.'

'Just to get an extra quid or two on his pension?'

'No,' Tyrell said softly. 'Just to give him a reason for getting through each day.'

'Poor old bugger.'

The DI smiled at Clarke's comment. It would have angered Mortimer but the words and tone had carried a wealth of sympathy and respect for the sick man.

'Inspector Tyrell!' Maria Gilbert had been as busy as all the other personnel. 'Major Clawson.'

'Clawson?' Tyrell thought of the houses in the village. 'Orchard Cottage.'

'That's the one. I noticed he'd had a few tours of duty in Cyprus, one of them was about the time my brother-in-law was stationed there. I rang him.'

'Any luck?'

'Eddie remembered Captain Clawson, as he was then. A good officer, strict, tough, with an obsession about Turks.'

'Sounds promising. Did he love or hate them?'

'Hate – and then some, according to Eddie.'

'Go on.'

'Something happened when Clawson was first in Cyprus.'

'The Turkish connection?'

'I don't know but, as Eddie put it, "he hated them more than the Greeks did – and that's saying something".'

'So, Tolland has a Turk-hater. Is there any evidence linking Orhan with Cyprus?'

Brian Clarke leaned on Mrs Gilbert's terminal as she tapped the keyboard. Emma Paige had been listening intently and she bent to read the changing screen.

'No indication,' Mrs Gilbert said. 'Home town a place called Usak. Mainland Turkey by the looks of it.'

Tyrell was thoughtful. 'I know it's already being done but can you double-check Orhan? Anything the DSS can tell us – or a relative of yours who happens to work somewhere useful,' he said with a grin.

'Of course.'

'When I've finished here I'll get round to the Claw-sons.'

Maria Gilbert continued to chase information electronically.

'I didn't know you could handle one of these so well,' Brian Clarke said admiringly. 'I thought you just used it for typing.'

'Two teenage sons. I have to try and keep up with them or they'd con me rigid.'

'Are you any good at computer games?' he teased.

'I'll take you on any time and beat the pants off you.'

Emma Paige raised a hand in horror. 'That, I do not want to see.'

The anger of Tolland mothers, ousted with their toddlers from the village hall, was reaching crisis point when Sir Edward offered the use of a room in the manor. The original kitchen had been vast and draughty, unused since the Land Army vacated it. Swept out and made welcoming with worn carpeting and colourful toys, it provided a place where the under-fives could carry on learning to be sociable.

Elaine Poynter did her best to run the playgroup in its new setting. In her first session she was upset when a child wanted to use its imagination and shut itself in the cupboard of an antique dresser. That panic over she was horrified as a tiny blonde angel began hammering a small boy to his knees.

Eventually, all the children played together fairly harmoniously but the parents were a distraction she could well have done without. With a murderer to be caught they were not prepared to leave their offspring and stayed in a corner of the room. There, they dissected police methods, compared reporters' nasty habits, exchanged gossip and, thanks to a grandfather dozing near off-duty police in the George, were able to circulate the news that the vicar's son had AIDS.

The pub hummed with activity. Sam Roberts was in his shirt-sleeves as he pulled pints and kept the customers orderly while they waited for meals.

Lunch hour in the George had become very elastic. CID men and women, like the reporters, arrived to be fed when work, not the clock, dictated. Uniformed officers were a little more regular but looked just as tired until one of Agnes Morse's hot dishes put life into them again.

PC Cole put his head round the door. 'Briefing in five minutes.'

Food disappeared quickly, glasses were emptied, stray journalists following the police for crumbs of news. The bar was quiet as Myra and Kate, the barmaid, cleared the tables.

An elderly man stirred, apparently after a good snooze. 'They buggers can put away grub,' he grumbled.

'They're working hard,' Sam told him as he wiped the bar.

'Aye, going round the clock to put one of us inside.' Tossy Reynolds nodded his head like a decaying mandarin.

'It's the price of murder.'

'For a bloody foreigner? It's not right!'

'Come on, Tossy. It mightn't be anyone local who's done it. They don't even know who the dead man was.'

'Yes, they do. Have done since yesterday. He's from Birmingham. A Turk.'

'You've been ear-wigging again, letting them think you were asleep. Tossy Reynolds, you'll get run in for that one day.'

'It'll be in the papers tomorrow,' Tossy protested. 'I was saving you buyin' one.'

133

'What else did they say?' Cyril Mitton moved from his seat by the bar, the better to listen.

'Griping, they was, having to go through the whole village again, looking for a Brummie connection.'

'And a Turkish one too, I expect,' Sam said. 'Just as well we don't go anywhere posh for our holidays, love!' he called to his wife.

Myra laid a tray of glasses on the bar. 'Chance would be a fine thing. Turkey.' She was puzzled. 'Who went to Turkey this year?'

'David Bryce and his wife,' Kate told her as she went past with stacked crockery. 'And last year. They like it there.'

'No, it wasn't them.' Myra pursued a wisp of memory.

'Your young Pam likes going on they package dos.' Tossy Reynolds had a wicked glint in his eye as he teased Cyril. 'Her'd go anywhere hunting a man.'

Sam laughed. 'She wore out the men and the boys at home.'

Cyril refused to be angered by his granddaughter's antics. 'No go in 'em. Same wi' all you youngsters – '

'Mr Maynard!' Myra exclaimed. 'That's who it was. He flew out and went sailing.'

'I thought he liked Greece?' Kate said.

'He does but last time it was Turkey.'

'If it's him they're after, no matter,' Tossy Reynolds decided. 'He's not one of us.'

Orchard Cottage, larger than its name suggested, rested double-fronted in a dream of a garden. The DI and his sergeant admired the setting as they waited for their knock to be answered.

Mrs Clawson was in her sixties and a lady on duty in cashmere and pearls. Warrant cards were read carefully and the policemen were invited into a pleasant room scented by bowls of flowers.

Brian Clarke spotted signs of wear in the furniture as well as mementoes of service life spent in exotic postings as the DI took stock of the major. The army man's handshake was firm but Keith Tyrell saw the care with which he moved. Under the neat moustache there was a white line around lips that were distinctly blue.

Seated, Major Clawson's colour improved. He straightened the cravat at his neck, regimental colours muted in the silk. Inspector Tyrell began the routine, going over the dates and times the Clawsons had given the last police questioners.

'And the Friday evening?'

'The Masons came from Newnham. For bridge. They didn't stay too late.' Mrs Clawson smiled at her visitors. 'We keep country hours.'

It was all very civilised. Tyrell steered his questioning to cover Major Clawson's first Cyprus posting.

'1955. I was a young subaltern, not long out of Sandhurst.'

His eyes lost their sharp focus and Tyrell sensed the old man was back in the hot sun of the eastern Mediterranean.

'All hell was breaking loose. The Turks wanted control of the island, so did the Greeks – except for patriots who insisted, very loudly, on complete independence from Athens. God, the noise! Greeks like shouting.'

'And fighting?' Tyrell asked.

'Being Greeks they had to fight – second nature to 'em. They fought the Turks, they fought us and they fought each other. I don't know if you're aware of the Greeks as warriors, Inspector, but even Hitler respected them.' The major's tone suggested Hitler was not alone.

'The Turks?'

'Same sort of thing, really.' Major Clawson sighed, an old man's sigh. 'It was one hell of a mess.'

'Tell them,' his wife begged.

He smiled at her. 'If you think I should, my dear.'

There was a pink spot of colour high on each cheek bone as he faced Tyrell. 'December '55. Two of my men set off for Nicosia. They were just a couple of National Servicemen off duty and wanting to see something of the island. Had they been regulars they might have been more cautious but they were due for demob in a couple of weeks. I know I did my damnedest to warn all of them what could happen.'

The pink spots had become an angry red flush. Mrs Clawson began to move towards her husband, stopped by a gesture from the inspector.

'They disappeared,' the major told them. 'At first it was thought they'd gone AWOL. It was two days before their bodies were found on the road to Kythrea, north of Nicosia. Turkish territory. That didn't mean much. It could just as easily have been EOKA madmen trying to make the Turks look guilty.'

'How could you be sure they were killed by Turks?' Tyrell wanted to know.

'You make it sound very quick, very clinical, Inspector. I'm afraid it wasn't like that. I was in charge of the patrol sent to recover the bodies. They'd both been tortured for hours before their throats were cut.'

He was silent, mourning his men afresh.

'I wanted to get my hands on the bastards responsible but facts were hard to come by. Neither side was prepared to help the British. In the end, Army Intelligence pulled in a few informers and sweated them. Word was passed on a group of Turks who had been boasting about what they'd done – how the brave British soldiers squealed like frightened little lambs before they were slaughtered.'

'Proof?'

'No forensic teams in those day, Inspector. No DNA. All we knew were the names of the killers.' Exhausted, the major lay back in his chair. 'There was one consolation. Informants not only brought in information, they also took it out. Patriots were purists and murderers

136

were dealt with quickly. Four fewer psychopaths for the new Cyprus.'

Mrs Clawson led the way to the front door. 'Tell me, Inspector Tyrell, why do you want to know about my husband's experiences in Cyprus?'

'The man buried in the churchyard was originally from Turkey.'

'Oh, now I understand. You had to follow up any possible link.'

'I'm sorry it was necessary,' Tyrell assured her.

'It's not your fault, Inspector. We chose to live in Tolland and make friends here. Whoever committed the crime involved us all.' Anxiety was back in her eyes. 'It's the nightmares, d'you see. Because of those boys in Cyprus Peter had terrible dreams. Even after we married they came back to haunt him, especially when he was stationed there. There were nights he'd wake sobbing – absolutely shattered. When he knows this man was a Turk I'm afraid they'll start again and the doctor insists Peter must be free of stress. During the day I can keep everything calm. When he's asleep, I'm helpless. If his heart starts pounding too much . . .'

Pigeons in a nearby tree called to each other as Tyrell and his sergeant walked down the path. Once in the car they sat in silence.

'If the nightmares get bad enough to give the major a heart attack that kills him . . .' Brian Clarke said.

'Our murderer will have bagged another victim.'

The DI switched on the engine and gripped the steering wheel.

'We've got to get him – and fast.'

Chapter Seven

'Paige.'

The girl looked up at Tyrell. 'Sir?'

'We've just been to the Masons in Newnham. They back up the bridge session at the Clawsons'.' He turned to Mrs Gilbert at a nearby terminal. 'Would you enter it, please.'

'They're in the clear?' she asked.

'There's no way Major Clawson could have lifted a shovel, let alone a corpse, without having a heart attack. If Clawson killed it would have to be in a fair fight and then he's the sort who'd have turned himself in.'

'What about money?' Emma Paige wanted to know. 'Could Orhan have been blackmailing them?'

'Over something that happened so long ago in Cyprus? It's possible but Orhan's friend, Kemal, seemed to think there was cash for the taking. The Clawsons live comfortably but carefully. I'd guess pension rather than capital.'

Brian Clarke was not so sure. 'They looked well off.'

'Appearances can be deceptive. If they had money in the bank do you think the major would be waiting in line for a heart op?'

Emma Paige and Maria Gilbert were going through a list of the newer residents, some of whom Tyrell had already visited.

'Burfield and Phipps,' Emma said.

Maria Gilbert began to read from the data on the

screen. 'Dennis Burfield, aged fifty-one, lives at Green-bank. Writes articles on gardening and cookery for the glossies so he's quite well known. Nothing on him in our records. Martin Draper says the wife died seven years ago – that's when he moved to Tolland.'

'Background on Phipps?'

'Nigel Phipps, forty-two, tutors would-be writers by post. He's also a reader for one of the big publishing houses.'

'Family?'

'Parents in Norfolk, brother in Australia, wife in a mental home.'

Tyrell raised an eyebrow. 'No care in the community?'

Maria Gilbert shook her head. 'According to Martin she's bad and it's progressive.'

The DI had no doubt. 'He won't divorce her – not the man I talked to.'

Emma went back to her list. 'What about the Walkers, sir?'

'No. Both of them are gormless. They'd never have done anything risqué enough for blackmail.'

'Then the nearest is Mrs Poynter – originally from Tipton.'

'Staffordshire. It's close.' The inspector hesitated. 'There was something about that house.'

'They're being checked out now, sir. DC Edison was allocated them.'

Emma Paige pointed to a young man intent on his computer work, the light of a fanatic in his eyes.

'What I'm after may not be easy to find out that way. It's Mrs Poynter. She's listed as an Oxford graduate and had all the right photos on the walls, even one of a punt on the Isis – which is a bit extreme.' Tyrell frowned. 'There was something wrong with the pattern.'

'What college, sir?'

'Maybe that was it. There was a Wadham crest in the hall but she talked of living with just women. It should have been St Hilda's. See to it, Paige. You may have to go and nose around a bit. Tell me if you do and I'll clear it with Oxford CID.'

Tyrell went on an inspection tour of the incident room. He expressed pleasure when he found work completed efficiently, frowned over any detected slackness.

Emma Paige watched him. 'If the Poynters aren't really suspects, why does he bother?' she asked Brian Clarke.

'I used to wonder when I first worked with him. Lots of guvnors pride themselves on spotting the suspect early on, then concentrate everything on nailing them. Tyrell now, he spots them OK but still insists on covering all leads.'

'Why? Surely it's a waste of time and money?'

'He says not. The CPS are more likely to go ahead with a case if they know it can't be thrown out because of police bias. If every possible suspect's been investigated, the defence can't cop a plea of police victimisation.'

'It makes sense.'

'Modern methods for modern villains – with all their rights and privileges.'

'And less chance of the case being thrown out on appeal. The DI will have heard his father go on about lack of proper evidence.'

'Which is what you'll get from Tyrell Junior if you don't sort out Mrs Poynter.'

'What's she like?'

'Thirties, not pretty but she does what she can.'

'There's not a lot of personality – she's very keen on copying Lady Driffield.'

Emma Paige chuckled. 'And him?'

'An accountant in Gloucester,' he said slowly, his heavy brows drawing together.

'What's the matter?'

'There didn't seem to be much cash around, know what I mean? An accountant?'

'I'll leave all that to Mark Edison. What I need is a photo of Mrs Poynter.'

'And her maiden name,' she was reminded.

'Yes, Sergeant Clarke,' Emma said, sounding like a grandmother not in the habit of sucking eggs.

The percolator plopped to a climax and Dennis Burfield stopped chopping vegetables to wipe his hands across the blue and white apron he wore. He rapped a message on the window then called, 'Mrs Baker!' at the foot of the stairs and returned to his chore, a well-built man with a pleasant, pudgy face and thick grey hair curling into his neck.

A pile of bed linen hid the person hurrying into the kitchen. 'I'll just get these going first,' a woman mumbled as she made for the washing machine in the scullery.

The door from the garden opened and closed.

'Coffee? Just what I need.'

Nigel Phipps was of medium height and rangy in old slacks and a check shirt. Exposed skin was weather-beaten and topped by fine brown hair which flopped over one eye. Dennis pushed a mug of black coffee towards his friend and he sipped appreciatively.

'Where's Mrs Baker?'

'Here I am – and gasping for my elevenses!'

Dennis smiled at the woman in an enveloping overall. She was stout, with frizzy light brown hair and protruding eyes behind large glasses. Her coffee, heavy with cream, sugar and a dash of rum, was sampled. Mrs Baker beamed at the two men as she licked her lips.

Nigel pushed the biscuit tin towards her. She reached in and the three sat companionably quiet in the large, homely kitchen redolent with good food past and present.

'Any news from the village?' Dennis asked her.

'Oh, it's all murder these days. Bad enough all those

141

bits of kids in Gloucester but when it's on your own doorstep, so to speak . . .'

Nigel selected shortbread. 'It must be very disturbing.'

'I should say!' Mrs Baker swallowed more coffee. 'Visitors in the George pushing the regulars to one side – though Stan says Sam Roberts is very good and don't stand no nonsense.'

'Are the reporters much of a nuisance?' Dennis asked.

'They're not too bad. They like to sit and talk big about murders they've been on. Mind you, there was one got his hand on Kate and then there was a to-do. Myra Roberts flared up and set about him. Right temper Myra's got if her staff get upset. Well, I mean to say, she needs to keep 'em happy, the trade they're doing. My God, but those coppers can eat! Stan says Myra Roberts must be making a packet on food.'

'Are they getting anywhere? The police?' Nigel asked.

'Dunno. They don't say much, just ask questions all the time. Most seem harmless and ask what's expected.' Mrs Baker stared at her mug. 'One or two are rougher than they need be. Myself, I think they get a kick out of it.'

She drained her mug and Dennis dutifully refilled it, adding the extras discreetly.

'Who've they upset?' Nigel asked.

'The Bryces, David and his wife – and old Noah at death's door. It's not right.'

The fresh coffee was sipped. Mrs Baker's cheeks became red and her views increasingly forceful.

'Just because David likes going to Turkey on holiday and there's plenty of cash in the family, they decided he was being blackmailed by this man from Birmingham.'

'Is that the only reason they picked on him?' Dennis wanted to know.

'So Stan says – he heard it in the George. The police

142

have been on to anyone in the village with money who's been to Turkey.'

'What about the Driffields?' Nigel said. 'They're wealthy.'

Mrs Baker shook her head. 'August, it's shooting in Scotland. January it's skiing with the boys. If they fancy a bit of sun it's usually the Bahamas – there's a house out there. No, only David and Megan fitted the bill. He had her in tears, you know. Megan Bryce.'

'Who did?'

'The sergeant who pestered them. Big man, oily hair and always wears black. The things he wanted to know!' Mrs Baker leaned forward. 'Their sex life,' she whispered. 'Megan told Sally Lumsden she just feels dirty all the time now.'

'We must've been lucky,' Dennis said. 'Inspector Tyrell was very civilised. So was his sergeant.'

'Efficient, though,' Nigel added.

'He certainly was,' his friend agreed. 'I wouldn't like to have a dark corner in my memory. He'd suss it out in thirty seconds flat.'

Nigel finished his coffee. 'Just as well we've got a clean bill of health.'

'That reminds me,' Mrs Baker said as she stood up. 'I'll finish your bedroom today, Mr Burfield, and give Mr Phipps a good do next time I come. OK?'

Collating all the information pouring into the incident room was a massive job. WDS Rogers proved her worth assembling, linking, sorting, enabling the inspector to be kept up to date with essential data.

'The Perkins family, Church Road,' Penny Rogers said. 'Their details came through very quickly. He and Mrs Perkins settled here three years ago and fitted in well. He works for a plumber in Lydney.'

'They came from?'

'Leicester – where his real wife lives.'

'Nasty for him,' Tyrell said and grinned.

'He's going berserk in case she gets hold of his address and demands maintenance.'

'Children?'

'Not with her. He's had two since he arrived in Tolland.'

'Two in three years? It must be something in the water. Let's hope no one gets the idea of bottling it. Anything else?'

'Not a lot. The other families check out clean. There's no GBH, ABH, not even domestic violence reported. Tolland's definitely the place to live if you want peace and quiet.'

'DCI Whittaker is due back tomorrow morning. There may be something by then.'

'The super rang while you were at the Clawsons. I updated him as far as I could. All he seemed to need was the assurance everyone was being investigated thoroughly.'

'How did he sound?'

Penny Rogers looked sharply at Tyrell. 'Tired.'

'He's still damned good at his job,' the DI said. 'Did he make any suggestion?'

'No. He said you had everything well in hand.'

Tyrell met speculation in Penny Roger's eyes, perhaps the beginning of respect.

'We're still no nearer an answer. Get a list of the most likely suspects from each of the teams and check them out again.'

'Any special ones you want targeted?'

Tyrell knew Whittaker would look for any sign of a neglected lead. 'All of them – without exception.'

'It'll take time.'

'I agree – and it's time which is helping a murderer cover his tracks. I'll say one thing for him. He's got nerve.'

'Are you so sure it's a man? Couldn't a woman have done the killing?'

'Oh yes, no doubt about it. If that were all I think we'd have the murderer by now but there's a man in it too. Strong enough to carry the body and bury it. Canny enough to slow us up by getting rid of clothes, finger-prints, facial features. Even the wreaths were put back in exact order, with just one ninety degrees out.'

'The one that upset your friend Mrs Slade.'

There was a commotion at the far end of the room. The DI and Penny Rogers turned to look at the source of the noise. Elsie Slade was hatted and ready for battle.

'He's busy, Mrs Slade.'

Penny Rogers chuckled. 'Talk of the devil.'

'I'm going to see Inspector Tyrell, so just get out of my way,' she shouted at the very tall young man in uniform who was trying to keep order.

'It's all right, Constable,' Tyrell said.

Having got what she wanted, Elsie Slade drooped, became small and tired.

'Could you find us some tea, please?' Tyrell asked the policeman.

'None of that weak stuff, mind,' Mrs Slade insisted.

With a grin the PC went off to do her bidding and Maria Gilbert came to help.

'Mrs Slade, it's nice to see you again. How's your daughter?'

'Agnes? She's all right. Why shouldn't she be?' Agnes' mother back in fighting mood.

'No reason. Come and sit down. The inspector's busy but I'm sure he'll find time for you.'

Tyrell seated himself beside Elsie Slade and accepted a mug from the constable, thanking him.

'Mrs Slade, how can I help you?'

Eyes averted, she sipped from her cup. The DI noticed Maria Gilbert had produced good china for the visitor. The cup was placed carefully in its saucer and the teaspoon straightened. She was hesitating to speak and he sensed the source of her distress.

'You're still worried about your husband.'

145

His words were gentle, consoling, and the difficult tears of old age started. Elsie Slade pulled a tissue from her pocket and blew her nose.

'It's not proper. I should be able to take Fred flowers and talk to him like always.'

Tyrell had seen the grave. It was tidy again, the dead flowers discarded. Only the widow's wreath remained, watered regularly by Reg Warren.

'What stops you?'

'That other man. It's just as if he's between us. I can't tell Fred what I want to with him listening.'

'No, you're quite right, you can't. Have you talked to Reverend Hatton about it?'

She snorted. 'He don't go about the village like he used to – and his wife. Shut themselves away, they have, since all this fuss come. How could he help, anyroad?'

Because it was his job, Tyrell thought. 'Do you want me to have a chat with him?'

'Would you?' The little eyes gleamed. 'He'd listen to you.'

The buzz of noise in the room was of many people working.

'What they all doing?'

The inspector explained as simply as he could. He kept from Elsie Slade that the main objective was to lay bare the past lives of everyone in Tolland if it became necessary.

In spite of the massive coverage of investigations in and around Gloucester, there had been no let-up in the media attention in Tolland. Every time Tyrell walked between his car and the village hall it was a quiet battle to fend off persistent journalists. He remained courteous and referred all questions to the police press office so that it was interviews with residents which filled columns and satisfied the ghoulish curiosity of an invisible public.

Mrs Fell grieved in front of the cameras for the demise of the community spirit. She blamed the latest murder and police activity for her loss of trade. Elsie Slade snapped at the reporters, advising them to 'Bugger off and leave us in peace.'

The rest of the village remained tight-lipped, refusing comment. In the George the exceptions to the rule of silence were Cyril Mitton and Tossy Reynolds. They sat in their respective corners and fed crime reporters and sundry strangers enough imaginary gossip to maintain a steady supply of ale.

The pace of work in the incident room was relentless. Searches by computer, fax and phone produced a mass of data. It was hard, intricate work, with only an occasional reward.

'Guv – Sir!'

Tyrell went swiftly to the detective who had called him.

'What've you got?'

'I rang Leamington and asked about Mrs Gallagher.'

'Gallagher?'

'Yes, sir. Widow. Big new bungalow on the Gloucester road – Southfork, the locals call it – and she's not been there long. She retired to Tolland but was born here so wasn't on the "new to area" list. Someone mentioned she and her husband kept a pub in Leamington so I rang the local station on the off-chance.'

There was an air of suppressed excitement about the man, whose eyes were tired from monitoring the screen of his terminal.

'And?'

'One of the sergeants had lived in Leamington all his life. He had the idea the Gallaghers moved in from Birmingham.'

'Great! Well done,' Tyrell said. 'Put them both through

the wringer. If you can find out Mrs Gallagher's maiden name, put that through too.'

'Yes, sir. By the way, Mrs Gallagher's credit rating's good. Very good. I wouldn't mind having one like that. She could've got a pile of notes together very quickly.'

'It sounds promising. Let me know what you get.'

'Yes, sir. Where will you be?'

'The vicarage.'

'Inspector Tyrell.'

There was a chill in the courtesy from Reverend Hatton when he answered the DI's knock.

'May I talk to you?'

'You have no sergeant with you. Is it an official matter?'

'No, sir. I'm here more as a messenger.'

The atmosphere thawed slightly. 'I never suspected you of having winged feet, Inspector. You'd better come in.'

'I was hoping you'd walk to the churchyard with me.'

'If you wish.'

The two men went towards the place where so many had come and gone in the last few days. The marks of many feet remained in the turf and on the gravel of the paths but Reg Warren had done a good job. The mound of earth that was Fred Slade's grave had a simple dignity again.

'You've come from Mrs Slade, of course. I should have been to see her . . .'

The spectre of an anxious boy stood with them.

'I understand, sir.'

The vicar looked up at Tyrell. 'Yes, Inspector, I think you do. So, what does Mrs Slade want now?'

'To talk to her Fred.'

Nicholas Hatton smiled. 'It's a habit she'd have great difficulty breaking. How does it involve me?'

148

Tyrell explained the silent listener. The vicar pursed his lips, clicking his tongue against the roof of his mouth as he considered the problem.

'It may be she's merely having difficulty coming to terms with an extra body buried there, even if it has been moved. On the other hand, she could be aware of an unsettled spirit.' Reverend Hatton gnawed a thumb joint. 'I doubt anything I did would be of use – I'm too familiar.' He gnawed some more, then nodded, his mind made up. 'Father Andrew would be perfect. Very high church, Father Andrew, very learned in church rituals. If there is a way of moving Mr Orhan's spirit, Father Andrew will know it and carry out the appropriate offices.'

'Bell, book and candle?'

'Perhaps not excommunication, Inspector,' the vicar chided. 'Mr Orhan was not of our faith but Father Andrew may have the means of helping the poor man back to his own spiritual world.'

'As long as it means Mrs Slade can get back to talking to her Fred.'

Reverend Hatton's expression was serious but his eyes were merry. 'Are you sure, Inspector, that is what her Fred wants?'

Keith Tyrell found it good to stretch his legs on the way back to a pile of paperwork demanding his attention. No journalists watched for him. It was the start of the George's lunch hour and reporters would be pushing hard to get the first of the meals hot from the oven.

As the DI neared the hall he heard the sound of an argument, then his name was mentioned. He slowed, trying to identify the verbal combatants. Without a doubt Elsie Slade was one and she was giving some poor soul hell. Tyrell stood in the lee of the wall surrounding the pub's car park and listened.

'You've got to tell him, Steve. It's no use expecting

Terry to do it for you – he wouldn't give them the time of day. Anyroad, you was the one driving.'

'It's not right! He's still one of the village.'

'No he's not, he's a foreigner. If one of they buried that poor little devil with my Fred, then the sooner the bugger's locked away the better.'

'You don't know he's the one did it, so what's the use of me telling?'

'Then why'd he run?'

There was no answer, the man stumped for a reply. Curiosity made Tyrell move, his feet crunching loose gravel on the side of the road. Elsie Slade spotted him.

'There he is! I told you, Steve. He'll listen to you.'

The DI recognised Elsie's companion, a stolid man of middle age, his broad features unhappy.

'Mrs Slade, I've just seen Reverend Hatton and he's taking action on your behalf. He'll be coming to see you.'

'I told you he wasn't like the rest,' the doughty little lady scolded her companion.

'Is there a problem?'

Tyrell looked from Elsie Slade to the worried man who stood beside her.

'This lummox is Steve Perry, he's foreman to Noah Bryce and he's got some information you should know about. Go on!' she said as she dealt Steve a sharp blow in the ribs with her elbow.

Few men dared to argue with the little lady and Steve Perry was not one of them.

'The morning the skeleton was dug up.'

'Something happened?'

'I was driving Terry Butcher to the field where he was digging the drainage ditch.'

'This was early?'

'Before eight o'clock. Quarter to, I'd guess. We'd not long turned in off the Gloucester road and I wasn't going fast – Terry was ready for once. Anyway, this car came at me and I had to get out the way or hit it. There was a wide bit of grass there so we didn't come to no harm, just stalled.'

'You were forced off the road by a car being driven very fast and coming from Tolland?'

Steve nodded. 'Bloody madman, he was.'

'Did you get his number?'

'No need. There's not that many BMWs this way so you get to know who has what.'

'The driver?'

'Maynard.'

'He lives at Puddle Cottage,' Elsie Slade added importantly. 'Worked in London, somewhere like that, and had a breakdown. Retired early.'

'Early! Lucky bastard. He's not much older than me. I can't see Noah Bryce letting me take it easy before I'm sixty-five.'

The DI needed to be sure. 'If he was travelling so fast, how can you know who was driving?'

'I tell you, it was him.'

'It's important, Mr Perry. Did you recognise the car and guess it was the man?'

'No. He's got red hair and I saw his face. He looked weird, like he was driving in his sleep. I don't reckon he even knew the van was in his road.'

Once Tyrell was in the village hall he moved quickly.

'Maynard.'

Penny Rogers looked up from her work. 'Maynard, Puddle Cottage. He wasn't here at the relevant times.'

'Who says he wasn't?'

She sorted through the files muttering 'Maynard' to herself until she found the right one.

'A Mrs Munt, cleaner,' she read. 'He's often away and she keeps the place aired. Maynard, Jeremy James, left for London the Monday before the Slade funeral. He hasn't been back since.'

'Oh yes, he has, and I've at least one witness prepared to say so. Jeremy James Maynard was seen leaving Tolland at seven forty-five on the Monday morning after the funeral. I don't know how long he'd been home but he was going like a bat out of hell when he left.' Tyrell smiled at Penny Rogers. 'I think we should have a word with Jeremy James, don't you, Sergeant? With his BMW he shouldn't be too hard to trace.'

Penny Rogers set the hunt in motion. 'How did you find out about him?' she asked the DI.

'I didn't. It was Elsie Slade wearing her deputy's badge. Is there someone free to go and get a statement? It'd better be done quickly. I think Perry's nervous about being seen helping us with our enquiries.'

Penny Rogers was annoyed. 'He should come in.'

'Perhaps he should but don't forget he's got to live in Tolland after we've gone. We've caused enough of an upheaval without adding extra bother.'

'Bother? You've that Mrs Slade coming in every whipstitch.'

'She's by way of being a Judas lamb, you might say. So, who's free?'

'Mark Edison could do with stretching his legs.'

'Then get him off to Steve Perry's house. The end one of the council terrace on the Blakeney road.'

'Which end?'

'Edison can show us just how good he is – and find out,' Tyrell said with a grin. 'I'll take DS Clarke and see what Mrs Gallagher has to offer.'

'You'd better be careful,' Penny Rogers said, trying hard to keep a straight face. 'We looked her up under her maiden name of King. Several arrests for prostitution many years back and mostly in London. Another two charges were for keeping a house of ill-repute.'

'She was a madam?'

'And then some.'

'Where?'

'Birmingham. The vice squad up there don't remember her personally – before their time, they'd have me believe.'

'And she came back here to live,' Tyrell said softly. 'If she wanted to keep her past quiet . . .'

'It would make a very good motive for blackmail but she was out of the village that weekend – in Ireland. She checked out clean.'

The very new bungalow sprawled magnificently. Tyrell could understand why it was called Southfork by the villagers when the name on the gatepost spelled 'Dungannon'.

Mrs Gallagher opened the door to the ring of the bell, its chimes rich and fluting. As Tyrell and Clarke extended their warrant cards they realised they were being assessed by a pair of very shrewd, tawny eyes.

Tyrell had half-expected her to favour leopard-skin print, revising his ideas of the lady when he saw the paisley silk of her dress was cut in a style more Sandringham than Soho. Her hair was stylishly blonde and make-up perfect on wide-boned features.

'Inspector Tyrell.' The voice had the roughness of too many years of cigarette smoking and early coughing. 'I've heard of you. I must be important if you're here yourself. Come on in.'

Mrs Gallagher studied Brian Clarke, her eyes lingering on strong thighs as he walked past her.

The house surprised Tyrell. There were no satin drapes or cushions, no plush-covered chairs. Instead there was a feeling of air and light. An occasional vibrant colour in the glass of a huge vase or a wall-hanging punctuated the simplicity of pastel fabrics and well-designed furniture.

Mischief hovered in Mrs Gallagher's smile. 'Welcome to my home, Inspector. I'd offer you a drink but you're not the man to take one when you're on duty. How about tea?'

153

'Maybe later?'

'Get comfortable, then. I guess you want to know all about my past – the bits you haven't already got in your computer.' She tossed her head at DS Clarke. 'Will he take notes?' Her eyes were on the sergeant as she waited for the DI's reply.

'Do you mind?'

'Not a bit.'

Mrs Gallagher nestled into the corner of a chesterfield and crossed her legs, silk swishing over the fullness.

'You were born in Tolland?'

'Not actually in the village, Mayhill's out a bit. The Kings never had much to do with Tolland – except on Sundays. My grandfather was very keen on church-going.'

'Then the Mr King who farms Mayhill is . . .'

'My uncle. There's no use asking him about me. As far as he's concerned I died years ago. In fact he prefers to pretend I never existed. Well, I've returned and I'm the proverbial thorn in his side.' She turned the full beam of her smile on the two men. 'I was a bastard. My mother had me after a romp in the hay with a Yank she met in Gloucester.'

Tyrell raised an eyebrow. 'Any particular Yank?'

'Danny McNaughton from South Dakota. He was one of those killed on D-Day.'

'You're sure?'

'Sure he was killed?'

'That he was your father.'

'Positive. My mother died when I was ten and I found the letters he'd written her. And his photo.'

Heavy gold gleamed as her fingers pointed to a silver-framed photo on a nearby table. Tyrell picked it up and saw the same wide cheek bones and firm nose in the father as in the daughter. Danny McNaughton had been a large, blond, smiling man.

'After your mother's death?'

'It wasn't much fun.' There was bleakness in her

154

voice. 'I didn't live as part of the family. My grand-mother did her best but she was a poorly little thing and ashamed of me. The Kings were all so good, you see, and God had punished them by giving them a bastard to raise. I got out as soon as I could.' A past hell flickered across her face. 'I'd been fair game on the farm, all the men trying it on – like mother like daughter. By the time I left all I wanted was to make men pay.'

'Where did you go?'

'London – where else? A pimp picked me up on the station and tried to force me in a car but I kicked him in the balls and ran. A girl on a street near Paddington took me back with her. She had a room in a house owned by a Mrs Baghurst. Fanny Baghurst was ugly, old and scarred.' A manicured finger drew a line from throat to forehead. 'She was kind to me in her way, even if she made a fortune out of the rent she charged. Still, she got us seen to if we were knocked up, made sure we ate properly and kept clean. It wasn't a bad life and I was saving hard.'

'What for?'

'I didn't know. Just something better.'

Tyrell smiled. 'You obviously got it.'

'It was slow. I managed to buy my own flat and built up a good set of clients.'

'Did you want a different kind of life?'

'Get off my back, you mean?' Suddenly, she was tired and looked her age. 'What else did I know? I'd had it rammed down my throat often enough. "Seed of a whore". My grandfather loved calling me that. Whoring seemed like the family tradition. I just worked hard at making it a profitable one.'

'This is still in London?'

Mrs Gallagher nodded.

'When did you go to Birmingham?'

''74. Gerry Hancock, one of my men friends, he came from there and suggested I move up. His wife had died and the travelling was getting to him. Gerry was in the building trade and had a good nose for property. He helped me invest. When he died I settled down a bit.'

'And ran a house of your own?'

She chuckled. 'My social work.'

'Mr Gallagher?'

There was a softness about her. 'Martin, God bless him. He came to do the roof and treated me like a lady. Martin was a big man in every way. He said all he'd ever wanted to do was run a pub – not that he drank much and that's strange for an Irishman. He got what he wanted but not in Birmingham – said Leamington was more my sort of place. Bless him, he wouldn't have me working behind the bar or in the kitchen.'

'How long did it last?'

'Until he died. Three years ago last month.' Curves in her face became angles of desolation.

'You still miss him?'

'Every day.' The silence was sad before she stirred and became brisk. 'Come on, Inspector. You're not here to talk about my love life.'

Brian Clarke showed her the picture of Orhan and outlined the man's background.

'So, because I lived in Brum you want to know if I ever met the man buried with poor old Fred.'

'Did you?'

'Not to my knowledge. I didn't have much to do with Turks, they mostly keep to themselves. I'm guessing you think he was here to put the black on someone. I've a bob or two in the bank and property in Birmingham, I'm the most likely person.'

'One of them.'

She laughed, a deep-throated, happy sound. 'Not me.'

'Why should I believe you?'

'Why not? I've nothing to hide. Tolland's my village. Everyone knows how I got my money and they envy me every penny of it – that's the way I want it. Don't forget, I'd have lost everything years ago if I hadn't learned how to take care of myself. My money came the hard

156

way and I'm not letting anyone get their grubby paws on it. If any little toe-rag had come near me wanting an early pension, I've still got contacts who'd give him a right seeing-to. There'd have been no mess on my doorstep and I wouldn't have to do more than lift the phone.'

'Any joy with Mrs Gallagher?' Penny Rogers wanted to know.

'An interesting visit,' Tyrell said, 'but she's in the clear.'

Brian Clarke hunted through his notebook. 'Her dates and times rule her out. She'd left for Ireland before Fred Slade died and didn't return until a week after the funeral. Flew from Cardiff and drove herself both ways to the airport.'

'It all matches the original statement and we checked that. What about the Birmingham connection?'

'That's all it is, a connection,' Tyrell said. 'Mrs Gallagher's come back to Tolland to make her family realise she's a damn sight better off than they are. There's no way she's trying to hide her past. If anything, she wants to rub her uncle's nose in it.'

'I gather the lady impressed,' Penny Rogers said. She had caught grudging admiration in Tyrell's defence of her.

'So much so,' he said, 'that if she needs us at the house for any reason, for God's sake don't send Clarke or we'll never see him again.'

'But what a way to go,' that gentleman said with a blissful smile.

'Anything new?' Tyrell asked Penny Rogers.

'The DCI phoned – or rather, Pete Simons did on his behalf. They've got some interesting details but he wouldn't say what.'

It hung unspoken in the air that DCI Whittaker would keep anything useful to himself.

'Maynard?'

'Not located yet,' Penny Rogers said. 'He does consultancy work for his old firm, Maynard, Webster and Bailey. I tried to talk to the partners but both were unavailable, Webster in conference and Bailey away on business.'

'The other two aren't our pigeons, Maynard is. Keep up the pressure to find him.'

Tyrell went to where Brian Clarke was typing up his notes.

'There's nothing more you can do tonight. Get off home to that poor wife of yours.'

'Thank you very much! She'll just have time to get me mowing the lawn,' the sergeant groaned.

The DI grinned. 'Do you good. You need some hard, physical effort to get your mind back up to your brain – from where Mrs Gallagher sent it.'

'She's some woman!'

'She certainly is,' Tyrell agreed. 'Tolland seems to breed 'em tough.'

After his sergeant left, Tyrell sat deep in thought. Tolland breeds them tough. An idea bubbled. He ambled over to Penny Roger's desk and leaned on the terminal.

'You know, we've all been so busy looking for a link with Birmingham we may be ignoring the obvious.'

'Which is?'

'Our man's home-grown. Have all the village people been processed through records?'

'Everyone listed. Men, women, juveniles. There were the usual traffic offences, driving bans, shoplifting – that was juvenile. There was nothing Martin Draper didn't know about.'

'Was there anything he did know that wasn't in the data bank?'

'Nothing that hadn't been through the courts.'

'It's here,' Tyrell said softly, 'and it's staring us in the face.'

'Orhan came from Birmingham. It must be relevant.'

The DI shook his head. 'That's just a diversion, I'm sure of it.'

'Inspector Tyrell!' Maria Gilbert held a phone towards him. 'Your wife.'

It was unusual for her to ring him at work. 'Jenny, is everything OK?'

'Yes, darling. I just wondered when you'd be home. Clay Gifford's coming to dinner. He phoned here to find you and I invited him. Is that all right?'

'Of course. Whittaker's not due in until tomorrow morning so I'll be on call.'

'What's new, pussy-cat?'

Her voice was light, amused, with no undercurrent of bitterness. The DI thanked God yet again for the miracle that was Jenny.

'I'll be home as soon as I can.'

'Promises, promises,' she said with a laugh and the line died.

He watched the flow of movement in the room, the intensity of concentration with which men and women sought answers from their computers. Tyrell itched for action.

'I'll take a walk round the village,' he said to Penny Rogers. 'I've got my mobile if you need me.'

'Looking for ghosts?'

'Something like that.'

As evening approached the air was fresh, cool. Tyrell strode down the lane that led the short distance to the river. The Severn flowed beyond the slimy grey of the mudbanks and he saw the direction of the tide. The current was north, towards Gloucester, the force of the water swirling shoals near the bank.

Tyrell looked down at his shoes and was annoyed to see the grey mud that spattered them. Tussocks of tough grass helped him clean off what he could before he walked back towards the village.

The air of Tolland moved past him and he closed his eyes, savouring the place. Was the smell of frying bacon real or only in his imagination? The sound of a door banging and a deep voice grumbling came from the direction of the George. The pub would soon be occupied by its regulars as they washed down their evening meals.

Human life was hidden from him by stones and bricks. Somewhere one, perhaps two, moved as did their neighbours but they were his prey. He could not see them, did not know their faces, but he knew they were there.

The DI walked on and leaned on the lychgate into the churchyard. He looked towards the plot where Fred Slade slept alone. 'Well, almost alone,' he said to himself and smiled. Father Andrew would arrive in the next day or two and put Elsie Slade's world back to what was right and proper.

'Better sleep while you can, Fred,' the inspector advised the distant grave.

Back in the hall he found Penny Rogers immersed in files.

'Aren't you going home? There's nothing more can be done tonight, surely?'

'I've nearly finished.' She pushed her hair back with strong fingers and looked young, vulnerable. 'Everything has to be ready for the morning.'

Tyrell had heard of a relationship between the DCI and Penny Rogers but Colin Whittaker was not the man to let anything as human as love or affection impede his race to the top. Then there was Mrs Whittaker. She was unlikely to accept an extra-marital hiccup gracefully. If her Colin strayed he would find the ladder of his ambition kicked away very noisily and very publicly.

'You've worked hard,' Tyrell said. 'The DCI won't find anything out of place. Go on home, Penny.'

'Isn't there something you want done before I go?'

'One thing but it can wait until morning.'

'What?'

'The tyres of the Merc used – they were examined. I'd like to know what was tucked in the treads.'

'I can tell you that without looking it up. It was mostly leaf mould. Oak leaves.'

Keith could hear voices in the kitchen, Jenny's light and quick and a deeper voice, broad-vowelled and familiar. There was the smell of garlic mingling with herbs and a marvellous sense of homecoming. The tiredness which had become part of his bones as the day progressed vanished like mist in the sun.

'Keith? We're in the kitchen.'

Clay stood and his hand was out, ready. 'Great to see you again. I hope you don't mind me intruding like this?'

'I'm delighted. You'll cheer up Jenny.'

Keith explained Whittaker's absence, the extra hours of duty it had entailed.

'And tomorrow he's back and finding fault with everything you've done?'

'You read him well.'

'I've noticed one or two like him at the embassy but the ambassador's great, so what the hell?'

There was an opened bottle of wine on the table. Keith poured himself orange juice, cold from the fridge.

'Still on duty?' Clay asked.

'Until Whittaker marches in, yes.'

'How's it going?'

'Like chasing will-o'-the-wisp.'

'Pardon me?'

Jenny smiled at the American's puzzlement and told him of the methane gas lights dancing over a marsh. Keith watched her face as she spoke and was disturbed. There were shadows under her eyes and her cheek bones stood out sharply. He had been too busy with his own concerns to notice the recent changes in his wife.

'What about Gordheimer?' Clay asked.

'On hold until tomorrow and Whittaker takes over again. If I'm lucky he'll let me have time on my own case.'

'The longer that takes you, the happier he'll be,' Clay warned. 'That guy wants you to fail.'

'It's not that hopeless. I'm keeping Elsie Slade sweet. She's helped me a lot, one way and another, even in the Orhan case.'

'No nearer with that one?'

'Not really. Whittaker's convinced the answer's in Birmingham and I'm sure it's in Tolland.'

'You disagree on most things, why should this case be any different?' Clay laughed. 'One thing I came to tell you, the Gordheimer brother and sister are coming down tomorrow. They're resting up in London and there's a hire car taking them to a Gloucester hotel. The plan is for them to drive around and see where their brother was based – get the feel of the Forest of Dean.'

'How sad for them,' Jenny said. 'It's a pilgrimage, isn't it? What are they like?'

'Dignified,' Clay told them. 'The old lady's very frail but the brother, Aaron, is good for his age.'

'I'll give Reverend Hatton a call. He promised a service, now he can arrange a date. The poor man's being kept very busy.'

Keith explained to Clay the need for Father Andrew.

'It must be a helluva ghost if it can stop Elsie talking,' the American decided.

Jenny dished up the chicken casserole and saffron rice

that had been awaiting Keith's return. It was a happy meal, disturbed twice by phone calls from Tolland. Neither of them demanded Keith's presence in the incident room, merely his decisions.

After Clay left it took little time for the supper things to be cleared, the kitchen tidied. Keith held Jenny, then turned her face to his.

'Tell me.'

Her eyes were shuttered, defensive.

'Something's bothering you – and badly.'

'No.'

'If there's a problem I can help.'

'There's nothing wrong – and if there was I can't talk to you about it.'

'Of course you can.'

'No.' Tears threatened. 'The same way there're things you can't tell me.'

'The job?'

She nodded.

'Is it one of the staff?'

Jenny shook her head. 'Something I noticed.'

'Have you talked to anyone – told them what you've seen?'

'Not yet.'

'Then do it tomorrow. Promise me you will.'

'If I get a chance.'

The morning came all too quickly after an uneasy night. Jenny had been restless at first but, in the shelter of Keith's arms, she slept. He had stayed awake, organising his ideas and his problems with the faint hope that when he woke his subconscious mind would be ready with the answers.

It was raining. On the narrowest part of the road the DI took to Tolland, a tractor delayed him. When he pulled into the car park at the village hall Whittaker was just going in the door.

'Glad you could spare the time,' was the DCI's greeting.

Behind him DS Simons smirked.

'Good trip, sir?'

'Well worth it.' Whittaker was not finding it easy to keep excitement at bay.

Emma Paige hurried in, shaking raindrops from her hair.

'Sir,' she called to Tyrell, 'you were right. No joy at Wadham or St Hilda's. Neither had heard of Elaine Marie Sims, Mrs Poynter-as-was, not in any capacity. I got lucky in one of the secretarial colleges. It had her on the list of past students.'

Brian Clarke wished them good morning, then yawned. Mark Edison walked over and looked approvingly at a glowing Emma Paige.

'Did I hear you say Poynter? I got him sorted out after a bit of a search. He did try his final accountancy exams but failed too often. It means he can work as an accountant but not being fully qualified he can't take responsibility for accounts and audits – nor can he get the big fat pay cheques.'

'Poor little sods,' Brian Clarke said. 'All they're guilty of is trying to con the neighbours.'

'They also live in fear of the neighbours finding out,' Tyrell added.

DS Clarke heaved his massive shoulders as he stretched. 'They're not the only ones around, I bet.'

DCI Whittaker called, 'Briefing!' and cleared his throat. He waited for silence.

'Our victim, Mehmet Orhan, was not known to his local police. His friend, Halam Kemal, is someone who interests them very much indeed. As he claimed, Kemal does have an electronics firm of sorts. He trades in TVs, video recorders and so on. Over the years he's been suspected of receiving – nothing proved against him. But – Kemal lives far too well for the returns a business the size of his would make legitimately.'

164

A rustling grew as men and women moved in their chairs, sensing the DCI was close to revealing vital information. They settled and there was a hush.

'According to Mrs Orhan her husband helped Kemal in the evenings and at weekends. She told us it was warehouse work and gave us an address he'd once mentioned. It was what the CID up there had been waiting for and they went in with warrants. They found a video factory, copying machines producing a dozen at a time. They also found a lot of plain brown wrappers.'

A whoosh of voices rose as each person realised the implications. Whittaker held up his hand and the talk subsided.

'It should have been easy to get the names and addresses of clients but Kemal believes in modern technology. The data was all on a floppy disk which he destroyed. Labels already printed were going through a shredder as the CID broke down the door.'

'If Kemal's that clever, he'll have back-up disks,' Mark Edison volunteered.

'Guess what we've left their CID looking for,' Whittaker said. His expression hardened. 'I'm lucky. I don't have to spend hours examining the videos taken in the raid but some poor devils will have to. DS Simons and I saw enough.'

'Hard porn?' Penny Rogers asked.

'Yes and the filming involved children. Kemal, with the help of Orhan and various like-minded individuals, was supplying paedophiles.'

Chapter Eight

An hour later the village hall was almost deserted. Two uniformed women sat at computers while at Whittaker's desk the youngest of his CID team tidied documents and sorted files. Maria Gilbert was busy typing up reports and Emma Paige was helping her stow the resulting paper in manilla folders.

No one looked at the inspector. He sat immobile in a corner of the room, apparently studying a file intently, while all the time Whittaker's words resounded deafeningly in his memory . . .

'You don't look convinced, Inspector.'

Whittaker had commented loudly enough to make sure everyone turned to look at DI Tyrell.

'No, sir, I'm not. It's more likely any blackmail attempt would have been made by Kemal and not by Orhan if the target was someone on the list of clients. From all I've heard of the two men, Kemal wouldn't pass up a chance like that – and he wouldn't send Orhan to cream it off for him. It just seems logical the link with Tolland was personal to Orhan and not related to the paedophiles.'

'So, Inspector Tyrell, you'd be quite happy to let perverts who prey on children off the hook?'

'No, sir, never. That's not what I meant.'

'Then I can't see you having any objection to our

investigating probable members of that network as scum as we hunt down Orhan's killer?'

'There's no evidence to tie deviants in with the killing. No one living in Tolland is on any list of convicted child sex offenders and there's been no whisper of anything odd. If there had, PC Draper would have picked it up.'

Whittaker smiled, a fisherman with a fat trout taking his bait. 'Ah, Tolland. The magical village that casts its spell on all unwary members of the force who get taken in by the natives. There's none so blind as those who won't see and none so deaf as those who won't hear. What one has to do to keep in with the locals!'

A riffle of amusement ran through the DCI's henchmen and Tyrell knew he must tread warily.

'It's a very tight-knit community, sir. Anyone coming in from the outside can miss so much if they're not careful.'

'Are you accusing me of being inefficient?'

Whittaker had spoken quietly but no one had missed his words in the sudden hush.

'No, sir. Not at all.'

'I'm just wrong when children might be at risk?'

Tyrell felt anger beginning to override caution and he dug fingernails into the palms of his hands to make pain steady him. Whittaker was determined to press home his advantage.

'If your wife ever takes time off from her career to present you with children, Inspector, you'll know how the rest of us feel.'

There was a pounding in Tyrell's ears, a mist before his eyes distorting what he saw. He forced himself to breathe evenly, steadily, and the danger subsided. Around him eyes were glistening with the excitement of the confrontation and tongues moistened dry lips.

Whittaker scented victory. 'Well, Inspector Tyrell, since you're not happy with this line of enquiry I suggest you return to your dry bones and finish that report

– it's taken you long enough, for God's sake. You can keep WDC Paige to help you. Clarke's a father, I'll have him with me.'

'Inspector Tyrell did too well while the DCI was away,' Emma Paige whispered to Maria Gilbert as they watched him.

'It's typical of Richard Whittaker that he felt he had to even things up and humiliate him in public.'

'Did he have to go that far?'

'Little men sometimes wear big shoes. I know my husband thought him a good copper but always on the lookout for any advantage that could be turned his way. It's just Keith Tyrell brings him out in spots.'

'I suppose it's because the DCI likes everyone to know how clever he is and how hard he works while Inspector Tyrell gives the impression everything is so obvious and logical.'

'It is – to him.' Maria Gilbert was thoughtful. 'If Whittaker's on the mark with the paedophile lead, it'll be a feather in his cap. He's got to do all he can while he's the senior man and that can't be for much longer – unless Inspector Tyrell can be pushed flat on his face somehow.'

Emma Paige shook her head. 'It's the DI who's right about Orhan. It is something private. Who would the man come to see? We've found no hint of any link to Orhan. Could it have been the coincidence of a new grave ready for an extra tenant?'

'No,' Maria Gilbert said. 'I'll stick with Inspector Tyrell. It's a Tolland crime.'

'What about Whittaker's concentration on paedophiles?'

'It can't do any harm – if they do exist in the village. Wherever vermin like that go to ground they need clearing out. It's just that every inhabitant's been under such

168

intense investigation and there's never been even a hint of child sex. There can't be any paedophiles here.'

'Why not? They can look just like you and me and a quiet place like Tolland would be ideal cover them. Someone might think paying a blackmailer could be worth while.'

'If they do exist they can't stay hidden – not the way Whittaker's concentrating on men who could be possibles.'

'There's only that pair that live at Greenbank,' Emma Paige said as she frowned.

'Burfield and Phipps? Someone told me they're marvellous cooks.'

'It doesn't make them child molesters, any more than the average hetero male,' Emma Paige protested.

'I doubt Tolland would have let them settle if they were perverts of any kind.'

'Would the villagers know?'

'You can bet your boots they would. It's not like a town where you can keep secrets. Any hanky-panky, even in private, and those men would have had their lives turned into a living hell. From what I've heard, they're very popular.'

Emma Paige was not happy. 'Whittaker will still take them apart.'

'That's not all.' Maria Gilbert's whisper was even quieter. 'Mark Edison's been put on Barry Warren.'

'Who's he?'

'You'll have seen him hanging about. A big, simple lad, more a child really.'

'Him? But why?'

'He watches the kids playing.'

'Is that all?'

'It's enough for Whittaker – and Pete Simons.'

Across the room a phone rang and was answered. The two women watched a young DC make notes and a promise. Emma Paige turned to Maria Gilbert.

'Orhan wouldn't have come this far unless there was

169

a real chance of cash. The Warren boy doesn't look as though his family's well off.'

'They're not – far from it. His father's a labourer and gravedigger and his mother's a cleaner,' Maria Gilbert said. 'I overheard Whittaker giving orders the boy was to be pushed hard in case he could give a lead to a possible child sex ring in the area.'

'Is it likely?'

As Maria Gilbert shrugged her shoulders in reply, beyond her Keith Tyrell tidied his papers, pushing his chair back as he closed the dossier. He walked towards the two women, his step firm, his expression pleasant, resolute.

'I'm just off to see Reverend Hatton,' he told them. 'The Gordheimer relatives are due today and the sooner the vicar holds the memorial service, the better.'

'Do you want me to come, sir?' Emma Paige asked.

'There's no real need. Is there something you can do here?'

The DI saw the two women exchange glances.

'Can you give us a minute, sir?' Emma Paige asked.

'Of course.'

'You see, sir . . .' the girl began, then looked at the older woman.

'You were right about Orhan,' Maria Gilbert told him. 'It would make sense if the investigation continued along the lines you started.'

'Against orders?'

'They're your orders, sir, not ours. We could go on with the search for Maynard and carry on working through the list of your suggestions. Maria's an absolute whizz with a computer. She'd make a dangerous hacker.'

The inspector considered their proposition, then he smiled.

'Go for it. What would you start with?'

'A follow-on from your idea. Orhan must have met

170

someone from the village, maybe a long time ago,' Emma said.

'We can keep Maynard in mind and I can hunt through records some of these youngsters don't even know exist,' Maria Gilbert promised.

The DI was impressed by their keenness. 'If that's what you want to do, OK. Any objections, you have my permission – such as it is.'

Emma Paige was delighted. 'Great!'

Tyrell smiled at her enthusiasm. 'There're three main points that need clarifying. Firstly there's "who" – who killed and buried. Secondly, "how". Forensic suggested a rough piece of oak wood. It could have been a log ready for the fire but the DCI's searches have been very thorough, added to which there's no hint of anyone getting extra washing or carpet cleaning done to dispose of bloodstains. My guess is the murder occurred in the open air.'

Maria Gilbert sighed. 'Fair go to Whittaker, he's had every square yard covered – twice. Nothing. No sign of blood, no clothes buried.'

'You said three points, sir,' the WDC reminded him.

'We need to know when the victim and the murderer first met. I'll go bail it was before Orhan settled in the Midlands. I've a feeling Birmingham's as false a trail as the paedophiles.'

'If Orhan's not an illegal immigrant, he must have acquired the right to stay somehow. I'll see what I can find out.'

Maria Gilbert wrote a swift list and settled at one of the new computers.

'What about me?' Emma Paige asked.

'How hungry are you?'

'Not very.'

'Tough. You'll just have to suffer for the cause,' the DI told her with deceptive solemnity.

The girl's eyes widened. 'That woman who feeds you?'

171

'Elsie Slade,' Tyrell said, and grinned. 'She's not too sure about women in the police force. See what you can do to put her mind at rest. While you're doing that, get from her all the details you can of everyone, and I mean everyone, who's moved into Tolland in the last ten to fifteen years.'

'For God's sake, sir!'

'Don't worry, there won't be that many. You'll find Elsie will love dishing the dirt on foreigners, as she'd call them.'

The young woman looked up at Tyrell. 'Not bad, sir. You get information which may lead to the Orhan killer, yet it looks as though I'm chasing fifty-year-old facts.'

'If Elsie volunteers anything useful in the Gordheimer case, handle her gently. She's a nosy old besom but she could let drop a thing or two if she chooses. This village has one dead murderer and one live one. Because it's all happened here, what we turn up in one case can help us solve the other. It's wise not to be blinkered.'

'Just lift up the stone and see what crawls out?'

'Or who,' Tyrell said.

The vicarage looked even more depressing, flowers needing to be dead-headed and bags of rubbish waiting for collection. Reverend Hatton opened the door and expressed pleasure at the news of the arrival of the dead American's relatives.

'His sister as well? I thought she was too ill to travel?'

'That's why the delay. The brother wanted to come immediately but waited for the doctors to get his sister fit for the journey.'

Tyrell explained the tour of the Forest, the visiting of the site of the huge holding area for D-Day.

'Will the camp still be there?'

'No, it was cleared completely as soon as the troops left. Major Gifford has been in contact with the Pentagon. Official records have been dusted off, I gather, and maps sent over.'

'I'm very glad, Inspector. The poor boy clearly didn't plan to desert and it makes it very hard the stigma of cowardice has been in place for so long. Now his family has agreed to the service, we'll try to make it an occasion worthy of him – after all, he was buried so long in our midst. Many of the villagers have expressed a wish to be present. When do you suggest?'

'Could the day and time be decided when we know the state of the sister's health?'

'Of course. I'll have the benefit of Father Andrew's advice by then. He'll be here in time for matins tomorrow and sometime later will proceed to isolate Fred Slade once more.' The vicar shook his head. 'Poor Fred.'

Deep in thought the inspector closed the vicarage gate behind him.

'Keith!'

It was Clay Gifford who had called his name. Tyrell smiled at his friend and shook his hand.

'Good to see you again. What've you done with the Gordheimers?'

'Mrs Mandel is resting up but the professor will be here shortly. I came on ahead to see you and suggested he meet me in the George. Care to join us?'

'Good idea. I could do with a cup of coffee.'

Sam Roberts greeted them pleasantly enough. 'Morning, gentlemen. What can I get you?'

They watched him pour coffee and reach into a fridge for a jug.

'It's quiet this morning.' Clay Gifford said.

Sam Roberts pursed his lips. 'Early yet. There'll be a few come in for a half before their dinners, then the reporters and coppers come in for a good feed. Lunch, we have to call it for them.'

'Is everyone in Tolland a good cook?' the American asked. 'I know your wife is. That steak pie . . .'

'It's the best beef she uses – and the beer. It makes the meat as tender as a maiden's kiss.'

'For God's sake, Sam Roberts, come off it and give me my usual,' Cyril Mitton grunted, mumbling to himself and glaring at the two young men until a full glass claimed his attention.

'Yes, we eat well in this part of the world,' Sam Roberts said when the old man moved away to his seat. 'You've been feeding up at Elsie Slade's, I've heard. It's a wonder you can still walk. Her Fred enjoyed his grub and his missus always kept a good table, even before their Agnes went off to learn how to do things properly. Worked here for a while, Agnes did.'

'When was that?' Tyrell asked.

'It was a while back – after old Sir Hilary died. Agnes cooked for him and his sister, Miss Caroline, until the new Lady Driffield moved in and wanted things posh. Agnes was upset but she did well by the George until Miss Caroline helped her get the catering business going. That upset Lady Driffield.'

Sam Roberts began to laugh, his massive frame shaking until a bout of coughing brought his wife out of the kitchen.

'Go on, Sam. I'll see to things here.'

Myra Roberts might be small and dainty but the fingers working the beer pumps were sinewed with steel. Sharp eyes flicked rapidly, seeking out any trouble spots in the bar. Satisfied there were none she smiled at her two customers.

'We've all been a bit busy since the day you arrived in Tolland, Inspector.'

'I'm sorry.'

Tyrell's apology was merely a courtesy. The two murders had made trade in the George soar.

'No matter, it did no harm, though it was sad about

the poor young soldier buried so long. Shot, wasn't he?'

'I expect you know more than I do.'

Myra Roberts looked smugly pleased. 'You hear a lot behind the bar. Where else would journalists sit and gossip? They kept on at old codgers like Cyril, there, wanting him to say who had shotguns in the war.'

Clay Gifford sipped his coffee as Keith Tyrell leaned on the bar.

'What did Cyril tell them?'

'After a few pints it was "every bloody farmer and all they buggers in the Home Guard".'

'There's no way he'd grass up poachers, even after all these years?'

'No, that's not the way of things in Tolland.' She snapped her lips into a thin line.

'You're a local girl?'

'Well, girl's pushing it a bit but yes, I was born in Murren.'

Her gaze dared him to comment and Tyrell kept silent his admiration of the guts and hard work it must have taken for her to climb away from the slum of houses across the fields and reach the respectability of life at the heart of Tolland.

'Did you always live round here?'

She shook her head. 'When I was old enough I got taken on as a chambermaid in a hotel in Gloucester – live-in. It was hard work in the day and even worse at night, trying to sleep. Men think you're easy meat in a job like that.'

'You didn't get further afield?'

'I didn't get to Birmingham, if that's what you're after,' she retorted. 'Besides, I thought you'd been taken off that case? Mind you, if that Turk was making dirty videos with kids, he got no more than he deserved.'

'I was just curious,' Tyrell said, hiding his amazement at the speed with which police information reached the

George. 'You've got too much going on here for it to have been learned locally.'

'I did get to London. None of the flash hotels, mind you. It was the Wellingborough in Kensington I ended up in. A good, solid sort of place and a nice class of people stayed there. Worked my way up to house-keeper,' she said.

The door opened and there were customers to be served. The two men took refilled cups to a table tucked away where it was quiet but from where they had a good view of the door.

'You're never off duty, are you?' the American said and chuckled. 'You almost had me believing you were fascinated by her story of "how I made good" but the facts are all stored away. When you get back to base they'll be handed over for verification.'

'Murder's the ultimate crime, Clay.' Keith Tyrell swished the dregs in his coffee cup, watching them swirl and ebb. 'Orhan was what you'd call a minor hoodlum but, like any other murder victim, his wounds can't heal. He can't stagger out of a hospital in a few weeks' time and go back to his family or to jail. It makes no difference what his crimes were, no one has the right to take on the job of his executioner. So, until we've got his killer, not one of us is off duty.'

A very tall stranger walked into the bar and curious villagers watched him over the rim of their glasses. The clothes he wore had the comfortable, well-cut look of the English aristocracy, his skin darker than might be expected. The man's nose was large and truly aquiline, the mouth firm, yet sensitive. Dark curls frosted with white were neatly clipped and brushed above keen brown eyes which surveyed the men and women present until they found Clay Gifford. The newcomer headed in his direction.

As Keith Tyrell rose he held out his hand. 'You can only be Professor Gordheimer.'

'Am I so obviously an American?' The words were clipped, precise, the accent minimal.

'No, sir. I've studied a photograph of your brother. Had it been computer-enhanced by fifty years he would look as you do now.'

There was sadness in the dark eyes. 'Ben and I were very alike when we were boys.'

Myra Roberts brought fresh coffee, another cup and saucer, fussing around them as she tried to satisfy her curiosity.

'Your war service was in the navy, I understand,' Tyrell said when, at last, the three men were left alone.

'Yes, Pacific fleet. I was lucky, I went home.'

The inspector had seen the elder Gordheimer's war record. Luck did not account for two of the decorations.

'Clay tells me you've nearly completed your enquiries.' Tyrell prepared to outline the progress made when he became aware of a movement nearby. A young man was inching closer, trying hard to look as though he was watching the elderly Cyril indulge in a monotony of complaints.

'Mrs Mandel has not been too troubled by the travelling, I hope?' the inspector asked, amused by Professor Gordheimer's puzzlement at the sudden switch in conversation.

Clay Gifford grinned and nodded towards the pair of ears, pink with exertion, at the next table. The professor understood.

'She's quite well but missing her family. They live in Vermont. Have you ever visited that part of the States, Inspector?'

'No, sir.'

'Then you must do so.'

With brown eyes twinkling, the academic gave his listeners a brief history of that corner of New England.

He went on to list its tourist attractions until the eaves-
dropper could stand it no longer.

'Inspector Tyrell, is it true you've been dropped from
the case?'

'As I'm on duty at the moment, it hardly seems
likely.'

The words had been pleasant enough but the news-
hound's eagerness was cooled by the chill emanating
from the policeman.

'But DCI Whittaker – '

'Is in charge of one case, while I have responsibility
for another.'

'You've been working on the Orhan murder.'

'We all have – as and when we're needed. DCI
Whittaker is a very efficient officer and can manage
without me this morning, which is why I'm free to get
on with my own work.'

'But I heard – '

Tyrell held up a warning hand. 'I'll make you a promise. If you don't believe all you hear, I won't believe all
I read.'

Scudding clouds threatened rain as the DI made his way
back to the incident room. He hoped the two Americans
were not too drenched by the time they reached the
vicarage. In the hall Maria Gilbert, fingers on a mouse,
was intent on the screen of a monitor as she delved into
the past of Mehmet Orhan.

A uniformed sergeant raised a hand. 'Inspector
Tyrell!'

The DI waited for the man to approach. Malcolm
Thompson was yet another who had resented Tyrell's
speedy promotions in the county force.

'Mrs Gilbert's accessing the national computer for
records on Orhan and Kemal and says it's on your
authority.'

'Is that a problem?'

178

Thompson pursed his lips disapprovingly. 'DCI Whittaker excluded you from the Orhan enquiries, I heard him do so myself.'

Tyrell gazed steadily at the sergeant and the man's fleshy face with its bold eyes began to show signs of discomfort.

'Mr Whittaker wants a result, Sergeant, and he expects backing from all of us, including me. As a result of the DCI's order, I am able to continue with my own investigation. I don't need Mrs Gilbert's help at the moment, so I have left her following an idea or two which might prove useful. If you're asked for confirmation of my authority, I'd be grateful if you cleared it.'

The words were polite but the stiffness in Tyrell's voice and manner had Thompson straightening to attention, his cheeks reddening with the implicit reprimand. There was still truculence.

'And WDC Paige. Sir?'

'She is with Mrs Slade. Should anything relevant to the DCI's case come up in Mrs Slade's memory, the information will be passed on immediately.'

'Yes, sir.'

Thompson took himself out of reach of the DI's tongue as fast as possible and Tyrell turned to a pile of case notes. He was ready to settle to work when Brian Clarke thrust the door open and shook raindrops from him like an angry dog. The DS checked data on a computer, then punched a number viciously into the nearest telephone.

'Social Services? I want to speak to whoever's in charge there.' He gave his personal details as well as the temporary station from which he was calling. 'It's a confidential matter at the moment. Check me out and ring me back – but only when I've got the top person to speak to.' He slammed the handset back in place.

'Trouble?' Tyrell asked.

'It's a witch hunt – a soddin' witch hunt!' A massive fist punctuated the words as it pounded the desk.

'I imagine Tolland's seen a few of those over the centuries.'

Clarke looked up at the inspector. 'You interviewed those men, sir, and you've got a good nose. Did they seem iffy to you?'

'Which men?'

'Burfield and Phipps. Greenbank. Up the end of Nelson Lane.'

'I'd no reason not to clear them, nor any private suspicions,' Tyrell said. 'Their dates and times checked out and there's a nosy little old man lives at the end of their drive.'

'Eric Summers. Widower aged seventy-eight. Lived in Tolland all his life.' Sergeant Clarke sounded miffed enough to have met him.

'That's the one. He watches their comings and goings like a hawk. I gathered Burfield and Phipps did his shopping for him and ferried him wherever he needed to go. There's no way they could have driven one car past him, let alone two in one evening.'

'The DCI's got the bit between his teeth. He's convinced the videos are what link Orhan and the village. Pete Simons is egging him on – making out Burfield and Phipps are the only possibles in the villages. Pete's been going after them like there's no tomorrow. I thought he wanted the two men to burst into tears when he laid into them.'

The phone bell interrupted. DS Clarke scooped it to his ear and listened. Tyrell read through sheets in his own file, aware of Brian Clarke's half of the conversation.

'At this stage, Miss Leonard, I must insist it's only an enquiry, a request for information – not for action. I don't want this call to trigger off any intervention on your part. Have I got your word on that?'

The sergeant looked dubious as the voice went on in his ear. At last he nodded. 'OK then. All I need to know is whether a Timothy James Bunting is on your list of children at risk?'

Tyrell heard the boy's age and address sent north and saw Brian Clarke frown.

'No, Miss Leonard, I'm not prepared to say why the boy might be at risk. I just want to know if he's already on your list, that's all. I'll wait here for you to let me know.'

When the phone had been replaced Brian Clarke got up and paced with short, angry strides.

'It's being in Whittaker's sights puts Timothy James Bunting at risk,' he told the inspector, then the big man swore softly, fluently, obscenely.

Tyrell waited for the stream of words to cease. 'Is there any evidence the two men are paedophiles?'

'Evidence? Who cares about evidence? The DCI and Simons kept them talking until the warrant arrived. After that the house was turned over – and then some. Pete Simons went berserk. He was taunting them about being gay and they kept telling him they weren't. It was as if he had to humiliate them. They've got separate bedrooms, single beds, just like monks. Pete didn't notice.' He wiped his face with a hand that still trembled. 'I've seen some rough searches in my time – nothing like that.'

'Perhaps DS Simons is afraid of the sexuality of others,' Tyrell said, remembering Jenny explaining such people and the terror they endure.

'He's anti-women, that's for sure. I put it down to a bad divorce. If you're right, maybe that's why the ex-Mrs Simons had it on her toes.'

Tyrell wanted to ask what the DCI had been doing while the rule book was being ignored but he knew he must make no overt criticism of Whittaker.

'It doesn't help the investigation if Burfield and Phipps are being harassed, which is what's happening if they're innocent. PACE appears to have gone by the board.'

'If that were all,' the sergeant groaned. 'They found photographs of this boy, Timothy Bunting. He's Phipps' nephew and Pete Simons is insisting there must be an examination for signs of abuse.'

'God, no! If the relationship's innocent . . .'

'Then some poor sod of a medico will be the one to abuse the boy – on Pete Simons' say-so.'

'Surely there's got to be hard evidence before that can happen?'

'You know as well as I do there're ways round that. A word in the ear of a paranoid social worker and another happy family bites the dust. The police won't get a look-in until it's too late.'

'And if we try to stop it – '

'We'll be accused of wanting to let pervs have a field day. Whittaker's already tried that tack on you.'

Brian Clarke waited for the answer to his enquiry and Tyrell leaned on Maria Gilbert's monitor.

'Problem?' she asked.

'Can you find out for me if the Birmingham CID have got any nearer a list of Kemal's subscribers?'

'That came in a while back.'

Tyrell's shock showed. 'You're sure?'

'Positive. There was no client in Tolland – not even in this area. The nearest was Coleford and that was a woman. There were two in Gloucester. All three were already in county records – along with others from further afield.'

Tyrell reached for a radio link. 'DCI Whittaker needs to know.'

'He's been told – at least DS Simons has. I heard Sergeant Thompson pass on the message. He even reminded Pete to tell Whittaker.'

'Mrs Gilbert, can you verify when that data came in from Birmingham?'

'Of course. It's all time-tagged.'

'And Thompson's call to Simons?'

'That too.'

182

'The search warrant issued with respect to the house? Greenbank, Nelson Lane.'

Maria Gilbert quirked an eyebrow at the inspector. 'I'll make sure of the times it was signed and delivered. Do you want print-outs?'

'Please. Put them somewhere safe – and not too obvious.'

The sharp ring of a phone bell interrupted them.

'He's not on the list? Great!' Brian Clarke listened, then dismay grew. 'What's that? Because of my query you'll have to do what? I don't believe you! I specifically asked you to take no action.' The arguments coming along the line were clearly not convincing him. 'Look, if we get any evidence, even a smell of it, that there's possible abuse, you'll be the first to know. Go ahead with taking the boy into care and insisting on a medical examination before that and I'll offer myself as a witness for the parents when they take you to court!'

The crash of the phone as it skidded into place was deafening, the silence that followed thick with emotion.

'You've done all you can,' Tyrell assured his sergeant.

'Have I? Not if the Bunting boy gets dragged away from his family. There's too much child abuse around as it is without soddin' social workers doubling up on it!'

It was a relief for the DI to get into his car and drive the short distance out of Tolland to the Bryce house. Rain was still swishing down in a way which could only please water companies and ducks. He dashed to the shelter of the porch, feeling wetness seep through trouser legs.

'Come in, Inspector Tyrell.' Mrs Bryce allowed only a brief flicker of surprise when she opened the door to her unexpected visitor. 'Take off your coat, do.'

Carefully, she hung the soaked article in a way which

allowed it to drip harmlessly, then led the way to her immaculate sitting-room. It still felt unused, even with a bowl of fresh flowers. Mrs Bryce stooped and switched on the full heat of an electric fire. Tyrell caught the smell of long-dried dust burning away on the elements as Mrs Bryce rose awkwardly. He waited for her to settle in a chair.

'You've been to the hospital this morning?'

A brief nod answered him. 'My husband's condition has stabilised and David, my son, insisted I came home for a rest. He's staying in the ward.'

'David, your son.' Tyrell looked steadily at Mrs Bryce. 'The relationship between David and your husband is a good one?'

There was a widening of her eyes, a slight flare of the nostrils. Mrs Bryce calmed herself with steady breathing.

'Noah thinks the world of him. He'd have liked David to have a brother or a sister but it wasn't to be.' A faint smile hovered. 'Mumps is such an embarrassing illness for a man.'

'Your husband would be glad you were able to have David in the early days of your marriage.'

Tyrell spoke gently but the import of his words reached Mrs Bryce. She sighed, a defeated sound.

'You know about David?'

The DI nodded.

'Who else have you told?'

'Major Gifford, from the American Embassy. Ben Gordheimer is his responsibility too.'

'No one else?'

'No.'

She looked hard at Tyrell, seeking reassurance. When she found it there was bewilderment in her expression.

'Ben Gordheimer? What's it got to do with him?'

'I had to keep in mind the possibility he was David's father. Was he?'

Her smile held pity for him. 'Heavens, no! When I told you I'd never met Ben that was the exact truth.'

'Then who? Forgive me but it is important. Most things are clear. It's David's parentage that clouds things a little.'

Mrs Bryce let her head fall back on the cushioning of her chair. The curves of her body told of tiredness, resignation.

'It has to be talked about. Legally, David is Noah's son. He was born soon after we married and Noah knew he wasn't the father because of the mumps. He'd had the illness in 1939 and thought he'd never have a child of his own. David was the next best thing and Noah's his father in every way that matters.'

'Noah Bryce also married the woman he loved. I'd guess your husband has always thought himself a very lucky man.'

There were tears in her eyes as she shook her head. 'I did all I could but part of me died after D-Day. When my baby was born I wanted him named after his real father. David Harrell,' she whispered. 'David Harrell.' This time the sound was firm, proud. 'He was one of the Americans who trained in the Forest. Ben Gordheimer was a friend of his – they were both Jewish.'

'And yet you never met Ben?'

'No. I got the impression he was quiet, reserved. Like the rest of the boys he came to the manor in the truck but always dropped off at the edge of the village. David told me Ben liked to walk on his own. If it was light enough he'd sit and read – he always had a book of some kind in his pocket.'

'So, Ben didn't fancy the partying and the land girls?'

'Never. It was understandable. We were a complete mix. Take Kate Scrivener. She'd been ready to go up to Cambridge when she got called up. Then there was Nolly Bell. She was nice, a heart of gold, and she'd grown up in the back streets of a town in the Potteries.

When Nolly first arrived at the manor she'd religiously change her underwear every week. It just never occurred to her to do any washing in between, not until Miss Scotland, the warden, had a chat with her.'

Mrs Bryce's face softened with her memories. As Tyrell watched her he thought that faced with a Nolly Bell he would have preferred a walk in the woods.

'Ben Gordheimer was always alone?'

'At first, then David told me Ben had met a girl from the village. They had the same interests but her family would be furious if they ever found out she was meeting a GI. It had to be kept a secret.'

'Did you ever have any idea who the girl was?'

'No. I only knew from David that she and Ben were in love. Remember, Inspector, it was just before the invasion. You fell for someone and it was very intense, very private. Perhaps secrecy was part of the enchantment.'

It was hard for Tyrell to see in the controlled, elderly woman a girl capable of great passion.

'Noah. Where did he fit into all this?'

'I met him when I first arrived at Tolland Manor. My father was a lay preacher so it was natural for me to go to church regularly. Noah got home at weekends when he could and he went to church with his parents. That's how we met. He never made any secret of the fact he loved me.'

'It was one-sided?'

'I suppose so. I liked him well enough – as a friend. He used to tell me all he was going to do when the war was over. It was so good to listen to someone who believed we'd win the war and everything would go back to being normal again.'

'Then you met David?'

'Yes.' There was a softness in the fine, wrinkled skin. 'Then I met David.' Tears misted her eyes. 'He was such fun to be with, yet even then he was so sure he'd never survive the invasion. It didn't make any difference, we just made the most of every second we had together.'

'And Noah?'

'He was hurt and angry. Very angry.'

'Did they ever meet?'

'I didn't think so, then I discovered Noah thought he had met him.'

Tyrell frowned. 'I don't understand.'

'The last time I saw David, Noah was home on sick leave – he'd broken his wrist. He'd heard the truck was due that night and knew David and I met away from the manor. Noah went round the lanes and met a GI. He decided it was David and hit him, very hard. I don't know if it was with his good hand or if it was the plaster cast on the broken one which did the damage. Noah left him lying in the road and stormed off. Later on he saw me in the distance with David and realised he'd punched the wrong man. He only told me all this after you came to the house that day with Sergeant Clarke. You showed us that photo. That's when Noah realised who it was he'd attacked.'

'Exactly where had he left Gordheimer?'

'By the gateway into the field where he'd been buried.'

'The discovery of the skeleton must have come as rather a shock.'

'Not when Terry Butcher first dug up the remains, Noah wasn't bothered then. When he knew they were those of a GI he began to worry but it was after he found out the GI was the man he'd hit, he really panicked. Only then did he tell me what he'd done that night. He thought the man he'd had a fight with had picked himself up and gone back to the base in the truck. It never occurred to him the soldier might be dead.'

Mrs Bryce looked into the fire, its radiant stripes giving an illusion of comfort.

'Fifty years,' she whispered, 'and then Noah had to face the fact he might have killed a man.'

'And buried him?'

Sheila Bryce shook her head. 'He knew he hadn't

done that. He convinced himself someone had come along, found a dead soldier in the road and didn't want the police and MPs nosing round. He decided this mysterious person must have dragged the body to the field and buried it in a crater.'

'Surely, when your husband heard the death had been caused by a shotgun he knew he was innocent?'

'If anything, that made it worse. After all this time there'd be no fingerprints, nothing to prove he didn't do it. His father had a shotgun and everyone knew Noah took it rabbiting when he was home.'

'All he's guilty of is striking a soldier. I'd look a fool trying to charge your husband with assault after all this time,' Tyrell said. 'Does he really expect to be charged with Gordheimer's murder?'

'Yes. It's eating at him and there's nothing I can do.' Mrs Bryce gazed at the inspector. 'Would you . . .?'

'You want me to go the hospital and let him off the hook?'

'If you can spare the time?'

'Of course. First, I'd like you to make a statement of what you know about that night – for the record.'

'David's father?'

'I see no need for him to be named.'

There was animation at last in Sheila Bryce. 'I'll do it now, the statement. Then can we go to the hospital?'

'I'll drive you there myself.'

The DI got behind the steering wheel and made contact with the incident room.

'WDC Paige, please.'

While he waited he watched a grey-haired woman being helped to a car. Keith Tyrell did not need to be told she was grieving, it was arced into her body. He was deciding a hospital car park could be a grim place when his radio crackled.

'Sorry, sir. She's not here at present.'

'Mrs Gilbert?' he asked and summoned up patience.

The young man with the sad woman stood by his own car door and stretched, weariness evident, as well as resignation.

'Maria Gilbert, Inspector. How can I help?'

'Is Paige still at Elsie Slade's?'

'Yes and no. She came back about half an hour ago and we went through her notes. One or two items needed amplifying so she's gone back.'

'It'll mean another meal.'

'Not for Emma – she's tough.'

'Good. Now, can you get hold of Major Gifford? He should be at the vicarage or in the church. Tell him I'm on my way to the garden centre run by Peggy Phelps' family. I'd like him and Professor Gordheimer with me when I go in.'

'No problem. They're in the George, waiting to hear from you. I'll take the message personally.'

Tyrell drove out of Gloucester, pulling into the busy garden centre and parking where he could watch the entrance. He did not have long to wait.

'I'd better warn you. The smell inside is horrendous,' he told the Americans as they made their way to the house.

'Thanks!' Clay Gifford said.

Professor Gordheimer straightened as if going into battle as a young woman answered their ring. She was wearing paint-smeared overalls and in one hand held a brush glistening with white enamel. The reek of decay and neglect was not as overpowering as on Tyrell's last visit and what remained was masked by the strong smell of fresh paint. The DI showed her his identification.

'I'd like to talk to Mrs Phelps.'

'I'm her granddaughter. Detective Inspector Tyrell,' she read from his card. 'You were here before. Who're these?'

The DI introduced his companions and explained the need to see Mrs Phelps.

'It's OK, I suppose.'

'Jessica! Who's there?'

Peggy Phelps appeared, feeling her way past sheet-shrouded furniture.

'It's that inspector and a couple of Americans. One of them's from the embassy. They want to talk to you.'

'Bring them in!'

Peggy Phelps clapped her hands and led the way. The walls and ceiling of the sitting-room had been newly decorated and movement was only possible in the centre of the room, a tiny arena surrounded by stacked furniture.

The old woman turned and faced her visitors, peering closely. Keith Tyrell was inspected and received a gracious nod. Clay Gifford was next and Mrs Phelps beamed up at his strength and good looks. Professor Gordheimer had been a silent onlooker, standing in the shadow of a bookcase. When he moved into the light from an uncurtained window, Peggy Phelps put her hands to cheeks from which all colour drained.

'You're dead,' she whispered. 'They told me you were dead.'

The inspector released his breath slowly as Clay Gifford stared at her. The import of her words had startled the professor and he tried to see in Peggy Phelps a young girl who had known his brother.

She was panicking. It should have been as the frantic beating of a moth's wing against the objects in the room but Peggy Phelps was clumsy with age and stiffness. The men watched helplessly as she lumbered backwards and forwards, keening as she went.

'Grandma!'

The girl's voice acted as swiftly as a dash of cold water. The woman was still, her eyes unseeing, tortured, as her fists beat the air.

'Come on,' she was cajoled as her granddaughter

190

patted her with a paint-streaked hand. 'You'll be scaring the daylights out of your visitors.'

'They said he was dead,' she whispered.

'You've got three live ones here, Grandma. No ghosts.'

Peggy Phelps drew on her courage to peer again at Professor Gordheimer. Her dim eyes brushed away the signs of age in him and she saw the man his brother had been.

'You used to wait for her. Sometimes you read a book.'

'Did you never speak?' the elderly American asked gently.

She shook her head. 'No. I didn't want anything to do with any of you. You were all going away to die.' Tears began a slow trickle down her cheeks.

Tyrell bent to her. 'You said he used to wait for her. Who was she?'

She was silent.

'Did you ever see the girl?'

'When I heard her bike squeaking, I hid. It's not nice to pry.' For a moment she was dignified.

'You had no idea who she was?'

'She wasn't one of us.'

'Not a land girl?'

'They were all at the dance.' Peggy Phelps shuddered. 'Dancing with dead men – I wanted no part of it.' She pulled at Tyrell's sleeve. 'Why did you bring him?'

'Professor Gordheimer wasn't in Tolland fifty years ago. He's come from America to meet anyone who might have seen his brother, Ben, just before he died. When all that's done, he'll take him home.'

Reality flickered for an instant in the dulled eyes as she understood his words. Hesitantly, she faced the old man.

'When the men came from the camp I used to go for a walk in the fields – there was peace there. He was always by the same farm gate, just outside the village.'

She cocked her head to one side and smiled with a wistful remembering of happier days. 'He'd pull a book from his pocket but all the time he kept looking up the road. If I saw her coming in the distance, or I heard her bike, I went away.'

'Was there a night she didn't come?' Tyrell asked.

Long white hair swung as the old head nodded. 'Yes,' she whispered. 'He was worried and marched around a bit, looking at his watch. The Yanks had such nice watches,' she told Clay Gifford.

The smile on the broad, fair face was reassuring. 'Did you see what happened to him?' the major asked her.

'No.' Her eyes were vacant as they dwelt in the past. 'A motor bike. I heard a motor bike coming, so I went away.'

Tyrell had to be sure. 'That was the night the girl didn't come?'

'Yes. The Yanks didn't come back after that night. They disappeared.'

Professor Gordheimer eased muscles to attention as he remembered friends who had vanished from other camps to lie in huddled, bloody masses on French beaches.

'If I write down what you've just said, will you sign it?' Tyrell asked.

The granddaughter was ready to object. 'You want her to make a statement?'

'I do,' the DI said. 'This is a murder enquiry and your grandmother was one of the last people to see the victim alive.'

'Fifty years ago!' the girl retorted.

'It's probably fresher in her memory than what she had for breakfast this morning. If you're concerned, you can check the statement for her.'

'I'll do better than that,' Jessica said. 'I'll write the damned thing myself.'

Chapter Nine

'What now?' Clay Gifford asked Tyrell when they reached the cars.

'I need to go back to the hospital.'

'If I can be of no more use, Inspector, I'd be glad to see my sister – tell her what's happened.'

Professor Gordheimer was relieved but exhausted. There had been a blueness around the man's lips for some time.

'Of course, sir. I'm very glad you were here today. Without you there's no way Mrs Phelps would have opened up as she did.'

'I found it an interesting experience, Inspector.'

'One that must have been hard for you?'

'It was. At least I know now Ben was happy before he died.'

After the Americans had driven away, Keith Tyrell sat in his car and made notes, diagramming a flow chart of work to be done. That task completed, he turned the key in the ignition and drove to Gloucester and the hospital.

David Bryce and his mother were keeping vigil. They readily gave their permission for the DI to question the still form that was Noah.

'Mr Bryce, I need to know one more thing.'

Only the man's eyes were alive in a face twisted awry by damaged muscles.

'There's no need for you to worry, no reason at all.

I have to know how you got to Ben Gordheimer that evening. Did you walk?'

The barest movement of his head sideways gave the DI his answer.

'Did you drive there by car?'

Again denial.

'Cycle?'

Noah lay still, watchful.

'Not a bicycle then. A motor bike?'

An eyelid closed and the invalid nodded slowly.

'Thank you, Mr Bryce. I've no need to trouble you again. Please, just rest and get well.'

Even as he spoke, Keith Tyrell realised the futility of his words. In a short time Noah Bryce had gone from being a powerful force in Tolland, in the county even, to a silent wreck of a man. Would it have happened if Ben Gordheimer's bones had lain undisturbed?

As he made his way into air unpolluted by the smell shared by all hospitals, the inspector thought of the professor and the release that old man had gained from knowing the truth about his brother's death. Aaron Gordheimer would not have to go to his grave with the burden of his brother's apparent cowardice.

'Swings and roundabouts,' he muttered as he linked with traffic moving west out of Gloucester.

Elsie Slade was nearing the door of the shop when it flew open and a distraught woman collided with her.

'Chrissie! What's the matter?'

Chrissie Warren stared at her, her eyes wide with misery.

'Come on, girl.' Elsie took the arm of the middle-aged woman. 'You can't go about like this. Come home with me and have a cup of tea.'

The woman hesitated. Her dull brown hair was speckled with rain and she wore a drab raincoat which

194

drained what little colour there had been in her cheeks.

'I gotta get back.'

'When you've had a cup of tea,' Mrs Slade insisted and pulled her captive in the direction of her cottage.

There was the sound of someone moving in the kitchen when Elsie guided her guest into the house with a firm hand.

'Agnes! Put the kettle on, there's a love – and get the whisky bottle.'

'You all right, Mother?'

'I am – but Chrissie needs something.'

Deprived of her mac, Chrissie's thick body was clad in an old black skirt and an electric blue jumper she had knitted for herself from yarn no one else wanted. To dry the air, Elsie had kept a small fire going and the flames drew Chrissie's attention. She stared at them, soothed by the warmth and mesmerised by the flickering lights in the small heap of coals.

Agnes quietly put down the tray she carried, poured a strong cup of tea and added a good dollop of her mother's whisky.

'Sugar, Chrissie?'

The woman shook her head, her eyes fixed on the radiance in the hearth. Only when most of the tea had been drunk at Elsie's urging, did colour begin to return to the heavy features.

'Who's been getting at you, Chrissie?' Elsie wanted to know.

Haunted eyes searched Elsie's face, then that of Agnes, finding only concern.

'Mrs Seymour was in the shop. She asked what the police wanted with Barry. I had to get away.'

'She wouldn't have meant no harm,' Agnes assured her.

'He did. Harm. You could see it in his eyes. He wanted to hurt our Barry.'

'Who did?'

'The policeman.'

'Which policeman?'

'The big one.'

'Inspector Tyrell?' Agnes asked, surprised.

'No, not him. A sergeant. Simons, I think he said he was. All in black.'

'What's he been doing to upset you?' Elsie wanted to know.

'Going on and on at our Barry. Asking who his friends were, who he spent his time with. The sergeant kept saying Barry's friends were bad and so was Barry – but he's not! You know him. You know he's not a bad boy.'

'What made him think so, this Sergeant Simons?' Agnes asked.

'He says Barry's a pervert and got dirty videos. Then this foreign man comes to Tolland to get money out of Barry and he killed him.' Sobs racked her and Agnes soothed and patted.

'Bloody rubbish!' Elsie declared. 'Barry doesn't have dirty videos, does he?' she asked, a spark of interest making her little eyes shine.

Chrissie Warren shook her head, then drained her cup. Courage began to flow back.

'Just 'cause Barry's not like other boys he's not daft or dirty,' she insisted. 'The police turned the house upside down and took every video they could find. There was only what Barry had – and one of the Queen Reg give me for Christmas.'

'What were Barry's?' Agnes asked.

'Most were Ninja ones and Barry cried when they took them away. That sergeant laughed at him.'

'Anything else?'

'*Lion King.* T'was Barry's birthday present and he watched it over and over. I liked it too,' Chrissie added defiantly.

'And why not?' Elsie said.

Agnes took the opportunity to pour more tea and add liquid courage. Chrissie drank thirstily.

'Did this Sergeant Simons give any idea why he was so down on Barry?'

Chrissie flushed at Agnes' question.

'He made out our Barry was – you know – queer.'

'Liked boys?' Elsie Slade was astonished. 'He doesn't, does he?'

'Not that way. Barry's just a kid himself, anyone can see that.'

Elsie nodded. 'Just like his Uncle Billy. Nice lad, Billy. Your Barry reminds me of him. Oh, a hard worker, Billy was.'

'So's Barry,' his mother protested. 'Them at the manor, they don't want the likes of him working there. Too stuck up by half they are.'

'Sir Edward's all right,' Elsie said. 'It's just that cow of a wife of his.'

'Mother! You shouldn't talk about Lady Driffield like that.'

'Why not? It's true. It's their place to give a job to the likes of Barry but she's too ignorant to know it. She's not proper bred to her place,' Elsie confided to Chrissie.

Agnes began to clear away the tea things. 'That doesn't help Barry. Have the police finished with him?'

Chrissie Warren bent her head as tears welled up. 'No,' she whispered. 'That sergeant said unless he was told who Barry's friends were, he'd prove Barry killed the man and it was Reg opened up the grave to bury him.'

'Silly bugger!' Elsie was furious. 'Reg was there. It was Reg who was sure the grave had changed. He said so and Inspector Tyrell got it dug up and found the foreigner.'

'I thought it was you.'

'I kept on about it but it was only when Reg agreed with me anything was done. It stands to reason, if your

Reg had put that bloody heathen in with my Fred, he'd have kept quiet about it.' She nodded her head at Chrissie like a little female mandarin. 'I bet Inspector Tyrell wouldn't have been as big a fool as this Simons feller.'

'But Inspector Tyrell's off the case, Mother. The one in charge, Whittaker I think he is, he had a row with the inspector in front of everyone. Martin Draper told me and I expect he's let a few know how things stand.'

'Inspector Tyrell's still working hereabout. I had a girl he sent sitting in that very chair this morning.'

'That's because the inspector's been put back full time on that business of the American soldier.'

'All these bloody foreigners!' Elsie stormed. 'Why'd they have to come here in the first place?'

There was a strange quiet in Tolland village hall when the DI returned. DCI Whittaker was absent and Pete Simons, sitting at a terminal, glowered across the room before he marched out, knocking papers flying as he went. Keith Tyrell was conscious of glances his way, and whispers. He picked up a file on the Gordheimer death and found the forensic report, frowning as he read and reread.

Emma Paige and Maria Gilbert were working together at a computer, both so intent on the screen they did not notice his approach.

'Progress?'

Emma grinned. 'As well as indigestion, sir? You expect too much.'

She handed him a list of names. Some of the men and women on it were known to him.

'The last fifteen years. Everyone.' Emma sighed. 'You were right. I bet Elsie Slade could even have told us the dates they had their hair cut.'

'Well done,' Tyrell said.

He smiled and Emma's chin lifted with the praise.

198

'It'll take quite a while to process them all,' Maria Gilbert warned him.

Tyrell agreed. It was a task that should be carried out by a team of detectives in a normal investigation. Such a use of labour would never be condoned by Whittaker in his present mood.

'I'm very grateful to you, Mrs Gilbert.'

There was barely time for a quick smile before the next screen-load of data rolled into place and drew her attention.

'Anything else helpful from the Slade household?' He asked Emma Paige.

'Apart from the fact I'll have to skip lunch and dinner for the next three weeks?'

'Not breakfast as well?'

'Never miss breakfast! My mother would have my guts for garters if I did.'

'Did Elsie drop anything useful?'

'Mostly, she wanted to talk about the old days. For some reason she'd got old Sir Monty on her mind. She was insistent he was very fair to his workers but he sounded a bit of a pig where his family was concerned – even locking his daughter, Caroline, in her room one night. He had a massive stroke near the end of the war and even that didn't change things. The butler – '

'Everett.'

'That's him. He acted for the old boy.' Emma rubbed her forehead. 'It's strange. I never realised how much the class system mattered to people like Elsie. Perhaps it's the village way.'

'In any healthy community there's a flexibility. No sense of repression on one side or useless assumptions on the other.'

'By your definition Tolland became unstable with the arrival of the latest Lady Driffield – if listening to Elsie's anything to go by.'

'It's possible. Her ladyship's superiority is a particularly useless assumption.'

'It's caused anger, frustration – you name it.'

'Agnes' job at the manor?'

'Not only Agnes. Lady Driffield got rid of Reg Warren's wife from the house and his son from the gardens.'

'Did Elsie say why?'

'I got the impression it was because they were simple and looked it. There's no way Agnes is simple so why sack her?'

'To make room for a chef who only lasted six months. Lady Driffield had met him in London when she worked there.'

'Wow! She keeps that quiet. What else is she hiding?'

'Her record's harmless – she was one of the first investigated. A country girl working her way in London, she met an eligible bachelor and eventually became lady of all she surveys. It's odd the Warrens and Agnes had to go almost as soon as she gets to Tolland. Was the aggro worth it, I wonder?'

'Chrissie Warren has plenty of work and is better paid than before, so is her son. As for Agnes, she's quids in financially – according to her mother.'

'The resentment's nothing to do with money. In a place like Tolland there's always been equality of value, each person with their own special skills the rest of the community needs. It goes from the squire to the ditcher but Lady Driffield doesn't see it that way. She expects the villagers to accept she's better than they are.'

'Because she's got a title? Some hope!'

'And she lives at the manor, remember. In a functional village that's the seat of power. The occupants may live a privileged life but there's a price to be paid. For every ounce of privilege there's two or three to be handed back in responsibility. They have to ensure the welfare of everyone the manor affects. Workers, villagers – even the vicar. Lady Driffield wants the status for free.'

Maria Gilbert replaced the phone she had answered. 'Reverend Hatton says Father Andrew will hold the service in the churchyard at eleven thirty tomorrow. The vicar is of the opinion that since you started the grave clearance, your presence is essential.'

Tyrell groaned. 'A bit of exorcism is just what I fancy.'

'Can I come?' Emma asked.

'If you're back in time.'

'Where am I going?'

'To find Everett's nephew.'

'How on earth – '

'You're the detective, Miz Paige. If it helps, Elsie Slade once mentioned Painswick.'

'That means I've to go back to Elsie's.'

'Not necessarily. I'll make a guess the Driffield's solicitor acted for Everett. They might have a copy of his will and that should give the heir's name and last known address. Then you can try the agent who sold the house for him.'

'Yes, sir. If – when I find him?'

Tyrell listed for Emma what he hoped the butler's nephew might provide.

'By the way, any news of Jeremy James Maynard?'

'No sign of him or the BMW,' Emma said. 'Maria tried his secretary again, about an hour ago. Still no contact.'

The narrow road leading to the river was deserted as Barry Warren walked home. He could see the roof of the cottage, a stream of smoke from its chimney bellying and stuttering in the breeze. There would be stew on the hob. He could almost smell it and his steps quickened.

Barry was in his twenties and the clothes that hung on him had seen their best days on his father. He had the body of an undersized man, topped with a thatch of brown hair on a boy's head. His small slab of a face had the clear, smooth skin of a very young child and his eyes

shone with a happy expectancy. Barry's stomach gur-
gled and his pace became a lop-sided shamble as he
hurried towards his mother and his supper.

'Hello, Barry. Going somewhere?'

The figure that stepped from the shelter of a tree was
between Barry and safety.

'There's only you and me, Barry,' the man said. 'No
Mammy doing your crying for you and getting everyone to feel sorry for you. Look, Barry – no solicitor to
make sure you don't say a word. There's not even PC
Draper wet-nursing you like a fuckin' nanny.'

The boy's arms went round his body, giving him the
illusion of warmth and protection. His hands clutched at
the fabric of his father's old coat. The small head dropped to one side and, as he looked up at his tormentor,
the saliva of fear drained away in a steady dribble.

'I got nothin' to say to you,' Barry moaned. His words
were high-pitched with terror and immaturity.

'Oh, but you have, Barry. You like playing with children. There're others round here who do too. I want
their names.'

'No! It's not true, Mr Simons.'

The man glowered. 'Detective Sergeant Simons, Barry,
remember that. Detective Sergeant. That means I can do
what I like with you – unless you tell me what I want to
know.'

Pale skin and greased hair swept back into a shiny
peaked cap gave the sergeant a forbidding mask above
the dark mass of his clothes. Simons pulled out thick,
black leather gloves and put them on slowly, stroking
each finger sensuously before flexing his hands into
fists. The movements mesmerised his victim.

'Look at me, Barry.'

The boy lifted his head and leather and bone crunched under the guard of his arms, deep into the soft
tissue of his gut. As he bent double in agony he was
hauled upright by the scruff of his neck.

'I'll tell on you!'

'It's your word against mine. Who's going to believe
a little shit like you?'

A second punch followed, a third. Barry was sobbing
and gasping for breath. His nose ran, the mucus disgust-
ing the sergeant.

'You make me sick, you and your sort. What is it gives
you a thrill? Putting your filthy hands up little girls'
skirts?'

'No! No!'

'It's little boys, then. What do you do to them, Barry?
Sodomy, it's called, did you know that? Did you know
that's the name of what you do to little boys?'

'No!' Tufted hair shook wildly. 'You got to believe
me!'

'Why, Barry? Why should I believe anything you say?
Can't you manage it on your own, is that it? Who helps
you?'

'Nobody.'

'So you do it on your own. Did you practise on the
sheep first, Barry? Was it because they stood still for
you? That's a kind of sodomy as well and I can get you
jailed for it – but you'd like it in jail, Barry. All those men
just like you.'

'No! Please!'

The pathetic little hulk wiped his sleeve across his
face, clearing tears and slime.

'All you've got to do is tell me who you're with when
you play with little boys.'

'I don't. There's no one.'

The sergeant's wafer-thin patience snapped. Swinging
Barry round he punched him hard above the kidneys
again and again as the boy let out animal cries of
pain.

'Tell me!' Simons snarled, the sibilance of control long
gone. 'You're not fit to live, a half-wit like you. If I had
my way you'd be buried with the rest of the rubbish.'

Barry tried to jerk away from his tormentor.

'You can't get free of me,' Simons taunted. 'Even if

you get home I know where you live. I can come and get you any time I want. You'll never be safe from me there.'

'My dad'll stop you.'

'Your dad?' Simons' laugh flooded the boy's brain. 'Your dad and mum aren't human like the rest of us. They should've been put down by the vet for having an animal like you. If I had my way there'd be a rope round your neck and you'd be strung up like the rest of the vermin.' He pulled Barry's face close to his, the boy's feet dangling. 'I'll only leave you alone – and them – when you're hanging from a tree, dead. Do you hear me? When you're dead!'

Simons flung the wretched boy from him, keeping hold of the lapel of Reg Warren's old coat. Barry pulled himself free and went through a gap in the hedge. The sergeant followed him but rain clouds were making the sky darken rapidly and only Barry could find his way easily.

'I'll get you wherever you try and hide.'

The shouted promise defied the wind and the sounds of Barry's escape. The sergeant listened intently for a few minutes then went back to the road. He brushed his clothes free of leaves before he took off his gloves and searched for cigarettes and a lighter. With the first smoke easing out through flaring nostrils, DS Simons began to relax.

He started to walk back to the village. As he did so he became aware of warmth, wetness, between his thighs.

Not an entirely wasted day, he decided.

It was quiet in the bar of the George, the lull between the early and late evening drinkers. In a corner Cyril Mitton and Tossy Reynolds droned in turn of days gone by. Sam Roberts counted mixers and Myra shed her apron. She stretched out on a settle, kicked off her shoes and wiggled her toes. Kate filled two mugs with coffee and carried one to Myra.

Myra let the first hot rush of coffee begin to work. 'God, it's been hectic!'

Kate sipped more slowly. 'It felt different today.'

'How? It was as mad as ever in the kitchen.'

'I don't know. Just – different.'

'Locals, reporters or police?'

Kate had no time to decide before the door was thrust open and Joan Baker stumbled in. Although still wearing her overall she was not her usual tidy self. Wisps of hair lanked either side of staring eyes and her cheeks were pale, clammy with sweat.

Sam stopped filling shelves. 'Mrs Baker. We don't often see you in here. What can I get you?'

The woman lifted herself on to the nearest stool and steadied her fingers on the gleaming wood of the counter.

'Brandy. A double.'

For a big man Sam could move quickly and the small goblet was soon being cradled by Mrs Baker as she breathed in the fumes rising from it. Myra Roberts approached noiselessly in her stockinged feet, Kate at her shoulder.

'Are you all right?'

'Just give me a minute.'

The shaking of Mrs Baker's hands swirled the brandy. Myra helped her hold the glass; the warmth of contact calmed the woman and she was able to drink. She shuddered as the neat spirit seared her throat.

'We only had a drop of port at home.'

Myra had an arm round Joan Baker's shoulders and was shocked at the tension she encountered.

'What's happened? Has there been an accident?'

Mrs Baker shook her head and gulped down more liquid.

'Your Stan?'

'No, he's at work. So was I. It's one of my days at Greenbank.'

She finished the brandy, not noticing Cyril and Tossy edging near.

'It was same as usual till the police come. Two cars full of them, there were. Polite to start with – the one in charge.'

'Inspector Tyrell?'

'Not him. A chief inspector?'

Sam nodded. 'Whittaker.'

'That's the one.' Colour was crawling snail-like back to Mrs Baker's cheeks. 'It was all like you see in *The Bill* then, I don't know – it went nasty.' She stared into the depths of her glass.

'What do you mean, nasty?' Myra asked.

'The one in charge and a young lad had gone in the sitting-room with Mr Burfield. Mr Phipps had to go to the study with that dark one as smothers himself in Brylcreem. Sergeant something he was – and another young one.'

'Where were you?' Sam wanted to know.

'I was in the kitchen with a policewoman and Sergeant Clarke. He's the one looks like he's going to bust out of his suit any minute. He just wanted to know how long I'd worked there, what days I went in, what I did around the house. I made him a cup of tea – and the girl. I couldn't hear what was going on elsewhere. All the doors were shut and stayed that way for ages. Then another car come but I didn't see what happened.'

Mrs Baker's eyes were unfocused as she relived her memories. The others waited, shocked and silenced by her distress.

'It was awful.' Tears rose and trickled down her cheeks. 'They just took the place apart. I kept saying, "What you looking for?" but nobody listened. Poor Mr Phipps. They took away all his computer stuff and boxes and boxes of papers and photographs – everything they could find.'

Kate pushed a mug of hot coffee between the woman's hands.

'Have the police gone?' Sam asked.

She nodded. 'I wanted to help clear up but Mr Burfield said not to. I tell you, I was worried for him. I thought he'd have a stroke he was so angry. All the years in that house and I've never seen him like that – and why not? Burglars couldn't have made more mess. The kitchen!'

'Why didn't he want you to clear up?' Kate asked.

'He said he was going to get a camera and photograph it all. "Just remember what it looks like," he told me. Remember? I'll never forget it, nor that sergeant. The questions he asked me after Sergeant Clarke went!' Mrs Baker's skin had a greenish tinge as nausea rose.

Myra was curious. 'What kind of questions?'

Mrs Baker looked at Sam and Kate, then back at her questioner. Leaning close to Myra, 'He asked if I'd ever caught them – you know,' she whispered.

'In bed together?'

'I told him they had separate rooms. He only laughed and asked if they had separate jars of Vaseline as well. Don't know what he meant by that.'

Myra did. 'Are they gay?'

'No way! They're as normal as you and me.'

'Then why would the sergeant ask?'

'Him? He's sick, if you ask me.'

'Did he arrest the men?' Sam wanted to know.

'No, but the sergeant said they'd be back.' Mrs Baker had recovered enough to be getting very angry. 'If they do come, I hope it's to clean up the mess they left in the kitchen!'

'The paperwork you asked for.'

Inside the manilla folder Maria Gilbert had given him, Tyrell found the print-outs of the day's events and the times of their occurrence.

'Very efficient, Mrs Gilbert. Thank you.'

The DI settled on a chair next to her desk, reading carefully. She roamed through digital files searching, cross-checking, discarding. Occasionally, she printed.

'That's the third one clear.'

Bridget Mary Walker, Tyrell read, had been born in 1960. Listed for him were details of her schooling, employment, marriage and children, and her move to Tolland in 1982.

'Nothing mysterious.'

'No, nor in the others I did. There's Amanda Dalton, teacher in Lydney, with no gaps, no oddities. It's the same for Teresa Sampson, except for one hiccup. Her wedding date is six months after the first child was born.'

'Normal for these parts and in this day and age. How many more?'

'Fifteen – and that's just the women.' She stifled a yawn. 'It could take days. What would make it easier is knowing where Orhan perched when he first hit Britain. It would narrow down the search considerably.'

'I doubt it was Birmingham. London's the place most immigrants go to – at least to begin with.'

'London's a big city. What part are we looking at? It could be anywhere.'

Maria Gilbert's tiredness echoed between them. Tyrell lifted her jacket from the back of her chair.

'Leave it for today and go home. You've done more than enough.'

'If you're sure?'

He helped her on with her jacket.

'Go!'

The DI watched the woman walk towards the door, realising how the subtle movements of a person's back gave so many clues to their state of mind. He guessed Maria Gilbert would sink in a chair and kick off her shoes as soon as she had shut her front door behind her. With luck, one of her sons would make her a cup of coffee. When that had done its work she would lift herself out of her exhaustion and organise her evening as thoroughly as she had kept control of his day.

'You heard about it, then?'

Brian Clarke, beaming with satisfaction, stood over Tyrell. The DI raised an eyebrow.

'Brum CID got one of their whizz-kids active and he salvaged Kemal's client list from a disk. There's no Tolland connection, not even close. It'll get the Bunting boy out of danger from the Social Services. Whittaker went dead quiet when he was told.'

'When was that?'

'Late this afternoon.'

'After he'd finished with the searches at Greenbank?'

'Way after.' DS Clarke froze like a dog on point with a strong scent in its nostrils. 'Why?'

'No reason. I was just curious.'

Tyrell knew that tucked away under a mound of folders was written dynamite. The news from Birmingham had arrived in the incident room forty-five minutes before the warrant was signed which resulted in the wreckage of a home shared by two men.

Pete Simons had taken advantage of his closeness to Whittaker to play his own game. Much as he disliked the DCI, Tyrell knew he would be furious when he learned of Simons' manipulations.

'Where's Whittaker now?'

'Gloucester.' Brian Clarke stretched. 'Fancy a pint?'

The DI grinned. 'Are you buying?'

'If you can make it to the George.'

The two men began to march the short distance in step. Brian Clarke was the first to speak.

'Where's Emma?'

'Hunting a lost heir.' Tyrell explained her task.

'So, what's the state of play with the American body?'

'We've got eyewitnesses to Gordheimer's last hour.'

The inspector described the waiting soldier, his

anxiety when no girlfriend appeared. Noah Bryce arriving on a motor bike and trying to fight a man who would not retaliate. Then had come the shooting and burial.

'You're still sure you know who fired the gun?'

'As I ever can be. I need corroboration and it won't come easily from anyone who's kept the secret for so many years. I'm banking on the Gordheimer brother. He shocked a statement out of Mrs Phelps.'

'Christ! Did he have a peg on his nose at the time?'

'Actually, the house didn't smell as bad as I remembered. The place is being completely redecorated. Some of the land girls want a reunion and may visit.'

'Rather them than me.'

The DI was still chuckling as he pushed open the door of the George. The two men leaned on the bar and waited to be served.

Hairs rose on the back of Tyrell's neck. He sensed he and his sergeant were under close scrutiny by everyone in the room. Animosity was building behind them and he turned casually, a pleasant half-smile hiding the thoroughness with which he took stock of the pub's customers. If eyes met his there was no problem. The stares were at the broad back of Brian Clarke.

'Have you been in here much?'

'Me? Not often.' He heard urgency in the inspector's question. 'Why?'

'For some reason the natives are restless. Perhaps they just fancy you in their cooking pot. At the very least they'd take a sharp knife to you. What've you done?'

'Nothing. I've been part of the enquiries, as we all have.'

The DI knew Clarke's methods. The brawny frame gave an illusion of slowness of body and mind. It was very deceptive, as a large number of men and women locked away in prison cells could testify. He was quick-witted, tough and always courteous, a true policeman and a caring one. He would never have initiated any course of action which could have given rise to the anger behind them in the cosy bar.

Sam Roberts was not hurrying to serve them, listening to Cyril Mitton as the elderly man moaned on.

'There's something up if the landlord prefers hearing that old chap complain non-stop to taking our money.'

Tyrell gazed at the publican until he reluctantly came to serve them.

'Good evening, Inspector. What can I get you?'

'A pint of bitter for Sergeant Clarke and a half of lager for me, please.'

The lager was presented in a matter of seconds but the beer took longer. Much longer. Sam even stopped half-way through pulling the pint to go into the kitchen. It was some time before he returned and finished serving the sergeant.

'That'll be £2.90, Inspector.'

Brian Clarke handed over a note and his change was delivered without Sam Roberts looking at him directly. They took their drinks to a quiet corner.

'You're right. Something's up,' Brian Clarke said. 'In this job you get used to aggro but it's just me they're narked at.'

They had almost finished their drinks when the door was pushed open by DS Simons. With his forbidding looks and dark clothes he hulked at the bar like a carrion crow. Tyrell heard him demand a whisky from the silent publican, then Simons stared at the villagers, contempt in the curve of his mouth.

Brian Clarke chuckled. 'Are there still witches round here who can make spells? If there are, Pete Simons is in for a rough night.'

Tyrell neither moved nor spoke. Brian Clarke had attracted a certain amount of passive animosity. When Simons appeared, dormant malevolence had become alive until it was almost possible to hear it snapping and crackling.

'You've been with Simons today?'

'You know I have. Whittaker had those two men in his sights and we had a search warrant.'

'Was Whittaker there all the time?'

'To begin with, then he got called away.'

'Simons?'

'I can't be sure. There was a half-hour or so, late on, when I didn't see him – I assumed he was still in the house. He was certainly there earlier when the DCI ordered a second search over the radio. Simons didn't find what he wanted and was in a right paddy. He sailed into Phipps and then went berserk in the kitchen.'

'Whatever Simons was doing he's managed to upset a lot of people.'

'Even more than me?'

'Yes, Sergeant, even more than you.' Tyrell pushed aside his empty glass. 'And I'd like to know why.'

Keith had a sense of homecoming. There was light in the house, more than the ones which switched on automatically at dusk.

'Jenny?'

There was no answer, no rush of feet.

He was puzzled. 'Jenny?'

'In here.'

The sound of her voice made him afraid and Keith hurried to the sitting-room. Jenny was tucked in a corner of the couch, a whisky glass clamped between her hands. She looked at him with huge eyes.

'Bad day,' she said softly and drained her glass.

He knew she hated whisky. 'Is it a private party, or can anyone join in?'

'The more the merrier.'

There was desolation in the words, mixed with a determination not to lose control. Keith poured himself a shot of whisky and splashed soda.

'Another for you?'

She shook her head and he caught the glint of tears. 'A patient?'

Jenny closed her eyes and nodded. Keith sat in the opposite corner of the couch, near but taking care not to touch her.

'Dead?'

Her hair swung in a silky 'No.'

Keith savoured his whisky. 'Do you want to talk about it?'

'I can't.'

'OK, I'm not prying.' He smiled at her. 'It's funny, I bet both sets of colleagues expect us to swap all the gory details.'

There was a half-smile on her lips, an easing of tight muscles in the slim figure.

'I can pick your brains though,' he said. 'Child abuse. Talk to me about the people who see it everywhere – I don't mean the experts called in to deal with individual cases, but the ordinary man in the street.'

'Or in a police station?'

Exultation leaped in him. She was diverted and he sensed the tension in her retreat a fraction.

'I'd better not say.'

Jenny smiled, a wan effort. 'No comment?'

'Very apt. Go on, then. Quote me a textbook.'

'I'm too tired. You'll have to make do with a précis – highly personalised.' With great care she placed her glass on the table beside her. 'Most people assume child abuse means parents molesting their children and, of course, it can be. The pity is there's far more child abuse than anyone can imagine. It's not only by adults, children can be just as guilty of committing it. Abuse ranges from name-calling in the playground to fatal beatings and persistent rapes, taking in every kind of torture on the way. If you include them all, hardly any child escapes. Mostly, it's minor and the average child weathers it, growing up in the process. They learn to answer back, stand up to bullies, avoid situations they

213

can't handle. It's a bit like being a woman,' she said and tried to smile.

'Cheeky!'

Keith was relieved to see Jenny's colour was returning.

'It still leaves far too many children whose lives are badly damaged in the short term – and in the long term as well. Physical trauma can heal and disappear. Emotional, sexual, mental? Altogether different. Which is it you want to know about?'

'Sexual. It's no secret now the newer of our murder victims was helping produce and market porn videos, some involving children.'

'At least he's not in a position to do any more harm.'

He understood her bitterness. Too much of Jenny's working day was spent helping to heal casualties in such a war.

'Pimps, drug dealers, porn merchants, there's not a lot to choose between them,' he said.

'All are the worst kind of criminals but they wouldn't exist without customers anxious to buy,' Jenny retorted.

'I'm trying to find out about those who see child abuse everywhere they turn, even when it doesn't exist.'

She slipped off her shoes and lifted her feet on to the couch. 'They're the worst kind of menace. They often project an image of respectability, yet each one of them can destroy innocence as quickly and surely as a rapist.'

'Without the physical damage.'

'You think so? Remember, he or she can get a kick out of making sure the child's examined by an expert. Depending on the child's age and emotional state, the examination alone can cause severe trauma.'

Keith thought of Timothy Bunting. 'To trigger all that off the person would have to be deranged.'

Jenny nodded. 'Sometimes they do it to achieve a

sexual climax as well as an emotional one. For them it would be well worth the price paid by the child.'

There had been Brian Clarke's anger. The sergeant might not have used Jenny's words or understood the reason for his fury but he had detected evil and a child at risk.

'The mental state of someone in that situation?'

'Vicarious sex? Imaginative voyeurism? I could give you a dozen names for it. Each individual has their own collection of hang-ups and would need thorough analysis before the problem could be pinpointed.'

'Suppose it was a man?'

'Attracted to boys or girls?'

'Boys, I think.'

'Is he married?'

'Has been.'

'An obvious possibility is that he's gay – bisexual at least – and denying it. The marriage may have been a cover and by doing the puritanical thing where children are concerned he's getting all the turn-ons without physically committing the crime himself.'

'When his wife left him, would that have caused changes in his behaviour?'

'Almost certainly. He'd feel exposed, vulnerable . . .'

'And might lash out?'

'It's possible. Just don't forget – if he was able to hide his sexuality so well he'd make sure any violence was hidden too.'

'No witnesses,' Keith said.

'None. He needs his safety.'

'And his status.'

This train of thought was interrupted by the sound of a car's arrival. Keith went to the porch as an engine was switched off and saw the gleam of a limousine behind Clay Gifford.

'On loan for the evening with the Gordheimers' compliments. I'm instructed to take you both out to dinner.'

'I don't know – '

'You wouldn't have me disobey an order? The ambassador might get to hear of it and send me somewhere very cold.'

'Jenny's tired.'

'Then a quiet evening out with me will do you both good.'

Keith held his hands palm upwards in the age-old sign of surrender.

'The professor asked to be excused. Today tired him more than he expected.'

'Heart trouble?'

'Angina. He's OK but he has to pace himself.'

'And he'll be dreading the service for his brother. Come and see if Jenny can be persuaded. Please, don't push her too hard.'

Once inside the house Clay beguiled Jenny with all the expertise of a burgeoning diplomat and it was not long before the three of them were being chauffeured to a bistro in Gloucester.

The evening passed pleasantly with a little wine and a lot of laughter. By the time Clay and the limousine left them at their home Keith, as well as Jenny, had benefited. They were ready for sleep.

'Tomorrow,' Keith began as Jenny switched off her light.

'What about it?'

'Talk to someone at the hospital.'

'Like who?'

'I don't know. The patients aren't your sole responsibility. Who's in charge?'

Her breathing become rapid, shallow. 'I'm trained. I should be able to cope on my own.'

'None of us can. Not you, not me – although we like to think so. We have to work in a team to get the hellish jobs done. That means talking out problems as well as ideas with others.'

216

Jenny nestled against him. 'You're right. I'll do it tomorrow.'

Keith thought of the rapport building with Brian Clarke, with Emma Paige, Maria Gilbert, Martin Draper, even Penny Rogers. He was part of an excellent team.

'So will I,' he said and closed his eyes.

'We drew a blank with the two gays yesterday,' DCI Whittaker admitted at the next morning's briefing. His attitude suggested the failure was entirely the fault of Dennis Burfield and his friend, Nigel Phipps. 'Info from Birmingham says there were no Tolland paedophiles in the list Kemal was using.'

'It doesn't mean there's no pervs in this God-forsaken hole, Guv,' Pete Simons protested.

'Of course not. Orhan had a reason to be here and we've got to find it.'

'Are you still going with blackmail, Guv?' a girl called from the back of the room.

'Yes. The finances of the most likely have been put under the microscope – no sets of suspicious payments. It could be the target wasn't wealthy. Orhan would make his demands and, if his victim had to rob a blind grandmother of her savings, he wouldn't lose any sleep. Birmingham says Orhan was always on the make, even for pennies, from the moment he arrived.'

'Is that known, sir?'

Tyrell's question had heads turning his way.

Whittaker hesitated, unsure of the question.

'When he arrived in Birmingham?'

'Not exactly,' the DCI said. 'The first mention of him is in '83, suspected of handling stolen goods. The DPS, as it was at the time, dropped the charges. Since then he's had a few tugs but never made it to jail.'

'Is there any idea, sir, when he got to this country? Did he land and go straight to the Turkish community in Birmingham?'

'Good question, Keith. I know you've got your own enquiries which are important, so Marriott, check that out, will you? If you've to go up to Birmingham, liaise with DCI Barraclough.'

Whittaker was being pleasant and Tyrell was not the only one to decide yesterday's egg on the DCI's face might not have improved his temper but it had worked wonders for his manners.

'We haven't been given the easy way in,' Whittaker said. 'It means we have to hunt for the connection. I want every likely magazine subscription checked.' His order was greeted by a chorus of groans and he frowned. 'I know it'll be time-consuming but it must be done.'

'Guv, the Yard should have lists we could use,' Pete Simons suggested.

The DCI was agreeing when Sergeant Thompson interrupted. 'Chief super wants a word with you, sir. Urgent.'

When Whittaker went to the radio bay at the other end of the room the chatter-level rose. The workforce was not kept waiting for long.

'Gloucester,' Whittaker said, the name bringing an instant hush. 'There's another possible in Hucclecote. Someone had a patio laid very early one morning. It's well inside the time-span. Keen, Parfitt, Towers, get off as soon as you can and make sure you've got overalls. The rest of you are on standby in case there's more digging to be done.'

'When we retire we can all become bleedin' archaeologists,' came from the back of the group. There was uneasy laughter.

'At least then there'd be no parents to see,' a WDC added quietly.

In a moment of silence each had their own thoughts, until Pete Simons thumped a desk with a folder.

'Possible magazines and contact numbers. Let's get to it – we've a murdering pervert to nail.'

He made sure the workload was distributed before advancing to where the inspector sat with Brian Clarke. Many in the incident room watched Tyrell and waited for his reaction.

'With your heap of bones you're into archaeology already. We'd better have DS Clarke with us.'

The DI looked up from his files and saw Simons had been over-generous with his Brylcreem that morning.

'If he can be spared, I'd like him with me today. We've a service to attend.'

'And another tomorrow? You are busy. I'm sure the rest of us can manage – sir.'

It was a vain hope journalists would remain in ignorance of Father Andrew's ceremony. They massed at the entrance to the graveyard, the jostling and shouting creating a physical barrier. Cameras of every size were aimed at anyone allowed through the lychgate.

Clay Gifford's height and easy manner had him through in seconds. Churchgoing villagers had a little more trouble. Caroline Driffield and her brother, Bobby, calmly ignored all questions and remained dignified. Their nephew and his wife fared less well, mainly because Lady Driffield stopped to argue with a TV reporter who had thrust a microphone in her face.

Elsie Slade and Agnes were escorted in by Martin Draper, his uniform attracting the greatest barrage of questions for his charges. On Tyrell's orders Brian Clarke was ready, his shoulders barrelling a path through the scrum for the two women.

The DI had arrived early and stood against the church wall as the congregation assembled. After talking to Mrs Slade and Agnes, Clay Gifford joined him.

'Any surprises?'

'None, as far as I can see. Most are here to support Elsie and Agnes.'

He recognised a number of faces. Mrs Seymour and

Mrs Gallagher were part of the old village, Mrs Poynter and the Clawsons representing the new.

'I expect the major prides himself on never missing a church parade. Of course, the Driffields are here in force.'

They saw Bobby moving awkwardly, shifting his weight from one leg to another as pain soared. Caroline chatted to Agnes while Elsie Slade was a quiet figure. Beside her, Lady Driffield still trembled after her battle at the gate and Sir Edward slipped a hand around her elbow. It was a moment of closeness in the squalls of wind which whipped at faces and skirts.

'Jeez, look at that!' Clay Gifford repressed a chuckle.

Father Andrew had come from the church. As he walked, immaculate white lawn frothed like a bridal gown from underneath a long black cape. He was a tall man, eyes shining in a face burned lean by his zeal. A crest of white hair blew in the wind, mocking the wisps of Reverend Hatton who walked alongside, carrying a silver-gilt chalice.

'Can we go nearer?' Clay asked.

They moved forward, halting at the back of the crowd assembled round the grave. Father Andrew stood at the foot of the bare heap of earth which covered Fred Slade. He began his mission in rich tones, archaic words swept away by the gusting wind. The rolling, sonorous voice and uplifted hand of the man impressed everyone present.

Jenny would have loved this, Tyrell thought. He remembered a college room and cheap wine. Jenny and he had been among the listeners while a soon-to-be psychologist informed them on the principles of public speaking. 'It doesn't matter what the hell you say, it's the authority you say it with that counts.'

It was working. Some of the faces in the crowd reflected awe and a measure of fear. Keith Tyrell looked at each in turn and made mental notes.

Water was blessed and sprinkled lavishly. Exhortation

followed which could even be heard by the crowd gathered beyond the churchyard wall. Father Andrew bent his head, his body an arc of compassion. There was a quiet prayer for a soul displaced, sending it on its journey.

Martin Draper handed a wreath to Fred Slade's widow. She laid it in place on the mound, twitching it gently as she might a blanket covering a sleeping child. Only Tyrell's eyes moved as he watched expressions, unguarded emotions.

'Inspector Tyrell.'

He looked down at Reg Warren. The man's face was working, his eyes tortured.

'Please. I dunno what to do.'

'What is it?'

'It's our Barry. 'E's gone. Since fust light I bin out lookin'. I can't find un anywhere.'

Chapter Ten

Clay Gifford escorted Elsie Slade home. As the chief mourner and her daughter left the scene, the rest of the village trickled away, reporters in hot pursuit.

It was quiet in the church. The DI sat with the worried father as Reg Warren rubbed a calloused hand across his eyes.

'I bin everywhere.'

'Has Barry any special friends?'

The big head shook. 'Barry gets on well w' most folk but 'e never stays away from 'ome. Never. 'Is mother 'ad 'is supper waiting last night. Stew, it was. Barry knew it was stew an' 'e'd never miss that. Likes 'is stew the way his mum makes it.'

The inspector took Reg Warren through Barry's movements on the previous day. The family had breakfasted together and the boy had worked in the Clawsons' garden that morning, going home and playing in the shed with his ferrets when the rain had become heavy. He had eaten a sandwich at midday with his mother, then returned to the Clawsons' in the afternoon.

'Do they know he's missing?'

'The major was fust I went to see. 'E took me round the back to where they keeps the mower and such like. T'was all tidy. Barry 'ad cleaned up after 'isself,' the father added with pride.

'What time did he leave the Clawsons?'

'Five o'clock on the dot. The major watched 'im on 'is way 'ome.'

'It would be best if you came to the village hall and reported him missing officially then we can – '

'No!' Reg Warren slid back along the pew in his anxiety. 'I'll not go near! It's they drove 'im away.'

'Who did?'

'That big copper and 'is boss. Day afore yest'day they come and scared Barry. Took away all 'is videos. Cryin' 'e was. When they went the missus 'ad to give un a dose Dr O'Brien left to quiet un.'

'Did anyone come back to see Barry yesterday?'

'I dunno, not for sure. 'Is mum went to the shop in the mornin'. She said Elsie Slade made 'er go and 'ave a cup o' tea with 'er an' Agnes. When she got back Barry was playin' with the ferrets an' that allus cheers un up. 'E's good wi' animals.'

'You go on home to your wife, Mr Warren. I'll start things moving.'

Leaving Martin Draper to take Reg Warren home, Inspector Tyrell went back to the incident room. Colin Whittaker was installed at the main desk, going through a pile of print-outs. He listened to Tyrell's account of the disappearance.

'Right,' the DCI decided. 'I'll go and see the father.'

'He won't talk to you, sir.'

Whittaker stopped. He swung slowly in his chair until he faced Tyrell. 'What did you say?'

'He won't talk to you – or to Sergeant Simons. I tried to get him to come here. He refused point blank.'

'I presume Mr Warren gave you a cogent reason for doing so?'

Tyrell was aware of silence in the big room. He knew every word of the conversation was being picked up by experts in nuances.

'The questioning of Barry which implied he had paedophile tendencies seriously disturbed the boy.'

'Boy? He's twenty-three!'

'In years, sir, yes. His mental age is considerably younger.'

'And his sex drive, Inspector? How old is that? If he can get it up who's he most likely to go for? The kids he plays with? Eight-year-olds?'

'Dr O'Brien, his GP, could tell us of what he's capable sexually. In the meantime, perhaps we could initiate a search?'

'Search?' Pete Simons asked as he came from the toilets. 'Who's missing?'

Whittaker glowered at him. 'Barry Warren.'

Few missed the sergeant's elation. 'Great! The little shit's given us all the proof we need he's involved.'

Whittaker's half-smile should have put Simons on the alert. 'I don't think Inspector Tyrell agrees with you.'

'Well, he wouldn't, would he?' Simons' eyes swivelled to where Tyrell stood and fingers were raised to his forehead in a mockery of the Scout salute. He turned to the DCI. 'Let's go get him, Guv.'

Tyrell barred his way. 'Not a good idea.'

It sounded like advice but had the feel of an order.

'Sir?'

Pete Simons faced Tyrell as a boxer would an opponent, his weight evenly balanced.

'We need the help of the village to find him. If you're seen out there we won't get it.'

'What are you suggesting? Sir?'

'According to his parents, it's your questioning of Barry that's led to his disappearance. They've not kept quiet about it, so the rest of the village knows.'

'His parents are as thick as he is,' Simons said. 'Anyway, I go by the book. Inspector.'

'Which book, Sergeant? If it's not PACE you'll have more than a missing witness to concern you.'

Whittaker intervened. The DCI was aware he was too short-handed to conduct a proper search, yet it was essential Barry Warren be found quickly. Pride was swallowed and he asked Tyrell to take charge.

'We need the full assistance of the villagers,' the inspector repeated to the officers rapidly mustered for a

224

briefing. 'They'll know the odd corner where someone like Barry might hide away.'

Martin Draper was already contacting anyone willing to help in the hunt. He made good use of the phone and, in a remarkably short time, cars and Land-Rovers arrived, their drivers and passengers swelling the crowd of men and women waiting for Tyrell's orders.

A woman he recognised was amongst them. 'Miss Driffield?'

'Inspector. I know the woods, especially round the manor where Barry used to work.'

'Of course. Thank you for coming. I'll put one of my men with you, if you've no objection. There's no knowing what you might find.'

'I know Barry,' she said softly, 'and we must hurry.'

With Brian Clarke beside her, Caroline Driffield led the posse of police and Tollanders, many armed with long sticks for searching undergrowth.

'What do you want me to do?' Maria Gilbert asked Tyrell in the suddenly empty hall.

'In spite of this search, the pressure must be kept up to find Orhan's killer. Carry on working through your lists.'

Sergeant Thompson and a WPC manned the radio and phones as Tyrell studied a large-scale map of the area, coloured pins marking the position of search parties. In a corner, Whittaker and Simons were ploughing through files when the door was thrust open and Superintendent Mortimer walked in.

'What the hell's going on, Colin?'

Whittaker and Simons shot to attention.

'Missing witness, sir.'

'On top of this complaint we've had? Some high-powered lawyer's making harassment noises. No proper grounds for a warrant which arrived late anyway. A house ransacked by your squad and massive damage done. He's even muttering defamation of character and God only knows what else.'

Tyrell bent closer to the map, hoping his own back did not reveal too much of his state of mind. Burfield and Phipps might have appeared vulnerable but they were neither stupid nor weak. They knew Simons had behaved improperly and were already fighting back. The DCI was not a man who would forgive Simons' activities, especially if they dented his own career.

Whittaker, trying to wriggle away from a messy complaints procedure, produced sheets of paper for DS Mortimer to read. Unfortunately for the DCI his superintendent was no fool. A check on the timing of events had Mortimer questioning intensively. Whittaker's occasional glare at Simons promised future discomfort.

With the radio messages from the patrols Tyrell began to see a pattern emerge. The teams of hunters had moved deeper into the woods and fields around Tolland. Some had even reached the river bank.

The inspector was deeply concerned. If Barry had lost his footing in the night, the notorious Severn mud would not release him. Tyrell looked again at Simons, deferential beside Mortimer's chair. There was a distinct sense of anxiety in the hunch of the sergeant's shoulders.

'DS Clarke for you, sir,' Sergeant Thompson called.

Tyrell reached for the handset. 'Brian?'

'We've got him.' There was desolation in the crackling voice. 'I've cut him down – left the knot intact. I'd say he's been dead hours. It looks like an own job.'

'Where exactly are you?'

'On a cart track through the woods. It goes behind the manor, almost parallel to the road out of Tolland towards Lydney. We came over a stile by the village end but Miss Driffield says there's a gate. It'd be easier to get a vehicle in that way.'

Sergeant Thompson had been listening to the message, tracing the route on the map. 'Here it is, sir,' he said, pointing to a pair of dotted lines that meandered.

'You may need bolt-cutters, Inspector.' It was Caroline

Driffield's voice on the radio. 'My nephew will have the key but he's out searching. It could take an age to locate him.'

The DI thanked her before giving orders for the hunt to be called off and the machinery for dealing with a sudden death put into its well-oiled motion.

Tyrell approached Superintendent Mortimer. 'Excuse me, sir.'

Lucidly, he made the senior man aware of the situation as Whittaker stiffened and Simons' eyes gleamed, then were shuttered.

'What d'you need?' Mortimer asked.

'If you could make a point of thanking the searchers personally, I think it might help.'

'Damage limitation?'

'Yes, sir. It sounds like suicide and you know what village gossip can be like.'

'I do. They'll all believe we pushed him into it.'

Tyrell kept his expression non-committal. He flicked a glance at Simons and met the wariness of defence.

'I'll go out to the scene.'

'Get off, then,' Mortimer said. 'What about the family?'

Muscles around Tyrell's jaw whitened. 'I'll go myself, sir. After I've seen the boy.'

There was a nod of dismissal and Tyrell picked up his jacket. 'Get someone with bolt-cutters to the gate as soon as you can,' he told Sergeant Thompson.

It was a short drive past the deserted George and the silent church. The dark bulk of the manor with its lighted windows was imposing in the early dusk. In the smaller houses he could see the glow of TV screens as families settled for the evening.

The DI found the gate, anchored to its post by a rusting chain and a newish lock. It was dark in the wood. After climbing the gate he used the light of his torch to help him inspect the track as he walked. Puddles of water filled ruts dug by the wheels of tractors and carts. Undergrowth was encroaching and branches of hazel whipped him as he passed.

There were voices, torchlight. 'It didn't take you long,' was Brian Clarke's greeting.

'I'm surprised how near the road this is.'

Caroline Driffield kept her back to the dark shape lying on the ground, its head shielded by a woman's scarf. Tyrell thanked her for her help and saw the glint of tears.

'I watched him grow up. He loved these woods – they were his playground.'

'How did you find him?'

'We took the route he'd use to get from his home to the lake.' She pointed into the darkness. 'You turn off just down there.'

The DI had noticed no path and wondered why he had missed it but there were other matters claiming his attention. He stooped to the body and lifted the scarf. Brian Clarke directed his torch and the DI saw bulbous, staring eyes and a bitten tongue from which blood had dribbled, gargoyle features in white skin mottled with blue. There were deep gouges in the jaw line and neck. Tyrell examined Barry's hands. Broken nails and smeared blood bore testimony to the boy's last writhings.

'It's a sycamore. Easy to climb.'

Brian Clarke shone his torch into the branches above them. From one end hung a rope, its cut end swaying in the breeze.

'He must have got up on to that lower branch and tied the rope above him. Then, when the noose was in place, he jumped. Poor little sod, he choked himself to death.'

Tyrell flashed his torch again at the hideous mask that had been a face.

'It must have been suicide. His hands were free and he was too active in his death-throes for anyone to have heaved him up that tree.'

'Could someone have persuaded him?' Brian Clarke asked quietly.

The DI made sure Miss Driffield could not hear them. She was yards away, leaning against a tree and with her back to them.

'You've got a reason for asking?'

'Take a look at his feet.'

The inspector used his torch. The thick, studded boots were caked with mud.

'What am I looking at?'

'On the sole the mud's darker. I know it's difficult in this light, but it's probably the usual red mud you've just walked through.'

The inspector's rubber boots bore witness, the mud on them still wet. He looked more closely at the layers on Barry's boots. Above the dark mud was a pale line.

'River mud?'

'Maybe. Certainly not from this track. He'd splashed through somewhere else before he started along this path.'

'You're right. It's higher up the leather. It could be days old.' He examined the boy's feet again. 'No, by damn, it couldn't. Look at the polish. His father was so proud of his thoroughness.'

'I bet he washed his boots every night and polished them in the morning.'

'Poor little devil.'

The men stood in silence, each thinking of the agony of the parents.

'That mud, sir.'

'What about it?'

'Last night in the George. I got some that colour on my trousers. Brenda gave me hell when I got home. I tried getting it off but it'll mean the cleaners.'

'In the George?'

The DI relived the scene in his memory. A man on a bar stool. A swinging foot.

'God, no! Simons? You think it's the same mud as on Barry's boots?'

'Yes, I do. My bet is Simons was on his own when he had a go at Barry and the boy ran away from him – ending up here.'

'We could never prove it.'

A car was being driven towards them and lights flickered through the trees. Chris Collier was the first from the police car. The preliminaries were brief, his examination careful.

'Dead.'

A PC held a torch, the doctor wrote his notes and looked at his watch.

'Rough guess, twenty-four hours. Judging by the marks I've seen it was anything but the easy way out, God rest his soul.'

'Suicide?' Tyrell asked.

'Most probably – the pathologist will need to confirm.' Chris Collier packed away his kit. 'And they say village life is dull. Two murders and a suicide in as many weeks?'

'In fifty years,' the DI reminded him. 'It's not too bad an average but it's still three deaths too many.'

'Knowing he's dead will be hard enough for them but having to see the poor little sod . . .'

Brian Clarke shook his head in despair as he pushed open the gate. The cottage was very small, light from an uncurtained window revealing the front garden as a square of grass surrounded by trimmed privet.

'I'll try and delay identification until he's been tidied up a bit,' Tyrell promised.

There were footsteps. The door opened and Reg Warren blinked at them, hope naked in his eyes. He looked at the DI, meeting sympathy, and the best part of him withered and died.

'You'd better come in.'

'Before we do, you should know where we found him.' Brian Clarke could be very gentle.

''Oo found Barry?'

'I did,' the sergeant said. 'And Miss Driffield.'

'Where?'

'On a track through the woods. Barry used a sycamore tree, perhaps because they're easy to climb. I cut him down. He'd been dead for hours.'

The father was bewildered. ''E's dead and nobbuddy killed 'im? 'E weren' murdered?'

'No, I don't believe he was,' Tyrell said.

Reg Warren shook his head to clear it. ''Anged 'isself? Why? My poor boy, 'e 'ad no reason. 'E never 'urt no one in his 'ole life. Never,' the man protested. 'I must see un.'

'Of course, Mr Warren,' Tyrell said gently. 'We need you to identify him but the morning will do.'

'You'm not sure it's Barry?' Hope flared, shocking in its violence.

'I'm afraid it is Barry but we need you to say the body we have is that of your son. It's a formality.'

''Is mum'll need to see un too.'

'I wouldn't advise it.' Tyrell's words were gentle but firm.

'Why not?'

'Barry died quickly, Mr Warren, but he died hard,' Brian Clarke explained.

The father swayed, rocking in his agony, his hands covering his face. Reg Warren wept silently.

'What's happenin', Reg?' Chrissie Warren called. Keith Tyrell gripped Reg Warren's shoulder. The man straightened and led the way into a cramped little room. Agnes Morse was there, an arm around Chrissie Warren, anchoring her to a narrow couch covered with a blanket of brightly coloured woollen squares. Chrissie's eyes were red-rimmed as she looked up at her husband's face streaked with tears. Transferring her gaze to Tyrell she saw his sadness.

'You found him then,' she said, with no tremor in her voice.

'Yes, Mrs Warren. I'm so very sorry.'

Reg Warren stumbled to his wife and Agnes Morse rose, leaving room for him to sit and be held by Chrissie's strength.

'I knew last night,' she said. 'I felt him sufferin' – then he was gone.'

She lifted her head to cradle her husband. With dawning horror, Tyrell and his sergeant saw marks on her neck where nails had gouged deep lines almost identical with those they had seen on her son. Brian Clarke took an involuntary step towards her but the DI held his arm in a tight grip.

'What time was that, Mrs Warren?' Tyrell asked, almost conversationally.

'Late. 'Bout nine, it was – when it were peaceful again. I knew then he weren't in pain no more.'

'You knew . . .?' Brian Clarke began but Tyrell stopped him with a warning look.

'Do you want to talk about it, Mrs Warren?'

'No.' The mother had a strange dignity. 'There's nothin' to say.'

'I'll make some more tea,' Agnes Morse decided and began gathering up discarded cups. 'Sit down, do.'

The inspector pulled out a chair from under a table in the corner of the room and squeezed into the narrow space. 'How long have you been here?' he asked Agnes.

'Since last night – when I knew Barry was missing. Reg was all over looking for the boy and Chrissie needed someone with her.'

She carried cups towards the door, almost filled by Brian Clarke's bulk.

'If you want to make yourself useful,' she told him, 'you can go and get a bottle of whisky from the George. It'll be a long night.'

Before he could move there was a knock at the door

232

and Agnes hurried to answer it. 'Come in, Vicar,' they heard her say. There was a low murmur then, 'Yes, they've heard.'

A car was being driven fast, then braked. Tyrell looked through the window and saw a figure moving slowly, awkwardly, towards the cottage.

Reverend Hatton was bent over the grieving parents, his words of comfort barely penetrating their misery. A brief rap of knuckles and Bobby Driffield limped in. He handed a bottle-shaped package to Agnes.

'You'll need this.'

She smiled her thanks. 'I've got to get Chrissie and Reg to sleep somehow.' Agnes turned to Brian Clarke. 'It's saved you a journey. You can come and help me with the tea.'

'Reg, my dear chap. I came as soon as I heard.'

Bobby Driffield's hand was on Reg's shoulder, the warmth of contact reaching him as no words had done.

'Mr Bobby!'

'No, Reg, you stay where you are. Caro told me. She helped find Barry, you know, along with Sergeant Clarke – said the sergeant was marvellous. Very quick, very gentle with your boy. He did everything he could for Barry but it was too late. Way too late.'

Tyrell felt superfluous. The village was beginning to pull its skirts around the tragedy, protecting and consoling as it did so. He was aware of Chrissie Warren's stare and turned his head to meet it. He had no idea for what she was searching but he let her assess him as she chose. She had earned that right.

There was the slightest of nods. 'In the mornin', I'll see Barry.'

'Perhaps just your husband?'

'No. We birthed him, we'll see to him – and his buryin'.'

'What time, Inspector?' Bobby Driffield asked. 'I'll ferry them wherever necessary.'

233

Tyrell told him the place and the time then caught his sergeant's attention and gestured towards the door. They paid their respects to the Warrens and left.

'She's a weird one!' Brian Clarke said when they were safely in the car.

'Weird? Maybe. Some would call her simple but she's kept a lot the rest of us discarded when we stopped being children and became officially grown-up and civilised.'

'You really think she was "in tune" with Barry as he died?'

'It's possible – you saw the stigmata. We can't prove or disprove it.'

'Like we can't prove or disprove Pete Simons drove the boy to kill himself. I wonder what he said to Barry last time they met?'

'Let's hope Chrissie Warren wasn't mystically listening in on that conversation.'

Tyrell watched bushes loom into sight and disappear behind them in the darkness. Brian Clarke glanced at the DI and saw his grim expression.

'Supposing he did?' the sergeant asked.

'Then God help Simons!'

Keith heard music as he put his key in the lock. A Chopin étude. Jenny liked the measured control of the piece when she was in a contented frame of mind. His own disquiet lessened as he walked to the kitchen and a wife flushed by the heat of the stove. Jenny moved into his arms and the agony of the day became more bearable.

'Did you talk to someone?' he asked when a boiling pan disturbed them.

Jenny was being very businesslike with vegetables, a sauce. She nodded as she concentrated on seasoning.

'Dr Pyecroft. Then we had a team meeting. Everyone was so very supportive I wished I'd done it sooner.'

234

'Problem resolved?'

'In this case it never can be. We're trying new tactics.' She became concerned as she saw Keith reach for the whisky bottle. 'What sort of day have you had? Was it the memorial service?'

'No, it was the ghost-clearing one this morning. That was the easy bit.'

He told her of Barry Warren.

'Darling!' Jenny whirled to him. 'You've always said a murderer claims more victims than the one he kills. Could this suicide have been prevented?'

'Oh, yes.' Keith's voice echoed with the bitterness he felt. 'No one would listen. Whittaker's career needed a high-profile investigation and child abuse was just what he could use to his advantage. Simons egged him on and, hey presto, we have one dead boy, a very nasty case against the police for harassment and a village completely turned against us at a stroke. As to finding Orhan's killer, we're further away than ever. A good day all round you might say.'

The vehemence of his words drained him and he sipped his whisky, wishing he were on Islay and walking across a moor in misty rain.

'When's the service for the American? Tomorrow?'

He nodded. 'After that, with luck, I can finish off the Gordheimer report.'

'At least your investigation into that murder produced no extra casualties.'

Keith thought of Noah Bryce's helplessness. 'No?'

In spite of driving rain Detective Superintendent Mortimer was on duty early next morning. He was as immaculate as ever and the blueness in his lips and fingers eased away after he had been seated long enough to read through the latest reports. DCI Whittaker hovered nearby.

'Everything's as it should be, Richard.' DS Mortimer

235

smiled. 'You've made it very easy for me to carry on where you've left off.'

'Carry on? I don't understand, sir.'

'You're needed elsewhere. The drain on manpower's enormous – there've been so many missing girls. Anyone who's ever had a building job done by that bastard wants it dug up and searched for a body. The ACC asked me to recommend someone for secondment to a course the Home Office is running in Liverpool. You were first in line. Call in at HQ and collect the paperwork. You'll be briefed before you leave.'

'When does the course start, sir?'

'Tomorrow morning.'

'You haven't said what it's about.'

'They'll tell you in Gloucester.'

Whittaker controlled his fury. 'Thank you for giving me the opportunity, sir.' He was past caring if sarcasm surfaced.

'My pleasure, Richard. I'm sure you'll do us all proud. Where's DS Simons?'

'At the dentist, sir. He's due in at ten thirty.'

'I'll see him then.'

'Is he being moved too?'

'As I said, drain on manpower. Last night a query came in about a driveway in Charlton Kings. The digging'll be heavy going in this weather but, if a body shows up, we do need people who can be sensitive to the situation, don't we?'

Mortimer's eyes blazed and Whittaker could only agree. There was some consolation in Simons slogging outdoors in a downpour.

'Anything you wanted to mention, Richard?'

'No – thank you, sir.'

'Then cut away. You'd better not keep the ACC waiting.'

Across the incident room Keith Tyrell had been working with Maria Gilbert. She had print-outs for him to read and messages.

'By the way,' she said, 'I had a nice chat with a CID man who knows Terrington St Clements well.'

Tyrell laughed. 'Where?'

'Norfolk – Lady Driffield's original home. Her father's no wealthy farmer, as she'd have the locals and the glossies believe. He runs a smallholding. Very basic, I gather. This chap provided an interesting snippet of information, though it's not strictly relevant to the enquiry.'

'Get on with it.'

'Lady Driffield has a sister who is – what's the politically correct term? Educationally challenged? There's also a nephew, the sister's son, who has similar problems.'

The DI whistled. 'So that's why Chrissie Warren and Barry had to go – too much like home. Anything else known about her?'

'No. The neighbours respect her for getting out and getting on. There's admiration of a sort for her ladyship.'

'As long as it's at a distance. Does she go back much?'

'Never. A regular allowance for the family arrives from Sir Edward.'

They were interrupted by Sergeant Thompson. 'Mr Mortimer wants a word, sir.'

The DI left Mrs Gilbert to carry on.

'Sir?'

'As of now I'm in charge of day-to-day investigations in Tolland.'

'Yes, sir.'

'It's no reflection on your abilities, Keith, far from it. It's been agreed we continue as we are and no new DCI will be drafted in unless we cock up – it's yet another measure of how thinly spread we are. Now, I've had a quick look at the files but I want your version. Firstly, the apparent suicide.'

'Sergeant Clarke is doing the identification with the

parents now. After that we'll just have to wait for the PM results.'

'You're sure it's suicide?'

'Ninety-nine per cent, sir. Barry wasn't tied up and he wasn't dead when he fell, in fact he struggled like mad. There's no evidence of any other person there. Mind you, it was dark when we got to the scene. SOCO might have more luck but this weather won't help.'

'Last night I sensed undercurrents. Are we responsible? Off the record.'

'The force as a whole, no.'

'Someone in particular?'

Tyrell searched for the correct words. 'Even if there was, sir, I wouldn't imagine it could be proved.'

Mortimer had seen the effort to be fair and was satisfied.

'You've never believed Orhan was killed because of the child sex connection and blackmail, have you?'

'Blackmail – yes, sir, but it would have been Kemal in the grave if it had been a local pervert. Mrs Gilbert's found a gap between Orhan landing in the UK and arriving in Birmingham. I think that's when he met the killer. Something happened that gave him an edge and he came down here to exploit it.'

'Why wait so long?'

'That's another puzzle. Mrs Gilbert's been working miracles checking the background of every newcomer. She could do with some help.'

'I'll see to it. Now then, this American body of yours. It'll keep the top brass off our necks if the case is finalised quickly. What's the present situation?'

The DI outlined the facts of the case which were backed up by statements.

'The rest is just guesswork, sir. WDC Paige is following a line of enquiry in the Painswick area. There's a message from her to say she hoped to get something later this morning.' Tyrell looked at his watch.

'The memorial service?' Mortimer asked and Tyrell

was surprised to see wry humour in the older man's expression. 'Yes, Keith, I do read the reports. Don't be late for it – and before you go make sure Mrs Gilbert and her helpers know exactly what it is you want from these damned expensive bits of machinery. If it means hacking, don't tell me about it. I'll settle for the end results.'

Tyrell sat alone in a corner of the organ loft and watched the congregation assemble. He recognised most of the villagers. For each of them there was a file in the incident room, data in electronic memories.

Tolland was turning out in force and the buzz of gossip rose as the church filled. The DI was pointed out and whispered about. He kept his expression pleasant, meeting curiosity with a steady gaze.

'Where's Major Gifford?' Brian Clarke asked as he sat next to the inspector.

'In the vestry with the Gordheimers. I've asked him to bring them in only when the service is due to start.'

'Who is it you want me to watch?'

'No one in particular.'

'I thought you knew?'

'I need an unbiased observation.'

'OK. It's a good turn-out, in spite of the rain. Pissing down, it was, when I came across.'

'Let's hope the ones we want don't stay away.'

Two of the land girls they had visited were already in place. Mrs Mitchell sat with her son and daughter-in-law. She turned to the Clawsons in the pew behind her and they chatted like old friends. Mrs Bryce and David were together, talking to no one.

Mrs Gallagher walked proudly to a pew on the right and near the front. Tyrell guessed it was the one habitually used by the King family. He smiled to himself. She was staking her claim to acceptance in Tolland and Ken Downing, the churchwarden, was not stopping her.

Mrs Hatton switched on the organ. The pipes wheezed and coughed and she began to play. From where he sat Tyrell could see anxiety in every movement of her body, the music reflecting her panic. At least it meant the service would soon start.

The Driffields were late arrivals. Sir Edward and his wife led the way up the aisle, his aunt and uncle following and stopping briefly to greet friends. At the first pew, under the eagle holding the Bible across its wings, Lady Driffield became increasingly impatient.

Brian Clarke's chuckle was quiet but infectious. Her ladyship was determined to make the older couple take the inner seats of the pew and her fury increased as she was kept waiting. Sir Edward soothed her with a word in her ear and a touch on her arm.

'He's nuts about her,' the sergeant said. 'I'd rather him than me. Brenda can fly off the handle but she's certainly no snooty cow.'

Brenda Clarke was little and feisty. Tyrell reflected that, like Jenny, she was a good policeman's wife, making little fuss over the odd hours and inconvenient holidays. As for the Driffields, Sir Edward turned a blind eye to his wife's pretensions and made life as easy for her as he could. Brian Clarke was right on both counts. Sir Edward adored his wife and she was a snooty cow.

'Any news from Emma?'

Tyrell shook his head. 'I hoped she'd be here by now.'

The vicar genuflected at the altar and arranged papers at his stall in the choir. Ken Downing hurried forward, pointing to his watch and whispering urgently in the vicar's ear. Above the heads of the congregation Reverend Hatton looked at the DI. Tyrell nodded and the vicar went back to the vestry.

Someone raced up the stairs to the loft. Emma Paige was breathless, her eyes shining. She handed a package to Tyrell.

'He only found it this morning.'

The inspector unwrapped a book. It was small, and the thin, fragile paper and tight printing were witness to the austerity of the war years. *Far from the Madding Crowd* by Thomas Hardy, he read from the cover.

'Well done,' he whispered as the choir appeared, most of them very senior citizens.

The watchers in the organ loft were still, only their eyes moving as Professor Gordheimer led his sister into the church. The vicar took his place at the altar as the elderly couple, followed by Clay Gifford, walked slowly to their seats across the aisle from the Driffields. Villagers stretched their necks as they wriggled to watch the newcomers settle.

'Anything, sir?' Emma asked in a whisper.

'Yes. It worked.'

With the appearance of the man Ben Gordheimer might have become, the DI had seen sudden rigidity. Intense shock had flooded a body but he guessed that even while back muscles revealed it, the person's face had not lost its composure.

The vicar announced the service was not to be one of darkness and despair but the celebration of a life. There were hymns and prayers, some familiar, others with words so appropriate to the occasion the vicar must have spent a great deal of time and effort in preparation. Clay Gifford read a Bible passage, the words of the Old Testament conveying a sense of timelessness.

'Are you sure you saw something?' Emma asked. 'I've been watching but I saw nothing unusual.'

'I got my proof.'

'So did I,' Brian Clarke said. 'Let's hope we got the same person.'

'Who?' the girl persisted.

'Shh.' Tyrell laid a finger on his lips.

Below them Reverend Hatton climbed the steps to the pulpit. When the rustling ceased he welcomed the Gordheimers to the service and the village. As he dwelt on the half-century of uncertainty, he linked them with the millions of families in the war who had suffered loss.

From his vantage point Tyrell could see the elderly brother and sister, their faces in profile. The angles of their bones were as old and proud as humanity.

'He's good.' Brian Clarke sounded surprised as he inclined his head towards the cleric.

'Not bad,' Tyrell said.

The tone of the sermon lightened, the vicar giving thanks for the young men and women who had fought tyranny whatever the cost. Subtly, Ben Gordheimer joined their ranks and the DI watched his prey. The tilt of a head confirmed his first observation.

The service drew to an end. In the closing prayers Reverend Hatton held up a hand.

'Go in peace to that place appointed for you,' he begged the dead American.

Tyrell was intrigued. The words had been used in Father Andrew's service. Were they part of an exorcism? The church was certainly doing what it could to tidy up lost souls.

The congregation began to file past the vicar, waiting in the porch with the Gordheimers. Brian Clarke's radio crackled. He listened to the message.

'Back to base, sir. DS Mortimer wants you – on the run.'

Tyrell, with his sergeant and WDC, returned to an incident room humming with activity.

'Sir?'

Superintendent Mortimer looked up from the report he was reading.

'You've had an alert out on a Jeremy James Maynard?'

'Yes, sir. He seems to have disappeared.'

'And reappeared at HQ, demanding to know why his

242

name had been bandied about the internet as a wanted criminal.'

'Where was he?'

'Spain. He discovered we needed a word when he flew back yesterday. As for the weekend of the Orhan murder his alibis are intact. Names, addresses – all highly professional. He was in Surrey until the Monday morning and he can prove it. DCS Hinton dealt with him and was not highly amused. He let me know Mr Maynard is a very vocal lawyer – and hopping mad.'

'Too bad, sir. He was on the list of those with cash, on the list of those holidaying in Turkey. He was in Tolland that weekend and seen leaving the village early on the Monday morning. He could have killed Orhan in Surrey and brought him here to bury with Fred Slade.'

'Not on the Friday.'

'Why not? If he could be here unseen on the Monday, why not the Friday as well? As a lawyer he should know every lead has to be followed up. If he doesn't like being involved, tough.'

DS Mortimer smiled. 'I'd like to be a fly on the wall when you explain that to DCS Hinton.'

There was no sign of dogs and the knock on the door was quickly answered by Caroline Driffield, still in the charcoal grey suit she had worn to church.

Bobby Driffield limped towards them. 'A problem, Inspector?'

'Not really, sir. I would like to talk to Miss Driffield.'

His quarry's head was bowed then, proudly, she lifted her chin. In her eyes was agony, acceptance, maybe relief.

'It's time,' she said. 'Come in. May my brother . . .?'

'Of course.'

The policemen were ushered into a comfortable sitting-room made cheerful with flowered linen covers and fragrant with bowls of jonquils.

Caroline Driffield waited for everyone to be seated. 'Well, Inspector?'

'I guessed in the first days of the enquiry you were the girl Ben Gordheimer came to see.'

'Guesswork, Inspector Tyrell? You disappoint me.'

'Caro – '

Her brother was stopped by Brian Clarke's warning hand.

'I had to have proof, Miss Driffield, corroboration at least. That's what's taken the time. The final piece of evidence reached me today.'

He handed to her the book brought from Painswick. She held it carefully, her expression one of disbelief. Opening it, the musty smell of reality reached her and she focused on the name and date. 'Ben Gordheimer. May 1944.' The writing was round, the letters carefully formed, the ink only slightly browned with age.

'I believe that to be the book Ben was reading shortly before he was killed. The stamp on the fly-leaf is from a bookshop near the cathedral. Ben could have bought it for himself but I had the idea it came from you.'

'Why?' Tears roughened the question.

'The writing is that of a young girl and you're the only person in Tolland who's quoted Hardy to me.'

Caroline was barely listening. With a gentle finger she traced the writing.

'How fortunate you're well read, Inspector,' Bobby Driffield said. 'Is that all you have to go on to accuse my sister of murder?'

'Not at all, Mr Driffield, and your sister's no killer. When Ben Gordheimer died she was locked in her room.'

Shock drained her of colour. 'It was that night?'

'Yes. Ben didn't know about the row you'd had with your father, nor its result. He was waiting for you, as usual, at the gate near the crossroads. There was a fight with another man – '

'Who?'

'It's not important. Let's just say Ben was left a little dazed. Unfortunately, that was also one of the evenings your father decided to go out and bag some rabbits. He walked through his fields and saw an American soldier waiting for his girlfriend. What happened then I can only conjecture. Sir Montague may have realised the GI waited for you. There may have been an argument. We do know the shots might have been fired deliberately.'

Bobby Driffield was curious. 'Shots?'

'The pathologist confirmed pellets from two, slightly different directions. Both barrels of a shotgun in the chest.'

'One would be an accident . . .'

'Two would mean intent,' Tyrell said.

Like the smell of rotting meat the word 'murder' hung in the air.

'Why?' Caroline asked. A tear had dropped on to the cover of the book and she watched it glisten.

'You could give us some idea of your father's state of mind.'

'If it was the night he had his stroke, he'd been insufferable all day. He'd even threatened to sack Billy Warren.'

'Was it the first time you'd been locked in your room?'

'Yes – at least, the first time since I was little. He seemed to sense I wanted to go out and meet someone.'

'And you, Mr Driffield? I know you were overseas at the time but you knew your father. What was he like, as a man?'

'You must understand, Inspector, my father was very – English.'

'Sir?'

'The man he would see waiting was presumably in uniform and recognisably American. He would also obviously not be of English stock – if he was anything like his brother.'

'You're suggesting Sir Montague might have shot a man because he was Jewish?'

'No! Not at all – but if he thought this was the chap seeing Caro and he didn't know the family . . .' Bobby Driffield shook his head. 'Here and now it seems so bloody stupid!'

'There's no doubt my father shot Ben?' Caroline asked.

'No. That's how my report will read, Miss Driffield. As to who buried him, the shooting occurred very near the crater of a stray bomb. Your father may have had the idea of burying the body there.'

'But he'd know Ben would be missed.'

'He'd also guess quite a few men would go AWOL before the invasion. It's possible he dragged the body out of sight, even began the burial. It's most likely that when Everett found him, your father had already had a massive stroke. I've no doubt at all it was Everett who completed the burial and made sure the crater was levelled off by Billy Warren.'

Caroline dismissed the idea. 'You can't be sure about Everett.'

'No? For a butler he retired very comfortably indeed. He had a substantial financial settlement as well as a sizeable house in the village – all provided by Sir Montague.' Tyrell pointed to the book she held. 'It was in that house Ben's book was found when Everett's nephew inherited. That could only have happened if he, or your father, had handled the body.'

The clock on the mantelpiece ticked majestically, unheard by a brother and sister lost in their thoughts. Bobby Driffield looked up at the DI.

'Is that the end of it?'

'I'll submit my report and, if it's accepted, the case will be closed. I would like a statement from you, Miss Driffield – for the record.'

She nodded wearily, exhaustion and emotion taking their toll.

'There is one other thing. Mrs Mandel and Professor Gordheimer would like to meet you.'

The request shocked Caroline Driffield. 'I couldn't! They must blame me for his death.'

'Not at all – they're very realistic. They both know their brother's chances of surviving Omaha beach would not have been great. Major Gifford's done some research for me and he traced Ben's unit. Only two men made it as far as the beach and one of them died there. Ben's family are grateful he knew and loved you.'

She smiled at him, hesitantly at first, then with an enchanting luminosity.

'I always thought Ben had left me. Now I know that choice wasn't his.'

Tyrell handed DS Mortimer a file. 'The Gordheimer case.'

'That was quick.'

'I just needed Miss Driffield's statement.'

'No coercion?'

'None, sir. It was enough for her to see Professor Gordheimer.'

'Where is he now?'

'At the Driffields' – the cottage, not the manor.'

'Hm. That's one problem solved but I've been getting pressure from higher up for us to close down here.'

'Pressure from the chief super?'

'Higher than that. The effect our presence is having on the village is disastrous, apparently.'

'A discreet dinner party?'

'More like indiscreet.' The superintendent popped a pill under his tongue. 'Should we move?'

'No, sir. If we do it'll be a public admission the murderer's defeated us and that's not what happened.'

'You think the investigation took a wrong turn?'

The DI knew he must be careful. 'Every lead had to be followed. To DCI Whittaker the child abuse set-up appeared to be the most likely background for the murder. He made that decision in the absence of relevant data.'

'You mean Simons kept the list of paedophile clients from him?'

'No, sir. You're saying that.'

Mortimer's smile was sardonic. 'You'd make a bloody good politician, Keith. So, you know this village well. What would you suggest?'

'Something occurred which triggered off the blackmail and murder and the answer's here. We've got to stay and we've got to ride out the backlash to Barry Warren's death if we're ever to have credibility again.'

The superintendent mulled over the pressures influencing his decision. 'Get Draper. See what he says about the mood of the village.'

'I can tell you what he told me, sir. Diabolical.'

Reg sighed, the heavy sound making Chrissie look at him. He was suffering, every part of him longing for his dead son. Her own eyes ached with unshed tears, but deep inside her shell of calmness anger burned white-hot.

Chrissie got up, staggering a little and exhausted by lack of sleep. She put her hand on Reg's shoulder and he leaned against the mass of her as would a child. She patted him and released herself, going through the kitchen to the scullery.

The tin she tried to lift from a high shelf was almost beyond her reach but she succeeded. Barry had been warned time and time again not to open it. As a little boy he had smiled at the fading picture on the lid, the grey-bearded man in a funny uniform beside a stately wife, her neck ridged with pearls and her corrugated hair surmounted by diamonds. Chrissie stroked the faces of the royal pair. She tried to open the tin but rust had sealed it.

'Help me, Granny,' she whispered.

Her fingers found purchase on the lid and the tin box squealed open.

'No, Chrissie! You promised!' Reg had followed his wife and was horrified to see what she held in her hands. 'It's wrong. You know what vicar said 'bout Granny Phelps and 'er like.'

The woman did not even look at him, fascinated as she was by the misshapen lump she held.

'It's for Barry.'

'Chrissie, love, let un lie in peace.'

'Peace? There'll be none o' that while he stays alive – the one with Satan's marks.'

''E's a copper!'

'Without him Barry would be here, with us.'

'You don' know 'e made Barry 'ang 'isself.'

Chrissie gazed at her husband and he was afraid.

'Please, love,' he begged.

'Put the kettle on,' she said and sat at the kitchen table, warming the grimy wax between her palms.

The tea Reg made for her was sipped, forgotten. Only the movements of her fingers eased the hurt deep in her. In her head Chrissie could hear Granny Phelps' voice. 'Shut your mind to everythin', my dear. Let your soul into your fingers.'

As a child Chrissie had not understood. She had feared Granny Phelps, even as she tucked away the special wax Granny had saved for her. 'Dribbled down from coffin lights, my girl.'

Granny Phelps was banished to oblivion as Chrissie kneaded and moulded, hatred pouring from her into the rough body, the stumpy little arms and legs. She took care fashioning the head, gouging out eye sockets and a mouth, pinching up a nose and ears.

'Must make sure it's a man,' she murmured, pulling and whorling a penis to stand erect.

The tiny mannikin was a child's toy as it lay on the table. Chrissie reached into the tin for a paper threaded with long pins. They were rusty and difficult to remove. She smiled, chilling Reg as he watched her.

'They won't go in so easy,' she told him, revelling in the thought.

'Stop now, Chrissie.'

It was as if he had not spoken. Her hand hovered over the figure. Lightning-swift the penis was wrenched from the body. A whimpering sound reached her and she looked at Reg, pitying him.

'That devil's spawn weren't no man, any'ow.'

Chrissie picked up a pin and concentrated all her longing, all her grief, as she stabbed the rusted point into the heart. She chose another pin and drove it deep into the belly, twisting and turning her weapon with a fury that came from the depths of her being.

'That's enough!' Reg shouted, desperation making him rise above his own misery.

'I want him dead,' Chrissie wailed.

'Forget un, it's you matters. What's all this doin' to you?'

Drained by her vengeance, Chrissie let Reg lead her away. He took her to the tiny parlour, raking out the old fire and building up a new one, soot splashing down on his fists. Torrential rain went on bouncing down the chimney. It washed window panes and rattled on the roof.

'You sit 'ere warm,' Reg said. 'I'll get us some tea – an' a drop o' Mr Bobby's whisky.'

Chrissie still held the mannikin. She waited for Reg to go before she opened her hand. The embedded pins amongst the wreckage pleased her but she was not satisfied. Reg had stopped her too soon.

'You'll die,' she promised the little figure. 'When I'm ready.'

250

Chapter Eleven

Anne Gallagher pushed open the door of the village shop. She turned to shake the worst of the rain from her umbrella and stand it in the container Mrs Fell had ready.

'Ghastly weather!'

'It is, isn't it? June's going to be a real wash-out this year and no mistake.' Mrs Fell beamed at her customer, the only one in the shop. 'What can I get you?'

'I've come to pay for my papers and have a browse round. I fancied something different for lunch.'

'There's a lovely ham, boiled on the bone, or a piece of quiche? Agnes Morse makes them for me – and you can't get better than that.'

Mrs Gallagher inspected the offerings. She guessed Mrs Fell's mark-up on the quiche must be at least two hundred per cent.

'I'll take a tin of soup, asparagus if you have it – and a piece of quiche.'

Mrs Fell busied herself.

'How're Agnes and her mother coping?'

'Not too bad,' Mrs Fell said. 'I think Mrs Slade was hoping the service to get rid of the Turk would help but I can't see it myself. A lot of mumbo-jumbo if you ask me.'

'Still, if it works.'

'There must be something in it. It's the only time in the past few days we've had a proper dry spell. The Devil looks after his own, I say.'

A mischievous smile was repressed by Mrs Gallagher. 'The rain must have hit your business – putting people off walking here.'

'Too right, it's been dreadful. I just hope we get a bit of fine weather to perk us all up.' Mrs Fell began entering amounts in her cash register. 'Joe had a dreadful trip back from the cash-and-carry yesterday. There were times he could hardly see the road for water on the windscreen. Terrible, it was. The spray from the lorries, that's what was doing it – and there's so many of them. It's all because of the tolls on the Severn Bridge. The drivers go over free one way and use our road to get back. Disgraceful, I call it. The government should be doing something. Drivers overtake when it's tricky – and with all that water last night! Joe said it would have been all too easy to aquaplane – just like being on ice with no brakes.'

'Perhaps that's what happened at Highnam? I heard there'd been an accident there.'

Mrs Fell bridled with importance. 'Joe saw it. He could only see one car but it was a mess. Ambulances, police cars – '

'Was anyone hurt?'

'He couldn't say. Traffic police kept everything moving.'

'Where do they get all the police these days?'

'I know. All that digging in Gloucester – and what they find!' She shuddered. 'Then our murder.' Mrs Fell leaned over the counter. 'I did hear two of them, police, have been transferred from the village.'

'Which ones?'

'That stuck-up chief inspector and a sergeant – the smarmy one with greasy hair and black shirts.'

'So, who's in charge?'

'Well, there's a superintendent, I'm told, but he's not well. The one doing all the work is the inspector who came when Terry Butcher dug up that skeleton.'

'Isn't that business finished with yet?'

252

Mrs Fell smirked. 'Martin Draper was in here yesterday and said the case was closed. They know what happened and it may have been an accident. He told me everyone involved in it is long dead and gone.'

'Unlike whoever killed the Turk.'

'Why couldn't he have stayed in Brum to get murdered, that's what I'd like to know? Just because he's found in the village any one of us can be questioned any time of the day or night. It's made those two nice men at Greenbank think of moving.' Mrs Fell mourned the potential loss of custom. 'And look what it did to Barry Warren. Cruel, that was. The poor little soul couldn't stand the hassle.' She shook open a plastic bag and stowed in it Mrs Gallagher's shopping. 'It's his parents I feel sorry for. Bad enough having a son who's – well, you know – but to lose him like that!'

'When's the funeral?'

'Nobody knows. There'll have to be an inquest first. I expect the coroner'll see the police don't get blamed, more's the pity. Now, is that all?'

Mrs Gallagher erected her umbrella outside the shop and decided it was fortunate she had a good income. The price of village information came high.

In the warm and muggy incident room there had been a lively discussion on the new lines of enquiry to be followed now the supposed paedophile connection was a thing of the past. The lists started by Maria Gilbert and Emma Paige had been amplified, duplicated, distributed, and the hall was a scene of organised activity.

Detective Superintendent Mortimer watched his inspector staring into space.

'What's bothering you?'

'Sorry, sir. Something niggling.'

'To do with this case?'

'Maybe. It was when Barry Warren was found – but it was dark and I could have been mistaken.'

Mortimer looked round the incident room. It was still very early in the day, yet already Sergeant Thompson was entering data on the spreadsheets across a wall. Every terminal was in use and no one was idle.

'I can handle things here. Cut away and check it out – whatever it is.'

They were interrupted by a PC who had been dealing with a man at the door.

'Sorry, sir. It's a Mr Maynard. He insists on seeing the senior officer.'

Tyrell smiled. 'So, Jeremy James turns up at last.'

'You can just stay and see what he wants,' Mortimer growled. 'After all, you were the one had him billed with Interpol.'

Jeremy James Maynard was of medium height and sagging flesh. He had curly red hair around a bald spot and a bushy moustache which served only to emphasise prominent teeth and a receding chin.

'Superintendent Mortimer?' Angry eyes and voice demanded full ceremonial.

Mortimer inclined his head and invited the newcomer to sit.

'I prefer to stand – this is not a social visit. I'm here to complain, in the strongest terms possible, about the conduct of one of your officers, an Inspector Tyrell. I want to deal with the man personally before I instigate further action with the Police Complaints Committee.'

'Then you're in luck, sir. I'm Detective Inspector Tyrell.'

Maynard turned his head and was annoyed he had to raise his eyes to meet those of his adversary. Surprise parted his teeth and wafted a breath saturated with stale alcohol.

'You? You're very young.'

'Thank you, Mr Maynard,' the DI said.

Tyrell's meekness and air of schoolboy innocence caused Mortimer to pull out a handkerchief and hurriedly blow his nose.

'I suppose you're going to plead inexperience when I cite your appalling conduct?' Maynard's nostrils flared with anger. 'I'll sue you. You'll answer for slander, libel, defamation of character – '

'And you'd lose each case you brought because I can justify every action I took involving you.'

'How dare you! You've blackened my name across the whole of Europe and I'm supposed to take it lying down? You've tangled with the wrong man, Inspector Tyrell!'

Maria Gilbert, her eyes dancing, handed Tyrell a file. He thanked her, opened it and found the sheet of paper he wanted.

'According to the information you gave yesterday, you were not in Tolland from the 15th of last month.'

'That is correct.'

'No, Mr Maynard, it's not.'

'Are you calling me a liar?'

'You're very touchy, sir, if I may say so? And before you try sidetracking me, I have here statement from a driver you forced off the road early on the morning of the 22nd. He was within two miles of Tolland and you were heading away from the village, probably driving in excess of the speed limit.'

'So? I didn't stay in Tolland. I only went into my house to pick something up and left again immediately. There's no law against that – and before you try to tell me there is, I'd remind you I'm a lawyer.'

'I'm well aware of that, Mr Maynard. Not in daily practice I understand? You retired early.'

'I was – unwell. Nowadays I work from home.'

'Yes, you have ample finances to allow you to do so – and you like going to Turkey for your holidays.'

'You've been enquiring into my bank accounts? How dare you!'

'Because I'd have given him hell if he hadn't,' Mortimer said. 'Now, sit down – sir.'

Maynard subsided into the nearest chair and Tyrell returned to the matter in hand.

'Briefly, Mr Maynard, you've available cash which could attract a blackmailer, there's a Turkish connection and you were known to be in Tolland when you insisted you were somewhere else. You could have killed Mehmet Orhan away from the village. Knowing Fred Slade had just been buried you could have returned home to bury Orhan in the churchyard and come back again on the Monday to remove incriminating evidence.'

'This is farcical!' Maynard was furious, his eyes almost starting from their sockets as he protested. 'Who's this Slade?'

'An old Tolland resident.'

The moustache and teeth were lofted imperiously until Maynard resembled an arrogant rabbit.

'I only live here. I do not associate with the locals.'

'Then explain what it was made you return to Tolland on the 22nd.'

Maynard responded to Tyrell's implicit authority. He sank back in his chair and passed a shaking hand across his mouth then stared at Tyrell and encountered sternness.

'I need to speak in confidence.'

'We only use what's necessary for our investigation – unless a crime's been committed.'

'That's just it. I was trying to clear up an unholy mess. One of my partners – '

'Bailey or Webster?'

Maynard was surprised by Tyrell's knowledge. 'Philip Bailey. He'd been conned, he said, while working with an estate agent. Mortgage fraud. Ralph Webster found out and alerted me. That was on the 15th, a Monday, and I went straight to London. While Ralph kept the firm running as usual, I tried to straighten out the situation. Philip didn't like what it would mean to him, financially and so on. He emptied a client's account and flew to Spain. The weekend you believe I was disposing of some God-forsaken Turk, I was attempting to stop Claire Bailey killing herself. When her GP got her into a nursing home, I went to Spain to find Philip.' He glared at Tyrell. 'I had to race back in the early hours of that Monday to get my passport and be at Heathrow for a midday flight. Satisfied?'

'And the Friday night, the 19th? For our records.'

'Contact Claire's sister Jane. She and Dr Malone, the GP, can confirm I was in Esher. 14, Spindrift Lane. All night.'

'Thank you, sir. As to the offences committed by your partner – '

'Don't worry about that, Inspector. The bloody estate agent's blaming Philip – and he's already made sure the Law Society have been fully informed. They'll penalise us harder than the courts.'

When Maynard was occupied making his statement, Mortimer beckoned to Tyrell.

'That idea you had when you got to the suicide. Follow it up now. I'll see to Little Hitler.'

The DI parked by the gate he had only seen at night. The heavy rain had eased to a drizzle but it had left a legacy. The verge was a quagmire and Tyrell guessed the path through the wood must be a necklace of puddles. He changed his shoes for rubber boots stowed in his car and still muddy after the search for Barry.

Fresh wire held the gate to its post. The chain he had ordered cut hung loose, the marks made by the bolt-cutters already dulling. The inspector hefted the lock as he looked for scratches. There were none.

Deep in thought the DI climbed into the wood and walked along the path. He had not gone far when he stopped, puzzled by the realisation he was rubbing his fingers together. They were slippery and that could only have happened when he held the lock.

'Is DS Clarke available?' he asked Sergeant Thompson by radio.

'No, sir.'

'WDC Paige?'

'Yes, sir. Do you need her?'

Tyrell did not have long to wait before Emma Paige, wearing her wellingtons, joined him. The DI showed her the heavy lubrication and the lack of scratches.

'Someone got that lock ready to be used,' he said. 'When?'

'And why?' she asked.

They trudged through water and mud to the sycamore Barry had climbed.

'Where did he get the rope from?'

'At a guess, the manor. Barry used to work there, remember. Maybe he found it in one of the outhouses? Who knows?'

'I suppose it was suicide?'

'We'll have to wait for the pathologist but I'm sure that's what she'll confirm,' Tyrell said. 'Now, between us and the road where we parked is a track leading off to the lake.'

'I didn't see it.'

'Remember that fact. It's supposed to be down there on the right and we have to find it.'

It was harder to locate than Tyrell had assumed but they persevered. Two hundred yards away from the sycamore a fallen branch lay alongside the path.

'You know, sir, it's odd.'

'Go on.'

'That branch.' Emma Paige looked up at the surrounding trees. 'Where did it come from? There's no sign of a fresh scar up there. It must have been pulled into place.'

'Yes, it was, wasn't it. Let's see why – and make sure you don't put your big feet on any evidence,' he said and grinned at her.

258

Scanning the ground they moved through the clearing behind the concealing branch.

'Sir! Tyre marks!'

Tyrell picked his way to where Emma Paige was bent over a ridge of soil sheltered from the rain by a dense hazel bush. The marks were too indistinct to be used for identification but there was no doubt a vehicle had been driven there, away from the rutted track. He looked back at the fallen branch.

'You know, move that aside and you could get a car through quite comfortably. Even a Mercedes.'

In the garden, early roses were defeated. Only buds thrust upwards and were a sign of hope. Mrs Gallagher knocked at the door and waited, savouring the smell of wet earth and crushed greenery that was the aftermath of the rain.

The door creaked open. 'Annie King!'

'It's a long time since anyone called me that.'

Elsie Slade beamed at her visitor. 'You'd better come in.'

When they were seated in the tiny parlour Elsie studied her unexpected guest.

'Well?'

'You've had a lot of dealings with the police.'

Elsie nodded. 'So've you – if all the stories told are half-true.'

Anne Gallagher threw back her head and laughed, a rich, full-bodied sound in the stuffy little room, and Elsie saw again the fiery girl who had been Annie King.

'I doubt you and I have had the same sort of dealings with the coppers.'

'I'd be as well off as you if I had.'

Anne Gallagher looked around. 'You're pretty comfortable – and with a daughter who's a marvellous cook.

Does she know what Mrs Fell charges for her quiches when they're sold on?'

'Too much. Still, there's folks who can't get Agnes' cooking any other way. Is that why you've come? To get Mrs Fell done for over-charging?'

'No. I need to know about the police working in Tolland. In the old days I could suss out which copper would be a client – given half a chance – and the odd one who meant well. That was all a long time ago and things have changed.' She hesitated. 'Inspector Tyrell?'

'Ah, you've picked a right one there. Tell you who he reminds me of, that middle boy of the Crabtrees'.'

'The teacher's son? Andrew.' Anne Gallagher was thoughtful. 'I suppose he does. The same way of looking straight at you and seeing what you didn't want him to know.'

'Looks like him, too. You'd gone by the time he grew up and they moved away. Handsome boys, they were.'

'Inspector Tyrell?'

'Married.'

'As he wears a wedding ring I'd guessed that much.'

'He's been here,' Elsie said. 'It was because of him Fred's grave was opened when I said summat was wrong. For a young un, he's a good listener, I'll say that for him.'

'Can he be trusted?'

'Why? You got a secret?'

'No. I might be able to help him.'

'And you don't want the village finding out?'

Anne Gallagher nodded and, like a small bird on a twig, Elsie tilted her head as she studied her visitor.

'What's brought this on?'

'Barry Warren.'

'Poor little soul, he never had a chance born the way he was. Just like Billy, his uncle.' Elsie's mind roved the past. 'Billy's mother used to work for the Kings. You knew her.'

'Bessie. She was always kind to me. So were all the Warrens – much more than my so-called family.'

'Aye, good-hearted folk, the Warrens, but there's nothing you, or Inspector Tyrell, can do to help Chrissie and Reg.'

Anne Gallagher sighed and, for once, looked her age. 'I know. Maybe we owe it to Barry to make sure nobody else gets hurt.'

The SOCO team was in the wood photographing, measuring, making a cast of the tyre track.

'Not very clear,' one member grumbled as he poured a viscous liquid into the prepared site. 'I can't guarantee it'll be sharp enough to get anywhere near an identification, especially after all this rain.'

The cast-maker was another who resented Tyrell's youth. The DI went off to supervise the drawing away of the branch.

'Lift it! Don't drag it!'

Care was rewarded and two faint tyre marks were found underneath the foliage.

'These are even worse,' the cast-maker decided.

'What's important is the exact distance between them. If we're in luck it can give us the chassis size, maybe even a make – and that's hard evidence.'

Tyrell's radio crackled. Replying to Mortimer the DI wondered if the super was feeling rough, his voice sounded strained.

'Just wrapping it up here, sir.'

'Next step?'

'We need the measurements of the Mercedes Orhan drove, specifically between the wheels.'

'Right. You'd better get back. Leave WDC Paige there.'

* * *

261

The atmosphere in the incident room was subdued and Mortimer looked tired. Discreetly, he slipped a tablet under his tongue, his expression daring Tyrell to comment.

'One of the DCs flicked through the RTA reports and thought he recognised the number of a car involved in last night's crash at Highnam. DS Simons.'

'How bad is he?'

'Severe head injuries. The paramedics got him to Gloucester. After he was stabilised he was transferred to Frenchay. Life support.'

Tyrell knew the Bristol hospital and the good work it did. Simons was in good hands.

'Chances?'

Mortimer lifted a hand, its fingers splayed, and waggled it like the wings of a plane.

'Poor devil. How did it happen?'

'Heavy rain. I rang Gloucester to see if there were any more details. A witness had phoned in, said the driver was slumped over the steering wheel as the car spun out of control.'

'Was anyone else involved?'

'No, thank God.' Mortimer straightened in his chair. 'Well, what've you got?'

Tyrell outlined the new evidence, such as it was. 'I'll give it to DC Close to follow up, he's good with cars.'

'Agreed. As for you, you've been on Driffield land and no warrant.'

'Part of a murder enquiry, sir.'

'That'll be the best argument. Let the legal boys look into it, just to be on the safe side. You, my lad, will have to go and be polite to the lord of the manor – and do remember he carries clout.'

'"The Chief Constable's a friend of mine,"' Tyrell quoted.

Mortimer was gloomy. 'Try the Home Secretary and you'll be nearer the mark.'

'Sir Edward's always been very co-operative.'

'Maybe so. You weren't turning over his back yard then.'

'No – but we were when we found Barry Warren.'

'Damned villages!' Mortimer snapped. 'Everything knitted together like some bloody awful jumper. See if you can keep him sweet – and take DS Clarke.'

Sir Edward welcomed them. He was formally dressed, his dark grey suit superbly cut and tailored.

'Will this take long? My wife and I are due at a reception and it's one of those occasions when we must not be late – if you know what I mean?'

The DI did. On top of all the demands on the force, a royal visitor was due in Cheltenham.

'We'll be as quick as we can, sir.'

Tyrell apologised for going into the wood.

'Think nothing of it, my dear chap. The entire village considers that part of my property theirs by right.' He laughed. 'I've always wondered how many of the children I see about were conceived there. A frightening number, I've no doubt. Did you find anything useful?'

The DI explained the Mercedes' possible hiding place.

'How ingenious! And you say the lock on the gate had been oiled? Someone went to a deal of trouble.'

'Someone with a key,' Tyrell reminded him.

Sir Edward chuckled and Tyrell had a glimpse of the boy inside the man.

'Come with me, Inspector Tyrell. Sergeant?'

They followed him through the house and were stared at by a girl laying a table in the dining-room. Their host marched on, pushing open a green baize-covered door and going along a flagstoned corridor past the kitchens. He did not stop and they were in a yard, the stable buildings ahead of them. Only when the tack-room door was pushed open did Sir Edward stop and face them, smiling broadly. He pointed to a key hanging in full view.

'There you are, Inspector. I expect half Tolland could have told you where it was.'

'Are these buildings ever locked up?'

'What for? They're away from the house. Anyone who wanted to get in and rob us could do so, no sweat, even if we'd the latest in alarm systems. It's easier this way. If there're no bars and bolts, matey assumes there's nothing worth stealing.'

'Is there anyone in the house who could have seen it being taken?'

Sir Edward shook his head. 'It would depend on the time of day but I doubt it.'

'It's not been missed?'

'No one's complained.'

'Edward!' Lady Driffield stood at the kitchen door. 'We should be leaving. Now!'

She was a picture of well-bred elegance in a suit of jade silk, her chin tilted imperiously in the shadow of a wide-brimmed hat. Her husband started towards her, then remembered the policemen.

'Was there anything else, Inspector?'

'No, Sir Edward. Not at the moment.'

The two officers saw Sir Edward reach his wife and take her hand in his.

'Ah,' sighed Brian Clarke, 'what marriage is for some folks. It takes the shine off it a bit when you have to change the nappies and take out the rubbish.'

'Maybe, but for her he'd clean the Augean Stables.'

'You've been at the Greek gods again,' the sergeant said. 'In that case, we'd better find an oracle to tell us who nicked that damned key.'

'It's me, Mother,' Agnes called out.

'I should hope so. Anyone else and I might've been in the altogether!' Elsie shouted.

264

Agnes was relieved. Someone had perked her mother's spirits. Whoever it was received a silent blessing.

'You sound better.'

Elsie came down the stairs. 'Nothing wrong with me.'

'No? Since the service in the churchyard, and the one for the American, you've been real down.'

'Well, nothing more to fight for. With the rain so bad I couldn't even get to your dad to tell him about it.'

'So, who's been here?'

'Annie King.'

Agnes was puzzled, then her expression cleared. 'Mrs Gallagher.'

'Annie King, I knew her, and she still is to me.'

'What did she want?'

'A chat.'

'What about?'

'None o' your business.'

Elsie followed her daughter into the kitchen and inspected packages before they were put in the fridge.

'She hasn't changed much – Annie. Miss Caroline would like her, they'd get on well.'

'Caroline? What – ?'

'If Miss Caroline and Annie King got friendly, her ladyship wouldn't like it one bit.'

'Mother!'

Agnes shook her head. She was resigned to her mother's scheming and filled the kettle.

'Anything new in the village?' her mother asked.

'Major Clawson got rushed off to hospital last night – his heart trouble again. This time it's real bad and Mrs Clawson's hoping they'll do the bypass. If they don't he doesn't stand much of a chance.'

'Who's been telling you all this?'

'Mrs Fell. And the vicar's son hasn't got AIDS. His mother had a phone call yesterday to say he's in the clear.' Agnes poured boiling water into the rose-trimmed pot. 'That means he never had AIDS anyway, he was just being tested to see if he was HIV positive.'

'All these new-fangled – '

Elsie was stopped in full flood by a knock at the door. Agnes hurried to answer it.

'Major Gifford! What a nice surprise,' Elsie heard her daughter say. 'Go into the parlour.'

Elsie bustled towards the newcomer and Clay Gifford smiled down at his tiny friend.

'I do hope you don't mind, ma'am, but I've brought Mrs Mandel and Professor Gordheimer with me. They're on their way back to London and they wanted to thank you for helping uncover the truth about their brother's death.'

'Bring 'em in! Agnes, proper coffee – and heat up the scones.'

'The super wants to see you, sir. Like an hour ago,' Sergeant Thompson said when Tyrell returned to the village hall.

'Thanks. Where is he?'

Thompson grinned. 'His office.'

In the men's toilet Mortimer was washing his hands, grumbling under his breath at the soap, the paper towels, the state of decay of the urinals.

'Where the hell've you been?'

'Collecting information, sir.'

'Where from?'

'Can't say, sir.'

Mortimer scowled at his subordinate. 'A bloody nark. Anything useful?'

'Name and address of a contact of Orhan's in London. Someone he came with from Turkey.'

'Promising, I suppose.'

Mortimer sighed and went back to his desk. Tyrell

found a quiet corner in the incident room and sat deep in thought . . .

Even in the safety of her own home Anne Gallagher had been unwilling to talk freely.

'When I realised I could be a suspect,' she had said at last, 'I called in a couple of favours. I wanted to find out all I could about this Mehmet Orhan, in case our paths had ever crossed.'

'Had they?'

'No.' Again she hesitated. 'I've never been one to help the police . . .'

'Do you feel threatened in some way?'

She had shaken her head, hardly disturbing the expensive hairstyle. 'Barry Warren. He shouldn't have died.'

Tyrell sensed the reason for her unhappiness.

'You think that if you'd passed on the information you had, Barry would still be alive?'

She stayed silent, her head bowed.

'Put your mind at rest. There's no way Barry's death was your fault. Believe me.'

Anne Gallagher had twisted the rings on her wedding finger, watching the play of light on gold and emeralds.

'The information. It could be of use to us – in case there's anything CID missed. The best thing we can do for the Warrens is to get this case solved and then clear out of Tolland.'

He had been patient. Eventually, Anne Gallagher had gone to her desk and taken from a drawer two sheets of paper.

'It's Orhan's friends, contacts the police might not know about.'

The DI hid his excitement as he read swiftly. 'This address in Stratford?'

'It's Stratford, east London. A kebab house.'

'And Husseyin Suleiman?'

'Came from Turkey with Orhan. He stayed in London when Orhan joined Kemal in Birmingham. Does it help?'

Tyrell was drawn back to the present by Sergeant Thompson's request to 'Settle down' and Superintendent Mortimer braced himself for a briefing.

'Firstly, an update on Sergeant Simons. He's still in intensive care and on a ventilator. It's possible he had a heart attack just before he crashed.' Mortimer consulted the data he held and breathed himself into a steady rhythm. 'Apart from a skull fracture there are internal injuries. The spleen's been removed, there are crushed ribs, lung damage and a shattered pelvis.' He looked up. 'The doctors say he's stable and, at this stage, that's all that can be hoped for.'

Pete Simons' details were placed on the desk and a file opened.

'PM on Barry Warren. It was suicide, although there was extensive bruising, prior to death, on the abdomen and back. The pathologist confirmed the GP's diagnosis that Warren was sexually immature. Small stature, no facial hair, undescended testicles,' he read. 'It's rare and possibly genetic.'

'There was an uncle like him, sir,' Martin Draper said.

Brian Clarke stood, scraping his chair as he did so. 'The bruising on Barry, sir. Had he been in a fight?'

Mortimer looked down at the notes as everyone in the room waited for the answer.

'If he had been it was one-sided. No bruises on the boy's knuckles.' Mortimer glared at the assembly. 'Now, if any of you are still harbouring the idea Warren was part of a deviant ring, forget it. And there were no signs of damage to the rectum so he hadn't been abused.' The superintendent sipped from a glass of water. 'More information's come in about Orhan's early years in the UK. Keith?'

Tyrell rose from his seat, taking attention from Mortimer who slumped in his chair.

'There's no doubt now Orhan was in London before he surfaced in Birmingham. What we could do with are his details from the Home Office and Immigration. Any luck?' he asked DC Edison.

'No, sir. After we got confirmation of Orhan's British nationality, the Home Office told us there was a fault in the computer program. What they really mean is some novice cocked up and it'll be a while before the system's back on line.'

The inspector frowned. 'That's all we need.'

'Sir,' came from someone at the back of the room.

Heads turned to PC Cole, red-eared with the sudden attention.

'I know someone in Immigration in London. She's an investigator.'

Whistles and cat-calls made the young man flush but he stood his ground and the noise died away.

'Thank you, Cole,' Tyrell said. 'If you can get hold of the officer, try this name and address on them.' He wrote swiftly, ensuring Anne Gallagher's handwriting remained as private as her list. 'Immigration may have more leverage opening this particular oyster than a posse of CID.'

PC Cole collected the information and hurried to a phone at the far end of the room.

'We must concentrate now on everyone in Tolland who could have been in London between 1979 and 1984. Once that's been sorted, I want return visits. DS Rogers will have assignments ready for you.'

'What are we looking for?' DC Edison wanted to know.

'Anyone getting rattled.'

*   *   *

The early evening air was fresh, sparkling a little as the sun reached for the skyline and slanted rays. Tyrell stood on the steps of the village hall, took a deep breath, exhaled slowly and felt tension recede.

'If only we could open windows in there and get a breeze through, we all might think more clearly.'

'Blow papers all over the place and get damp air in the computers, sir? How could you? Sacrilege, blasphemy – ' Emma Paige began.

'Treason?' Brian Clarke added.

'Let's get that drink and see if it helps.'

There was activity in Tolland as the trio walked towards the George, cars delivering their occupants home from work, teenagers on bicycles and skateboards. No one greeted them, or even looked in their direction. When Emma Paige pushed open the door of the bar, the quiet murmur inside died away. Tyrell delved for cash as he faced Sam Roberts.

'A pint of bitter and two orange juices, please.'

Sam dealt with the order, proffered the ice bucket, gave change.

Emma shivered. 'They're not looking at us but I can feel their eyes.'

'I've known worse in here.' Brian Clarke washed half his bitter down a welcoming throat. 'Even old Cyril's not moaning, for once.'

'Definitely a silver lining,' Tyrell said.

He swished juice over ice and remembered his first visit to the George to meet Clay Gifford. The entire bar had been agog. This evening the CID trio was being completely ignored. Cyril Mitton's glass held a little beer but he was in no hurry to finish it and cadge another drink. Tossy Reynolds was his silent companion, the two old men drooping in their seats.

If there were journalists present they had lost all interest in the stories which had focused attention on the tiny curve of land in the elbow of the Severn.

Myra Roberts bustled in from the kitchen, a blue

and white striped apron emphasising her trim figure. Tyrell caught her glance and saw lips firming into disapproval.

'The sooner we can finish up here, the happier everyone will be,' he said quietly. 'Especially me.'

'Amen to that,' Brian Clarke said and drained his glass.

Bobby Driffield limped in. He ordered his drink from a more cheerful Sam Roberts and teased Myra into a smile. There were cheery words for Cyril and Tossy before he noticed the police presence.

'Inspector Tyrell! Talked about you at lunchtime.' He walked towards them, careful not to spill his brew. 'Mind if I join you?' He settled himself into reasonable comfort at their table. 'The Gordheimers came to lunch – pity you couldn't have been with us. Clay Gifford was their escort and we had quite a jolly party.' Bobby Driffield's good humour spread a little warmth in the dark room. 'We needed something to cheer us up, all that damned rain. If anyone else mentions "flaming June", I swear I'll swing for 'em, Inspector. By the way,' he dropped his voice to a confidential whisper, 'any news of the inquest on poor young Barry?'

'Thursday, I believe,' Tyrell said.

'It'll be good to get it over with and the sad little soul buried. I'm glad there's no more nonsense about unconsecrated ground. Very hard on the relatives, I always thought.' He sipped his beer. 'I'm sorry we'll be losing Major Gifford – charming chap and fine company. You'll miss him, I'm sure.'

Emma Paige excused herself and hurried out.

'I say, I hope I haven't driven her away?' The Driffield charm was pleasant, effortless.

'No, not at all. It's been a long hard day for us all,' Brian Clarke assured him.

Tyrell was concerned. He had seen tears as Emma bent her head and ran.

'I suppose you'll be nearing the end of your enquiries

271

here, Inspector? There can't be much left under the stones of the village after all your efforts.'

'It would be nice to think so.'

'And the suspicions? When you go – they'll stay. Wouldn't you agree?'

The DI gazed at his glass for a moment and then looked at his questioner.

'There're always people with grisly minds and the rest of us do our best to keep them in check. But, when there's a murder, suspicions bloom in seconds and crop heavily, sowing the seeds of doubt for years to come. That's why we have to be so thorough and investigate every possibility. It's important for us to clear the innocent as well as pinpoint the guilty.'

'Moral weeding, Inspector?'

'It was the murderer who made that necessary, Mr Driffield. He, or she, created the situation and has thrown the whole of the village at us while they hide.'

Bobby Driffield smiled. 'Tolland will survive, Inspector. Come here in six months and we'll all be back to normal.'

Tyrell's answering smile chilled. 'Not quite all, Mr Driffield – if I have my way.'

'Jenny?'

Keith closed the door, leaning against it as he waited for an answer. There were quick steps on the stairs and Jenny was in his arms. He breathed in her freshness and the day behind him dissolved.

'That bad?'

'Not really, though I've tried to keep the pressure off Mortimer as best I could.' He sniffed. There was the aroma of a good cigar. 'Who's been here?'

'Clay brought the Gordheimers on the off-chance of seeing you.' Jenny's smile was full of mischief.

'When was that?'

272

'Four o'clock.'

'It's lucky you were in.'

Her smile widened. 'Lucky, my foot. He'd phoned me at the hospital to find out what time I'd be home.'

'Clay? What's he up to?'

'Getting the Gordheimers here. They're delightful, aren't they? And so appreciative of the tact and discretion you used from the moment you unearthed their little brother.'

In the sitting-room Keith sprawled as he let his muscles relax. Jenny was beside him, hiding her anxiety as she saw the tiredness which invaded every inch of him.

'I don't think it did Rebecca – Mrs Mandel – any harm to have a quiet sit down and a cuppa before driving to Oxford. Aaron lectured there in the seventies,' she explained. 'And Aaron didn't miss the chessboard. He's left his email address on the pad. If you fancied a game sometime, he'd be delighted.'

'I suppose if he's too good for me I can pass him on to Stephen.'

'Clay's coming back at the weekend to take us out to dinner. He did ask a favour.' Jenny's expression was solemn. 'Would I persuade you to get Emma Paige to join us – make up a foursome?'

Keith began to chuckle. 'So that's why . . .' He described the tears.

'Didn't you notice anything?'

'Not a thing, I promise. I don't even remember seeing them together.'

'And you call yourself a detective? For that you can cook dinner. I did the tea-time entertaining – all you have to do is pull it out of the fridge.'

Later, it was luxury to sit in the conservatory and enjoy the peace of a summer's evening.

'Now it's dry again, I'll have to cut the grass.'

'The exercise will do you good. It'll take your mind off all things Tolland.'

Keith stared into space, his mind troubled and far from Jenny.

'Talk to me,' she pleaded.

He tried to arrange his thoughts into a coherent pattern. 'It's the waiting.'

'There's nothing new in that, surely?'

'I don't mean us. It's the village.'

He told her of the walk to the George, the silent customers, the sense of unease.

'It's as though the entire place is holding its breath.'

'May it soon be over, then you can pack away all the files and computers and get out of Tolland for good.'

Jenny went to brew coffee.

'I never thought, all those months ago, when I read that article on Tolland that we'd ever be so caught up by what's happened there,' she called from the kitchen. 'I only noticed it at the time because it wasn't far away from us. Not much – '

'What article?'

She was surprised by his sudden energy. 'It was in a magazine your mother brought over at New Year. You know she always packs a pile of the ones she hasn't had time to read.'

'Have you still got it?'

'Not in the house. It's probably in the shed, tied up for recycling. All that should have gone a long time ago but you've been so busy . . .'

Keith had not heard her, he was running to the lean-to that covered the lawnmower as well as plastic bags of cans, bottles, paper. Jenny followed and watched him slash apart her tidy bales.

'What was it called?'

'I don't know,' she said. '*Woman's* something.'

'That's a fat lot of help! Look, if I pass you the magazines, can you go through them and find the article?'

'I hope you're going to tidy all this up after – '

'Please!'

274

She settled on an old chair that needed painting. 'I could do with some more light.'

Keith ran to the garage, returning with a bulb on a cable. He switched on the light.

'Jenny, if you love me, find the damned article.'

'Calm down,' she said. 'I'm looking.'

Patience was summoned from the depths of his being as Keith watched Jenny flick through page after page, discarding first one magazine, then another. At last she stopped, turned back to a section she had passed.

'This is it.'

There was enough light for him to see the figures in the photographs alongside the prose. Reverend Hatton was with Reg Warren in the church porch. The Clawsons stood in the beauty of their garden. Sir Edward and Lady Driffield were working in the study at the manor. Elaine Poynter was surrounded by children in the playgroup. Mrs Fell guarded her cash-register while Myra and Sam Roberts were a smiling pair at the bar of the George.

'Is that what you wanted?'

Keith pulled Jenny to him and kissed her. 'You are a genius. All along it's been a puzzle why Orhan waited for years before he tried blackmail. He must have seen this article and recognised someone.'

'Who? Do you know?'

'Not that I can prove. We've still no real evidence. Maybe tomorrow.'

Chapter Twelve

The early morning promised warmth and Penny Rogers had already discarded the jacket of her lightweight suit. She smiled a welcome at Tyrell.

'Morning, sir. You're early.'

He handed her the magazine. 'Page 42.'

She studied the photos, then turned to the front cover to find the date of publication.

'December, last year? This must have been what gave Orhan the idea of blackmail.'

'Almost certainly. I rang the super last night. He's agreed full, but discreet, surveillance on the most likely suspects until we've got factual evidence from the Home Office or Immigration.'

Sergeant Clarke, yawning, his tie loose, ambled in followed by Martin Draper.

Tyrell beckoned. 'Just the man I want.'

Brian Clarke blinked himself awake and was relieved to see the DI's gaze on Draper.

'Sir?'

Martin Draper was presented with the magazine. Brian Clarke looked over his shoulder and was startled by the article.

'Christ! Where did this come from?'

'My shed,' Tyrell said. 'Why didn't we know about this?' he demanded of everyone present.

'But we did, sir,' Draper protested. 'I brought in a copy and showed it to DCI Whittaker. I saw him pass it on to DS Simons.'

'When was this?'

'The day the two of them came back from Birmingham.'

In an uncomfortable silence, no one mentioned the obsession which had pushed aside all other considerations. His team watched for Tyrell's reaction.

'It's all water under the bridge,' he said. 'Anyway, we still have to wait for a lead from Immigration.' The DI straightened his shoulders and turned to Brian Clarke. 'As soon as Cole gets in, sit with him and get something from London we can work on.'

Clarke was not happy. 'Civil servants won't be answering their phones until the second cup of coffee's gone down.'

'Immigration have to work our hours – more or less. If you start early you might get an unofficial angle from Cole's buddy.'

'It's his aunt, sir,' Martin Draper said.

'Whatever. Push it as hard as you can.'

Tyrell allowed himself the luxury of a brief smile, remembering PC Cole's flaming ears.

'Can you get an update on DS Simons' condition?' he asked Penny Rogers. 'The super will want to start his briefing with a report – and I'd like to know what progress he's making. After that, I'd be glad of your help organising the surveillance teams.'

Emma Paige joined the group around the opened magazine. Tyrell noted her pallor and dark shadows, deciding there were more urgent issues than cheering a lovelorn WDC.

'We can omit the Clawsons,' he began. 'Even if they are the guilty pair I don't see him doing a runner from an intensive care bed. To cover ourselves we'd better have an eye on Reg Warren and the vicar. As for the others, Mrs Poynter's an obvious starter but there's no way she could have heaved Orhan around in the middle of the night. Draper, what about her husband?'

'He looks weedy but he does a lot of cycling and he is a regular jogger.'

'Is he a possible?'

Martin Draper frowned as he concentrated. 'Unlikely – but he's best not neglected.'

'Right. Both Poynters under observation today, please.'

Penny Rogers returned in time to make a note of the names.

'Simons?' Tyrell asked.

'No change.'

Everyone made a point of avoiding eye contact.

'At least he's no worse – and he's very fit,' the DI added. 'If anyone can make a fight of it, Simons can. Now, the Fells.'

Martin Draper cleared his throat. 'Trying to separate Mrs Fell and her money would be much the same as a tigress and her cubs. As for Joe Fell, he never says much. He's good with his hands, moves quietly and can hump sacks of spuds or cases of tinned stuff, no sweat.'

'They're in,' Tyrell decided.

The same agreements were reached for Sir Edward and his wife as well as Sam and Myra Roberts.

'I'll leave the allocations to you,' Tyrell told Penny Rogers. 'I'd like minimum observation and monitoring of each household until the super's had his briefing – just so we're sure who's where.' The team began to disperse. 'Paige, a word.'

Tyrell suggested the weekend dinner with Clay Gifford and saw Emma become radiant.

'What can I do now?'

'Go to the shop and get some – biscuits.'

'But that's sexist!'

'Of course it is. Mrs Fell's more likely to gossip with you than DC Edison and I want to know that lady's mood.'

Emma calmed down. 'OK. It makes sense.'

'Thank you, Miz Paige,' Tyrell said with a grin.

The first teams were out, trying to look inconspicuous in a village that left nothing unnoticed. DC Edison sat in his car at a distance from the George, able to keep in view the front door of the pub as well as the main gates of the manor and the path between vicarage and church. Another DC had parked his car on the verge by Tossy Reynold's cottage. He appeared to be catching up with his sleep as, through slitted lids, he watched the Poynter house further along the road.

'Not much movement yet,' DC Edison reported by radio. 'Sam Roberts has opened up the cellar trap door. I'd guess a delivery's imminent. And there goes the vicar. He's trotting back from church and looking hungry.'

Martin Draper nodded sagely. 'Eight thirty communion. I expect he was the only one.'

'Poynter on the move. Car heading towards the lower road, most likely going to Gloucester.' It was a different voice on the speaker.

'It's where he works,' Tyrell said. 'Get his registration number to traffic police and monitor his route to the office. If he's going to be there as normal we don't want to waste manpower.'

'Poynter's late this morning,' Martin Draper said. 'I wonder why?'

There was no time for an answer as Superintendent Mortimer walked into a room full of people working hard. Tyrell, in his shirt-sleeves, was moving from a computer terminal to a group poring over data. He looked up and saw Mortimer.

The older man smiled approval. 'I see you've gone ahead with what we discussed last night. Good lad. Got a list for me?'

Tyrell handed him a sheet of notes.

'Simons is hanging in there,' Mortimer said. 'Let's get on.'

*   *   *

Summer had arrived and the vicarage garden was not ready for it. The lilac tree accused him, its white heads of flowers tinged with brown. It would all take so much time and there were more important matters to consider.

Nicholas Hatton turned his back on his problems and strode through the early sunshine, welcoming its warmth on his back.

'Good morning, Cyril. Nice day,' he called to old man Mitton going snail-like towards the shop and his paper.

'Mornin', Vicar.'

A police car whizzed between them and annoyed Cyril Mitton.

'It's all right for some folks goin' the length of the village in their cars. That rain was bad for my room-aticks. Comin' 'ere of a mornin', I could do with a lift.'

'It's keeping moving that's the secret, Cyril,' the cleric assured him. 'These young people in cars will rust up sooner than you or I.'

Reverend Hatton strode on, leaving Cyril to complain to himself until he reached the shop and Mrs Fell.

The road to the Warrens' cottage had dried quickly although there were still puddles in the ruts alongside its length. Water was retreating and the exposed grey mud puckered as it dried, matched by a fine dust that powdered the tarmac. The vicar inhaled deeply as he marched, ashamed to feel so well and full of hope as he neared the home of two devastated parents. Under his breath he chanted the prayers that calmed, his personal rosary of belief.

Nicholas Hatton paused with his hand on the gate into the Warrens' garden. There were no weeds to be seen. He shook his head and sadness reached his eyes, blurring what he saw. All too soon neglect would mar the ordered greenness, just as his had.

Humility welled up. His own son had been saved and

280

he must take what comfort he could to parents who were enduring the ultimate loss. The door opened and Reg Warren waited for him.

'Mornin', vicar.'

'Good morning, Reg. How's your wife?'

'Up and about.'

'Can I see her? Talk to her?'

Reg shrugged his shoulders and held the door wide. 'You can try.'

Chrissie Warren sat motionless at the kitchen table. The vicar went to her, sitting near and putting his hand on hers. She looked at him, her eyes deep pools of peaty water that washed his secrets from him.

'You bin there,' she said at last.

'Where, Chrissie?'

She nodded. 'You bin there.'

In spite of the close air of the room Reverend Hatton felt a chill across his shoulders and he suppressed a shiver. Gently, he spoke of Barry, the peace the boy had found, the joy of heaven that was now his. Chrissie's head swayed from side to side and her hands became fists under his fingers.

'Barry can't get to heaven while he's still alive.'

'He? Who's he, Chrissie?'

'The Devil,' she said simply.

With all his rhetoric the vicar tried to reassure the mother her son's soul was safe but he was made helpless by her implacability.

'It's no good, Vicar,' Reg said. 'She'll 'ave none o' it. I bin tryin' – God knows I bin tryin'. Chrissie grew up along o' Granny Phelps and that owd bitch saw Satan in ev'ry man as ever breathed.'

Reverend Hutton had heard tales of the old woman who would have been burned as a witch in days gone by. In reality she had only been an embittered female who played on the fears of the gullible. Granny Phelps had enjoyed the power she exercised over them, as well as the presents in cash and kind which were meant to keep her friendly.

'Just be patient, Reg,' the vicar advised in a whisper. 'Chrissie will come to terms with it in her own way. Once time has passed she'll remember Barry when he was happy and it will be as though he's with her again.'

Reg stared at his wife and even Reverend Hatton's confidence faltered. Chrissie had not moved and about her was a vague aura of menace.

'It may take a while,' the vicar amended.

'Maybe she'll be better when the boy's laid to rest. I'll dig 'is grave ready.'

Nicholas Hatton had already experienced the agony of imagining himself conducting Will's funeral service.

'No, Reg. I can't allow you to do that. It would be too much for you.'

Reg's mouth tightened. 'Vicar, s'only right I do it meself.'

The vicar sighed, defeated. 'As you wish. We'll pick him a good spot.'

'S'af'noon? Agnes Morse's comin' to sit wi' Chrissie.'

'This afternoon it is, Reg.'

As he closed the gate Nicholas Hatton looked back at the house. Such a simple abode, little more than a large hut, yet in it were perhaps the only two people in Tolland for whom God and the Devil were real and as human as everyone else.

'If I ever get captured by terrorists I'll know what to expect!'

Emma slammed down her shopping and poured herself coffee.

'Mrs Fell?' Tyrell asked.

'That nosy old bitch! She not only wanted to know every detail of the state of play here, she also asked if

I found red hair and freckles a disadvantage. I nearly thumped her!'

'I'm glad you didn't. You've been in the shop before. Has there been any change in her manner?'

'She's very uptight for some reason. When I went in she was nagging her husband.'

'Did you hear what she said?'

'She kept telling him they've got to hang on, no matter what.'

'Suggestive – no more than that. Make sure it's recorded.'

Emma took her coffee and herself to the desk she used as Penny Rogers approached the DI.

'I just wish we could get something through from London,' she said.

Tyrell looked across the room to where Brian Clarke was being handed a phone.

'Fingers crossed, this is it.'

They watched the sergeant listen carefully, his dark features lightening until he wore a broad smile. Swift notes were made and, after thanking the person who had cheered him, he passed the instrument back to PC Cole and headed, with rugby-jinking swiftness, towards the inspector.

'Bingo! Kathy Newman, Cole's aunt, didn't know of this Husseyin Suleiman when we first asked yesterday. Since then she's interviewed him and he's opened up for her, sweet as a nut. I gather he's furious with a chap, originally from Ankara, who lifted a couple of grand off him in exchange for British citizenship.'

'When was that?' Tyrell asked.

'1981.'

'He's not naturalized?'

'Thought he was and he's very aggrieved at being cheated. Because of that Suleiman's prepared to co-operate with Immigration. In return, he's hoping to be allowed to stay here with his Turkish wife.'

The DI could see Brian Clarke was delighted to be holding something back.

'And?'

'He's singing his socks off about a certain Yunus Murat the Home Office would be very happy to deport. Murat, amongst his other activities, arranged marriages to British citizens – supposedly all legal and above board. He did it for Suleiman and for Orhan but Suleiman wasn't at his friend's wedding so he's no idea of the girl involved.'

'1981 – two thousand pounds? Steep for those days,' Mortimer said. 'Something extra on offer?'

Brian Clarke beamed. 'Got it in one, sir. The deal included a divorce. After two years Suleiman signed the official papers that arrived. In due course he was sent his decree absolute and married a girl who came over from his home town.'

Tyrell was puzzled. 'Wait a minute. By the time this Murat has taken his cut and paid the woman her fee, there wouldn't be enough cash left for a divorce. Yet Suleiman had one – or rather, and I'm guessing, he didn't.'

'Spot on! The marriage to the British woman had to be legal for the Home Office to allow him to stay here.'

'But if the divorce wasn't kosher and if Suleiman's married again . . .' Penny Rogers said.

'It's bigamy,' Tyrell concluded. 'It is for the woman as well – if she's remarried.'

'Suleiman's more or less in the clear on that score,' Brian Clarke said as he checked his notes. 'He married his Turkish girl in a Muslim ceremony. They didn't have a civil one in front of a British registrar so he's made no false statements there.'

Mortimer was dismissive. 'That's for the legal boys to fight over.' He waited for the DI to carry on.

'What we need to know for certain is which of the suspects, here in Tolland, Orhan married in London. Which of the women was there in 1981?'

'I'm accessing the file.'

Maria Gilbert tapped the keyboard of the nearest computer. There was a moment's wait as she searched for dates.

'First one up. Elaine Marie Poynter, née Sims. In 1981 she was temping from an agency in Brixton.'

'She wouldn't make much money there,' Emma Paige said, 'so even five hundred pounds would have gone a long way.'

'Myra Stubbins, now Roberts. That year she was working in the Dawlish Hotel, St James's.' Maria Gilbert was intent on the screen. 'Helen Mary Tyler, better known as Lady Driffield, was employed in an insurance office in Holborn.'

'One more to go,' Tyrell said.

'And here she is. Eileen Mavis Murphy – Mrs Fell to you all. At the time in question she was a shop assistant in Kensington.'

'Damn it!' Tyrell was annoyed. 'We can't eliminate anyone.'

'We've just got to wait it out until the Home Office grinds itself to a start,' Mortimer said. 'There's always the General Register Office but that usually takes even longer. Did you ask Immigration if they'd got data on Orhan's marriage?'

'I did, sir. They said they'd do what they could but it would take time. "Don't hold your breath" was what they actually told me.'

Mortimer was ready to relieve himself in a bout of cursing but a tightness in his chest reminded him to be careful.

'Where are all the damned suspects anyway?' he growled.

'Poynter's tucked up at his desk, the rest are loose cannons,' Tyrell told him.

'Edison!' the superintendent shouted. 'Keep on at those bloody civil servants!'

*   *   *

The morning wore on. Surveillance teams changed at frequent intervals, ensuring no one guessed their real intent. Joe Fell was followed out of the village as was Sir Edward, half an hour later. Records of behaviour patterns showed there was nothing suspicious in either journey.

Mrs Fell continued to moan to her few remaining customers while Lady Driffield walked round the garden with secateurs and a trug, clipping, tidying, putting in order. Mrs Poynter was similarly engaged. She could be seen kneeling by flowerbeds and rooting out weeds. As for Myra Roberts, her morning was spent in the pub's kitchen, a fact easily spotted by the WDC monitoring her movements through the open back door.

Superintendent Mortimer was called to Gloucester. It might be fast approaching the time an arrest could be made but area meetings had to carry on as planned and he was needed.

'If you can get it wrapped up, Keith, we'll all sleep better,' the superintendent said as he waited for his driver.

'You don't want us to call you?'

Mortimer's smile was weary. 'With a week to go to retirement, feeling a collar's hardly likely to affect my chances of promotion. No, lad. You see to it.'

'Yes, sir, I will – if the Home Office ever coughs up.'

The DI returned to the incident room, annoyed by the lack of fresh air.

'What's the hold-up?'

DC Edison had his own exasperation. 'All they keep saying is they'll get back to us as soon as possible.'

'You have told them it's for a murder investigation?'

'Yes, sir,' the DC explained with heavy patience. 'Every time I ring 'em.'

'Sorry, Edison,' Tyrell said quickly. 'I feel we're so near.'

'You know who it'll be, don't you, sir?'

'Maybe, but I can't move an inch without proof,

286

written proof and not just uncorroborated hearsay. This time we've got to be a hundred per cent sure when we go in.'

The aftermath of the chaotic mess at Greenbank was still causing problems and no one wanted a repetition.

'Yes, sir,' Edison agreed. 'What about lunch?'

'Lunch?'

'We usually go over to the George. Would it be best to go on the early side today? We'd be ready for action then when the info does come from London.'

'Good idea. It's best we carry on as normal and give no hint we're near a solution. Go on and get your steak and kidney,' he said to Edison and grinned. 'And remember, all of you,' he called out, 'not a single word, even if you know for certain every one of the regulars around you has been certified dead.'

It was the signal for a discreet rush. In the sudden quiet Tyrell stretched his head back, feeling neck and shoulder muscles crack with their release from tension. Emma Paige offered him a plate.

'Some of Agnes Morse's quiche, sir?'

The DI examined his proposed lunch. It was fresh and smelled appetising but he was curious.

'When did you get this?'

'I went over to the shop half and hour ago. You wanted an eye kept on the lady. Put some profit in her till and she'll sing like a canary.'

Tyrell was enjoying Agnes' cooking, licking wayward crumbs into his mouth.

'Is Mrs Fell still on edge?'

Emma nodded. 'She was moaning on, fed up she'd been left on her own again, her Joe being at the cash-and-carry.'

The DI grinned. 'I wonder if she knows he spent time this morning at their bank in Gloucester?'

'She didn't mention it.' Wickedness flashed in a smile. 'Maybe he's cleared out the account and is running off to the Bahamas. I wouldn't blame him.'

When the quiche had been washed down with luke-warm coffee Tyrell reached for a file.

'Where's Fell now?' he called to Brian Clarke who was manning the radio link.

'Just arrived at the cash-and-carry.' He listened to a report. 'Sir Edward's having lunch with his mates – he was late getting there because his morning meeting in the council offices went on so long.'

'Poynter?'

'Sandwich bar near his office. Salad in wholemeal with coleslaw.'

'Sam Roberts will be pulling pints,' Emma said.

'No, he's not. He drove to Newnham and has just turned up the Littledean road,' Brian Clarke reported.

'Where's he off to?' she wondered.

The DI was not concerned. 'He'll have Homes and Waters tailing him. They're good.'

'The men are all out, the women at home,' Emma noted. 'It's like some game – and they're all playing it.'

'What about the women?' Tyrell asked Clarke.

'Mrs Poynter and her ladyship are still in their gardens. Mrs Roberts is in and out of her kitchen, very hot. She's told Edison and Co. she's off for a bath.'

'Mrs Fell?'

'A customer has just gone in, so she'll be making money.'

'And we wait,' Tyrell said.

Time dragged on, minute by minute, and DC Edison returned from his meal at the George. He would have enjoyed sleeping under a tree while the sunlight danced through the leaves but DI Tyrell was restless, a hawk ready to pounce on the slightest movement.

Only when Reverend Hatton appeared in the incident room was Tyrell's attention diverted from the investigation.

'I've been with the Warrens this morning, Inspector.'

Tyrell saw a ruddy glow in the vicar's cheeks, a fullness there that told of well-being.

'How are they?'

'Not good – as you'd imagine. I tried to comfort them as best I could but it's early days. After the funeral . . .' He sighed. 'That's really why I've come. Do you have any idea when Barry's body will be released?'

'We haven't been notified but Superintendent Mortimer should be back from headquarters later today. He'll be able to speed things up if anyone can.'

'I understand, Inspector.' The vicar smiled. 'Rank has its uses and we must all wait our turn.'

'Quite right, sir,' Tyrell agreed. 'I was glad to hear the news of your son. It must be an enormous relief to you and Mrs Hatton.'

'Indeed it is. We are at last beginning to be able to sleep at night. Unfortunately, we can also now see the "things which have been left undone", as it were. So many sins of omission, I'm afraid.'

'A situation in which we all find ourselves.'

The vicar's gaze went round the room. He could feel tension, an air of expectancy.

'Do you think you will be here much longer?'

'We'll be moved on as soon as possible, sir. Like every head office, ours saves money where it can. I've no doubt Tolland will be glad to see us go.'

'I'm not so sure.'

Tyrell was surprised. 'I didn't think they could get rid of us fast enough.'

'But when you leave, it will be because one of our number has been named a murderer.'

'Surely, knowing is better than all the suspicions?'

'Ah, each one who is not responsible for that poor man's death knows it already. Only the murderer has an uneasy spirit.'

'At least our departure would put an end to the gossip.'

'Inspector! A place like Tolland thrives on gossip.' The

vicar's features puckered impishly. 'If that were not so, how did you manage to get all your information?'

'You're right, of course, sir.'

After the door closed behind Nicholas Hatton, Tyrell called for an update.

'The women are in their homes and out of sight,' Penny Rogers reported, 'except for Mrs Fell. She's getting around that shop in a way that makes her very easily spotted.'

'The men?'

'Fell's back and the van's been unloaded. Draper's right. Fell heaves weights around like a navvy. Roberts went into a house outside Littledean. He was there about twenty minutes, then he called in at a hotel in Newnham for a drink. Last message – he was on his way home.'

'Poynter's still in his office, I expect?' Tyrell guessed and received a nod from Penny. 'Sir Edward?'

'Minsterworth. The way he's driving, it won't be long before he's turning into his own driveway.'

'Anything, Edison?'

'Immigration's still searching, and the other place won't pick up the phone. Fed up with me asking 'em to get a move on.'

'It's infuriating!'

Tyrell paced the room, noting the stacks of paper heaped on desks.

'Let's get busy. It can't be long now before we've got to pack up all this equipment. We can at least get ready for the move. Check all paper before you bin it and mark the sacks. There's to be no shredding, nothing to be destroyed – just in case.'

At regular intervals Edison phoned London numbers, losing patience fast. The DI was supervising stowage of all the paper that had been amassed on paedophiles when Edison became excited.

'Sir! They've found it. Home Office fax coming through!'

290

Tyrell raced to the fax machine which had begun to click, then hum. It took great self-control to wait until the message was complete. He lifted it and read the details of Orhan's 1981 marriage and his face cleared.

'Got 'em!'

There was no answer to the bell. Tyrell tried again.

'Maybe they've gone out the back way,' Emma Paige said.

'Covered,' was Brian Clarke's terse reply.

The girl shivered. 'I wish they'd hurry up.'

Footsteps approached on an uncarpeted floor. The door opened but the man peering out at them was not as any of them had seen him before. Dejected, he seemed almost oblivious to their presence.

'May we come in, sir?' Tyrell asked.

Eyes shot with agony looked up at him.

'Of course.'

With a shrug of his shoulders, Sir Edward led the way.

'What's wrong with him?' Brian Clarke whispered.

'Something's happened,' the DI said quietly. 'Play it by ear.'

The three of them followed Sir Edward to his study and they were invited to sit down. Their host went to a drinks tray near his desk and poured himself a large whisky, vaguely waving the decanter at the inspector.

'You appear to be on duty, so I'd better not offer you any of this.'

'I must speak to Lady Driffield,' Tyrell told him.

Sir Edward sat at his desk and regarded them calmly enough but said nothing.

'Where is she?' the DI asked.

Her husband rubbed his forehead, then covered his mouth with shaking fingers. 'Upstairs.'

A nod from Tyrell sent Clarke and Paige from the room. In their absence Sir Edward sipped his whisky, his eyes unfocused as thoughts tormented. The quiet comfort of the panelled room, enhanced by the measured tick of a clock on the mantelpiece, made his misery obscene.

The sergeant's expression and a greenish tinge to Emma Paige's normally healthy skin, explained the situation for Tyrell.

'You had a meeting and then lunched in Gloucester. Did you find her when you returned, Sir Edward?'

'How – ? Of course, we must have been under observation. For how long?'

'Complete surveillance, only today.'

'Am I to be charged with killing my wife?'

The DI glanced at his sergeant and Brian Clarke cleared his throat.

'I doubt it, sir. Lady Driffield was seen after you left for Gloucester.'

'What was she doing?' There was pleading in the question.

'She did some pruning this morning. After that she was walking around, touching plants. She stood under the cedar for one long spell, looking back at the house.'

'Saying goodbye.' Sir Edward took a sheet of paper from his pocket. 'You'd better see this.' He handed it to the inspector. 'I'd like it back.'

Tyrell read swiftly. 'You may, eventually, but we'll need it for the coroner.' He turned to the sergeant. 'Get things under way.'

'Now, Sir Edward, may we have your version of events?'

In a corner Emma Paige prepared to take notes as the man drained his glass.

'Where shall I begin?'

'The beginning?'

'For me that would be the first day I met Helen. For her, I suppose it would be when she made a break from her past. Orhan was part of it.'

292

'We know about the wedding in Bethnal Green Registry Office.'

'When?'

'The possibility of cash for an arranged marriage, in the last day or two. Details of it were faxed from the Home Office less than an hour ago.'

'There was a divorce – at least, Helen believed there was. It'd been part of the deal and she had the papers.'

'I'm afraid the marriage broker had been doing a little cost-cutting. It's not unusual. Headed notepaper, signatures that are impossible to read. The documents are cheap to produce and there're no legal fees, no court costs.'

'You're sure?'

'I understand it's very unlikely the divorce was genuine. Others handled by Yunus Murat have not been.'

'I wish to God the Orhan marriage had been illegal!'

'The authorities do check thoroughly and the brokers know it. They make sure the actual ceremony is carried out properly – it has to be to pass Immigration and Home Office scrutiny. The first marriage of any woman used is usually legal. If she's involved at a later date without correct divorce procedures, then it becomes unlawful. Bigamy, trigamy, you name it – depending on how often she's paid by the broker.'

Sir Edward stood, easing misery with activity as he poured another scotch and ignored the siphon.

'Our marriage was bigamous. There was no criminal intent but ignorance is not always a good legal defence. It doesn't matter. Our sons are illegitimate and always will be.' He swirled the liquid in his glass, gazing intently at the amber movement. 'Everything Helen had struggled for wiped out by that grinning, greasy little Turk.'

'You saw him?'

'Helen had been on edge all day. Although I'd no idea

of the cause, I was aware there'd been something bothering her for a while – weeks. I was concerned and that night I followed her when she slipped out. I only realised Helen had gone to meet someone when she opened the gate into the wood. A car arrived and she made the driver go along the track until he couldn't be seen from the road.'

Sir Edward stopped talking and his listeners could see he was reliving the scene.

'It wasn't easy keeping out of sight – meant I couldn't hear what was said. I saw her hand over money and I watched the man count it. Then he looked at Helen and said something which made her furious.'

The stricken man was back in the wood, his memories flickering in slow motion.

'I swear if I'd been near enough, I'd have killed him with my bare hands.'

The words were soft, so sibilant with hate Tyrell barely heard them.

'I must caution you, Sir Edward. You are not obliged to say anything . . .'

The DI continued the legal recital, grateful Emma Paige could bear witness to its due administration.

'Do you understand, sir?'

There was a nod of assent.

'You're entitled to have your solicitor present.'

Sir Edward shook his head. 'There's no need. I just want it over.'

'As you wish, sir.'

Tyrell glanced at Emma and she pointed to her notebook. The decision had been recorded and the inspector returned to his questioning.

'How did Orhan die?'

'He opened the car door, ready to get in. Helen picked up a piece of wood and smashed it across the back of his head. When I got to her she was still shaking with anger. As I held her she told me Orhan had threatened to sell the story to a Sunday paper. You can guess what kind.'

'Hardly a reason for murder.'

'You don't understand. It meant so much to Helen to be Lady Driffield, to be accepted as my wife here, in Tolland, and amongst my friends in the county and in London. What mattered even more to her was that Max would inherit the title – and the manor. It was so important to her that, through her, he'd been born to it.' Sir Edward slammed the desk with his fist. 'Orhan's threats meant Max would lose everything and Helen hit out at the man endangering her son.'

'When you got to him was Orhan still alive?'

'There was no pulse. The back of his head was a mess and blood had dribbled from his ear. He was dead.'

'Why didn't you get help – at least notify the police? The courts tend to be lenient with anyone driven to despair by a blackmailer.'

'Oh, come on, man! Prosecuting counsel demanding to know why? Let alone the mucky media? Can you think of a better way of broadcasting to the entire world our boys are bastards? We had to make the best of it.'

Anger was beginning to replace desolation. Tyrell knew he must get what information he could while the man was willing to talk freely. 'You were left with the body. What did you do next?'

'I got Helen back to the house as quickly as I could.'

'And this was Friday, the 19th?'

'Yes. About six o'clock.'

'So it was still light?'

'More or less. There was a risk someone might feel like a walk through the woods and see the car and Orhan. I raced back with plastic bin bags to wrap round the body, got the car off the track, then I lugged him back here.'

'You didn't consider the lake?'

'Not deep enough – besides, it was getting warmer

295

and children swim there, as well as spending hours fishing. One of them might have found him.'

'Why Fred Slade's grave?'

Sir Edward leaned back and closed his eyes as exhaustion swept through him. 'It seemed like a good idea at the time. We'd been to the funeral the day before.'

'Did you plan to leave Orhan there?'

'Until I could think of something better.'

'Wasn't that going to be hard on Elsie?'

'She'd never have known. Even if I'd left him where he was, no one would have been any the wiser until she died and the grave was opened up for her.' He looked at Tyrell, his expression rueful. 'It would have worked but for you. If you hadn't been so thorough about that damned skeleton, Orhan would still be where I put him.'

Sir Edward rubbed his forehead, pushing away tiredness, and Tyrell waited.

'A freshly dug grave seemed so sensible. There wasn't time to bury him properly and you do see I couldn't leave the body in the house or buried in the grounds.'

'Why not?'

'Privacy is one luxury we don't enjoy. There are few servants these days, Inspector, but they do have the run of the place. As for the woods, poachers and villagers know every inch of them.'

'Logical, I suppose. Who disfigured the body?'

'I did. I used a log from the basket in the hall and burned it with the rest of the rubbish.'

'The fingers?'

A shudder went through the solid figure. 'A grater from the kitchen.'

Nausea rose in the man and he gulped whisky. Only when he had regained his composure did the DI take Edward Driffield through the rest of the story. The quiet churchyard. Mrs Hatton's organ practice. Young roisterers from the George. Emma Paige wrote swiftly. Her

296

notes would help when the official statement was made. 'You're being very frank, Sir Edward.'

'Why not? Whatever you charge me with, I'll plead guilty. If everything's settled quickly, it'll be much less stressful for the boys.'

'Is that why you're prepared to tell me your wife killed Orhan?'

'No, Inspector. From choice, I'd have preferred to have been the one who took the life of that worthless piece of garbage. It would have given me a great deal of satisfaction. As it is, without Helen what's my life worth?'

'If it wasn't for your sons Orhan might have lived?'

'I suppose so. We could have seen to the legalities and quietly remarried. Helen would have been Lady Driffield again and no one any the wiser.'

'But your sons exist and are illegitimate.'

'Exactly. As far as the title and the manor's concerned, they always will be. That's what she couldn't accept. When Orhan laughed at Helen, he tipped her over the edge.'

Brian Clarke had opened the door and stood waiting. The DI rose and went to him.

'All in hand?'

'Yes, sir. SOCO and Dr Collier on their way. Draper's upstairs and Sergeant Thompson at the front door. Edison's back on radio control. Once the media get wind of this we'll need back-up.'

'That'll be the super's headache. He can put HQ's press boys to work.'

Tyrell nodded to the baronet slumped in his chair.

'Keep going with him. An explanation of how he got the Merc away would help.'

'Right, sir.' Brian Clarke pointed upwards. 'She's in her bath. Third door on the left.'

It was a graceful hallway, the flight of steps shallow and of aged oak, the dark red carpeting thick. As the inspector neared the bathroom he sensed freesias, the

297

smell stronger as Martin Draper pushed the door open for him.

Lighting was soft and discreet. At first glance the woman looked relaxed, her head to one side. Tyrell noticed dark roots to the blonde hair, then he moved to stand where he could see her face. She was asleep, her personality hidden from him as fully as when she had been alive. Her body was covered by pink-flecked foam and what could be seen of her above the water was marble-pale.

Helen Driffield had been dead for some hours and Tyrell took her last message from his pocket.

My darling Edward,

I am so sorry. You deserved a better wife and the boys a better mother. Please tell them I was only trying to protect them. I thought if I hurt him he might keep quiet but he died too quickly. You, Max, Oliver, are my life. There is no other way.

I love you,
Helen

Three shall crosses below her name were firm, tragic in their simplicity. Like the dead woman, they were indelibly printed in Tyrell's memory.

She would be hauled out into a body bag, her skin wrinkled by hours of immersion. The gashes on her wrists must be examined, photographed, and her stomach contents sampled to see if she had used narcotics or merely alcohol to deaden the last, sharp pains. Water reddened by her blood would be sluiced away and the bathroom could be used again.

He heard voices and the house began to fill. The police surgeon was the first to join him in the bathroom.

'For Christ's sake, Keith, how many more?' Chris Collier demanded to know. 'And if she's been lying in a bath, how the hell is anyone supposed to estimate time of death?'

'I expect among the software there's a chart or two that might help.'

'Then the bloody pathologist can see to it. She's paid more than me.' The doctor crouched by the body. 'All I'm prepared to do is pronounce her dead.' He looked at his watch. 'At 4.52 p.m. My God, but she bled!'

Tyrell watched the doctor take and record the temperatures of the body, the surrounding water, the air of the room. That done he stowed away his equipment and notes, snapping his bag shut.

'What a waste! Doesn't anyone in this village know how to kill themselves quickly?'

'Oh, she could kill quickly enough,' Tyrell assured Chris Collier. 'One blow with a log was enough.'

The doctor was startled. 'Orhan? Are you sure?'

'I'm sure.'

Chris Collier shook his head. 'And I suppose that poor sod of a husband's been haring round like a blue-assed fly trying to clear up the mess?'

'Technically, he's an accessory after the fact.'

'Are there any more bodies? Or can we all go home now?'

'You can. It'll be a while before I can get away.'

Tired as he was, Keith had an overwhelming need to soap and shower himself free of death and misery. It took a long time. When he finally slid between the sheets, Jenny stirred.

'What time is it?'

'Half-past two.'

She snuggled into him, her breath escaping in a contented sigh. 'Is it over?'

'Yes.'

Even as he said it Keith was not completely certain. Sir Edward had left nothing hidden. Every detail had

299

been explained, accounted for, even that the death of Barry Warren had caused Helen Driffield such secret misery she could no longer endure life.

'I wonder?'

'What?' Jenny was proving yet again she could listen and think when half asleep.

'Whether the boy in Norfolk was really hers and not her sister's.'

'Does it matter?'

'Not now.'

'Then go to sleep.'

Jenny drifted off but Keith stared at what he could see of the ceiling, exhausted and yet wide awake.

The questioning of Sir Edward had gone on for hours, this time a tape recorder collecting every answer, cough, rustle.

'I'm pleading guilty to anything you charge me with,' he had insisted. 'All I ask is that you let Aunt Caro get to the boys before those damned hacks. She'll look after them until I'm free, then I'll take them to France – or somewhere. Start again.'

Start again, Keith thought. It sounded so simple.

The village hall was beginning to reappear. Yesterday's onslaught had reduced today's paper sorting. Desks were quickly stripped and computers unplugged and boxed, ready for their next assignment.

'Is the super with him?' Brian Clarke asked.

'Driffield? Yes. He'll be processed today and on remand.'

'Bail?'

'He might swing it.'

'He's got plenty of influence, in which case he could be back here tonight.'

'You're probably right.'

A van backed up to the door of the hall and overalled workers transferred the valuable electronics.

'I'll miss those steak pies at the George – and Sam Roberts' home-brew.' The sergeant sighed.

Tyrell grinned. 'I bet Brenda has you on a diet within a week.'

Brian Clarke groaned. 'No takers. She's already going on about more salads now the weather's changed.'

The photographs of Mehmet Orhan's body were being collected into folders, the wall that had displayed them almost ready for playgroup drawings.

'Inspector.' It was Maria Gilbert. 'Mr Mortimer wants you for a meeting in an hour.'

The DI thanked her and walked slowly towards the door. He stepped out of the way of a desk being carried. While he waited for it to pass he looked back at what had been a busy incident room. Windows were open and a fresh breeze drifted away the smell of tired men and women, the stale cigarette smoke. In a matter of hours it would be as though the police had never held sway there.

Tyrell was just about to get into his car when, with a crunching of gravel, Mrs Gallagher drew up alongside him.

'I wanted to see you before I left,' she said. 'Tell me, the information I gave you, was it any help?'

'Very much so.' The DI could see the woman was uneasy. 'What's wrong?'

'I can't stop thinking that if only I'd given it to you sooner, Helen Driffield might still be alive. Barry, too.'

'If only,' Tyrell said slowly. 'I'm told they're the two saddest words in the English language. You made the choice that seemed right at the time. That's all Barry did – and Lady Driffield. You might just as easily blame a computer operator in the Home Office,' he said with a wry smile.

'You're being kind.'

'Not a bit of it.' He saw a suitcase on the back seat. 'Off somewhere nice?'

'Birmingham. I like to get round my properties and make sure everyone knows I'm watching them.'

'Good for you. Will you be away long?'

'Long enough.' She shivered, although the day was beginning to build up heat. 'I'll come back when it's over.'

'When what's over?'

'I don't know.'

Tyrell was surprised. 'You can feel it too?'

'Very strongly. Even the air's waiting for something to happen.'

Tyrell nodded. 'I thought it might clear when we got the answer we needed but no, it's still there.'

'Like the elvers,' she said, then smiled at his bewilderment. 'My grandfather had land by the river and it carried rights to elver fishing.'

Gloucestershire-born, Keith Tyrell knew of the tiny eels migrating in huge shoals up the Severn. Fried in hot bacon fat they were reputed to be delicious.

Anne Gallagher smiled and thought of happier days. 'All the old river men knew when it was time. Everyone would gather on the bank and wait. There'd be jam sandwiches – my grandmother used to make them for us. It would be cold and we'd all be hanging about for what felt like hours. Then someone would shout and you'd see the water boiling with elvers. It was a mad rush to haul in as many as possible before they swam on. Nothing stopped them but a strong net.'

Tyrell saw not a middle-aged woman but a bright-eyed child dreaming in the sunshine.

'I'm waiting for that shout now,' she said, 'but I've lost my taste for elvers.'

The DI looked at his watch. 'I'm sorry, I must go.'

'Of course. Give my regards to your Sergeant Clarke.' Her smile was sad. 'He's very like my Martin when I first knew him. Tell his wife to look after him – and keep him as long as she can.'

*   *   *

The only place the coffin could rest was on the table in a corner of the tiny room. She watched Cobbett's men manoeuvre carefully before they set Barry down for the last time in his own home.

The bearers tramped away and Frank Cobbett bent over Chrissie. In his most solemn voice he assured her of his respect, his sympathy. She had no word for him and he left her alone.

Reg was in and out of the room, or going to the kitchen, the garden, to Barry's ferrets.

'Come to bed, love,' he pleaded as the warm evening darkened.

Chrissie shook her head. 'Not tonight.'

Together they kept watch over their sleeping son, the hours that passed filled with memories of him. When dawn let them see the room clearly once more, they knew the time was fast approaching when he would be taken from them and laid in the deep bed Reg had dug in the churchyard.

Chrissie's fury rose with the sun, acid rising from her stomach and biting as it moved. She hid the anger and pain from her husband so that all he could see was the face he knew carved now from stone.

'I'll make us some tea,' Reg said.

With muscles stiffened by the vigil he lumbered towards the kitchen. Chrissie heard him click the door of the privy and knew she had a few minutes of solitude.

Kneeling in front of the hearth she pulled grasses from the blue and white jug that had been her mother's pride. Seeds scattered and were ignored as Chrissie thrust her hand into the depths of the jug. Her eyes gleamed, her lips were a thin line of hatred and breath flared through her nostrils. Sitting back on her heels she opened her fist. The little wax mannikin lay helpless, speared by two rusty pins.

'I've got him, Barry,' she whispered.

From the back of the house came the sound of the

privy door squeaking open and she knew she must hurry, Reg would stop her if he could. He had already buried the old tin and had hunted through the house for the deadly wax.

Standing beside her son's coffin Chrissie drew the two pins slowly from the doll. Crooning, she twirled one in her fingers as she had seen Granny Phelps do, then, with a hiss, she thrust it once more into the heart of the mannikin.

'Chrissie!' Reg shouted from the doorway.

The grieving mother had not heard him return to her. She spun the second pin before aiming it at the head. The point went into the right eye socket and she pulled the pin backwards and forwards, opening up the wax and destroying any semblance of a human shape.

Energy drained from her and she was limp, longing for sleep. The face she turned to Reg was calm, almost peaceful.

'It's done,' she whispered.